OTTO PENZLER is the owner of The Mysterious Bookshop in New York. An authority on crime fiction, he is the founder of The Mysterious Press and Otto Penzler Books. He received an Edgar Award for the *Encyclopedia of Mystery and Detection* and was honoured by the Mystery Writers of America in 1994 with the Ellery Queen Award for his contributions in the publishing field. He lives in New York City.

MURDER &
OBSESSION

Edited by

Otto Penzler

ORION

An Orion paperback

First published in Great Britain in 2000
by Orion
This paperback edition published in 2001
by Orion Books Ltd,
Orion House, 5 Upper St Martin's Lane,
London WC2H 9EA

A CIP catalogue record for this book is available
from the British Library.

ISBN 0 75284 331 1

Typeset by Deltatype Ltd, Birkenhead, Merseyside
Printed and bound in Great Britain by
Clays Ltd, St Ives plc

FOR MICHELE SLUNG,
my indispensable friend,
my indispensable colleague

CONTENTS

INTRODUCTION

More than twenty years ago, a man I know met the woman who he knew, instantly, was perfect for him. He fell in love on the spot and, after waiting a reasonable period of time (about twenty-four hours), he asked her to marry him. She said yes and so the deed was done. After fifteen years, she left him, and he wept every day for a year or more. He spoke of her constantly until only his best friends could bear to hear another word. To this day, he thinks of her a hundred times a day and recognizes that there is a hole in his heart that can never be filled by anyone or anything else.

More than thirty years ago, a man I know enjoyed reading mystery fiction and decided that, since his means were extremely limited and there was little competition, this would be a nice area in which to collect books. It started with Sherlock Holmes and moved on to other favorites. As he read more, he discovered more and more writers to admire. And to collect. Today, his collection numbers about fifty thousand first editions, after he decided some years ago that he ought to collect it *all* – a first edition of every book in the history of crime, mystery, suspense, espionage, and detective fiction.

More than forty years ago, a man I know (he was a boy then) saw some picture, or some movie, or read about a house that spoke to him. It was a big stone pile, vaguely Tudor in style, and he loved it. He knew that, no matter what, someday he'd live in a house like that. Every time a magazine crossed his desk with a picture of such a house, or some lavish costume drama was set in such a house, he was filled with longing. As the years passed and he had some success in his career, he decided to build that house of his dreams. And he did.

Would it be a surprise to know that all three of these obsessions dominated the life of a single person? He built the house for the wife of his dreams and his great book collection. The irony, as if you couldn't see it coming, is that she left him before the house could be completed, and to this day he hasn't found quite enough money to finish off one room in the mansion. The library.

To him, of course, none of this smacks of obsession. If you want something, you go after it and, with enough hard work, a little patience, and some luck, it will happen.

So where is the line, that narrow border crossing that separates the areas of normal drive, or desire, and obsession? My best answer is that it is impossible to know. What seems entirely normal, planned, and reasonable to one person seems obsessive to another. Missing someone you love, collecting a lot of books, and living in a nice house seem perfectly normal to, well, me, for one. It is the perception of others that moves it into the murky twilight zone of obsession.

Perhaps another good way to spot it (since I don't think it's possible to define it satisfactorily, the best we can do is compare it to art, or pornography – you may not be able to define it, but you know it when you see it) is when it is in violation of universal standards of behavior by such a wide margin that laws have been written to prevent it.

There are no laws to prohibit mourning a lost love, or to stop someone from assembling a library that some might regard as excessive, or to prevent one from living in a manor more suited to an aristocrat than to a guy who grew up in the Bronx.

There are, however, laws that are designed to inhibit the commission of a form of behavior that most of us would concede has stepped out of the arena of enthusiasm, even passion, into the zone of obsession. This is the subject, more or less, of the stories in this book.

In spite of its title, not all the stories are about murder. One is about a cop obsessed with catching burglars, another about a woman who simply cannot stand for one more instant the sight of her husband's collection of Chinese art, yet another about a man who cannot stop staring at the painting of a woman long dead.

Perhaps the story that best captures the notion of obsession is James W. Hall's 'Crack,' a double entendre only for those with filthy minds.

Obsession is rarely harmless. It may appear to give great pleasure to the obsessed (else why would they continue with the obsession? Because they can't help it, to answer the question), but there is usually a price to be paid. Sometimes, the price is affordable. Sometimes, as witness the following tales, the price cannot be paid by anyone.

– Otto Penzler

KENT ANDERSON

....

One of the pleasures of compiling an anthology is attempting to determine which authors are appropriate, which is to say who is likely to enjoy writing a certain kind of story and therefore more likely to deliver a good one.

In truth, when 'obsession' was set as the theme for this book, the first name that came to mind was Kent Anderson. Having read the two adventures of his protagonist, Hanson – Sympathy for the Devil, a Vietnam war novel, and Night Dogs, a darkly brilliant police novel – I knew this is a man who understands obsession.

I wasn't there, so I can't say for sure how many times Anderson rewrote this episode. I know of four versions, but that might be the tip of the old iceberg. Anderson is obsessive about getting it right, which partly explains why there have been only two books in more than a decade. But, if you've read his novels, you already know that he does get it right. The voices, the sounds, the details – they are all just right. And his character? Obsessive doesn't seem to do justice to the way this guy behaves.

BURGLARY IN PROGRESS

By Kent Anderson

Radio said it was a burglary in progress. The complainant, who lived next door, said she'd seen him go in a window.

Five Sixty's got the call and—

'Five Forty can cover.'

Five Forty's—

'Five Eighty's close, I'll go that way.' Zurbo's voice interrupted the dispatcher, jumping in before another car could take the cover. All cops love the chance to catch a burglar. Neal was on vacation and Zurbo was working alone. The precinct ran a lot of one-man cars in the summer, when the crime rate was highest.

Five Eighty covering with Five Forty ...

Hanson turned around in an out-of-business gas station and ran a red light, accelerating up Williams Avenue. 'Five Forty and Eighty, go to channel three,' Hanson said into the mike, flipping the radio frequency to the car-to-car channel.

'You guys there?'

'Forty here,' Bellah said.

'At your service,' Zurbo said.

'You guys want to take the back of the place? We'll check with the complainant and take the front.'

'Forty copy.'

'Roger dodger,' Zurbo said. 'We'll see you there.'

Hanson switched back to channel two and hung up the mike. 'Good,' he said, talking to himself. 'Very good. Let's hammer this motherfucker.'

They took cold burglary reports every day, two or three of them waiting from the day shift when they first hit the street. Crime reports, statements, lists of stolen property, serial numbers that could be peeled off, useless fingerprints. A lot of paperwork and a waste of time. No one ever got their property back, and it was almost impossible to get a conviction without an eyewitness or a snitch who was willing to testify in court. Paperwork for nothing.

He cut the lights a block away and stopped a few houses from the address, using the hand-brake so their brake lights wouldn't show. The interior light was disconnected so it wouldn't go on when they got out of the car. Hanson pushed his door quietly closed with a *click* and was halfway up the street before Duncan finally got out of the car and slammed his door.

Hanson had been working with Duncan, a rookie, most of the week, and they didn't talk much. Duncan was fresh out of the Air Force, where he'd been a lieutenant. He was a by-the-book guy who planned to make lieutenant in the department by the time he was thirty.

Hanson was using codeine and crank to take care of his hangovers. He'd talked the city shrink out of a prescription for the codeine after Dana's death, and a white doper from Tacoma had ditched a quarter ounce of crank under the seat of the patrol car a couple of weeks later, when Hanson was working alone. Hanson decided he'd rather have the crank than charge the guy with 'possession for sale.' Who cared? He'd used up the last of it that afternoon, snorting it out of a Contac capsule in the bathroom of the Town

Square. It had already started to lose its edge, and Hanson had a headache.

He sniffed and wiped his nose, streaking blood on the back of his hand. He wondered if Duncan might turn him in for using narcotics, then decided, no, it was too early in his 'career' for him to start rocking boats. He'd already begun studying for the sergeant's test, between calls and reports.

The complainant was standing inside the screen door of her house, the lights inside turned off. Her husband ignored them, watching the end of *Homicide* on TV, a bar of static lapping the screen every two seconds.

'He went to the door first,' she said, 'to see if anybody home.'

'Why don't you talk to Officer Duncan, ma'am,' Hanson said as Duncan came up to the door. 'I'll keep an eye on the place from here.' He ignored the look Duncan gave him and studied the neighbors' house, packset to his ear, the volume turned all the way down.

It was still hot from the afternoon. Hanson saw 580 pass the intersection at the next block, its lights out, the curve of the roof catching moonlight. He smelled magnolia, or maybe honeysuckle. 'The people who live there, the Robinsons, gone to Los Angeles to visit their daughter. She teaches junior high down there,' the complainant told Duncan. 'I don't know how she can live in that place . . .'

'The burglar, now . . .' Duncan began.

'Like I done *told* you, he gone to the door first, then around to the side, messing with the window. I went and watched him from the bathroom. I think he's inside, but I'm not sure. It took you so long to get here.'

'Which side?'

'*This* side. I can't *see* the other side.'

Duncan nodded.

'Five Sixty.' Zurbo's whisper came out of the packset like a burst of static.

'Five Sixty,' Hanson answered.

'We got both corners covered.'

'We're on the way,' Hanson said. 'She thinks he's still inside.'

They crossed the yard and slipped along the wall to the small louvered window. Zurbo was in the back, where he could see two sides of the house, the moon reflecting off his badge and leather gear. Hanson slumped, swept his open hand low in a James Dean wave – *Smooth*. He could see Zurbo's grin.

The burglar had broken the aluminum crank mechanism and forced the window partially open.

'I'll go in and open the front door,' Hanson whispered.

'Why not wait for him to come out? He's not—'

'Well, hell,' Hanson hissed, 'why not call a SWAT team? Or maybe you could call a fuckin' air strike on him? What if he's already gone? Here we are standing around with guns in our hands, looking stupid. Besides, I'm hungry. If we fuck around here much longer it'll be too late for supper. Okay?'

'Whatever you say.'

'Thank you, Lieutenant.'

'You got a nosebleed,' Duncan said.

'Must be all this excitement. Tension, you know? Does it every fuckin' time,' he said, wiping his nose, his eyes on Duncan's. 'It's a burglar,' Hanson said, trying to smooth things over some. 'We might nail the fucker.'

'Who gives a shit about these people,' Duncan whispered. 'I'm not gonna get my ass shot for them.'

'I'll let you in the front door,' Hanson told him.

The back of his neck and shoulders tingled as he tipped his head through the window into the smell of old food, stale cigarette smoke, and other people's sweat.

He put his head and shoulders inside, stopped to listen, then eased his chest inside – a tight fit – careful not to snag his badge or name tag on the sill. He worked his hips through, easing himself into his own moonlit shadow, walking on his hands, scraping his shins as he pulled them through the window, then carefully lowered his steel-toed boots, one at a time, into the foyer, poised on all fours like a sprinter waiting for the starting gun.

When he stood up, his own dark reflection in a mirrored closet door rose to his right and he spun toward it, reaching for his gun, then he smiled, straightened up, and swept his open hand low in the James Dean wave, relaxing as his adrenaline rose and leveled out – *Smooth*. His headache was gone.

His boots made more noise than he liked as he stepped – heel and toe, heel and toe – to look down the hallway to the living room. Some of the guys at North had taken to wearing black-leather running shoes for silence and speed, but Hanson preferred the steel-toed boots, an extra weapon and much better for kicking in doors. And he was *used* to combat boots. It seemed as if he'd been wearing them all his life. And they supported the ankle he'd broken in a night parachute jump four months before going to Vietnam. He'd splinted the ankle with pine branches and walked on it for a week in the North Carolina mountains – vomiting from the pain a few times when he'd slipped and put all his weight on it – rather than be Medevaced and held back from the training group he'd been with from the beginning.

He paused at the doorway, smelling fresh sweat and something else. In the back of the house a refrigerator kicked in, rattling and humming. Down the hall, an eerie blue light surged and plunged through the house like pure power trying to break out, the kind of light, Hanson thought, that must dance down in the core of a nuclear reactor. The light from a television screen. He peeled the safety snap on his holster so it wouldn't snap.

Hanson was on guard, on and off duty. All the time. On the street, in bars or supermarkets, he watched for assholes, psychos, the bulge of a gun in a woman's purse or under a twenty-one-year-old's T-shirt. Sitting at home, reading, he was prepared for men with shotguns to come through the door. His reaction wouldn't be *What? Who's that? What's going on?* He would only think, as he dove for cover and his own gun, *Shit, it's the guys with shotguns.* Most of the time that fear was, a psychiatrist once told him, 'inappropriate,' a nice word for 'insane.' But it was always there, when he took a shower or opened a door or turned a corner or woke up in the dark at 3:00 A.M. The guys with shotguns were out there. He'd spent enough time in the hills and jungles of Northern I-corps and walking the ghetto streets to know that was true.

But the fear *was* appropriate in this dark strange house with a burglar in it, and for now Hanson was 'sane,' relaxed. For now, the world made sense.

He backed to the front door, let Duncan in, and the two of them walked down the hall toward the blue light, unlit Kel-Lites like clubs in their left hands. The clear plastic runner covering the hallway runner crackled beneath their boots.

The hallway opened into a living room, stairs to the left, the room silent, empty. Across the room, behind a huge curving sofa, faced a silent TV, a 'home entertainment center' as big as a refrigerator. A weatherman, wearing a bow tie, crossed the silent screen. Like a magician, without looking at the map behind him, he swept his hand across Kansas, Missouri, then up to Nebraska, and blue raindrops, like a wallpaper pattern of blue hearts, began to pulse across those states.

All the furniture matched. A brand-new living room, bought on time like an automobile, Hanson thought, with high-interest monthly payments. The sofa, love seat, and upholstered chairs, the lamp shades, and the formal dining table and chairs were sheathed with clear plastic slipcovers. Everything had been dumped by the burglar. A china cabinet sloped forward, shards of dishes and cups smashed through shattered glass doors, letters and snapshots, spools of red and gold ribbon and yarn – a half-finished sweater. Silverware had been dumped from a chest of drawers. Framed photographs covered the top of the TV set and the mantel behind it. The biggest photo, in an ornate gold frame, was of a black kid in Marine dress uniform. He wasn't trying to look tough. He was smiling, and somehow Hanson knew he was dead now.

A sofa-size painting of a praying Jesus hung on one wall, the glass reflecting the weatherman and his map. Palms pressed together, fingertips just touching His chin, Jesus rolled liquid eyes up toward the Bobby Kennedy/Martin Luther King memorial plate mounted above Him like a ceramic moon. The TV weatherman, a Technicolor ghost, glided across the face of the painting.

The love seat beneath the painting was littered with potato chips, lunch meat, and beer cans, beer puddled on the plastic slipcover – obviously a meal break for the burglar. He'd also taken a shit on the floor.

Hanson glanced up at the ceiling, as slow footsteps creaked above them toward the head of the stairs. Duncan went into the kitchen, where he peered around the doorway. Hanson backed into the shadow on one side of the TV, giving him a clear shot at the stairway. Blue light from the TV rippled and jumped across the walls.

He could have taken cover behind the sofa, or in the kitchen with Duncan, but his angle on the stairs wouldn't be as good. As it was, he was exposed, and that meant the burglar would have a second or less to freeze if he had a gun. If he had a gun and moved at *all* or, hell, if he had a gun in his hand, period, he was dead meat, Hanson decided. He'd tell Internal Affairs that they'd yelled, 'Freeze, police officers,' and the suspect pointed the gun at them and they'd shot him. Zurbo and Bellah would back them up on that. Hanson wished he was carrying a throw-down gun, just in case the burglar wasn't armed. Then he could shoot and kill him and toss the throw-down nearby and say it had been the suspect's. Too bad, Hanson thought, adios, motherfucker.

He'd seen too many burglary victims. Every day he and Dana had sat down in their kitchens or living rooms and made lists of what had been stolen, the little bit they had. Toys taken from beneath Christmas trees of single mothers trying to raise two or three kids so they wouldn't end up dead or in the joint, which they probably would anyway, but they deserved a couple of Christmases before they were shot and went to prison. Old people who had lost their savings, cash kept in a coffee can in the freezer because they didn't believe in banks since the Great Depression. People who had nothing worth stealing, so the burglar slashed and smashed everything in the house.

Or they'd go to the hospital to take the worthless reports from men and women who had tubes in their noses and arms, who had walked in on the burglars, been beaten and raped, some put in wheelchairs for the rest of their wretched lives, living on dog food or the occasional visit from a social worker, their social-security checks stolen most months. The people who woke up at the wrong time or opened the door after dark. Burglars.

Cat burglars who got a rush walking into the bedrooms of sleeping victims, half-hoping, most of them, they'd wake up and have to be killed.

'Home invaders' who tied their victims up, beat and raped them for fun, then burglarized the house.

The TV news anchor picked up a stack of papers and evened up the edges on the news desk. The woman coanchor, a brunette with a dyed gray streak, glanced over at the anchor, then at Hanson – he saw her out of the corner of his eye – at Hanson and a hundred thousand other viewers – looked boldly into the camera, as if to say to Hanson, *I have to work with him, but I'd love to fuck you.*

Then the anchors were replaced – the 'news' was over – by footage of some kind of kids' dog show, the names of cameramen and producers and writers scrolling up the screen so fast it was hard to read them. The dogs were in costume. A poodle in a paper party hat trotted smartly past

15

the camera. A bowlegged boxer wearing sunglasses and a striped T-shirt swaggered up and looked into the camera, his distorted face filling the screen until a little girl grabbed his leash and jerked him away.

A little boy – a white kid like all the others – had to slide his collie in moccasins and feathered headdress past the camera, his legs braced against the leash. Another cute kid walked his sheepish-looking German shepherd past. The big dog's legs poked through the sleeves of an army fatigue jacket that buttoned up along the back and looked like a straitjacket. A floppy bush hat hung from his neck on a strap, hitting him in the legs with each step. The focus moved closer until the shepherd lunged, teeth bared, and the camera jerked back and up, like those old bits of war footage during the six o'clock news when cameramen walked into ambushes.

The footsteps were coming down the stairs now. Hanson thumbed the safety off his model .39 and took a two-handed stance, both eyes open at the stairs that jumped in and out of focus, brightened and dimmed, as the TV cut from shot to shot of a handsome, *confident* young man drinking blue mouthwash.

Come on, motherfucker, Hanson thought, show me your gun so I can shoot you, kill you, be sure you're dead so you can't show up in court to testify against me.

Internal Affairs would take them up into the bleak, bare-walled interview room and want to know why they hadn't waited outside for the 'suspect.' Couldn't they have avoided shooting the suspect?

They would have their stories together, even Duncan. 'We didn't know who was in the house. Maybe one of the owners had come home early and walked in on the suspect. Then, when the suspect came down the stairs, we announced ourselves as police officers, repeatedly commanded the suspect to freeze – he had a weapon in hand – it was shiny, it looked like a weapon in the light from the TV set – and when he raised it, pointing it at us, we had no choice but to fire first.'

Hanson checked the already thumbed-off safety, relaxed his hands and wrists, shrugged the tension out of his shoulders and back. Come on down, baby, he thought, come on.

'Couldn't you have taken cover before he came down the stairs?' IA would ask, air conditioner moaning overhead in the third-floor ductwork of Central Precinct. 'If he didn't have a clear shot, he might have complied with your commands.'

'There was no cover available at the time,' Hanson would say.

Black zippered boots and bell-bottom pants stepped into Hanson's sight-picture. Another step and Hanson saw that his pocket and shirt waist were stuffed, lumpy like the pillowcase in his hand. He took another step, and another, slow and heavy, the junk in his shirt and pillowcase clanking in his left hand, until his shoulders and sweating face came into view. Willie Barr, a heroin addict and asshole they'd arrested before. More than once. He was fucked up, his eyes heavy-lidded, the whites yellowish, his afro ratty and filthy in spiky tufts. He held a big silver crucifix in his right hand – *'I thought it was a gun,' Hanson could claim to Internal Affairs.* But fuck it, Willie Barr.

Hanson yelled, 'Freeze! Police officers! Freeze!'

'Get your hands *up*,' Duncan yelled from the kitchen.

'Get em *up* there, Willie,' Hanson shouted.

Duncan shined the beam of his cast aluminum Kel-Lite in Willie's face. The yellow pattern of light fluttered over his eyes and nose and lips like butterflies. Willie dropped the crucifix and rubbed his hand over his face, as if he could push the light away like a swarm of gnats. Annoyed.

'Hands *up*,' Hanson shouted.

'What?' Willie said. 'The fuck. Who's *that*?' He dropped the pillowcase, made a fist. 'I ain't *playing* now.'

Hanson holstered his pistol, said, 'Shit,' glanced at Duncan, and stalked the few steps to the stairs. He kicked sideways into Willie's shin, then grabbed him by his shirt. 'You want to *freeze* now,' he grunted, jerking him off the last stair. 'You want to help us *out*?' he said, throwing Willie into the wall.

'Wait now, I don't—' Willie said, and Hanson kicked his legs out from under him.

'You want to fuckin' freeze?' Hanson yelled as Willie hit the floor and Hanson drove his knee into the small of his back.

'Get that arm back here,' Hanson said, jerking the sweat slick right arm back for handcuffing.

'Wait now,' Willie said.

'God damn,' Hanson said, hammering him in the hollow between his neck and shoulder, cuffing one wrist, then the other. 'Get your arm back.'

'What's goin' on, man?' Willie said, the tendons in his neck cording as he strained to look back and up at Hanson.

Hanson holstered his pistol. 'You're under arrest, fuckhead,' he said as Zurbo and Bellah kicked in the back door.

'Arrest? Say what?'

'Burglary and Resisting Arrest. Anything you say can and will be used—'

'What?' Willie said.

'Anything you say can be used against you in a court of law. You have a right to an attorney—'

'Arrested? What you mean, arrested?'

Hanson flipped him over and grabbed him by the shirt. It felt good to do something. He liked the way his right arm felt as he twisted the material. He liked the resistance, the way the muscles in his forearm and shoulder bunched up when he pulled Willie's face close.

'For being stupid. For being a stupid, dumb asshole.'

Hanson grabbed the shirt with both hands, shook him, and slammed him into the floor.

'Don't interrupt me again, motherfucker,' he said, pulling him up. 'You understand? Like I said' – slamming him down again – 'you're under arrest.'

Hanson stood and lifted Willie onto his toes. 'You remember me?' he said. 'Look at my face, fuckhead.' He released the shirt with one hand and pointed at his name tag. 'Hanson. Hanson. That's me,' he said, a little out of breath now.

'I should have shot your dumb ass. Next time I will. If I ever get the chance again, I'll kill you. You understand me? If I ever see you in my district I'll kick your ass and take you to jail.'

'Yes, sir.'

'Now, shut up while I give you your rights.

'You have the right to ... Anything you say can and will ...' Hanson was out of breath, too angry to recite the meaningless Miranda speech.

Zurbo was laughing now. Hanson shoved Willie at him and said, 'Will you give dickhead here his rights?' He pointed at Willie.

'Goddamn people,' Hanson said, looking at the TV. Jay

Leno was laughing. Duncan, in the kitchen, looked bewildered. Hanson thought about punching him. Then he wondered where he could score some crank. How he could get through the rest of the night without kicking Duncan's ass. What he'd do all day tomorrow until it was time to hit the street again.

EDNA BUCHANAN

After fifteen years of covering the crime beat for The Miami Herald *in one of the crime capitals of the world, Edna Buchanan won a Pulitzer prize for her journalistic efforts.*

Covering the crime beat in such a fiercely competitive and violent world as Miami is also the job of Britt Montero, the hero of most of Buchanan's crime novels. She is tough, smart, talented, attractive, and totally dedicated to her work. The comparisons between author and heroine are inevitable.

After two successful nonfiction crime books, Buchanan followed her lifelong dream to write fiction and took a leave of absence from her newspaper to produce Nobody Lives Forever, *which was nominated for an Edgar Allan Poe Award by the Mystery Writers of America for Best First Mystery. Her second novel,* Contents Under Pressure, *introduced the intrepid Montero.*

Montero seems incapable of slowing down, racing from one case to another, and so does her creator. Buchanan, with more than eighteen years of experience as a crime reporter, continues to write novels, magazine articles and, happily, short stories.

THE RED SHOES

By Edna Buchanan

He stared from the shadows until the lights went out. He knew which apartment was hers, had conducted several recon missions to scout the layout of the building after following her home a week ago. She had been wearing narrow red sandals with little straps that night. The heels had to be four inches high. She wore them bare-legged, soles arched, each delicious digit of her toes spread like some exotic bird clinging to her elevated perch. Harvey's knees felt weak as he remembered, picturing the voluptuous curve of her in-step, and the right heel, slightly smudged, from driving. She should carpet the floor of her car, he thought, it would be a shame to ruin those shoes. Their sharp stiletto heels had pounded across the pavement and up the stairs, piercing his heart. Had to be at least four and a half inches high, he thought.

Suddenly her second-floor door swung open and some-one emerged, taking Harvey by surprise as he gazed up, lost in fantasy. A big man trotted down the stairs, stared for a moment, then brushed by, ignoring him. Though husky, the fellow was light on his feet, in running shoes, jeans, and a hooded yellow sweatshirt. Must be the boyfriend, Harvey thought, turning away as the stranger strode toward the parking lot. Harvey took the opposite direction, the

23

breezeway to the mailboxes, his head down, pretending to be a tenant coming home late.

His first instinct was to abort, to go home and watch another old movie, but instead he lingered. Nobody could know all the neighbors in a complex this size, he assured himself, aware that he was not a man most people would notice, or remember, anyway. A car door slammed and a big engine sprang quickly to life. Harvey relaxed as headlights swung out of the parking lot and melted into the night.

A close call, he thought, loitering behind the Dumpsters. From his vantage point he continued to watch her apartment. The lights were still out. He had read that the deepest sleep comes soon after the first hour. He was too excited to give up now. The wait would be worth it, he thought, and settled down.

Harvey had always liked women's feet. The roots of his obsession dated back to the moment he realized that he was the only one in his high-school art-appreciation class turned on by the bare feet of the Virgin Mary.

Women's feet became even more alluring after he stopped drinking. He had worked the steps, had a sponsor, and saw the truth behind an AA counselor's comment that 'You often replace one addiction with another.' How true.

Unfortunately, his recent expeditions had made the newspapers, forcing him to exercise more caution. But this one was worth the risk, more exciting than all of the others he had followed home.

Two of his encounters had apparently never been reported. That had perplexed him. He wondered if they had been too afraid or too embarrassed, or too lacking in faith in the local police? Perhaps they had liked it and hoped he'd be back. He pondered that possibility until, consulting the luminous dial of his watch, he decided it was time to make his move.

He silently ascended the open staircase. Glittery stars winked from above and Mars burned like an ember to the east. The rudimentary hardware on the sliding glass door was laughable. The high-school summer he worked for a local locksmith had been well spent. These people should know how little protection they have, he thought righteously, then slid the door open just enough to slip in sideways. The darkened dining room smelled of lemon furniture polish on wood and the fruity aroma of fresh oranges arranged in a ceramic bowl.

A pendulum clock's rhythmic tick was the only sound. It followed him to her bedroom, keeping time with his stealthy footsteps. His body quaked with anticipation. He knew the right room, always the last light out at night. Her faint form was barely distinguishable, a dim outline on the bed as he paused in the doorway. A jumbo jet roared overhead in ascent from Miami International Airport, but she never stirred. He waited until the airliner's thunder faded, replaced by the faint hum of the ceiling fan above her bed.

He did not need his penlight to find what he had come for. The stiletto heels, side by side, stood at rigid attention next to her closet door. She had slipped them off carelessly, without unfastening the tiny metal buckles and the skinny straps. That's how you ruin an excellent pair of shoes, he thought indignantly, then shivered with delight at her rash and wanton behavior.

In the beginning, during his early forays, he simply seized his prize and fled, pilfering their shoes, sometimes from the floor next to the very bed where they slumbered. Sometimes he snatched a bonus, a worn sock or nylon stocking from the dirty-clothes hamper on the way out. But one breezy and memorable night, his inhibitions had crumbled, along with his resistance. She was a shapely little waitress from Hooters, red-haired with a ponytail. Creeping in a window left open to the breeze, he had found her running shoes. They radiated a delightful, intoxicating aroma, a mixture of musky sweat, rubber, and Odor-Eaters. He was about to depart with them, when the blossoming full moon silvered the room, the sweet, alluring scent of night-blooming jasmine filled the air, and she stirred, murmuring in her sleep, and kicked off the flowered sheet. He stood frozen, the enticing arch of her bare foot beckoning, just inches away. Lord knows, he wasn't made of stone. Who could resist? He planted a passionate wet kiss on her metatarsal. She woke up screaming, of course, and he beat feet out of there, but the shared terror, the adrenaline, the flight were irresistible. He was hooked.

Since then, local papers and television newscasters had reported the unknown intruder's fondness for feet, announcing that police wanted him for eight to ten such escapades. The notoriety made it a more risky business. Couldn't they see how harmless it was? Nobody hurt. And no matter how many valuables, jewelry, cash, even drugs that he found scattered across dresser tops, all he ever took was footwear. He had his pride. Actually, he was doing them a favor, demonstrating their lack of security before some truly dangerous stranger paid a visit. This might be out of the norm, but it was certainly safer than driving drunk or ruining his liver. And it was so much more stimulating – and satisfying. Nobody could deny that.

Excited now, he heard her breathing, or was that his own? This one slept naked, sprawled on her back, her feet apart at the foot of the bed. His heart thudded as he stepped closer, hoping she hadn't showered. The polish on her blood-red toenails gleamed in the eerie green light from her bedside clock as he focused on the seductively plump curve of her big toe. He licked his lips in anticipation, the pleasure centers of his midbrain slipping into overdrive as he touched her, stroking her feet gently with his thumbs and index fingers, then leaned forward. The toes were cool beneath his warm lips. He could almost feel them stiffening.

The scream came as expected, but it was his own, as the moon broke free from clouds and he saw her clearly in the light spilling between the blinds. Eyes wide open and protruding, the twisted stocking grotesquely embedded in an impossibly deep groove around her throat. He gasped, stumbled back in horror, and tried not to gag. Instinctively he fled, then hesitated in the dining room and turned back, wasting precious moments.

He snatched the red stiletto heels off the floor near the closet, shoved them under his shirt without looking at the bed, and scrambled for the exit. The bulge beneath his shirt forced him to push the sliding glass door open even further to escape. What if someone had heard his cry? The door shrieked unexpectedly, metal rasping on metal, resounding through the night. In his haste, he stumbled against a plastic recycling bin outside her neighbor's door. It tipped over, spilling aluminum cans that clattered everywhere. He righted the receptacle with both hands and stood quietly for a moment, breathing deeply, his pulse pounding like a racehorse at the gate. A few feet away someone opened a window.

'Who's out there?' a deep voice demanded.

Harvey fled blindly, in panic, descending two and three steps at a time. Another window cranked open.

'What's going on?'

'There he goes!' someone else shouted.

He plunged headlong from the landing, stumbled, scrambled painfully to his feet, and hobbled across the parking lot, right ankle throbbing.

Lights bloomed, a concert of light behind him, as he glanced over his shoulder. Miamians are notoriously well armed and primed to shoot. He could not chance an encounter with some trigger-happy crime stopper. The cold metal of the dead woman's stiletto heel jabbed him in the belly as he flung himself into his Geo Metro. He winced at the pain as it broke the skin, fumbling frantically to fit the key into the ignition. His hands shook so uncontrollably that it seemed to take forever. Finally the engine caught. He tore out of the parking lot, burning rubber, lights out.

He took deep breaths, the car all over the road, his eyes glued to the rearview mirror. No one in pursuit. He forced himself to slow down, assume control, and switch on his lights, just in time. He saw the blue flasher of an approaching patrol car. It roared past at a high rate of speed, westbound, no siren, probably responding to the prowler call. Harvey whimpered, turned onto U.S. 1, and merged with other late-night traffic. How could that vibrant young girl be dead? Murdered. Her killer had to be that bastard, the man he saw leave, the man in the yellow sweatshirt. But the police wouldn't know that, they'd think he did it. His prize, the coveted strappy red sandals now resting uneasily against his heart, could send him to the electric chair.

Fear iced his blood and he shuddered involuntarily as he wrenched them from beneath his shirt, tearing it as a heel caught the fabric. He rolled down the window to hurl the incriminating evidence out by the side of the road, but could not bring himself to do it. It was not only because another motorist or some late-night jogger might see. He felt suddenly emotional about the final mementos of that lovely woman, so vivacious and full of life. The sort of lovely, lively woman who never would have given him a second look. He tried to think.

How could he explain? What would he say if they arrested him? 'I'm not a murderer, I'm only a pervert.' He said it out loud and didn't like the way it sounded.

How good a defense was that? Nobody would believe him. His favorite fantasies occasionally involved handcuffs, but their image now horrified him. Yet he could not bring himself to throw away her shoes like so much garbage, like someone had left her lifeless body, naked and exposed. He needed a drink, really needed a drink. Mouth dry, his tongue parched, he eased into the parking lot of the Last Chance Bar, but changed his mind before he cut the engine. Drinking was no answer, backsliding wouldn't help his situation. He needed to think clearly. He drove back out onto the street, toward Garden Avenue. The AA meetings there were attended in large part by restaurant workers and airport employees whose shifts ended at midnight or later.

The big room radiated light, fellowship, and the smell of fresh coffee. He was glad to see Phil, his sponsor, in the crowd.

Harvey sat and listened, sweating despite the cool evening and the laboring air conditioner. He wondered why nobody ever bothers to turn them off in Florida, even when the weather is comfortable. He sailed through the preliminaries when his turn came, then began, 'You don't know how close I just came.' He shook his head and ran his fingers through his hair, already thinning at twenty-six. 'Something happened tonight.' The shrewd eyes of a member named Ira lingered speculatively on Harvey's torn shirt.

'Old bad habits almost got me in big trouble.' Harvey licked his lips. His mouth felt dry again despite the coffee he'd had. 'You know how they always tend to come back and cause you problems.' He looked around. Several people he didn't know were present. 'Tonight, I was only trying . . .' Harvey's eyes continued to roam to the back of the room, to the coffee urn, where the man in the yellow sweatshirt stood watching him.

Harvey nearly strangled on his own words. 'I have to go,' he mumbled. His sponsor called his name, but he was out the door.

The Dew Drop Inn was quiet, a few regulars at the knotty-pine bar, an old martial arts movie on TV, and some guys and girls playing pool in the back room. Harvey swallowed his first drink in a single scalding gulp, quickly followed by another, then sat nursing the third, trying to focus on the taste, avoiding all other thoughts. The double doors opened, admitting fresh air and street sounds along with a new arrival. A dozen empty stools stood at the bar, but the newcomer chose the one next to his. Harvey knew who it was before he looked up.

'Fancy seeing you here.' The man in the yellow sweatshirt grinned.

Harvey squirmed, trying to look casual, his stomach churning. 'Just testing the waters again.'

'Me too.' The man paused and lit a cigarette. 'I can only take so much culture before I have to roll in the shit.' He looked at Harvey. 'They say it's the first drink that gets you drunk.'

'I'm on number three.'

The barkeep hovered expectantly. 'J.D. neat,' said the newcomer. 'And hit my friend here again.' He studied Harvey's glass, then raised hooded eyes as cold-blooded and hard as a snake's. 'What is that?'

'Stoly'tini, twelve to one.'

'I like talkin' to a man who speaks my language.' The big man in the yellow sweatshirt flipped a twenty onto the bar as their drinks arrived.

Harvey wondered if he could make it out the door if he decided to run for it. He might make it out the door, but not into his car. Was the killer armed? Would he pause to pick up his change before he came charging after him? If Harvey did make it to his car, the man would surely see what he drove, and his tag number – if he didn't already have them. Had he been followed? Or had the big man methodically checked every bar in the neighborhood? At this hour, Harvey's little Geo could easily be forced off the road with no witnesses. He could call the police, but how would he explain why he was at the murder scene? He would probably rot behind bars longer than the killer.

The big man sighed aloud in gratification after knocking back half his drink. 'The program really tends to ruin your drinking, you know?'

Harvey did not answer, his mind racing. The man half-turned to him. 'You were starting to share back at the meeting,' he said carefully, 'think you said something happened tonight, then you bolted like a deer who just saw Bigfoot. What the hell happened?' He waited for an answer.

'Nothing,' Harvey said weakly. 'Nothing that a few more of these won't cure.' The man wasn't as handsome up close, he realized, raising his glass. His skin was rough and craggy, a small scar dissected one eyebrow, and there was a mean curl to his thin upper lip.

'A woman,' the man persisted, a knowing undertone to his voice. 'Has to be. I bet that's it.'

Yeah, Harvey thought. It's a woman. The problem is, her lips are blue, she's dead, and you killed her. He nodded, unable to trust his voice. He felt his eyes tear and looked away.

'They drive us all nuts. Yeah,' the man continued philosophically, 'we all have our addictions, our weaknesses, that's why it's lucky that we all understand and support each other.' He took another gulp of his drink, then peered closely at Harvey. 'Haven't I seen you somewhere, other than a meeting? I'm sure we've crossed paths, I just can't place it.'

'I don't know,' Harvey croaked. 'I'm not good at faces.' He cleared his throat and got to his feet.

'You live somewhere around here?' the man persisted. 'Hey, where ya going?'

'Gotta go drain the lizard, be right back. Order us a coupla more. I shall return.'

Leaving his change on the bar, Harvey strolled past the rowdy pool players to the men's room, trying to look casual and nonchalant.

He had remembered correctly. There was a pay phone in the men's room and it worked. He punched in the familiar number, willing his sponsor to be home, willing him to answer.

'Thank you for your call,' the machine's robotic message began.

'Phil, pick up, pick up for God's sake!' Harvey muttered, glancing at the door behind him.

'Harv, that you? What happened at—'

'Thank God you're there, Phil. No time to talk, I need your help.'

'Where are you?'

'Never mind, Phil. That tall guy in the back tonight, by the coffee urn, the one in the yellow sweatshirt. Do you know him? Who is he?'

'Sure,' Phil said slowly. 'Quiet, intense type o' guy, shows up sporadically at the Garden Avenue meetings and the group over at St. John's. Left right after you did.'

'What's his name? What's he do?'

Harvey gasped as the door opened, nearly dropping the phone, but it was only one of the pool players, a bone-thin Oriental with dyed blond hair and a nose ring. The man went to a urinal, ignoring him.

'Where the hell are you, Harv?'

'Who is he?' Harvey hissed, his voice frantic.

'Calm down, calm down, son. Some kinda general contractor, he builds houses. Name is Ray, drives one o' them pickups, big blue one, a Cherokee, I think, with the company name on the doors. Can't think of it off the top of my head.'

'Ray. A contractor. Thanks, Phil. Later.'

'Wait a minute, Harv. Where—'

Harvey hung up. When the pool player left, he unlocked the narrow window and struggled to open it. His hands were sweaty and slippery. It had been painted shut and wouldn't budge. Panic-stricken, expecting his drinking companion to burst in at any moment, he upended a wastepaper basket and, ankle throbbing, climbed atop it to gain better leverage. With a desperate wrench he threw open the window, grasped the sides, pushed off with his good leg, and managed to half-drag and half-hoist himself through. He tumbled forward and landed on his hands and knees in the alley.

He lurched to his feet, wincing at the pain from his ankle, and tried to catch his bearings. The blanket of stars overhead earlier had vanished, and the night looked as murky and unpromising as Harvey's future. How had an evening he had looked forward to so much ever come to this? Tears flooded his eyes, but no time for regrets. The big man had to be wondering where he was. He would check the men's room any minute now. He would see the open window.

Harvey half-ran, half-limped to the parking lot behind the building. There it was. A blue Cherokee, RAYMOND KARP CONSTRUCTION lettered on the side. A built-in toolbox rested in the bed of the truck, double locked, then secured by a padlocked chain. Harvey memorized the tag number and the wording on the door, then scrambled into his Geo. As he looked back he saw no one.

He drove aimlessly, focused on the rearview mirror. Not until certain he was not being followed did Harvey head home. He knew the big man could track him down, but it would probably take him a day or two. Harvey parked two blocks from his own place anyway, then walked cautiously to his apartment, scanning the darkness. Safely inside, he felt weak with relief.

His locks were the best – he had installed them himself – but, straining and grunting, he pushed his mother's old china cabinet against his front door, just in case. He then lined up his coffee mugs and mismatched jelly-jar drinking glasses along the windowsills, and balanced saucers on a kitchen chair placed against the back door. He took a ball peen hammer from his tool shelf to bed with him, then tried to sleep, his throbbing ankle elevated on a pillow. But he was still wide awake as the sun rose, staring at the ceiling, waiting for the sounds of breaking glass or china crashing to the floor.

Before brewing his morning cup of English breakfast tea, Harvey channel-surfed the early-morning news. They all had the story. The murder was apparently the most newsworthy of that day's three Miami homicides. Channel 7 aired footage of the shrouded corpse being taken away. Harvey shuddered, the remote in his hand, watching as they wheeled her out and down the stairs on a gurney, an inanimate form beneath a blanket. He remembered her energy, her spirited and distinctive walk, and heard her name for the first time: Sandra Dollinger, twenty-four years old, receptionist at a South Beach photo studio. Somebody's daughter, somebody's child. Harvey wanted to weep, overwhelmed by mixed emotions. Why did he ever go there? Why hadn't he gone sooner? Had he been first, she would have been cautious, frightened, more security-conscious. Perhaps the killer never would have gotten to her. Never again, Harvey swore, if somehow he got through this, he would never again risk his life, his freedom, everything. Nothing was worth this.

'I can't believe it,' a woman neighbor was saying in the Channel 10 report. She looked pale and near tears. 'We've lived in this building for five and a half years, and nothing like this ever happened before. We didn't know her well. But she seemed nice, always said hello, always friendly.'

She and her husband heard the killer flee, the reporter said. 'I looked out, almost got a look at him,' said the husband, a chunky fellow wearing a mustache and a gold chain, 'but he ran, and by the time I pulled some pants on and got out there, he was driving off. We didn't know yet it was a murder.' They rapped on their neighbor's door but there was no answer. Her sliding glass door stood ajar. They alerted the manager who found the body, they said.

The victim's sister and best friend were assisting detectives in determining what was missing from the murder scene, a police spokesman said on camera. Harvey felt a thrill of fear at his words. Asked if robbery was the motive, the spokesman hinted that certain items might be missing, but he was not free to divulge what they were since it was crucial to the investigation.

'Do you think this could be linked to other cases?' a reporter asked. The spokesman lifted a meaningful eyebrow. 'No comment at this time.'

Harvey knew then what he had to do.

He limped into the kitchen first, to prepare his usual breakfast – two poached eggs, whole-wheat toast, orange juice, and tea. He had no appetite for anything, not even the high-heeled red sandals. He looked at them and felt only sadness. He forced himself to nibble at his meal the best he could. Maintain regular habits, he told himself, do not become overwhelmed by stress and fear. This was no time to go haywire. He stacked the breakfast plates in the dishwasher, then called in sick to his job as inventory clerk at Federated department stores. He had injured his ankle in a fall, he told them. No lie there.

Raymond Karp Construction was listed in the yellow pages without a street address. The man must work out of a home office, Harvey thought. He tried the number, carefully preceding it with star sixty-seven to block caller-ID.

'You have reached the office of Karp Construction, please leave a message at the sound of the tone.'

It was the big man's voice. Harvey hung up.

He stopped at a drugstore to buy an elastic bandage for his ankle and at 10:00 A.M. walked into the building department at city hall. He wore sunglasses, a baseball cap, and carried a notebook. His elderly mother was planning renovations, he explained, and he wanted to check out a potential contractor. A smart move, said the friendly clerk who confirmed it was all a matter of public record and helped him access the computer data base.

By noon he cruised his newly rented Ford Taurus past the modest ranch-style home of Raymond Karp Construction. The blue truck wasn't there. He found it at the second of three permitted projects Karp had under way, a two-story corner house on Northeast Ninety-third Street. The next forty-eight hours became a recon mission, as Harvey observed Karp from a distance, day and night, recording in his notebook where the contractor parked at each stop, and for how long. Karp seemed preoccupied during the day. He looked guilty, it seemed to Harvey, but, he reasoned, Miami contractors were notorious for their shoddy work and greedy post-hurricane rip-offs of helpless homeowners. They probably all looked guilty, or should.

Karp attended AA meetings at night, though, Harvey

noted, he never stayed long and went from one to another, as if looking for someone.

Harvey arrived home late. Headachy and hungry, he popped a Lean Cuisine in the microwave, then checked his message machine.

'Where ya been, Harv?' Phil's friendly voice sounded concerned. 'Is everything okay? That fellow you mentioned, Ray, the contractor, he's been asking around about you. What's going on?'

The clock was ticking down, no time left for further recon. Harvey set his alarm for 3:00 A.M. Somebody once wrote that it is always 3:00 A.M. in the dark night of the soul. He tried to remember who it was, before napping fitfully, anticipating the alarm.

When it sounded, he arose and reluctantly began to gather his collection. He cleaned out his closets, removing other souvenirs from beneath his bed, touching them longingly, reliving the special moments evoked by each one. The Salvatore Ferragamo slingbacks that had hugged the long narrow feet of that tall blonde with the swanlike neck and high cheekbones. He had trailed her from Saks Fifth Avenue all the way home to Coconut Grove. The soft suede loafers had been well worn by that long-haired young woman he had followed home from the library, and the black and white mules with their pointed toes and open heels unleashed a rush of memories. He had shadowed them all the way down Lincoln Road as she strolled, window-shopped, and chatted with friends. She seemed demure, so shy, so quiet, but screamed loud enough to wake the dead when she woke up as he fondled her feet.

He included the anklets, stockings, peds, and house slippers, all the little bonuses picked up along the way. He nearly forgot the silvery thong sandals tucked between his mattress and his box spring and had to go back for them. Finally he had dropped them all – the battered running shoes, the bejeweled evening slippers, the rubber flip-flops – into the maw of a big, black plastic garbage bag.

Each was a part of his life, he would miss them, but never again. The AA counselor was right, it was easy to replace one addiction with another, but now it was over. He wasn't going back to booze either. If he got out of this, it was time to exert some control over his life. His firm resolve felt good. He pulled the rental car up to his front door, checked the street, then carried the bag to the car. This would be his final caper.

The brisk Miami winter night was splendid, the temperature sixty-five, a star-studded sky, and the moon nearly full. The blue Cherokee was exactly where he expected to find it, parked in the driveway of the modest rancher. The house was dark. He stopped on the street near the foot of the driveway and wondered if the sleep of the man inside was as troubled as his had been.

Harvey sat in the car, watching, listening. He thought about prowlers gunned down by irate homeowners and trigger-happy cops on patrol. Even fifteen-year-olds had been shot for stealing hubcaps.

He wondered what this town was coming to.

As high-flying clouds obliterated the bright face of the moon, he made his move, melting like a shadow into the bed of the truck. There was an alarm on the cab but nothing in back. His penlight clenched between his teeth, he worked methodically on the padlock, then on the toolbox. It didn't take long. He cautiously lifted the creaky lid, then stopped to listen. A dog barked in the distance, but the house remained quiet and dark. The box was half full of tools, with rolled sets of plans on top. Harvey removed the plans and the tools, then replaced them with the shoes and other intimate items of footwear. He kept only a single red high-heeled sandal. He replaced the plans, closed the box, chained and padlocked it, sighing with relief as the lock snapped shut. He wrapped the tools in the empty garbage bag, scanned the street, then carried them back to the rental. He was about to start the car when he saw approaching headlights and crouched, holding his breath.

A Miami prowl car, two officers in the front seat. Harvey whimpered, some neighbor must have made a prowler call.

He thought he would faint when he heard the two cops talking companionably as their car pulled abreast of his, then rolled by, ever so slowly. He fought the urge to jump out, hands in the air, to surrender before they pulled their guns. But they kept moving and turned right at the end of the block. He must have a strong heart, Harvey thought, unlike his father. If ever he was to succumb to a heart attack, it would have been now.

He continued to crouch, body limp, heart pounding, until he was convinced they were gone, that no SWAT team was surrounding the block, then started the car, rolled a few hundred feet, switched into second gear, and turned on the lights.

He went to an all-night Denny's, suddenly ravenous, and ate a hearty breakfast. He read the morning paper as he devoured a stack of pancakes, syrup, and bacon, food he usually never ate. There was nothing more in the paper about the murder except a short paragraph and a telephone number, asking that anyone with information call Crime Stoppers.

At precisely 7:28 A.M. he was parked near the expressway entrance ramp three blocks from Karp's rancher. Karp passed by behind the wheel of the blue Cherokee at 7:31 A.M., on the way to his first job-site stop of the day.

Harvey's next step was more tricky. Neighbors were up and about, getting their children off to school. He approached on foot from the block behind the house and pushed through a thick hedge into the backyard. The back-door lock was a good one, an inch-long solid steel dead bolt that would take a lot of tedious time and work. He skirted the house and was thrilled to find the kitchen entrance, an old-fashioned jalousie door. It takes no smarts or training at all to simply remove a jalousie, reach in, and turn the knob. The kitchen was a mess. Dishes in the sink, a cardboard pizza box, empty except for a few gnawed crusts, a nearly empty Jack Daniel's bottle on a counter. The garbage can was overflowing. The living room was no neater. Neither was the bedroom. Harvey took the remaining high-heeled red sandal from inside his shirt, tucked it between the rumpled sheets of Raymond Karp's unmade bed, then left the way he had come, replacing the jalousie on the way out. He left Karp's tools just inside the door, still wrapped in plastic.

He called Crime Stoppers from a roadside pay phone.

'I believe I have some information,' he began. He told the volunteer he had overheard a stranger in a bar brag to a companion about the murder. The stranger also commented that he had to get rid of some evidence he had hidden in his vehicle. Later, he saw the man drive off in a truck. Just this morning he had spotted the same man, in the same truck, at a construction site. Harvey gave the address and a description of the truck and its driver. He was only a good citizen doing the right thing, he said, and was uninterested in any reward. Being a family man, he was reluctant to become further involved. Harvey hung up and went home.

As he heated some tomato soup for lunch, the Channel 7 news on the tube, a bulletin announced a breaking story, a police chase in progress. Harvey stepped away from the stove to watch. Police were in hot pursuit of a man they had approached at a building site that morning. The newsman said the suspect had given police permission to examine the contents of his truck, but when they found something suspicious, he had struggled with them, broken away, leaped into his truck, and fled. The station's eye-in-the-sky chopper crew was bringing live coverage from Interstate 95, where it was now reported that the fleeing driver was the suspect in a homicide.

Harvey turned off the burner under the soup and watched. How lucky, he thought, that Karp had made a run for it. How incriminating.

The chase was frightening. Other motorists were being forced off the road. Harvey's heart was in his throat. It looked to him as though the fleeing driver was headed home. Sure enough, the Cherokee sailed down the exit ramp into his neighborhood, trailed by wailing police cruisers. More were waiting. Karp's Cherokee skidded into a patrol car, then sideswiped a cement truck.

Harvey couldn't stay away, he had to see for himself that it was over. Galvanized into action, he dashed out to the rental.

The scene was chaotic, traffic was jammed. News choppers throbbed overhead, on the ground were sirens, camera crews, and a growing crowd. Just like an action movie, but this was real life.

Thrilled, he watched from a distance as Karp, dazed and bleeding from a gash on his head, was led away in handcuffs. Justice had triumphed, Harvey thought, justice for Sandra Dollinger. The police spokesman had convened a press conference and was addressing reporters. Microphones bristled, cameras zoomed in. Harvey edged up front, into the crowd.

The man arrested, the spokesman said, was the chief suspect in the murder of Sandra Dollinger. Physical evidence had been discovered that detectives believed would not only link him to the homicide but to a frightening rash of assaults on women – and identify him as the notorious serial shoe thief. Reporters gasped.

'Another classic case,' the public-information officer said wisely, 'of a deviate whose sex crimes continue to escalate in violence until culminating in murder.'

Puleeze, Harvey thought as he walked away. Whatever. He was free, he thought jubilantly. It had all worked. He smiled, safe at last, no cops, no killer on his trail. No drinking in his future, no more women's feet. This experience had turned him off both for good. He was free at last.

His smile lingered and caught the eye of a passing police officer. She smiled back. 'Helluva story, ain't it?'

'It sure is,' he said. 'What a town.'

She turned to direct traffic away from the scene. She wore the crisp dark blue uniform of the department and was attractive, in an athletic sort of way, her sandy hair pulled tightly back from her fresh scrubbed face. But that was not what caught his attention. Harvey's eyes were focused on her thick, shiny leather gun belt and holster. He heard it creak faintly as she walked. He breathed deeply and imagined how it smelled. Clipped to one side were an intriguing pair of black leather gloves, probably for man-handling suspects when necessary, he thought, and little leather compartments probably full of shiny metal bullets.

Harvey followed, longing to stroke the smooth leather and bury his face in her belly to inhale its aroma mingled with her perspiration. His face flushed, his knees felt weak. She turned, still smiling, and motioned the vehicles forward with a broad wave, raising her right arm, giving him the perfect opportunity to read her name off the metal tag pinned to her shirt pocket.

AMANDA CROSS

....

There is a long and great tradition of academics and scholars turning to the detective story, but it is mainly a British tradition. Dorothy L. Sayers, Michael Innes, Nicholas Blake, and others too numerous to list all had active careers at a university but found pleasure in reading detective fiction and eventually writing it – frequently under a pseudonym.

Amanda Cross will take no offense when it is pointed out that she is a bit anachronistic, following in the footsteps of the British masters of the Golden Age. Having built an extremely successful career as an academic, culminating with a full professorship at Columbia University, and having written influential scholarly works under her real name, Carolyn G. Heilbrun, she began writing mysteries in the 1960s because, as she says, she couldn't find any interesting ones to read. That was thirty-five years ago and, she continues, is a situation that has changed dramatically since then.

Her character, Prof. Kate Fansler, has starred in a dozen books, the success of each exceeding the previous one. The following story does not involve her heroine, but it does reflect the type of surprises of which the middle class is capable, not leaving crime only to the thugs.

THE DOUBLE-BARRELED GUN
By Amanda Cross

The telephone message had come for Detective McRae on Friday evening about seven o'clock. McRae had retired earlier that year, so the deskman sent it up to Farragut, who had taken over McRae's unfinished cases. Not that there were many unfinished cases, but there were some kept 'active' because they had neither ended in an indictment nor been abandoned. The message rested in Farragut's slot until Monday morning, and even when he found it there he was unsure what to do with it.

'The gun was returned today. Ursula Comstock.' That was the message. Obviously Ursula Comstock, whoever she might be, did not know that McRae had gone away to claim his pension and was now working as a security guard. Finally, Farragut wandered off to ask McRae's sergeant, who pointed to a file cabinet; the world of computers had not yet wholly colonized the precinct. There was no file marked *Comstock*, and Farragut had about decided the hell with it when he thought he would go so far as to look Ursula Comstock up in the Manhattan telephone directory; she was there, in a fancy building on East Seventieth. He dialed the number without bothering to write it down. He was answered by a machine; she was sorry she was unable to come to the phone right now, please leave a message after the tone or try her at her office, number given.

'And a good day to you too,' Farragut muttered. Then, while he was at it, as he told himself, he called the office number. He had not written that down either and had no intention of writing it down. If he didn't get her, so be it. McRae should have left better notes.

But she was there, or at least her secretary was; the secretary asked him his name, his business, and to hold. He glared at the sweep hand on his watch, hating to be on hold. But 'This is Ursula Comstock,' she said, before he could righteously hang up.

'Detective Farragut of the Fourteenth Precinct,' he said. 'Your message to Detective McRae was passed on to me; McRae retired.'

'Oh, I see,' she said. 'I thought he might want to know that the gun came back. But perhaps it doesn't really matter anymore.'

'What gun is that?' he asked, hoping it really didn't matter anymore and that he could let it go at that.

There was a long pause. 'It's rather a long story,' she said. 'If there isn't any record of it there, maybe it's not worth bothering with. You don't sound very interested, do you? I guess the whole thing just got to McRae; it's probably not worth anyone's time, particularly if there's no record of it there. Anyway, thanks for calling.' She hung up.

'Shit,' Farragut said. Conceding something, he wrote her business phone number down in his notebook and went in search of McRae's sergeant, an overweight man named Grusum, which name hadn't made his life any easier from boyhood on. He was now sore at having a new partner whom of course he did not like; Farragut doubted he had liked McRae at first. That was how it went.

Grusum was with difficulty persuaded to retrieve the Comstock case from his jammed-up memory. 'It was a loony case,' he told Farragut. 'This dame had reported her gun stolen, some nutty sort of gun, maybe a rifle, I forget the details. Then we had some shootings of bicyclists in Central Park, but I don't think they had anything to do with the stolen gun.'

Farragut studied Grusum for a minute, trying to decide what to say.

'The truth is,' Grusum conceded, 'McRae handled the bicycle crap himself; I told him I thought it sounded plain nutty, and the lieutenant told him to shelve it, so McRae sniffed it out on his own time. I don't know what, if anything, turned up. If you're interested in the gun that got returned, why not ask the Comstock dame?'

'What do you mean, shooting of bicyclists in Central Park? That doesn't sound like something the lieutenant would dismiss.'

'Oh, they weren't really hurt or anything. No blood, no damage. They just fell off their goddamn bikes. BB shot or something. My advice, which you didn't ask for, is forget it. I have.'

Later, Farragut would be unable to explain why he didn't forget it. Why he called Comstock back and asked for an interview. Why he ever bothered with the whole damn thing.

'You were fucking intrigued,' his sergeant told him when it was all over. 'You thought one day you'd write a goddamn book. Or maybe you don't get a chance to interview many CEO dames in big fucking Wall Street firms.'

'Maybe you're right' was all Farragut ever said. He and his sergeant had always got along fine, and Farragut was willing to take a lot of smart talk to maintain the status quo.

Ursula Comstock agreed to see Farragut in her office the next day at lunchtime. She had offered to get a sandwich for Farragut, but he declined, which he was glad of when he saw the salad mess she was eating out of a plastic tray with a plastic fork. If he were a CEO he would have ordered a sturgeon sandwich with caviar on the side, and a fancy beer. People who had money were always on diets, except for the thugs running crime organizations; they, at least, knew how to eat. He sat in the chair across from her desk and took out his notebook.

'Didn't McRae leave any record of this? I reported the theft of the gun to the police, and he was the one who got the report. Couldn't you talk to him about it?'

'I could,' Farragut said, 'but I'd rather hear it from you, if you don't mind taking the time. McRae might be a little fuzzy by now about the details.' Which was unfair to McRae, but Farragut didn't have to deal with the guy now he'd quit the force; that never worked out. Friendship, yes; cases, no.

Ursula Comstock ate salad for a while, chewing as though some dietitian had issued serious orders and expected them to be followed. Farragut began to wonder if he'd have to wait through the whole salad and decided no, no way would he wait; she might have been thinking while she chewed, but he couldn't tell.

'I'd like to see the gun,' he said, 'when you're finished eating.'

'Sorry; I was waiting for you to speak. The gun's not here; it's at home. That's where it was returned.'

'How?'

'How?'

'Did the person ring the bell and say, "Here's your gun, thanks a lot?" Was it mailed, delivered by FedEx or UPS?'

'It was left with the concierge in the lobby.'

'Someone handed the concierge a gun and said, hey, this belongs to Ms. Comstock, please get it to her?'

'It was in a large box, almost like a flower box, only longer. I didn't know what it was till I unwrapped it. There was my gun, same as ever.'

'It didn't look different in any way?'

'Not that I could tell; it's been a while since I last saw it, and once I had packed it to send it to New York from Florida with all my belongings, I never really studied it again. Wait a minute, though, there was something different. Whoever it was had taken out the screws that made the little dingus on the top work; the screws were in an envelope with a note saying "for safety." I still have the envelope,' she added, as though to comfort him.

'What little dingus, exactly?' He was beginning to think he'd been out of his mind to come.

'You're welcome to examine the gun if that would help in any way. But let me see, there was a thing on the top of the gun that chose one barrel or the other and made the trigger operable. I'm sorry that I seem to have forgotten so much about the gun. I used to be quite a good shot with it.'

'Why did you have to choose a barrel?' Farragut asked. She had finished her salad, chewing in between her sentences, and he about decided to finally let the whole thing go, now he'd got this far. Who chose barrels?

'It had two barrels; one was a shotgun barrel, the other was for bullets, twenty-twos. I tried a lot of guns at the time, and I chose this kind; bought it secondhand. I hit targets pretty well with the rifle part, which has a sight; the shotgun was in case I didn't have time for the sight.'

Farragut was uncertain what to say next. 'It's hard for me to picture a gun with two different kinds of barrels,' he said, not really knowing why. Certainly, he'd never heard of a gun like that but supposed it was something they used in the South, which might as well have been a foreign country for all he knew; still, there were rednecks there, and this may have been the kind of thing they kept in their pickups.

Ms. Comstock consulted her watch, as though it had become clear to her that she had better take charge of this interview. Well, she was a CEO, after all, and he hadn't sounded sure of himself, there was no doubt of that. 'I'll be home at seven, if you want to come by then and see the gun. Just give me a call first. Or if you want to skip the whole thing, that's fine too. I'm glad to have met you,' she added, rising and holding out her hand, trying to sound friendly. She strolled toward the door, so he rose and followed her. She managed somehow to suggest that her opinion of the police was not very high. Farragut hoped that that was mostly due to McRae. He took her hand, shook it, and departed.

Rather against his will, he called and went to see her that evening at seven, as she had suggested. She had laid the gun down on the coffee table in the living room, ready for his inspection. It was somehow larger than he had imagined, about four feet long, maybe a bit longer, and it must have weighed seven pounds, more when loaded. He had some trouble imagining her hefting it, let alone shooting it.

She seemed to follow his thoughts. 'I practiced for a while,' she said. 'I could handle it well in those days; quickly too.'

'Why did you want it? Because everyone in south Florida has a gun? To use on crocodiles in the Everglades?'

'We had a gun culture down there, no question,' she answered him, smiling. 'But I never shot any living thing in my life, not even an intruder, as it turned out.'

'The intruder was what made you get the gun?' He was still holding it, inspecting the two barrels and the place where the screws should have been. It certainly didn't seem to be a gun anyone could conceal; probably that was the point, to make it evident, easy to see. If a gun like that was aimed at him, even by a small woman like her, he didn't think he'd be inclined to find out how efficient a shooter she was.

'Not only an intruder. He tried to rape my daughter. I can speak of it calmly now, but not for many years, believe me. Fortunately, my daughter had been instructed, in case she was ever assaulted, to do what the rapist told you not to do, because – the theory went – what he told you not to do was what he was most frightened of. In this case the theory proved right. He said don't scream, and she screamed as loudly as she could. We heard her eventually, my son and I, and the man ran out of the house.'

'Was he caught?'

'My daughter picked him out from the pictures at the police station and out of a line-up, but he wasn't convicted because she couldn't say what color shirt he was wearing, even though she was able to recognize his face. The prosecutor wasn't smart enough to realize, or to let the jury know, that in a dim light, color, like the color of a shirt, is hard to distinguish, whereas a face is not.'

'A black face might not have been that easy to recognize. A black rapist, was he?'

'No,' she said, smiling into the detective's black face; her own face, he thought, was nice, getting on, but attractive. 'He was white and disgusting. And they caught him soon after. He broke into a house where the husband was home and chased him; he was caught and this time put away. Not that that made the three of us feel particularly safe. After all, he had known which room my daughter was in. I got the gun.'

'You just went to a gun store and bought it?'

'Not exactly. Wouldn't you like a drink? I would. I have a beer if that's your drink of choice; I won't tell anyone.'

'I just might do that,' he said. She got up to go to the kitchen. He knew she was offering the drink because he was black, and she wanted to let him know that didn't make any difference to her. She came back with a beer he'd never heard of and a fancy glass, which he refused. 'The bottle'll do fine,' he said. No sturgeon or caviar, but here was the exotic beer. She was drinking scotch, he guessed, or maybe bourbon since she came from the South.

'I had some women friends who were gun people, not for hunting, for shooting. It was called "blinking," practicing shooting, that was what the lower classes did. The upper classes shot at clay pigeons, called skeet, but to a certain extent guns were cross-class. Lordy, I haven't thought of all that in a long time. Anyway, the women advised me to try a number of guns, which they lent me from their own collection. I tried all sorts, going into Monroe County, in the Keys, to practice near the Everglades, shooting at cans. This was during the Cold War when there was fear of the bomb and a sense that one might have to take to the wilderness and survive; many who went in for blinking had been in the Army.' She sipped her drink; she seemed to be back there, he thought. She wasn't really talking to him, not really.

'Women were relatively rare as shooters; they practiced with women friends, or alone. In south Dade County and in Monroe County, there was water on both sides of the road; salt water, deep, with crocodiles. Crocodiles will put up with salt water; alligators stick to fresh water.'

'I'm glad to know that,' he said. They both smiled. He shook his head as she seemed about to offer him another beer.

'Well, that's it,' she said. 'When I moved up here to take the job I'd been offered, the gun just came along. I've got the ammunition somewhere; do you want to see it?'

'No,' he said. 'But I'd like to take another look at the gun if that's all right.'

She waved her hand toward the gun, palm up, meaning 'Be my guest.'

He picked up the gun, turning it to the light, and noticed there was writing on it. *STEVENS Savage Arms Corporation, Chicopee Falls, MA, USA,* it said. And underneath that he read, with some difficulty, turning the gun to the light, *Model 22–410, Proof-tested 410 bore, 3-inch chamber, .22 long rifle.*

He placed the gun gently back on the coffee table. 'So as far as you know,' he said to her, straightening his jacket and feeling his revolver in its holster under his arm, 'you reported the gun stolen, and then reported it returned. That's the whole story.'

'That's it.'

'Well, thank you for telling me all about the gun. And thanks for the beer.'

She stood and walked with him to the door. He felt he ought to say something else, something showing he'd appreciated hearing the story.

'I've never been to the South. Do you think I ought to have a look at the Everglades?'

'Well, they are interesting, and of course, they're endangered, like so much else in this country. We actually have to fight to preserve crocodiles. I may retire there someday and go back to growing avocados; that's what I did, in those years, before I went to work in an office.'

She opened the door; they shook hands again, and she closed it as he walked toward the elevator. He had wanted to ask if she were divorced or a widow but he hadn't known how to, and it wasn't any of his damn business anyway. Riding down in the elevator, he decided not to bother mentioning to anyone that he'd visited her. No reason to mention it; no reason at all.

But whatever reasons Farragut had for not mentioning his visit hardly survived a call from McRae that came some days later.

'Hey, Farragut,' McRae said, 'I hear the gun was returned to the lady who had it stolen. You know, at the time I never put the two things together, the gun the Comstock woman reported stolen and the shots someone was taking at bicyclists in the park. But now it suddenly comes to me, maybe hers was the gun shooting the bicyclists. Just goes to show you, you got to connect things up. Am I right, Farragut?'

'Right, McRae,' Farragut said into the phone.

'How about you and I meet to talk and connect things up together?'

'Well,' Farragut began, an excuse on the tip of his tongue. McRae heard the unspoken wariness.

'Come on; we'll have a drink and a talk. This damn case has been bugging me for a long time; I'll tell you about it. Talk about loony, this took the cake. Craziest damn case I ever looked into.'

'Where and when?' Farragut said before he found himself in the midst of excuses. No point trying to put McRae off, and, face it, he wouldn't mind knowing what the hell this was all about.

McRae told him where and when.

'Grusum tell you about it?' Farragut asked.

'Yeah. I called him to see how things were going, see if I could come up with some useful information he might need. He told me about the gun turning up.'

Farragut could guess what had happened. McRae was having trouble letting go of the tit, and Grusum gave him the only 'case' he didn't think really mattered; a good case, in fact, to fend McRae off with.

They took their drinks to a table. 'Okay,' Farragut said. 'Tell; I'm buying.' And why do I want to make him feel good by acting interested, Farragut asked himself. I encourage him now, he's going to make my life a misery from here on in. The truth was Farragut felt sorry for the poor mutt; who wanted to be retired, out of the loop, with no one giving a single goddamn about what you knew or thought or remembered?

'As I told you,' McRae began, 'I never connected the stolen gun reported by the Comstock dame and the loony case we had in Central Park. No reason I should have; still, I ought ... oh, the hell with it, never mind that. What first came to our attention was a young hefty guy who'd been knocked off his bicycle in Central Park by what he thought were bullets or shot but what turned out to be salt pellets. Someone in the park police came on him, lying on the ground next to his bike, which was kind of bent. He was mad as hell, and he kept saying it was that old broad, the old hag who had yelled at him. 'Why don't you go and find her instead of questioning me?' he said, so the cop rode back with the victim next to him in the car, and they found her, plain as day. Both of them got out of the car and confronted her; she seemed like a really old dame, sort of staggering along with a dog who must have been as old as she was. The idea of her shooting anybody was nutty, yet the guy who was on the bike kept saying it had to have been her.

'The cop asked him why.

'"I rode past her, close to the mutt but not touching either of them, and she yelled at me, "What's wrong with the road?" I yelled back, "What's wrong with you, you old bag?" And then, a few minutes later, I was shot."'

McRae finished off his drink, making a show of it, and Farragut got them both refills. 'No old lady with or without an old dog could have lifted that gun I saw,' Farragut said. 'The guy on the bike was dreaming, wasn't he?'

'The cop certainly thought so. They stopped to question the old lady, and she could scarcely understand them; deaf as a post. 'Why did she yell at you?' the cop asked the biker. 'She thought I should be in the road instead of the path,' he said. 'It was none of her damn business.'

'The cop pointed out that if he nearly ran her or her dog down, it was her business. Furthermore, the lady had a point. Since the road was free of traffic from ten in the morning until three in the afternoon just so bicyclists could ride there, why was he on the path? The guy said he wanted to go where the path was going; the cop pointed out that the road was running alongside the path and he, for one, didn't see why the guy didn't ride his bicycle on it. Anyway, they went back to where the bike was, and the cop decided to let it go at that. No need to bother with reporting it; a fluke, or a nutty guy, a typical Central Park complaint.'

'But you heard of it,' Farragut put in as McRae caught up with his drinking.

'It was a story, and it went around the way crazy stories do. I thought nothing of it at the time. Then, maybe three weeks later, maybe less, maybe more, around that, there was another incident, guys on Rollerblades this time.'

'Same path?'

'No, but nearby, in Strawberry Fields, the John Lennon place. There's a path that winds around, and one that's straighter; they're both hilly and come out in the same place. These college kids on spring break were Rollerblading down the curvy one and scaring people. Of course, the snotty kids paid no attention to people complaining or pointing to the signs about it being a place for 'quiet recreation.' I don't know about quiet recreation, but besides the tourists and Lennon worshipers, it's mostly old people and babies in strollers around there and it was a stupid place to go roaring down the hill on Rollerblades. This same old lady—'

'You're sure she was the same?' Farragut asked.

'Definitely. Same old dog, same cop, although there were two cops this time, one of them from the Fourteenth.'

'What happened to the Rollerblader?'

'Bladers. Plural. There were three of them. One of them yelled at her to get out of the way, together, you can be sure, with a description of her he didn't repeat. They kept going up to the top of the path, near where that plaque in the ground is that says *Imagine*, in memory of Lennon–tourists and people are always putting flowers there – and hurtling down. On one of the trips the front guy was shot – that's what he said – and fell down, tripping up the others.

'This time the cops looked for shells or whatever to see what he'd been shot with, and it was salt pellets.'

'So you didn't really know it was salt pellets the first time.'

'No. That cop just decided the biker had fallen on his own. Anyway, they then go looking for the old lady, who's back on the path she was on when the biker was shot, and this time they asked permission to pat her down and look in the bag she was carrying, but there was nothing. They even patted down the dog, who growled, or so they said. Nothing. *Niente.*'

'So they wrote a report this time, and the case got handed to you.'

'Not exactly. No one really thought of it as a case; they never did. But I asked the cop, the first one, to let me know if anything like that happened again, if he was on the spot or heard about it, and it did happen again.

'This time it was on the street, Central Park West, on the

park side. The old lady was walking along with the old dog, and a messenger flew by her at, she said, fifty miles an hour. She told us that if she'd moved an inch he would have hit her. He nearly hit the dog, though personally I think if he could have killed that mangy old mongrel it would have been a blessing. She called after him and he gave her the finger. Next thing, he's on the ground, pretty shook up since he was going so fast, and cursing like nothing you've heard, and I for one have heard it all.'

'Salt pellets?'

'Salt pellets. But by the time a cop got there, from another precinct, it just seemed like a crazy story, as it does the first time you hear it, and we might not have known about it in our shop except that again the story got around. We all laughed and said maybe the old lady was an alien with an invisible gun and anyway it served those damn messengers on bicycles right. I wouldn't have minded if there were more like her getting after them, if you want the truth.'

'I take it there was another time,' Farragut said, returning with more drinks.

'Yeah. This time she and the dog were crossing Central Park West, with the light, and a messenger on a bicycle shot out from behind a bus and all but knocked her over; scared the dog.'

'And he was soon thereafter knocked down with salt pellets farther down the road.'

'You got it. Only he was in the road in the traffic, and a car hit him. He wasn't hurt too bad, broken ribs, but this time we really had a case we had to follow up. Injured messenger, and a bus driver who saw the bicyclist nearly run over the old lady and the dog. The messenger and the company he rode for were fined, and nobody was suing anybody, so that could have been the end, except it was a reported accident and the guy driving the car that hit the bicyclist was claiming psychological damage and a dent in his new fancy vehicle. So I was told to track her down.'

'She must have been pretty rich if she lived near Central Park West.'

'She didn't look rich. But by this time I'd figured out that no way was she a bag lady; maybe she didn't take much care with her looks, but she sure had enough to live on, and my guess is she used to have more. Trust me, she was angry at the bicyclists and the Rollerbladers, but no way did she have a gun even if she was making herself out to be a crazy old dame.'

'And even if she'd had a gun strapped to the inside of her corset, she couldn't have hit a guy on a bike several blocks away,' Farragut put in.

'Yeah. Up to this point we still couldn't figure out how it was worked. I mean, when they patted her down she didn't have a phone on her. Of course she was a woman, and old, and they didn't have a female cop with them so they weren't exactly thorough, but they swore she didn't have anything as big as a portable phone, even the small kind.'

'So you questioned people in the neighborhood.'

'Right, but we didn't get stuck with much of that; she wasn't hard to find. By now I was really hooked on this case, partly because it was so loony, but also because I hate those bicyclists who won't use the road in the park and don't stop for lights and ride too fast. Some of those – uh – those messengers on bikes act like they want to run someone over.'

Farragut nodded. He knew that McRae had been going to

say 'black messengers' and stopped himself. 'They're damn good bicyclists though,' Farragut said, to keep himself honest. 'If people wouldn't panic they wouldn't get hurt.'

'They still get frightened, or they do panic and jump aside and that's when the shit hits the fan.'

'So you found her.'

'Yeah, I found her, by hanging around where she usually walked, she and the old dog. I followed her home.'

'Too bad no one nearly knocked her down while you were watching.'

'Who has that kind of luck? But I found out where she and her husband lived, between Columbus and Amsterdam in a brownstone; they had been renting two rooms there since before Columbus discovered America; cheapo, of course. The landlord or super, whichever, was happy to talk about her. They would have liked to get the old couple out, but no way. Still, they had a certain fondness for her; she'd once caught a bicyclist who knocked over a stroller with the baby in it right on their street and never stopped. She'd yelled at him and made a big fuss; so they were on her side, in spite of the cheapo apartment.'

'Some people might call her obsessive,' Farragut said. 'She couldn't just curse at dangerous bicyclists and bullying bladers like the rest of us and then just get on with her life. She had to get even; she had to let them know they were being punished by righteous people.'

'Sounds pretty fancy.'

Farragut cursed himself for forgetting to whom he was talking. 'I mean, she had this on her brain, it had taken her over, she thought about it a lot.' Farragut had wondered before this if McRae would have been drinking with him if he was still on the job and not lonely for cop talk. The others avoided McRae; Farragut knew that.

'You got that right.'

'Don't keep me in suspense,' Farragut said. 'How did it wind up?'

'I figured there had to be someone else, someone waiting for a signal. Once I'd got that part straight, it wasn't hard to find him.'

'Him?'

'Yeah, of course it had to be the husband, and he was old like her and the dog. But she wasn't as feeble as she made out, she wasn't really feeble at all, though the dog was, and the old guy wasn't feeble either.'

'How did she get in touch with him when she wanted him to shoot?'

'She yelled at the bikers something, like "What's wrong with the road?" She had some kind of microphone, a little gadget, stuck in between her breasts; when she yelled, he picked it up with a gadget he had. No problem, they told me down at the station; the sort of thing kids can work out.'

'But he had to be lying in wait in the same direction the bicyclist was taking.'

'That he did. If the bicyclists or whatever were going the wrong way, they got away with it, for that day at least. We don't know how many of the guys they hit just picked themselves up and went on without complaining. Anyway, I spotted the old guy, but I didn't let him know I'd spotted him. We decided to wait for the next time and get him cold. But I did watch him long enough to see how he carried the gun. He strapped it against his body and hid it under a big, raggy raincoat. Old guys get cold and wear coats even in the summer.'

'Did you catch him the next time?' Farragut was tired of having the story dragged out.

'No. That's the stupid part. A big case came up, and by the time it was over and I thought back to the old lady, she wasn't to be found. The dog had died – I went and asked the super in her building if she was still there – and she didn't go out walking so much anymore. I thought, the hell with it. And then they struck again.

'This time the bicyclist was a woman in a helmet on the path in the park who crashed into a baby darting in front of her. The mother and the bicyclist got into a screaming match, although the baby wasn't really hurt, just scared half to death, not to mention the mother, and the fracas went on while they called a cop. He took it all down, IDs and everything, and the bicyclist got on her bike and continued riding on the path, believe it or not. The old lady yelled and the bicyclist was down. They told me at the station that I had to arrest the old guy. I said I thought the bicyclist was the one to get, but she was being sued; that's how the rich handle these things. So I went in search of the old couple.'

Farragut looked interested, which was genuine enough, damn it.

'When I saw them right up close, they didn't seem all that old to me, but what do I know? For sure, they were nothing like as fragile as the lady had made out on the path when the cops caught up with her, and not deaf at all. Pretty spry, all right, probably could run farther than me.'

Farragut forbore pointing out that that hardly made her a marathoner.

'They told me it started after they'd had a dog killed by a cyclist who got clean away. The whole thing had taken over their lives; they didn't see why the police and the park rangers didn't keep the bikes off the paths; they certainly gave enough tickets to dogs off the leash who did a lot less damage. They showed me a picture of the dog that got killed. They were still mad.'

'So what did you do?' Farragut got out his money to pay, indicating he was ready for the end of the story.

'I didn't do nothing,' McRae said, standing up. 'I figured they didn't need to be dragged into the station and go through all that crap. I made them promise not to do it again.'

'And they haven't?'

'Nope, not as far as I know, and I think I'd know.'

'I hope so,' Farragut said. 'They might shoot someone in the eye or something.'

'Well,' McRae said, 'if I'm right about the gun being Comstock's, and I bet I am, it's been returned, so I figure that's the end of that.'

As the days and weeks went by, Farragut agreed that was the end of that. Yet the matter hardly dropped from his consciousness, not least because Ursula Comstock's face appeared between him and his forms whenever he was sitting at his desk filling out reports. Why he could not tell, neither himself nor any trusted friend or psychologist, should there be such in his life, which there was not. Finally, to try to put an end to it, he called her at her office, got her secretary, and, to his relief, Comstock, hearing his name, picked up at once. Which, he told himself, must mean she remembered who he was.

'I've still got the gun, if that's what you were wondering,' she said, laughing. 'Still in my closet without its screws, just as you saw it.'

'I'm glad to hear it; we're winding the whole thing up, and I hoped you could clear up a loose end,' he said, making it up as he went along.

'If I can. What's the loose end?'

'Do you know when the gun was stolen? It doesn't really matter except that the fact that it was returned to you suggests the person knew you and knew where you lived. My guess is that it was stolen from your apartment; that's how they knew where to bring it back.'

'Of course,' she said. 'I always suspected it might have been stolen during the large party I had just after I moved in here. I haven't had a large party since.'

'When you moved from the Everglades?'

'From Florida, anyway.'

'Did you know everyone at the party?'

'More or less. Everyone was intrigued by my having brought my gun up from Florida, and it went from hand to hand with considerable amazement on everyone's part. They were old friends from New York, where I lived when I was young, before I went to Florida.'

'With your husband, I suppose,' he said, hardly daring to risk offending her.

'Right. We were divorced and I stayed on in Florida. Which is why I got the gun and learned to shoot it. The rapist must have known there was no man in the house.'

'Could someone you didn't really know have come to the party?'

'I suppose so; I asked some people from the office; people I knew could have brought someone I didn't know. Isn't it rather late now to think about that?' she asked, as though it had just occurred to her.

'Yes, it is. But I thought they must feel friendly toward

you, considerate, to have returned the gun, even though we can't know why they chose that particular moment.'

'Maybe it was easier to return it than to dump it.'

'That's likely. I can't help wondering, though, how anyone could have walked out of your party carrying the gun; I mean, don't you think it was a rather large object to carry away without anyone noticing?'

'I think the very fact of its being so conspicuous is what made it easier. You might not have thought about it, being a policeman, but guns are far from common among the sort of people who would come to any party of mine. In fact, the gun aroused a good deal of innocent curiosity as it was passed around. I imagine that the couple must have watched its progress and made sure it ended up near the door. Then it would only be a matter of seizing it as one left and whisking it down to the lobby and out the door. Perhaps they held it between them as they walked into the street. It's astonishing, really, what you can get away with at a party if you go out of your way to be inconspicuous.'

'I'm sure you're right about that,' Farragut said, remembering some of the parties he had been to over the years. 'Well, thanks a lot for answering the question. It was on my mind.'

'Not at all,' she said.

He hung up feeling let down. Why, for God's sake? Was she supposed to ask him up for another beer just because he inquired about how the gun might have been lifted? Maybe she saw it was just an excuse. He thought not; anyway, he hoped not. It was a reasonable question. So that really is the end of that, Farragut assured himself.

And then two mountain bikers were shot in Central Park,

in the Ramble, this time not with salt pellets but with a real gun, a thirty-eight. They were not killed, but one was badly wounded and the other wounded enough to have to undergo abdominal surgery. The police knew the gun was a thirty-eight because one of the bullets had lodged in the back of the biker who was the worse hurt. The bullet was sent to forensics, but with no matching shell, bullet, or gun, they could determine little. The area was searched for shells, but none was found. The gunman must have retrieved them.

The Ramble is a woodsy section of Central Park, with winding paths and streams and places to hide out, should one wish. Long ago it was a meeting place for sexual prowlers of all inclinations, but the park rangers began patrolling it on horseback in pairs, and strollers walked there now. There were signs all over pleading with bicyclists not to ride off the paths, because it injured the plants and disturbed the ecology of the area. But these two on mountain bikes had whooped it up all over the place, frightening walkers, ripping up the delicate roots of the flora, and disturbing the birds nesting in the trees. There had been complaints from bird-watchers and others; the rangers had warned the bikers, but their enjoyment was the only imperative they recognized. The police, watching them carried off on stretchers, considered them lucky not to be dead.

The shooting had to be investigated, no doubt of that, but there was little clue to who might have hidden in the bushes with a gun. If he ever shot again, the police figured, they could match the bullets and perhaps get a lead. As it was, they kept a watch out, they questioned some of the rough types who hung around the park, but no one had a gun that matched the bullet taken from the biker. Anyway, the bicycles had not been stolen; theft was not the motive. Bikers had been attacked before in the park for their bicycles, but not this time.

After a while, the incident, which was not repeated, more or less vanished into the large collection of unsolved assaults. The police and the rangers thought the bikers had got what they deserved; the crime was not reported in the press, there having been no fatality, and all the overworked men and women, rangers and police were glad enough to see it fade away.

No one but Farragut knew that it did not fade away, that it was probably not an unsolved crime, that he was pretty certain who had shot the bikers, but he kept all this to himself. One afternoon, he was at the station when a call came in from a patrol car on the west side: two old people, apparent suicides, dead. Farragut went to the address, never doubting what he would find.

The super, not having seen the couple for several days, had hailed a patrol car and asked the police to accompany him as he unlocked the door and searched their apartment. The super was not long in America and did not want to break any laws. When he unlocked the door with his passkey – after the police had knocked and demanded to be let in, with no response forthcoming – the two were seen to be lying on the bed, quite dead, a gun between them. The police and the super were soon joined by Farragut.

'Looks like he shot her, then himself,' one of the patrolmen said.

'There's a note on the table.' The super had noticed that.

Farragut picked it up. It seemed rather long for a suicide

note, but a suicide note it was. Farragut read it over, and then read it aloud.

> There is an ancient Greek myth that tells how Jupiter and Mercury, seeking to test the hospitality of humans, could find no one to take them in when they disguised themselves as destitute travelers. Only one poor couple, Philemon and Baucis, welcomed them and shared food and warmth with them. When they left the next day, the gods revealed themselves and offered to grant the two any wish they might desire. Their wish was that neither of them would ever have to live alone. 'Grant that we may die together,' they said. The wish was in time granted them and has been granted us also, by our own hand.

'That seems clear enough,' Farragut said. 'I'll take the gun; you do the necessary.' He had already guessed that the gun was a thirty-eight. The address was the one McRae had told him. There were two small rooms, at the back of the house, as McRae had said. Farragut did not find it difficult to imagine their misery at seeing the Ramble invaded by those arrogant, macho bikers. Probably the old couple were bird-watchers too; he had seen a pair of binoculars on the dresser in their room. Perhaps they had heard, as he had, that a pair of red-winged hawks were living in the park, maybe in the Ramble; no bird-watcher would want red-winged hawks upset.

Where had they got the gun? he wondered. Probably bought it on the street; thirty-eights were as common as crack vials. He would turn it in, and forensics would discover that it was the gun that had shot the bikers. Well, no harm could come to them now. It was always possible, if he told forensics there was no rush about this gun, since there were no real questions left about it, that they would forget it forever; forensics was backed up at the best of times.

One thing was now obvious to him, and considering it gave him a jolt of pleasure. He had been right that the couple, or one of them at least, must have been at Ursula Comstock's party. He knew he was also right that they must have thought of her with affection. Whatever part of her life they were from, or however long ago they had known her, they had liked her a lot. Having used her gun for their revenge on domineering bikers and bladers, they had returned it to her before their final, perhaps fatal attack on the mountain bikers in the Ramble. They made certain no weapon for what might, intentionally or not, become a fatal shooting could be traced to her. They had given her back her gun, the screws removed for safety, as though that part of their task was finished.

They were obsessed, that pair; of course they were. Farragut had looked up *obsession* in the dictionary, which defined it simply as a compulsive preoccupation with a fixed idea. Watch out you don't become obsessed as well, Farragut, he warned himself.

But it was no use. He called her again at the office.

'Look,' he said, 'you may not give a hoot in hell what your gun was used for, but we've got the whole story now, and it occurred to me that you might be interested in hearing it. It's on the long side, but I could tell you on the phone, now or another time.'

'You might as well tell me this evening,' she said, 'if you'd like to stop by and have another beer. Did you like the kind you drank last time? I have others. Seven o'clock okay?'

'Any kind of beer will be a pleasure,' he said, smiling as he hung up.

JAMES CRUMLEY

....

Obsession can take many forms, but seldom can it be said to be a force for good. It is an emotion that causes its possessor to stop thinking rationally, and that is often the first step down a dark path. Or at least a stupid one.

C. W. Sughrue just can't help himself. Here, as in The Last Good Kiss *and* The Mexican Tree Duck, *he has no intellectual choice. If a woman needs his help, damn, he's just got to be there. It's not always what he wants, and it's not always good for him, but there it is. He's got to be the strong right arm or the consoling shoulder.*

While the intention in this collection of stories was for each of them to be brand-new, published nowhere else until between these covers, I made an exception for 'The Mexican Pig Bandit.' Crumley, one of a handful of my favorite writers, writes a short story about as often as I have an urge for broccoli. When I found that he had written this story exclusively for a limited-edition publication of three hundred copies, mainly for collectors, I thought it was okay to cheat – just this once.

THE MEXICAN PIG BANDIT

By James Crumley

After Nixon resigned, the sixties seemed to stumble into a coopted and unseemly halt, and C. W. Sughrue's major source of income – finding runaway minors in San Francisco – just disappeared. Either the kids had stopped running away, or their parents had stopped looking for them. So Sughrue did what any self-respecting unemployed private investigator might do: He cut off his ponytail, bought a brand-new El Camino, and headed for Mexico to avoid making a decision, preferring instead to live his life as a leap of faith.

After a couple of weeks knocking around the desert and the Sierra Madre, he found himself a couple of hours south of Mazatlán working on his tan, smoking a bit of great Mexican *mota*, and enjoying his vacation among the surfers, dopers, and various other Americans who had no more purpose in capitalist life than he had. They had all lodged like lazy ticks nuzzled into the shaggy hide of the Mexican Pacific coast in the quiet village of San Geronimo.

For three weeks, Sughrue enjoyed the wonderful simplicity of simply waiting. On that last peaceful morning, as he did every other one before, Sughrue ran on the cool beach, then devoured a room-service breakfast of *huevos rancheros*, propped his bare feet on the balcony rail, then popped the tab on a Tres Xs and fired up a joint of the primo dope he had bought from the two Texas A&M dropouts rediscovering the sixties in the suite next door. The ex-Aggies were playing Iron Butterfly yet again. But Sughrue tuned them out as he watched the Pacific waves break over the shallow bar at the mouth of the bay, just waiting.

During his three hitches in the Army, Sughrue had learned to wait. On the first two hitches, he waited for baseball or football season to begin as he sat around gyms passing out towels to Special Service gold-bricking jocks even lazier than he. Or sitting around the base newspaper waiting for something to happen worth reporting. Then on his third hitch he decided to become a real soldier with the 1st Air Cav. In the Central Highlands, he learned to wait patiently for the choppers to carry his squad into the bush, then wait frantically for the bastards to come back.

San Geronimo sure beat the hell out of Pleiku as a place to wait. In the early years of their conquest, the Spanish had tried to turn the small fishing village into a port. The ruins of the old fort still cluttered the tangled jungle along the steep ridge that divided the village from the shallow estuary. But the constantly shifting bar at the mouth of the bay, which sometimes made the surfing great, defeated the Spanish sailors over and over again until they abandoned any notion of making San Geronimo into a major port.

The village remained, though, strung out on the narrow strip of flat land between the fine white beach and the steep ridge, home to a few fishermen, some businesses that catered to tourists, three small hotels, and a string of *jalapas* that lined the beach until it petered out as the ridge dove sharply into the bay. A narrow, rough road led from the main highway to the village, where it split into two even narrower one-way streets. One ran south in front of the hotel, the other behind it and out of town. Sughrue had solitude without isolation, peace without boredom. Even in October the sun shone every day, and the offshore breeze kept the flies and mosquitoes at bay; the food was fine if uninspired; the beer cool if not cold. And the bright lights and painted women of Mazatlán were only a six-pack away.

Sughrue thought he might stay until his money or his tourist visa ran out. After that, who knew. Because he had a knack for finding people, one of the large San Francisco agencies would probably take him on. But for now he was content to wait for the *mota* and the beer to dull his edge, to wait for the sun to clear the ridge behind the hotel, its rays broken into spears by the ruined fort. Then it would be time for a siesta.

The inbound morning bus, a first-class, with its load of tourists but not many Mexicans, trundled beneath his balcony. Sughrue knew that the sunshine wouldn't be far behind. He had another hit off the joint, stubbed out the roach, and opened a new beer. Then he strolled around the corner of his balcony to wait for the sun. A man had to have some regularity to his day; the Army had taught him the benefits of that. As he leaned lazily on the rail, he noticed an old flatbed truck – it looked like a converted American Army deuce-and-a-half – parked in an alley just down the outbound street. Sughrue noticed it because it was black and lacked the gaudy paint and lights of most Mexican trucks. Also, he noticed a huge sow wearing a large red bandana around her neck, stretched out in front of the truck like a concubine who had just finished her nightly labors.

Down at the end of the beach the bus unloaded a few

passengers, picked up a few more, then bounced back toward the hotel. Beneath him, Sughrue heard something, more a bark than a word. The sow, surprisingly delicate and agile, rose to her feet and trotted to the center of the ratty pavement, where once again she stretched out full length, blocking the street.

When the bus arrived, the driver did the sensible thing; he stopped. Hitting a pig with a vehicle is very much like hitting a rock of the same size. The driver leaned on the horn for several seconds. Nothing happened. Not that time, or the next. Finally, much irritated, the driver charged out of the bus. He was a stocky, bowlegged man in cowboy boots and droopy jeans. When he nudged the sow with his boot, his shirttail popped out, revealing his butt-crack. Sughrue laughed. The driver looked up with a sneer, then turned back to the pig, kicking and cursing her. He might as well have been kicking his bus for all the sow's reaction. She didn't even raise her head. After several moments of this, the driver looked at his passengers and shrugged as if to say 'What now?' Several passengers climbed off to help. One middle-age American who looked like a farmer in a homemade jumpsuit suggested that the driver try biting her ear. Either the driver didn't have any English, or he did and knew better than to anger the sow. The old joke about the hogs eating your little brother wasn't a joke to anybody who had ever seen a sow protecting her litter. Whatever, nothing happened again. Sughrue liked that; it seemed a perfect Mexican moment. Most of the passengers, none of them as amused as Sughrue, climbed off the bus. One of them was a young Mexican woman dressed in a peasant blouse and full skirt, sunglasses, and a dark scarf, and clutching a cloth bag to her chest.

Then with a rattle of Spanish like a burst of automatic gunfire, half a dozen people dressed like comic bandits with red bandanas over their faces and wearing sunglasses and floppy straw hats stepped out of shadowed doorways and alleys. Four men and two women. One of the men – the leader, Sughrue assumed – carried a Thompson submachine gun with a drum magazine. Two others had M-1s. Another a pump shotgun. One of the women had a .30 carbine, the other an Army Colt .45. The leader, the stock of the Thompson lodged in the crook of his elbow, spit orders in Spanish too quick for Sughrue to follow. The man with the shotgun climbed on the bus, herded the remaining passengers out of the bus, then began to throw small bags out the door. The other men shoved the driver to the luggage compartment, which he opened, and they emptied, tossing luggage into the flatbed truck. The woman with the .45 opened a tow sack and forced the crowd of passengers to throw their watches, jewelry, purses, and wallets into the sack. Some of the passengers grumbled, but not too much after the woman clubbed the farmer in the jumpsuit on the elbow with the Colt.

Only the young woman resisted when the woman bandit grabbed her cloth carrying case. Sughrue had seen the young woman around town for a week or so, but she always seemed to be crossing to the other side of the street or just leaving the cantina when he entered. She struggled briefly until the woman bandit nestled the .45 lovingly into her neck. The young woman gave up the case, then seemed to collapse in tears. Sughrue thought he heard an animal's cry, but it was lost in the shuffling of the confused passengers and the leader's laughter.

The leader covered the crowd with his Thompson while

the others pulled a stepped ramp from the back of the truck. When he barked a command, the sow rose quickly and with some grace and elegance clambered up the ramp, her red bandana fluttering in the still air. Then the bandits piled aboard and drove quickly up the street out of town.

Sughrue just watched, as if stoned, but he hadn't been since the guy with the Thompson stepped out of the shadows. He thought he should have done something but didn't know what. His Browning Hi-Power, which he'd foolishly smuggled into Mexico, was locked under the seat of the El Camino. The suite didn't have a telephone, so he couldn't call the village's single policeman, Jesus Acosta, who also owned Sughrue's favorite watering hole, El Tiburon. And he supposed racing down the stairs barefoot and wearing only gym shorts to interfere in the robbery would have been even more suicidal than was normal.

The passengers, mostly middle-age Americans or young Europeans, milled in small confused circles, chattering in several languages, shuffling dust out of the thin asphalt. Then they began to drift quietly away, either like the stunned survivors of a natural disaster or people for whom this robbery was perfectly natural, leaving the young woman weeping in the middle of the street.

He'd always hated dealing with a crying woman. After his father came back from WWII, however briefly, then kept moving west for reasons he never bothered to explain, Sughrue's mother cried, it seemed, for years, cried until he quit high school and joined the Army. His most abiding childhood memory found him sitting across the table from his mother in the little lease house as she recounted her day of peddling Avon products and collecting all the gossip in Moody County, chain-smoking cigarettes, drinking short

Cokes spiked with Everclear, and weeping. Sughrue never found a way to comfort her, to stop the tears. Not his mother, or any other woman. And he never found a way to stop trying. A fat farm wife from Iowa would show up in his office looking for her runaway child; he would carefully explain to her the difficulties of finding anybody in the Haight in those days of peace, love, and drugs; she would cry; Sughrue would take her money, promising to try. Often he suspected his reaction to weeping women was either cowardice or a very stupid obsession.

Sughrue knew he didn't have enough Spanish to comfort the young woman, but he had to try, so he slipped into his T-shirt and started toward the stairs, but she looked up and shouted at him. Until she whipped off her scarf and sunglasses, Sughrue thought she was screaming at him in Spanish, but when she locked her brilliant blue eyes on him, he saw clearly that she was obviously a *gringa* with a great tan.

'What?' was all he could say.

'Why didn't you do something, asshole?'

Not just an American, but by the way her lips puckered when she called him an asshole, an American accustomed to giving orders.

'Don't you have a gun or something?' she shouted as she walked toward the back stairway. Sughrue wanted to stop her but, as with the bandits, he seemed paralyzed. As she came up the stairs toward his balcony, she shouted again. 'Aren't you a private detective or something? Don't you have a fucking gun?'

'Lady,' Sughrue explained – quietly because illegal firearms were a sure way to hard time in a Mexican jail or an extremely expensive trip to the border – 'I don't have a gun. And even if I did, there were six of them and they all had guns.'

'Right,' she barked as she arrived in front of him, then backed him around the corner to the small table, 'and a fucking dangerous pig!'

'Sows are dangerous. . . .'

'Whatever,' she said, then flopped into a chair, grabbed a Tres Xs and a chunk of lime, cracked the can, squeezed the lime, and gulped the cold beer.

'Just who the hell are you?' Sughrue asked.

'Don't play dumb, man,' she said. 'I know my fucking father sent you down here after me.'

'Hey, I'm down here on vacation.'

'Fucking lying prick!'

Sughrue didn't know exactly how to respond to that. This was nearly as confusing as her tears. Then the larger of the two ex-Aggies stepped out of the marijuana haze of their suite and leaned over the rail between their balconies. His red butch haircut hadn't grown out very far, and his skin would never adapt to the Mexican sun. He peeled a scrap of skin off his nose and asked, 'What the hell's going on. C. W.?'

'I don't know,' Sughrue admitted.

'Hey, you're an American,' the young woman said. 'How about giving me a hand here? My fucking jerk-off father sent him down from San Francisco to take me back to Mill Valley. Very much against my will, I might add.'

The young woman was pretty, and the ex-Aggie was a Texas gentleman, even if massively stoned. Sughrue saw him tense as if about to vault the short distance between the balconies, then saw him reconsider. The ex-Aggie knew Sughrue had shot men, both in and out of the war, and knew he had a right hand as swift and fast as a major-league fastball. Sughrue knew that the ex-Aggies had financed their Mexican sojourn by buying a hundred pounds of Mexican shake, then wrapping it in copies of the Bogotá newspaper and carrying it to New York City, where they sold it as Colombian. Sughrue also knew that the boys planned a major move in the dope business and that they couldn't stand any heat of any kind. So he just smiled at the ex-Aggie and said, 'Hook 'em Horns, dipshit.'

'Sorry, ma'am, it ain't none of my business,' he said, then disappeared back to the smoke and portable tape-deck sounds of their suite.

'Well, isn't that just lovely?' the young woman said, her face wonderfully composed for a woman who had been sobbing helplessly only minutes before. 'What are they? Your butt-fuck buddies?' she added, then hid her eyes with the sunglasses.

'Lady,' Sughrue said as he sat down across the table from her, 'I don't have the vaguest notion who you are, but I know this: If I was your father, I wouldn't spend a thin fucking dime to have you brought home. In fact, I'd pay somebody to keep your sorry, weeping ass in Mexico—'

Suddenly, she was sobbing again. Silently this time. Soft fat tears seeped from beneath her shades. Sughrue opened another beer, drank it slowly, praying this crying fit would be over before she asked him for something he couldn't provide. But it didn't abate a bit. He finished the beer, went into the suite for a quick shower, then dressed in Levi's, boots, and his next-to-last clean shirt. He had a strong feeling that he needed to be dressed for whatever happened next. He even thought briefly about getting the pistol out of the El Camino, but decided against it.

When he went back outside, the young woman still hadn't stopped the silent tears. The sun had already topped the rise. The siesta was hours away, but as soon as the sun hit the village, everything seemed to slow to a halt. The seabirds fluffed their feathers, the inhabitants sought shady perches, and the traffic dust seemed to hang in the stolid air. Even the Pacific became as flat as a dry lake. Forlorn surfers wandered back from the beach, their boards like bones over their shoulders. Everything stopped. Except the young woman weeping like a lost child.

'Hey, I'm sorry,' Sughrue said softly as he opened the last beer and offered it to her. She declined with a weak shake of her head. He drank it himself. Finally, through no fault of his, she stopped crying and dried her eyes. She mumbled something he didn't catch, probably didn't want to catch. 'Hey, I'm going to get some more beer, okay? Can't get to lunch without beer in Mexico. So you just wait right here, okay?'

Maybe she nodded. Maybe not. Sughrue picked up the breakfast dishes and the bucket of melted ice and started for the stairs, but she mumbled again.

'What's that?' he asked.

'I could use a couple of shots of tequila,' she said quietly. 'If you wouldn't mind.'

'No problem.'

'And maybe something to eat.'

'Sure.'

'No fish, though,' she whispered, 'please. I can't stand any more fish—'

'You came to the wrong town—'

'You're telling me,' she said.

'No problem,' he said.

As he headed down the stairs, she might have said 'Thank you.' But maybe not.

When Sughrue came back from downstairs carrying the ice bucket, the food, and a glass of tequila – he'd had a couple of shots himself while they rustled up a plate of *carne asada* tacos – the balcony was empty. He almost sighed in relief until he heard the squeal of the tiny shower. He set everything down, then looked in the room. Her clothes and huaraches were scattered every which way. No bra, of course. But a pair of white cotton panties hung on the bathroom door as if to warn him. Suitably warned, Sughrue shut the door as he went back to the balcony. She was in the shower a long time. Long enough for him to finish several cigarettes, a beer, and one of her tacos. As he stubbed out a cigarette, he noticed that the roach was missing from the ashtray. He stole a sip of her tequila.

When she finally came outside, her dark hair was wrapped in a white towel and she was wearing his last clean shirt, a white cowboy shirt he had been saving for a special occasion, should one ever arise in this sleepy village. She was a bit short in the leg and a little long in the waist, but she was trim and tan. All over. Her heavy brown breasts glowed through the white cotton of his shirt. Maybe this was a special occasion.

She sat down, salted the back of her hand, and picked up the tequila. Before she licked the salt, she looked up, her eyes shining, sporting a childishly seductive smile, her pink tongue flickering at the corner of her mouth. Sughrue realized she was younger than he had thought. And either tougher or more desperate. She gunned the tequila without a flinch. Then unwound the towel and shook her long, sleek hair in the sunlight. Against his white shirt, it gleamed like silk.

'So what are we going to do?' she asked as she picked up a taco.

'About what?'

'Those bastards took everything I had – clothes, money, ID, everything,' she said, then bowed her head as if to weep again. 'The fucking assholes even took my baby.'

'They what?'

'I told you a while ago. They took my baby. He was sleeping in the bag.'

'I guess I missed that,' Sughrue admitted, then remembered the sharp cry he'd heard when the woman bandit jerked the bag from her.

'Listen,' she said when she finished her taco, 'my daddy has ten thousand acres of irrigated land in the Central Valley and five car dealerships, so he's got just oodles and scads of money, and I'm sure he'd pay you whatever you want if you help me.'

'Maybe I can help,' Sughrue said, 'but I need to know a few things first.'

'Like what?' she said with a stubborn tilt to her face.

'Like your name,' he said, 'and what the hell you're doing down here.'

'Marina Forsyth,' she said. 'You ever hear of Forsyth Cadillac?'

'Yeah,' he said, then held out his hand. 'C. W. Sughrue.'

Marina shook his hand quickly but with a strong grip as she said, 'I know.'

'How the hell do you know?'

'Jesus, man, everybody in the Haight knows about the

Cowboy Detective,' she said. 'You were in all the papers when you shot that chick's guru—'

'He wasn't a *guru*,' he interrupted. 'He was a sleaze-bag smack dealer. And he shot at me first.'

'I heard it a little differently on the street,' she said calmly, 'but that's besides the point. Will you help me?'

'What the hell were you doing down here with a baby?'

'Do I have to tell you?' she whined.

'If you want me to help,' he said.

She took a deep breath, her eyes brimmed with tears briefly, then she said, 'I'm fucked if you don't help.' After a long pause, she looked out at the gleaming Pacific. 'I had a baby boy right after Christmas last year,' she said, 'out of wedlock, as my father likes to point out, and he made me give him up to some rich asshole friends of his. I found out who they were and that they were staying at their place in Acapulco, so I rode the bus down there and got him back. That's all.'

'Got him back?'

'Well, I sort of took him.'

'Took him?' Sughrue said. 'As in kidnaping?'

'They just wanted him because they couldn't have one,' she said. 'They buy two new Caddies from my father every year. For all I know, they bought my baby too. So I just took him back—'

'I'm sorry,' Sughrue said, 'but I don't think I need to get mixed up in a kidnaping down here.'

'That's what you did, though,' she said. 'You just kidnaped those poor kids who were trying to get away from their parents—'

'That's not the same,' he said.

'Why the fuck not?' she said, then stood up and stormed

around the balcony for a few moments. 'Why the fuck not?' Then she sat down and ate another taco.

Sughrue shut his eyes, tilted his face to the sun, and thought about it. Even if she was conning him, and he knew she wasn't telling him the whole story, she was stuck deep in Mexico with no way home. If he drove hard, he could get her to the border and be back on the beach in three or four days. Maybe somebody with money could meet them there. He could renew his tourist visa and vehicle permit, then stretch this early retirement for another six months. If the price was right, he thought, even as he hated himself for thinking it. Truth was, even if he'd only admit it to himself, he'd hated giving some of those runaway kids back to their parents. Sometimes the mothers stopped weeping as the kids started. And as he admitted that, Sughrue realized that he wasn't always happy in his work. It was just something he did well.

'So what are you doing, Mr. Cowboy Detective?' she asked. 'Working on your tan?' she added so snottily, he nearly changed his mind about helping her.

'You can call me 'Mr. Sughrue' or you can call me 'C.W.' or you can call me 'Sonny' like my folks did, but nobody but that fucking idiot reporter ever called me "the Cowboy Detective"—'

'Maybe it was "the Hippie Detective," ' she said. 'Didn't you have a ponytail? Why'd you cut it off?'

'Down here it's just asking for trouble.'

'I found the roach in the ashtray,' she said. 'You act like a hippie.'

'Smoking dope doesn't make you a hippie,' he explained. 'It just makes you stupid and happy for a little while.'

'That's for sure,' she said, waving another taco in the air

between them. 'If I hadn't been blazed that night, I'd never have let Mark inside me without a rubber. "I won't come inside of you," he says, "I just want to *feel* you." Then he came like a racehorse. Immediately. If the dumbfuck had let me on top, I might have gotten away from some of it. Jesus, shit ran down my leg for an hour. But not enough, obviously.'

Sughrue noticed that as he soaked up the sunshine and listened to Marina's faux tough hippie-chick chatter, he also watched her breasts bob and weave with the movement of her hand. The earlier stone crept softly back into his body on little cat feet. He caught himself quickly before he floated into the cool siesta shade of the bedroom, hoping she would follow.

'If I take you back to the border,' he said, 'would your father meet us there – you'll need a passport or a birth certificate to get back across, anyway – and maybe bring some cash for my trouble?'

'If he came,' she said, 'and I don't think he would, he'd try to give you a check then stop payment on it.'

'What about your mother?'

'She's out of the picture,' she said. 'She's down here somewhere – Oaxaca last we heard – living with a creep who calls himself a painter.' Then she paused dramatically. 'I've got an aunt in Scottsdale who might.'

'You know her telephone number?'

'Of course,' she said. 'How much cash were you thinking about?'

'Hadn't thought about it,' Sughrue said aimlessly. 'How about five hundred plus expenses?'

'If you help me get my baby boy back,' she said, 'I'd bet she would come with five thousand.'

'You've got a deal,' Sughrue said, sitting up suddenly, no longer drifting. 'You wait here while I check out some things with a friend of mine.'

'You don't want me to come with you?' she asked. 'I suspect my Spanish is a lot better than yours.'

'Honey,' he said, 'down here they can keep material witnesses in jail until they convict somebody.'

'I forgot that.'

'So if anybody asks,' Sughrue suggested, 'your stuff was on the bus, but you missed it.'

'Why?'

'You were up here with me,' he said, 'in the sack.'

'Now, who'd believe a thing like that,' she said, but tried her sly smile on him again. 'You think you could pick up some clothes for me? I don't want to go on a manhunt in your last clean shirt.'

Sughrue said he'd try, but he didn't really mean it. He thought she was kind of cute in his shirt. And after a few more drinks, he knew he'd think she was lovely.

Sughrue didn't bother stopping at the tiny police station with its single cell but headed straight for El Tiburon. The bar was silent, the transistor radio turned off for the first time Sughrue could remember. Roberto, the fat bartender, slept on the bar, stretched out with much the same languid grace that the sow had exhibited. Jesus Acosta sat at his usual place, a table by the back door and under the only working ceiling fan, a liter bottle of El Presidente brandy sitting on the floor beside his chair. Acosta was a lean man, dressed in stiff khakis, starched and ironed each night by his loving mother. He had a gaunt Indian face and wore mirrored sunglasses and looked like a man who would be happy to slice the eyelids off an American tourist before he staked him on a sunny anthill. Sughrue knew, though, that when Acosta removed his sunglasses and grinned, a grin full of impossibly white teeth, he became just a nice guy working as a police officer in his hometown. He had been to the States many times, and his English was more than serviceable. In fact, in the early evening when the brandy was nearly gone, Acosta became eloquent in the manner of television cops. Sughrue crossed the hushed bar to grab a Negra Modelo ale from the cooler behind the bar, then sat down at Acosta's table. The policeman wore his hat and sunglasses inside, and not a single sharp tooth gleamed from his dark, grim smile.

'Sr. Sonny,' he said quietly, 'please forgive me, but I have no time this morning to practice my English. You've heard, perhaps, of our troubles?'

'Rumors, no more,' Sughrue lied.

'Revolutionaries have robbed the *Tres Estrellas autobus* and broken the arm of an American tourist,' Acosta said solemnly. 'Very bad trouble. For everyone. Especially me.'

'Revolutionaries?'

'Communist filth,' Acosta said, then quickly added, 'but not Mexicans. The driver has told me that the leader's accent was very strange. Perhaps Salvadorians or Guatemalans. Not Cubans. He was very certain on that point.'

'I didn't hear that,' Sughrue said, thinking that a band of drunken thieves was one thing, a communist cadre quite another. Five thousand wouldn't be nearly enough. 'Nothing like that.'

'Yes.' Acosta sighed. 'There will be much trouble for me ... when it is reported.' Acosta removed his hat and tossed his sunglasses in it. His eyes were terribly bloodshot for noon. He lifted the brandy, three quarters gone already, drank from the neck, and complained, 'I will be replaced. Yes. Who will take care of my wonderful mother? And my business? *Me carnales*, they will rob me blind.'

'I'm sorry,' Sughrue said. Then added without conviction, 'I wish there was something I could do. . . .'

Suddenly Acosta became very excited. 'You are a famous detective, Sr. Sonny,' he said, 'you can find them. I will owe you my life.' Acosta's hand darted across the table, and Sughrue had no option but to shake it. As if a deal had been struck, Acosta continued. 'They will be near water. The pig needs water. This is only their third job. They will not be hard to find.'

'Stranger things have happened,' Sughrue said. 'You could ride along.'

'No,' Acosta said, standing as he replaced his hat and sunglasses. 'No, I cannot. Even now my mother prepares lunch for the passengers. I must keep them happy until the telephone is repaired—'

'The telephone is broken?' Sughrue asked, looking at the only working telephone in the village, sitting like a dumb plastic toy on the bar.

'And the bridge also.'

'The bridge? How will I get out of town?' Sughrue asked.

'My cousin Flaco, he waits at the bridge. He will show you the *vado*.'

'Of course.'

'Bring me their bodies.' Acosta smiled, showing teeth this time, as he picked up the brandy and headed for the doorway. He paused in the doorway. 'Or their heads will do,' he said to the empty street, then stepped into the burning sunshine, only listing slightly.

Sughrue snagged another ale, lit another cigarette, and leaned on the bar to stare at his reflection in the ragged mirror. No answers there, he decided, then turned to face the open doorway. He watched the street as he sipped the ale. Nobody passed. Perhaps the whole town was down at Acosta's house, swilling his tequila and chewing on his mother's great *carnitas*. Or maybe they were hiding from the revolutionaries. No answers there either. And no clothes for Marina, Sughrue thought as he walked back to the hotel. All the stores were dark and empty. It looked as if she was going to have to hunt *bandidos* in her dirty clothes. Or his last clean shirt.

Flaco's jeep blocked the bridge over the Rio Escondido, but because Sughrue was the good friend of Jesus Acosta and for a gift of a hundred pesos, he moved his vehicle. When they reached the highway, Sughrue turned north toward Mazatlán. Dutifully, he stopped at every roadside business – cantinas, fruit stands, revulcanization shops, and places that would rewind your generator by hand, even at groups of confused peasants at bus stops – but nobody had seen a flatbed truck loaded with luggage, bandits, and a trained pig. In Mazatlán Marina burned down his credit cards and came up with a fairly classy wardrobe for a hippie chick who had been engaged in Mexican felonies in a native costume. Then he drove her to the post office, where she made her call.

'All set,' she said as climbed back into the El Camino. She fluffed her white lace dress around, then stared at her toes, winking from her new white sandals.

'Not exactly your rat-killing clothes,' Sughrue suggested.

'See if you can't find a drugstore or a supermarket or something,' she said.

'Why?'

'I think my period's about to start.'

But when she came out of the *supermercado*, she had turned a handful of his pesos into a bag of cosmetics, a bottle of Herradura tequila, a bottle of *sangria* for a chaser, and an armful of fruit.

Sughrue grabbed the register receipt and tossed it into the glove box. He didn't see any tampons, though. Marina made him wait while she fixed her face and painted her nails.

'You ready?' he asked, then headed north out of Mazatlán.

'Where do you think you're going?' she asked as she dried her fingernails in the air conditioner's blast.

'If we drive all night, we can make Nogales by morning.'

'My aunt can't make it down for a couple of days,' she said calmly. 'So let's head south and see if the bastards went that way.'

'They're probably long gone by now.'

'You're not afraid, are you?' she asked. 'They're just a bunch of pepperbelly jerks.'

Sughrue took a deep breath, then said, 'Hey, you know who you sound like? A bunch of kids I flew to Vietnam with. "Just a bunch of little pissant gooks," they said. A lot of kids are dead or crippled now. You don't have to be John Fucking Wayne to pull the trigger of a Thompson, kid.'

'I'm not a kid,' she said, 'and I'm sure as hell not afraid.'

'Maybe you should be,' Sughrue said. 'But, listen, if we find these *bandidos*, promise you'll let me go to the authorities.'

'Sure,' she said blithely, 'but it might be a little harder than finding a stoned hippie kid on the streets of the Haight.'

'Harder than you might think,' Sughrue said.

'And I just thought of something. . . .'

'What?'

'On the back of that truck,' she said, 'there was a pile of boards and a tarp.'

'That makes a difference,' Sughrue said. 'If we're heading south, we better get some lunch.'

For the first time since she'd climbed his stairs, she agreed with him.

'By the way,' she said offhandedly, 'your Spanish sucks. Maybe you better let me handle the questions tomorrow.'

And for the first time, he agreed with her.

Sughrue knew a little place across the boulevard from the beach, so they had a long lunch of ceviche and crab omelets. Marina didn't talk much, just sat there looking like a beautiful American woman and occasionally asking questions about his work. Sughrue did his best not to defend himself and just told her the funny stories, not the sad ones. He hadn't talked to an American woman in months, it seemed, and he talked to Marina, told her about his mad father who had come back from WWII convinced he was a Comanche Indian, about his mother, the weeping Avon Lady, who knew all the gossip worth knowing in Moody County, Texas, and his life as a football bum. Marina kept trying to get him to talk about Vietnam, but Sughrue artfully dodged that question. But he talked until the sun drifted toward the misty horizon.

'It'll be dark by the time we get back to the turnoff,'

Sughrue said, 'so maybe we should crash here tonight and get an early start in the morning.'

'I hear the El Camino Real is nice,' she said with a quiet smile.

'I know more people at La Playa,' he said, and once again she agreed with him.

When Sughrue asked the desk clerk for two connecting ocean-side rooms, the young man didn't even glance at Marina, he just smiled politely and found them rooms, a sweet Mexican smile that seemed to say 'Some days, life is a gift.' The less sophisticated bellhop who carried Marina's purchases and Sughrue's duffel up to the rooms just grinned. As did Pablo, the one-eyed bartender who served them margaritas as they sat at the open-air bar and watched the sun sink between the rocky islands of the bay.

'You've been here before,' Marina said, 'with women.'

'I've been here, right,' he said, 'but not with women.' But he had met women sitting at this bar. A tall, lanky lady probation officer from Denver, and a tiny Air France stewardess from Paris. 'It's a good hotel,' he added. 'Right, Pablo?'

'Man does not live by fish tacos alone,' Pablo said in passing.

'Jesus, you jerks,' Marina said with a sneer, then gunned her second margarita. 'If the gods didn't mean for you to eat it, they wouldn't have made it smell like a fish taco.'

Then she drank two more margaritas quickly without a word, then ordered a hamburger and fries, ate half of it, then said she was tired and intended to go to bed. But she wasn't too tired to be snotty when Sughrue suggested that he might go downtown to check out some 'sources.'

'Sources?' she slurred sweetly. '*Las mujeres de la noche*?' Then she walked toward the lobby, her slim hips swaying a bit more than necessary, her sandals slapping loudly on the tile floor.

Pablo poured them two large glasses of tequila, opened two beers, then raised his glass. 'It's too early to go downtown, sarge.' Pablo had lost his eye to a short round in the Iron Triangle with the 25th. 'Or maybe you could just follow your *gringa* up to the room.'

'She ain't mine, man,' Sughrue said. 'She belongs to *el diablo*.'

'Where do you find them, my friend?' he asked. Which was the same thing he asked when the probation officer cold-cocked a vacationing San Diego fireman for slapping her on the butt and calling her 'Shorty.' 'Or do they find you?'

'You're a cruel man, trooper.'

'I learned it in Fresno,' Pablo said, 'shoveling chickenshit for twenty cents an hour.'

They clicked glasses, wishing each other health, happiness, money, and the time to enjoy them. And bad luck to redneck chicken-fucking egg farmers.

It took Sughrue until nearly midnight to find Antonio Villalobos Delgado sitting at his favorite table at his second-favorite whorehouse, La Copa del Oro. Villalobos was a large, burly *abogado* with a wealth of flaming red hair on his head and face. La Copa was nothing like the border-town whorehouses of Sughrue's south Texas youth. The working women were, if not beautiful, certainly nicely dressed and nicely buffed. And they didn't hustle drinks or hassle customers. They just sat at the bar, consumed with an

elegant boredom, waiting quietly until a prospective cus-
tomer drew them to their table with a glance. Most of the
customers were wealthy by Mexican standards, drank
expensive whiskey rather than tequila, and talked business
before indulging in pleasure. At least it looked that way to
Sughrue, who watched from the bar as Villalobos talked
quietly to three men sitting at his table.

Villalobos didn't seem to be the man in charge of
Mazatlán's shady side, but Sughrue suspected he worked for
the *familia* that was. Sughrue also suspected that as an
American who always skirted the edges of the law, he
couldn't know enough Mexican lawyers so had cultivated
Villalobos's friendship. They had shared drinks and dinners
and laughter. And once had driven into the mountains
toward Durango, where Sughrue had taught Villalobos how
to field-strip an M-16 blindfolded. He'd also tried to teach
the redhead how to fire short bursts on full-automatic but
with less success.

When the three men left his table, Villalobos waved
Sughrue over to the table. They exchanged *abrazos*, then sat
down to engage in the polite conversation so necessary
before talking business in Mexico.

Then Villalobos ordered two more Chivas Regals on the
rocks and leaned across the table. 'I hear you've been
looking for me,' he said in unaccented English – Villalobos
had done his undergraduate work at Yale – 'I hope it's
nothing serious.'

Sughrue explained his problem.

'You are not the only one looking for these *cabrónes*,'
Villalobos said. 'The *federales* think they are communists
because they give clothes and money to *los indios* and *la
gente*. But I think not. They've stopped three buses with the

pig and no one has been hurt. Not communists, I think. But no one knows who these people are. They pay no respect to anyone and they are very bad for business. It is a great mystery.' Villalobos drank, then looked at his empty glass for a moment until the waiter appeared with another.

'I have some friends who would be very generous should you find these people,' Villalobos continued. 'And should you find them dead ... Well, think of a villa in Acapulco where a man might live like a sultan for as long as he wished.' Villalobos took a card from his wallet.

'I've got your card.'

'But not this number,' the lawyer said as he scribbled with a gold Mark Cross pen. 'Call anytime, of course, but call me tomorrow night for sure.' Then he laughed. 'I will put my ear to the ground; you put your shoulder to the wheel. Perhaps I will hear something. Perhaps you will run something down.'

'Sure,' Sughrue said, but wondered how many more clients he would find before he found the pig bandits. As he started to stand, Villalobos waved him back to his chair.

'See those two blondes at the end of the bar?' he asked. 'They claim to be cheerleaders from Phoenix. Perhaps we should check out their English. And the color of their *conejos*. My treat, of course.'

'Perhaps I should get an early start—'

'Ah, the curse of the *norteamericano*,' Villalobos interrupted. 'It took an extra year, amigo, but I graduated from Yale without ever taking a course before noon.'

Sughrue, who had a B.A. in history courtesy of a batch of junior-college gut courses for football players and the University of Maryland Extension Service, and who even had an M.A. in English courtesy of a domestic spy operation for the Department of Defense Intelligence Agency, realized that he'd never taken a class before noon either.

'Thanks,' Sughrue said to Villalobos, 'but I think I'll pass on the women. There is one thing you could do for me, though.'

'Your wish is my command, amigo,' the lawyer said. And he meant it.

Back at the hotel, oddly reluctant to go up to his room, Sughrue stopped to have a couple of beers with Pablo. After he came back from Vietnam, Pablo had taken his disability and moved back to Mazatlán, where he had been born. He bought a small place just out of town to raise avocado trees and children, but he enjoyed tending bar until the trees matured. The one time Sughrue had been out to Pablo's house for dinner, he found himself sad with envy for Pablo's life. So they drank a beer and talked aimlessly about life. As they always did. After they discovered they were both vets, they never talked about the war.

But when Sughrue rode the elevator up to the room, he found himself thinking about his nine months in the bush. Sometimes he thought it had been the finest time in his life, but he sincerely hoped that he hadn't become an adrenaline junkie as so many of his buddies had. They had to be cops or criminals or maniacs. Then he had to laugh. Surely he was half cop, half criminal, and to judge from the frightened looks of the young American couple with whom he shared the elevator, more than half crazy.

In his room, Sughrue found both the balcony and the connecting doors open and Marina snoring softly in his bed, her half-covered body and spray of hair as dark as noon shadows, a black hole drawing him inexorably into it. He took a step toward the ripe young woman in his bed, then stopped. She had crashed in his bed on purpose, he suspected, hoping to seal the deal with her body. Of course, she had no way of knowing that she had already nailed him down with her tears. *Stupid fucking obsession*, he thought as he grabbed the Herradura and the *sangria* and stepped outside, where he sipped the tequila, chased with the fiery widow's blood, and watched the quarter-moon slip into a cloud bank far out over the Pacific. 'Fuck a bunch of early starts,' he said to himself. He knew he'd find the bandits. And whatever happened, he wasn't waiting anymore. Sughrue also thought seriously about firing a round into the next tearful face he saw. Even if it was his own.

When he saw where the pig bandits had gone to ground, Sughrue gave up any notion that they might be hard-hat commie revolutionaries. They had trapped themselves in a small cove down a heavily jungled dead-end dirt track, trapped themselves without a single guard or listening post. They had even stacked their weapons against a jagged boulder. At least they hadn't built their fire on the beach but had snuggled it beneath a rocky overhang, where they had also parked the truck. Facing the wrong way, of course, for a speedy retreat. The bandits didn't seem to have any more camping experience than they did combat experience. One of the women was trying to cook something in a large cast-iron stew pot on the fiery fringe of a raging bonfire. She kept getting longer and longer sticks to keep from burning off her fingers. Without much success. While Sughrue watched, the woman set fire to her shirtsleeve, dropped the pot, and spilled its contents into the blazing driftwood, where whatever it was smoked like a tire. The woman glanced nervously over her shoulder at her partners in crime, but they were huddled under the overhang, gathered around a Coke-syrup bottle of what he assumed was homemade mescal and a case of Tecate beer. Except for the leader, who sat on the other side of the fire, his straw hat off, his blond hair blowing in the stiff onshore breeze and a baby bouncing on his knee. And the sow, who had found a warm sandy wallow against the rock face.

Sughrue was surprised that the baby really existed outside of Marina's mind.

Once Marina and Sughrue started looking for an army truck with a canvas-covered bed, and with the addition of her surprisingly fluent Spanish, it didn't take them long to locate the bandits. They started south of the San Geronimo turnoff, where they found people who had seen the truck, then drifted down the highway until they found people who hadn't seen the truck, then slowly backtracked as the late afternoon darkened under a storm front that rolled in off the Pacific. Sughrue spotted the tracks of the large lugged tires where they plowed through the shallow barrow ditch and into a seemingly impenetrable screen of thorny jungle. Then a pile of newly turned stones rolled into a roadblock. Even the leaves on the brush the bandits had cut to hide the entrance to the narrow path were already withered and drooping morbidly.

'Shit,' Sughrue said, 'I should have seen this place when we came by the first time.'

'I still don't see it,' Marina said.

'They don't teach tracking at Mill Valley High?'

'Or pig farming either.'

'I guess I'll wait till it's a little darker,' Sughrue said, 'and let you watch the car while I do a little reconnoiter. Then hit them just before dawn—'

'I told you this morning, cowboy,' Marina huffed, 'it's my baby boy, and I go where you go.' She had dipped into his funds again before they left Mazatlán to buy jeans, a denim shirt, and black tennis shoes.

'Then we've got to find someplace to stash my ride.'

'What's wrong with right here?' she said.

'Might not be much left when we got back,' he said.

'You're not prejudiced against Mexicans, are you?' she asked archly.

'No,' he said. 'But I'm not stupid either. I don't leave my car parked on the highway anywhere.'

Sughrue found a sandy loop about a mile down the road where he could park the El Camino behind a rocky hummock, then made Marina help him brush out the tire tracks with a blanket he kept stashed with his surveillance gear behind the front seat.

'I thought you were supposed to use a branch or something for this,' she said as Sughrue shook the sand from the blanket.

'Branches leave scrape marks,' he said as he spread out the blanket on the hood of the El Camino and set the cooler on it.

'Is it your work that makes you so paranoid?' she asked as she grabbed a burrito and a Coke from his cooler. 'Or does it come naturally?' Sughrue didn't bother answering. 'Or from that shitty little war you were in?'

'You know what the three most important things in combat are?'

'No, what?' she sneered.

'Preparation and luck.'

'That's only two.'

'And keeping your mouth shut, baby-cakes,' he said, thinking that might shut her up. But he was wrong. Sughrue let her rail for a few minutes, then stopped her with a question. 'What's your baby's name?'

'What?'

'Your baby,' he said, 'he's got a name, right?'

'Earl,' she spit.

'Earl?'

'After his daddy,' she said.

'I thought his name was Mark?'

'Mark Earl,' she answered quickly.

Sughrue didn't have anything to say to that, so he dug out a handful of *taquitos* and a beer. Marina didn't seem to have anything to say either. They ate in silence, leaning on opposite sides of the hood. Marina stared into the distance as if she could actually see something but sharp rocks and tangled thorns. Sughrue started to tell her that she was pretty when she ignored him but thought better of it. So he got the weapons and a cleaning kit out of the cab, then laid everything out on the blanket. Marina cast a bored glance over her shoulder as she finished her Coke, then she threw the can on the ground and confronted him.

'What the hell is that?' she wanted to know.

'Pick up the can.'

'What?'

'Pick up that fucking can and stow it somewhere,' he said calmly.

'They don't have any littering laws in Mexico,' she said, stomping her foot.

'Actually, they do,' he said, 'but I was thinking more about your fingerprints.'

'Oh,' she said, undeterred, asking again as she tossed the can back into the cooler, 'what the hell is that?'

Sughrue held up the Browning in its shoulder holster. 'This is a 9mm semiautomatic pistol—'

'No,' she said. 'That.'

'This?' he said, touching the M-16. 'This piece of shit? Superior firepower, I hope, since the fucking lawyer wouldn't lend me his Czech-made AK-47.'

'What lawyer?' she shouted, then without waiting for an answer added, 'You dumb son of a bitch, you don't think I'm going to let you shoot that thing around my baby, do you?'

'With any luck,' he said, 'I won't have to. But if you don't keep it clean, it has a tendency to jam when your ass is hanging in the wind.'

'And you're probably a great shot too.'

'Knock the dingleberries off a gnat's ass at fifty meters,' he said, but she didn't smile. Just turned away.

As Marina sucked on a beer and sulked, Sughrue broke both weapons down, cleaned them, then did it again. Finally, Marina finished her beer and her sulk about the same time, then asked for a cigarette.

'I didn't know you smoked,' Sughrue said as he stepped around the El Camino to give her one.

'I don't,' she said, and from the way she puffed on the cigarette, he agreed with her.

'It's okay to be nervous,' he said. 'Only fools and children aren't afraid.'

'And you think I'm both?'

'I suspect you've got more guts than sense,' he said, 'but I don't think that will be a problem. As long as you're willing to do exactly what I say. No more, no less. And do it when I tell you.'

'Yeah,' she said, her chin cocked. 'And if I don't?'

'I'll knock you on your pretty little ass,' he said. 'I didn't sign on to get killed because a stubborn teenager refuses to do what I tell her. Either do what I say, or hope you don't lose any teeth when I pop you.'

'You're serious, aren't you?'

'As serious as seven hits of windowpane.'

'You've never dropped acid,' she said, chuckling.

'Only until my fillings dissolved,' he said, and she laughed for the first time since he'd met her, laughing so hard she had to lean her palms on the hood. But the laughter quickly became hysterical, then she disintegrated into a heap of wet sobs. Sughrue took the cigarette from between her fingers before she burned her face as she fell on the backs of her hands. He butted their cigarettes into an empty beer can, then put a hand on her back. Marina turned quickly and fell into his arms, where she wept as he held her and patted her back ineffectually for what seemed like a very, very long time, his obsessive need to comfort the woman unfulfilled.

The dark clouds lowered above them as they rolled swiftly past. A skein of large, hard raindrops rattled through a gust of wind. Then the wind dropped, and a fine drizzle filled the air. Sughrue remembered how much he hated and feared setting an ambush in the triple-canopy jungle, the heavy monsoon rains washing out sight and sound, the black-clad Vietcong slithering through their watery world like the venomous ghosts of sea snakes. He shivered slightly, but she didn't notice. Maybe the drizzle would hold, the deadly rain hold off.

'I'm sorry,' she sniffled as she stepped back, knuckling snot off her pouty upper lip. It was all Sughrue could do to keep from kissing her soft, wet mouth. 'Sometimes I'm too tough for my own fucking good, man, but listen, you tell me jump, I'll say "How high?" You tell me to shit, I'll say "Where, how much, and what shape?"' Then she paused, raised her head, rubbed her eyes, and added, 'I want my baby back, man, and I thank you for the help.'

'And my patience,' he said, smiling.

'And your patience, you asshole,' she said, but she was smiling too. 'By the way, I haven't been a teenager in a long time.'

'Whatever.'

Sughrue checked the magazines, shrugged into the shoulder holster, and grabbed two black zippered sweatshirts from the El Camino. He tossed her one. Then he wrapped the M-16 in the blanket, shouldered it, and said, 'Okay, baby-cakes, let's do it.'

'Where's my gun?' Marina asked.

'You don't think I'm going to have you at my back with a weapon, do you?' Sughrue said, and was pleased to see her smile as she lifted the sweatshirt hood to cover her hair. Then he dug an extra El Camino key and a wad of pesos out of his wallet.

'What's this for?' she asked.

'If anything happens to me, you know where the car is parked,' he said. 'Head for the border and don't look back.'

'Just leave you here?'

'Like a shapely turd,' he said.

Her smile was uncertain, but a smile nonetheless. Then

she grabbed his face and kissed him quickly, more like a punch than a caress. 'Why didn't you climb into bed with me last night?' she asked.

'Saving my strength,' he said, then moved out.

'Fucking men,' she bitched as they jogged toward the highway.

As dusk seemed to rise like a dark fog out of the ground, Sughrue led Marina along the edge of the rough track through the tangled and thorny jungle, moving swiftly but silently. The track was so rough the bandits could have managed it only in the all-wheel-drive truck. Even then, it was obvious that they had to stop occasionally to remove large stones or chop down small trees. At first, Sughrue took fifty carefully placed steps before he stopped to listen. Then, when the track switchbacked down the slope toward the beach, they lost most of their cover, and he reduced the number of steps to twenty. Behind him, he could hear Marina's impatience in her short, frightened breaths. At the beginning of the first switchback, as dusk eased into darkness, Sughrue crouched and motioned Marina to his side.

'Wait here,' he whispered. 'I've got to check out the guard positions. Alone. I'll be back.'

Sughrue left the track to angle across the slope. He checked all the likely positions but found nothing, which confused him. He checked unlikely positions. Again nothing. It was full dark before he eased back to the track.

'Nothing,' he whispered. 'Maybe they're not here.' Marina stood up. 'But we have to act as if they are.'

She followed, as quietly as she could, as he led her down the three switchbacks to the beach. The tracks of the truck went north along the loose sand above the high-tide mark. The drizzle had become a foggy mist that sailed with the shifting breeze, but even through the heavy air, Sughrue could hear the crackle of a fire, the pop of beer cans, and the mutter of aimless conversations. They scuttled quickly to the edge of the cove, then pulled up behind a rough, wave-worn boulder, a position with a clear field of fire into the bandits' camp.

'Who the fuck are these clowns?' Sughrue whispered.

'Clowns,' Marina answered softly.

'Somehow I didn't think there was a baby.'

'Asshole,' she murmured, but Sughrue didn't know who she was cursing. 'What now?'

'As lame as these guys are,' he said quietly as he switched the M-16 to single fire, 'I don't think we need to wait till dawn. When the blond-headed Mexican puts the baby down, I'll put a round in his head, then a burst into the rock face—'

'No,' Marina pleaded quietly, 'please, no. He's not a Mexican, he's a fucking Mormon. A Mexican Mormon from Casa Grande. He's Earl's daddy.'

'That's pretty fucking interesting,' Sughrue said, perhaps louder than he meant, but his words were lost in the crash of the rising waves. Sometimes the waves beat the storm to shore. Maybe this was one of those times. 'But we don't have time for lengthy explanations,' he added, 'and I'm fucking sick of lying clients and runaway teenagers. You want your baby back?' Marina nodded damply. 'Then stay the fuck out of my way.'

'Don't shoot anybody,' she whined. 'They . . . they used to be my friends.'

'Well, baby-cakes, your used-to-be buddies better not

make a move toward their weapons,' he said, then belly-crawled around the shore side of the boulder and along the rock face toward the overhang.

It might have worked without bloodshed, but the sow either heard him or sniffed him out. She raised her head and grunted loudly, then squealed wildly as she scrambled to her trotters and darted toward him. Sughrue jumped to his feet. One of the bandits dashed for the stack of weapons. Sughrue tried for his leg. It should have been an easy shot. The bandit was clearly outlined by the fire. But the round hit with a solid thunk, and the bandit tumbled loosely and unmoving to the sand. Nothing to do about that. A quick round into the rock face over the others' heads, which froze them, and another into the fire, which exploded the cast-iron pot into shrapnel. The cooking woman grabbed her face and spun to the sand. And the last round into the sow's charging head. She squealed once, then plowed a furrow in the sand and lay still. Nothing to do about that either. *Carnitas*, maybe. Sughrue advanced out of the shadows, his weapon solidly trained at the leader, who stood up, the crying baby in one arm, the Thompson in the other.

'Marina!' the blond guy shouted. 'What the fuck are you doing?'

'Put the baby and the Thompson on the ground, buddy,' Sughrue yelled, 'and back away. Now!' The blond guy moved the baby in front of his body. 'Asshole, you're worth a hell of a lot more money to me dead than you are alive. Put the baby and the Thompson down and back away. I won't tell you again.'

The blond guy hesitated briefly, sighed, cursed, then complied. Sughrue sighed himself as Marina rushed past him to gather up her son. He wondered how much of her story had been a lie, but he didn't have to wonder about her joy at finding the baby.

Sughrue slipped the M-16 sling over his shoulder and covered the group of kids with the pistol as he unloaded the weapons and tossed them into the rising surf. Then he checked the wounded. Luckily, the man had taken his round on a Buck knife in his pocket; his hip was probably broken, but none of the metal fragments had caused anything but surface wounds. The cook had a piece of the stew pot sticking out of her forehead – the skin, not the bone – but she wasn't badly hurt. He gathered the unwounded members of the bandit gang on their faces beside the fire, and Marina backed under the overhang to get her baby out of the drizzle that threatened to become rain.

'You didn't have to murder my pig, man,' the leader said, muffled by the sand beneath his face. 'I've had that sow since high school—'

Sughrue, still trembling with the adrenaline, so jacked he thought the mist might be sizzling on his face, stepped over to the blond guy and kicked him in the thigh.

'You shut the fuck up, man,' Sughrue said as the blond guy hit the sand. 'I didn't kill your goddamn pig. She did. With her fucking lying, crying, and bitching, you stupid son of a bitch. So shut up before I rip your head off.' The fucking kid started crying. Then Sughrue turned his anger on Marina. 'What the hell is going on, lady?'

Marina looked up from her baby, who had stopped crying and started gurgling happily in his mother's arms, her face white in the firelight against the dark rocky shadows. 'He's a Mormon,' she began to explain, 'he's already got a wife—'

'Two wives,' the blond guy sobbed.

'– and he thought a hippie chick off the streets of the Haight would be perfect ... But I didn't want to be—'

'Jesus,' Sughrue said, 'who the fuck are these other people?'

'Earl's daddy's got a ranch on the American side of the border,' Marina said. 'They work there ...'

And suddenly Sughrue didn't want to hear any more explanations, no more silly teenagers or lying parents. He pointed the M-16 toward the dark Pacific and emptied the magazine into the rolling waves. He didn't even bother replacing the empty magazine with a loaded one. For a few minutes, anyway.

'Marina,' he said, 'what do you want me to do with these idiots?'

'I'm not sure,' she whimpered. 'I didn't think about it, you know, afterward.'

'No shit,' he said. 'These people are all American citizens, right? Even the Mormon?'

'Right,' she said. 'They're all from El Paso. Mark was born there so he could have dual citizenship—'

'And your aunt is meeting you at Nogales with my money, right?' Sughrue interrupted.

'Of course,' she said, as if he would believe her now.

'You fuck this up, baby-cakes,' he said, 'and I'll hunt you down like a dog.'

Marina nodded, and Sughrue told her how it was going to work.

Perhaps because the poor pig, the only innocent one, was dead, it worked.

After everybody had left, Sughrue stayed on the beach

until dawn, apologizing to the sow's ghost and to the deep rolling Pacific as he drank most of the mescal from the jug – it had the good smoky bite of a single-malt scotch – and all of the beer. In spite of the drink Sughrue was still ready for gunfire and blood, still trembling on the angry edge of death and disaster when he drove the deuce-and-a-half, grinding slowly in compound, up the steep slope to the highway. Where Villalobos stood beside a four-wheel-drive pickup full of armed things, his red beard fiery in the gray light, the smoke from his cigar as ashen as the illumination.

'Are they all dead?' the lawyer asked as Sughrue climbed down from the truck, the plastic assault rifle dangling like a toy from one hand, the jug from the other.

'Not dead but gone,' Sughrue said. 'All the stuff from the robberies is in the truck. I'll take it to Acosta in San Geronimo, let him work it out.'

'You let them go?' Villalobos said. Sughrue nodded. 'It would be better if I had a body to take back,' the lawyer said, looking angrily at Sughrue, then jerking his chin toward the pickup.

'They won't take my body without taking yours too,' Sughrue said, then smiled at the prospect. For a moment it seemed the brightest prospect in his future. 'Or we can be civilized, Tony, and have an eye-opener,' he said, holding up the jug.

Villalobos smiled suddenly, his tobacco-stained teeth almost the same color as his beard, then reached for the jug and said, 'What's the point of an Ivy League education, if it doesn't make one civilized.'

Sughrue had a snort too, then suggested, 'Why don't you explain it to me, *hermano*, on the drive back. . . .'

Villalobos's chuckle was the heart of civility.

But when Sughrue parked the pig bandit truck full of loot in front of El Tiburon, Acosta's laughter was full of brotherly love. The laughter lasted for three solid days of food and drink, lasted until Sughrue woke with a boring hangover and decided it was time to move on. He wanted to ride the bus to the border, but Acosta insisted that Flaco drive him in the open jeep. The trip cost Sughrue another three days and four hangovers – plus a stop for lunch and a siesta in Culiacán – but finally he arrived at the border crossing at Nogales, where he crossed without incident. Sure enough, Marina had left his El Camino parked in the lot just on the Arizona side. She had stuffed his extra set of keys and the wad of pesos in his glove box. But no five thousand dollars. Not even a note of either apology or thanks. She hadn't cleaned up the baby puke in the front seat or the bloodstains in the pickup's bed either, and the gas tank was almost empty.

At least he had his ride, Sughrue told himself as he filled the tank at the nearest station. It wasn't a total loss. Except he regretted not climbing into bed with the crazy kid. As if he might find her down in Mexico, Sughrue turned around and drove straight back to Mazatlán, where he blew the rest of his money on two mad weeks at La Playa. He knew Villalobos knew he was in town, but the lawyer didn't seek him out, and Sughrue seemed to have lost his taste for fancy whorehouses.

At the end, dead broke and hanging like death in a hammock behind Pablo's house, peaceful in the chatter of children, the stirring of leaves, and the peeping of chickens, Sughrue dreamed that Marina came to him, her white lace dress slipping from her tanned shoulders, her black hair shining like satin sin, her blue eyes blazing like retribution.

Sughrue woke in a cold sweat, borrowed a hundred dollars from Pablo, and went home.

Well, if not home, at least his apartment above Washington Square, telling himself that he wasn't expecting any word from Marina. Which was good, because he never got one, but as he drove around San Francisco looking for adult work, he found himself checking out every dark-haired woman on the streets. And even though he easily found Marina's father's address in Mill Valley and sent him a bill, no money ever appeared. After a week, Sughrue took the first job offered, chasing down a druggist from Redwood City who had fled to Montana with an aging hippie chick. Sughrue followed him without looking back, following their trail of junkie sniffles and thin tears. He had always been too damn good at that.

PHILIP FRIEDMAN

....

While many people seem to allow an affection to grow into a passion before it ultimately mutates into an obsession, others have it thrust upon them. Innocent bystanders, they happen to be in the wrong place at the wrong time and find their lives consumed by outside forces that they had never previously had in their consciousness.

That is what happens to the poor guy in Philip Friedman's story. At first a minor annoyance, as all of us who have lived in big cities have experienced, the irritation mushrooms to the point of outright assault. As you read this story, you will feel a tension, a knot forming in your belly, that evokes memories of the times you felt this same helpless frustration.

Philip Friedman is known for his big courtroom thrillers in which intellects play such important roles. Here, it is precisely the opposite. Blind arrogance and stupidity unleash unthinking rage.

It could happen to anyone.

DOG DAYS
By Philip Friedman

Harry Burton had been around long enough to know that losing your job meant losing your place in the great heavenly hierarchy of voicemail. He'd already been through the list of contacts he'd taken with him when the ax fell at work. He had learned to consider himself lucky if his calls were even returned. He was down to the last name and number now, like looking in the last pocket for your wallet: If it wasn't there, you'd really lost it.

The return call came quicker than Harry had expected, but the conversation didn't last long.

'There's nothing here,' said a man he'd mentored for years and saved from a major career crisis. 'You know I wish I could help, but things are tightening up here as bad as everywhere else.'

So there it was. He was well and truly on his own. He held tight to the knowledge that he had to get past it. You couldn't let yourself get desperate – they could smell desperation the way a dog smelled fear.

He and Vickie went to the movies that night. He hadn't had the spirit for socializing for weeks. She knew he'd left his job, he couldn't have kept that from her, but he didn't dare let her know how bad he really thought things were.

'How's it going?' she asked him while they waited for their tickets.

She meant well, but what was he going to say? In the couple of days since she'd last asked that question he'd had no results, unless you called that last door closing on him a result.

'Well as can be expected,' he said.

'Anything from the headhunters?'

'Not yet, but it's still early for that. I'm starting to look seriously for consulting work while I wait.'

'Oh. Well, that's good. It's better to have something to keep yourself busy.'

Harry made it through the weekend the same way he had the others since they'd fired him – at the desk he'd set up by the window in his living room, combing the Internet and the Sunday paper for leads, trying not to think of how bad things might turn out to be. He had some severance and a cushion after that, but it wasn't that much and he expected to be alive for a long time.

Monday started out to be another draining day, making phone calls to people he didn't know and checking and rechecking the Internet. When he got discouraged or distracted by dogs frolicking in the park or a car alarm or a passing automotive boom box, he got up and walked around the apartment or went into the kitchen for some coffee or a sandwich. He didn't dare get too far from the phone, and a cell phone was a luxury he wasn't allowing himself for now.

Harry was fast reaching the point of not caring where the job was as long as he could find one. And then, surprisingly, something seemed to pay off. A guy he'd worked with so long ago they barely remembered each other had given him a name and a number to call, and lo and behold there was someone at the other end who needed a restructuring plan for his sales, service, and customer-development departments. He was interviewing consultants and listening to presentations.

For fifteen minutes after he got off the phone, Harry couldn't contain his excitement. This was a chance – if he got this contract it meant good money and a great credential. And then he began to focus on the *if*, and he started to clutch. It took him a long time to talk himself down to the point where he could begin going over his notes on the call and reconstructing the rest of it. In the morning he'd get a package of data about the company, but he wanted to use every bit of information they'd given him. And he needed to start working on a revised résumé that would fit the job.

A few minutes after ten, the nighttime dogs came out. He'd first noticed them not long after he'd begun to spend all day every day at home, and too many nights as well. The nightly commotion in the park across the street sometimes lasted an hour or more. He tried to think of reasons why after all these years of peace he was suddenly being assaulted this way, but there was no apparent answer.

He'd been trying to believe it was a transient problem. When it got bad he took a walk outside – at least he didn't feel so chained to the phone at night, even though there was plenty he could still be doing at the computer. He'd tried playing music, but it didn't really do the job. He couldn't enjoy the music, either, because the barking was so loud and insistent. This time it was over before it jangled him too badly.

He went to bed at eleven-thirty, lying there restless, needing sleep but too wired with the possibilities of this interview and presentation and with fear he'd screw up somehow. Fear, in fact, that screwing up would be his fate from now on, that he'd been let go not because of some general downsizing but for some actual fault or flaw of his own.

His eyes were finally closing when they were popped open by a deep-throated roaring bark and then another and then a discordant unison of them. On and on it went, piercing and aggressive, so he couldn't just lie there and listen. He got up and made himself a small pot of decaf. In the kitchen he could hear them even more clearly, like a lot of rowdy kids playing a shouting game.

He went back into the living room and flicked on the television to catch some news. The ruckus under his window would be over soon. It had to be, because he needed his sleep, he needed a clear head to prepare his presentation. There was so much riding on it.

He tried not to think of it as his entire career. But he wanted to be on top of everything, and each time he'd try to put his thoughts together the dogs would shatter whatever was forming in his mind.

It was beginning to make him angry, but he was determined not to let it get to him – they were only doing what dogs did. He sat down with his notepad in the living-room easy chair and appreciated the view of the late-night skyline across the river for a moment before trying to pick up the thread of his thoughts from only minutes ago. But he couldn't: He needed to go back over his earlier notes, to get back into the rhythm. And just as he did, just as he felt like he could see where he had to go next, there was another savage burst of noise – four dogs, five, a dozen, he couldn't tell.

He looked at the clock: It was after midnight.

What were these people thinking of, letting their dogs go on like this at an hour when scores and scores of people within earshot were trying for a little sleep? People who needed the psychic repair that only sleep could bring.

Harry went to the window and looked out, not knowing what to expect. The park across the street looked empty at first, as it should. No one went into the park at night; that was for fools and the people who preyed on them. He scanned the street along the park's edge and saw only a couple of joggers. And then he saw a group of people under a streetlight on one of the main park paths at the top of a hill, about a hundred yards to the south. A loose circle of conspirators; he counted six. And around them, swirling . . . dogs. Eight at least, maybe ten. Three big black dogs, a smaller black dog, and others in shades of brown and white. Sparring with each other, sniffing each other. Running off down the hill but then coming back to bark for attention, until the people reacted.

Some of the dog people had long hair, some short. All wore jeans or khakis. One, probably a woman, wore a thigh-length orange slicker. Another, long-haired but androgynous at this distance, wore a leather bomber jacket. The turmoil among the dogs and the intermittent barking increased until finally the man(?) in the bomber jacket threw a ball and all the dogs took off madly down the hill after it. At the bottom, almost out of sight, they piled together in a competitive snarl, all yelping in enthusiasm or hostility or from some other drive he wasn't enough of an anthropomorphist to imagine.

The winner – one of the bigger black dogs, Harry thought it might be a standard poodle – bolted up the hill followed by the others in a tight pack, some still barking, milling around the poodle as he presented the ball to the leather-jacketed thrower, who took it and teased them all with it until they were clamoring in a unison of frustration, then finally threw it again.

The whole spectacle was more than he could believe. It was almost one o'clock now and these people were standing in the cold, socializing and paying almost no heed to the dogs, rowdy for attention, which were the ostensible reason for their being out.

He looked down the curve of the avenue along the mute wall of apartment buildings, window upon window upon window – a silent backdrop like the face of a cliff, except that each of those windows sheltered a human soul. People asleep or trying to sleep – not that sleep was likely in the face of this unceasing, unavoidable clamor.

As he watched the dog people alternately ignore and torment their animals, seemingly in search of the precise pattern of frustration and encouragement that would inflame them to bark their loudest and most constant, he could feel his anger feeding on itself, feel his blood pressure rise, feel the anger build still higher.

He tried again to sit down and work but he couldn't. He kept getting up and going to the window, and when a few of the dog owners said their good-byes and started home he went to bed, hoping it was over for the night and perhaps forever. Perhaps this gathering of insomniac dog fanciers had been more coincidence than convocation, and perhaps the lateness of the hour had been an aberration. After all, why would anyone – much less six people – be out walking the dog after midnight except on rare occasion?

Tuesday night it happened again and he tried to wait it out. He went for a long walk, telling himself it was a way to let his thoughts about the Cleveland presentation sort themselves out in his mind. He couldn't let himself admit that he'd been driven out of his own house. It was bad enough that he'd been forced out of a career he'd been building since college.

Wednesday night he couldn't wait around for them to go in. He needed his sleep too badly. And he had to get up at six to make the plane to Cleveland.

He remembered a box of earplugs he'd bought for long plane trips. Put them in and discovered an oasis of quiet. The traffic noise was gone. No dogs. Relief.

He lay in the dark staring at the ceiling, heart beating too fast, trying to calm down as he visualized the presentation he'd be making in less than twelve hours.

It was quiet now. Maybe the crazy people with the dogs – it was the same ones every night; he hadn't been able to keep himself from looking and looking and looking, as if he could stare them into going away – maybe they'd finally taken their dogs home. Just as he was finally drowsing into a sleepy contemplation of his strategy for the morning, his mind set for productive sleep despite it all, there was another explosion of animal noise, not playful at all but a battle royal full of fury punctuated by yelps of pain.

It was as if he had amplifiers in his ears, not wax plugs.

He pressed his hands to his ears, hard, harder. It helped dull the sound, but it didn't eliminate it.

He sat bolt upright, heart pounding again.

He thought the meeting in Cleveland went as badly as it could have. They said he'd hear in a week or so if they were giving him the contract, but he expected nothing. He told himself it was all foreordained anyway: The client – client! Fat chance of that – had decided whom to hire long before he ever began his presentation. He told himself there was nothing he could have done. It wasn't his fault. It wasn't that he'd screwed up because he hadn't slept for days, his nerves were frayed, he was haunted by the sounds of hostile, contentious dogs ...

Back home, Harry had to steel himself against sitting immobile, waiting with hope and dread for the phone call from Cleveland that would never come. But when he did try to think of a new strategy or find a new contact, any train of thought he developed was sure to be derailed by the daytime barking that instantly triggered replays of the agitation caused by the worsening noise at night.

When he went out now, he saw dogs everywhere. Big dogs, barking dogs. He'd lived in the city forever, but he didn't remember anything like it. He asked his friends: Have you noticed? Some of them looked at him oddly, others thought about it and agreed – more dogs, bigger dogs, louder dogs.

They were at it again, out in the rain, the rain Harry had been sure would protect him this one night, keep them inside.

He decided, finally, that it was stupid just to endure it. Maybe they didn't understand the effect of what they were doing. The cliff-wall of apartment houses that overlooked the park did seem inanimate when you looked at it from street level, more like a feature of the landscape than a matrix of sensitive ears and psyches.

He got out of bed and got dressed in whatever came to hand, threw on a raincoat and a hat, and went downstairs. The late-night elevator operator was surprised to see him.

Outside it was raining harder than he'd thought.

Down the slope, slipping in the mud. There had been grass here, a welcoming hillside for lounging, sunbathing in the summer, but most of the grass was gone now, dug up and cast aside by scurrying claws.

It was dark here, but Harry could make out the shapes of two people standing in the mud, Longhair in the bomber jacket – a man, after all – and the woman in the orange slicker, the same clothes they wore every night.

'Hi.' He wanted to be pleasant, not to confront. After all, if this was innocent in some way . . .

'It's really late,' Harry said. 'I wonder if you realize how hard it is to sleep with all the noise your dogs are making.'

'You're not the first person to come out,' Longhair admitted, to Harry's surprise. 'But the park police said it'd be all right if we were down here.'

'Well, I don't know why they said that, because they were wrong. This hill is shaped like a megaphone. It just channels the sound upward. It's very loud.'

'Okay,' Longhair said. 'But the dogs really need the exercise.'

'I'm not saying they don't. But they don't need to bark like this. I've lived here a long time and I've never heard anything like this. I mean, you can train them not to bark. Traditionally, city dogs don't bark at all.'

That seemed to make Longhair angry. 'You're telling me that my dogs are the only ones that bark.'

'No.' Harry was in retreat. Antagonizing this fellow would destroy any possibility of making things better. 'I'm just saying there are a lot of people here' – waving at the apartment buildings looming over them – 'and it's very late at night.'

Longhair smiled, the anger seemingly past. 'I'm glad you came out and told us. We'll try and be careful.' He held out a hand. 'My name's Curt.'

Harry shook Curt's hand. 'Harry.'

Except for Curt's burst of anger, the exchange had been pleasant enough, but it left Harry feeling he was being yessed. He said thanks, he appreciated the consideration, trying to sound like he meant it. He walked up the hill, slipping as he went. The dog owners stayed where they were, with their still-barking dogs.

Two nights later, Harry and Vickie came back from a movie and spent a pleasant hour in bed. She went right to sleep, but he was plagued by fear that he was never going to get a job as good as the one he'd just lost, that his career was at the beginning of a downward spiral from which he would never pull out.

He knew he had to do something constructive or he'd go nuts lying here, not a good thing to do with Vickie sleeping next to him. He got up and started working on a presentation piece he could send to potential consulting clients. If he was going to do it, it had to be convincing enough to attract attention, and that meant it would be expensive. He thought it would be worth it, to make himself look like a going concern instead of a guy out of a job.

His concentration was shattered by the dogs, back again. He got up and looked out the window. There they were, the same people – Curt in his leather jacket, and Ms. Orange Slicker, and others he recognized – standing and chatting, looking exactly as if they were picking each other up at a bar. And the black poodles and the other dogs, agitated and ignored. It was almost twelve-thirty.

He closed the window tight, even though choking off the outside air quickly made the room feel close and uncomfortable. Worse than the stifling air was the feeling of being out of control of his own life, having to defend against an assault that now felt intentional. When the dogs snarled and yelped and quarreled with each other, or demanded attention, their owners couldn't take refuge in claiming ignorance. They had been made aware of the disruption they were causing, personal assurances had been given, but they continued anyway. And that wasn't paranoia speaking either, Harry reassured himself. Curt had said Harry wasn't the only one who'd come out to complain. So not only did they know, but they knew it was a lot of people they were disturbing.

He told himself to put it out of his mind. It was just part of the landscape, nothing he could do anything about. But he was seething, he couldn't concentrate. It brought back the nights before his presentation in Cleveland, the damage that might have been done to his life by how sleepless and on edge he'd been.

There was a lull in the din. He closed his notebook and went to bed, quietly, carefully, not wanting to disturb

Vickie. Lay there again – he was coming to expect this part, the too fast, too hard beating of his heart, the difficulty drawing a full breath. He lay and waited to calm down enough to sleep, earplugs solidly in place, hoping that this time they might work.

And again another eruption of sound, loud and unending. The earplugs were no match for it even though he pushed them deeper into the chambers of his ears. On and on it went, echoing off the building walls along the sidestreet. It was too much. He sat up.

Next to him, Vickie rolled in his direction.

'What's wrong?'

'It's the dogs.'

He'd mentioned the problem before, told her about his foray out into the rain.

She listened a minute.

'I never really heard them before,' she said. 'I grew up in the country, and you learn to tune it out.'

She listened more. 'You're right, though. If it was like this where I grew up, people would complain. You couldn't get away with that kind of noise at this hour.'

He was grateful for the corroboration. He leaned over and kissed her.

'I'll be right back.'

He pulled on jeans and a shirt, the good black loafers still caked with the mud of two nights before.

'How hard is this to understand?' he asked sharply when he came within earshot of them – they'd been watching him approach. 'It doesn't seem like a difficult concept. It's way past midnight, and people are trying to sleep.'

This caused a burst of barking from the owners as feral as anything produced by the dogs.

'Who are you to come out here and talk to us like this?'

'We have our rights.'

'If you're going to be a jerk, then fuck you,' Curt yelled. 'Last time you came out and talked to us like a person. Don't come out here and be in our face and be a jerk. I live right up there in that building' – he pointed – 'and I never hear anything. I don't know what you're talking about. Why don't you just yell out the window if it bothers you? Just don't come out here and be a jerk.'

This was beyond what Harry had been prepared for. He stood mute until they were done, shocked by the fury of it.

'Look,' he said as calmly as he could, 'the whole point is I'm trying *not* to be a jerk. Shouting out the window, that's being a jerk. I'm coming out here and trying to make you see the discomfort you're causing because I don't think you want to do that. It's not just me – there are people in these buildings who are old, who are sick, who need to get up early for work and need their sleep.'

The woman in the orange slicker – she always wore it, rain or shine – said to him, 'Why don't you get double-pane windows?'

'I *have* double-pane windows. I wear earplugs too.' He was feeling frantic now, thrown off by their apparent failure to hear what he was saying.

'Well,' she said, 'you could build something inside the windows that would block the sound.'

He stared in disbelief. 'I'm just asking for a little consideration,' he said.

One of the dogs came over to examine him. It was a little more than knee-high, a biggish dog but not huge, not a breed he could identify. Big brown eyes and a doggy grin. He reached down to pet it. Beyond it, the other dogs were milling around the legs of their owners. One mounted another unsuccessfully, then retreated from a volley of barking and to avoid being bitten. The owners didn't notice or didn't care.

'I don't have anything against the dogs,' Harry said. 'I know they need their exercise. I just don't see why they need to be barking at the top of their lungs at one in the morning.'

He walked away. Curt ran after him. 'We really don't want to disturb people,' he said. 'If it was just me I'd go down into the park, but the women are afraid to go down there alone. They like to stay up here by the lights along the path.'

'Okay, but maybe there's someplace else, too. Can't you at least try to find different places different nights? Why always here?'

There was no reply to that, and Harry thought he'd pushed beyond Curt's impulse toward accommodation.

Harry crossed the street and walked toward the apartment-house entrance feeling like he'd been a wimp, going over in his mind what he could have said, what he should have said. None of this was within their rights. There were leash laws – for the dogs' safety, too, if you thought about it – and there were laws against dogs making too much noise, and they were violating all of them.

And it might be true that big dogs needed plenty of exercise, but who had forced these people to buy and keep animals that should never have been penned up in city apartments in the first place? Was that their right, too? To imprison for their own pleasure animals whose recent ancestors had been bred to work on farms or to hunt in fields or forests?

And these people thought of themselves as animal lovers.

As he walked into the apartment-house lobby he heard a dog panting eagerly behind him and turned. It was one of his neighbors with his energetic young dog pulling hard at the leash. Harry stepped aside so they could get into the elevator ahead of him.

'They bother you, huh?' the neighbor said.

'Only if I want to sleep.' Harry couldn't tell if the neighbor was being sympathetic or simply distancing himself from the others for the duration of the elevator ride, or even mocking him.

The next day he tried to work on his self-promotion piece and tried not to think of Cleveland, but he could barely keep his eyes open. He weathered the daytime dogs, but as eleven o'clock approached he could feel the dread building. But by midnight there were no dogs, and he thought maybe he'd been wrong, maybe they were listening to him, after all. He watched a little television to decompress and went to bed.

He'd been asleep, it couldn't have been a minute, when a machine-gun volley of barking popped his eyes open. He twisted around, tangled in the sweaty sheet, so he could see the clock on the headboard shelf.

12:26.

He let himself down onto the bed and adjusted the pillow and closed his eyes, but his heart was pounding too violently for him to sleep. He thought that if it hadn't been dark in the room he'd have been able to see his heart punching up out of his chest with each beat, as if he were a cartoon movie creature.

It was hard to believe it had come to this. He'd lived in this same apartment for ten years. He'd always thought of it as a kind of paradise – not the biggest one-bedroom apartment in the city, and far from the most luxurious, but paradise for him. There was a broad view of the river through large windows, and the old building had stout walls and thick ceilings so he wasn't always hearing his neighbors and he didn't have to worry very much that they were hearing him. There was a bus route that passed by, eight stories below, but the buses didn't run very often and it was easy to tune them out. The swoosh of cars passing was as much a part of the environment and as soothing in its way as a river or an ocean.

He lay waiting, hoping his heart would slow enough to let him sleep before it came again. But no, there they were, the dogs in full voice – savage, contentious, even a touch exuberant.

He lay there that way, waiting for it to end, still hopeful enough to be fooled by two minutes' silence here, four minutes' there, each time jolted from the beginnings of relief by the reality of another assault.

He began to think of what he could do. This was no longer just a nuisance, it was a personal matter. They were doing this to Harry Burton, directly and specifically. And he wanted to hurt them the way they were hurting him.

But hurting them wouldn't do him any good, and anyway there was no way he could inflict this kind of pain. If he stood outside their windows – assuming he could learn where they lived – and played loud music in the middle of the night, he'd be as bad as they were, hurting the innocent people who lived near them.

Maybe he could do something that would just keep them away. There had to be some kind of dog repellent – what did you do if you wanted to keep your dog off the couch? If there was a spray or something, he could dump a lot of it all over the ground in that area ... but the expense would be unbearable and it would get washed away anyway. Better might be spraying the dogs themselves. What would a dog do if its own hair was soaked with dog repellent?

He thought about spreading some other substances on the blacktop path they used – tar or motor oil – and then he began to think of things that might hurt some of the dogs, not badly but enough to make it seem dangerous to run them on the hillside. Thumbtacks in the grass.

The next morning, bleary and unfocused, Harry showed up at the office of his outplacement counselor – fancy name for a shrink. His severance included a six-week crisis package, though the therapist had let him know he could extend it if he was willing to self-pay. That didn't seem likely – if he needed it he wouldn't be able to afford it, and if he could afford it he wouldn't need it anymore.

Lying on his back looking at the ceiling, Harry talked about his night's torture and the helpless anger it had created – a fury that had eaten at him even as he imagined gaudy revenge and was as responsible for his wakefulness as the noise itself.

The therapist, in response, told him the story of a patient he'd heard about – a woman who'd been struggling with her inability to sustain a relationship with a man. She'd finally gotten to the point where she'd been with one man almost six months, an eternity for her. He'd even asked her to marry him. She wasn't ready for that, but she thought maybe she could move in with him, and then she'd learned that he'd once strangled a dog with his bare hands. He'd lived next door to this dog for a long time, he'd told her, and it barked night and day. He'd talked to the owner many times with no results and finally he'd just gone over and choked the dog to death. She'd been frightened and confused by this and had asked her therapist what she should do. The therapist, being new to the game, had sought advice from his colleagues.

'I asked him, how long ago did the guy do this, and he said five or six years. So I said as long as he hadn't strangled any other dogs since then I didn't see any problem.'

'That's some story.'

'Well, I'm not suggesting you go out and strangle dogs, just that you shouldn't feel too crazy if you have fantasies along those lines. The sound of dogs barking can be powerfully upsetting, especially if you have other reasons to be more sensitive to your surroundings than usual. The trick is to get to a place where you don't hear it so well.'

Easy for you to say, Harry thought.

He was helped a little by astonishing news from Cleveland. He'd gotten the job. He flew out that afternoon to talk to them about the details, and he saw right away that it wasn't quite as good news as he'd thought. Of the three executives involved in the restructuring decisions, only the company president seemed to be fully behind him. The COO was skeptical at best. And the head of the combined divisions that he'd be studying was clearly looking for him to screw up because he had a candidate of his own who'd been passed over in Harry's favor.

So this was a setup for failure if he wasn't careful. He was starting with a week in Cleveland, then he'd go back home to digest what he'd learned and develop new lines of inquiry for his return to Cleveland for two days so he could fill in whatever blanks he found in his knowledge of how the company worked. At the end of the fact-finding and the strategy sessions with the three executives, he was supposed to write a report. Total elapsed time, one month.

Harry got home after the first week in Cleveland a total wreck. He'd been virtually living at company headquarters, with side trips to the branch offices. Working as a consultant was infinitely harder than having a job, he'd discovered, and this job was only made worse by the subtle obstructionism of the division chief, whose support he needed to get access to and cooperation from people who saw him as a threat to their very existence.

As soon as he arrived home and settled in to work, he discovered a new addition to his tormentors – a fat old Alsatian that was walked at least four times a day, emitting a noise more howl than bark from the moment it waddled out of the house across the street from Harry until the moment it crossed the threshold coming back home. Its owner was a small old woman who walked excruciatingly slowly and stopped often to chat with other dog owners. Harry had no idea where she'd come from: He'd never seen her before.

Worst of all, she took her dog for its first morning walk no later than 6:15. Dawn was coming earlier now as spring approached and Harry was often brought to near-waking by the light, as he had been all his life. In the past he'd always simply rolled over and dropped deeper into sleep. Now that was impossible. His sleep was hostage to dogs at both ends of the night, and the maximum uninterrupted time was no more than five hours on the best nights. Sometimes it was less than four.

Bleary and tired as he was, he couldn't afford to be sidetracked from working on his interim report for Cleveland. He got out an old fan that he never used because of its noisy motor and tried to use that as a white-noise machine. Its rattle and clank was an annoyance all its own. And it was a constant reminder that his life was being distorted by the selfishness of people who had no reason to beleaguer him like this.

Encouraged by the session with his outplacement therapist, he helped himself get into a sleeping mood by fighting back with fantasy. He even imagined a way he could repay pain with pain, if not to the owners, then to the dogs. He imagined a recording or a machine of some kind that played sounds only dogs could hear and that he could blast out his window so the dogs would be made as crazy by it as he was being made by them, and he wouldn't be hurting anyone innocent. And maybe if the dogs went wild every time they were near by, Curt and his pals would start taking them somewhere else.

Being under so much career pressure increased Harry's sensitivity to the dogs, but it didn't incline him to go out and talk to Curt and the others again. He already felt their behavior as a personal attack. If he complained again, tried to reason with them further and they still didn't respond, then this really would be something they were doing to him. And that would make him angrier and interfere even more with his sleep and his ability to concentrate on the work that he now saw as being the key to his entire future.

He did make one attempt with the old woman who walked the Alsatian. He was particularly careful to be warm and neighborly and not sound like he was accusing her.

'My dog doesn't bark.' She was absolutely indignant, in a thick French accent. 'You are mistaken. It is some other dog.'

And indeed, as if to vex him, this mangy, bowlegged beast that in Harry's experience was never silent a moment – howling its way out and back with a voice and delivery as distinctive as Sinatra's and as unpleasant as Old Blue Eyes' was soothing – stood mute. Until at its mistress's moment of triumph it found its voice and howled anew.

'You see,' Harry couldn't keep himself from saying. 'Like that.'

But if he was unwilling to go out and confront Curt and friends again, he couldn't keep himself from leaping out of his desk chair every time there was an extended period of barking, day or night. There was something about that particular noise that made it seem plugged directly into his nervous system. It was like a baby crying – you couldn't ignore it. And, like a baby crying, the effect was cumulative: Even if you could ignore the first few minutes, after ten minutes or so every second was enough to make you want to run screaming for relief.

At any given time of day it was always the same people. He did call the park police, and they assured him they were aware of the off-leash problems under his window and were on top of it. By Harry's assessment they were so far on top of it as to be invisible. The one time he saw them cruise by and spot a leash-law violator they took so long to stop their cute park-police SUV and lumber out after the culprits that owners and dogs were in full flight off the hillside before they could be admonished, much less ticketed.

And the park police couldn't help him with noise, they told him, that was up to the real cops. Assaulted as Harry felt, he couldn't bring himself to distract the police with a few jerks whose worst crime was to encourage their animals to disturb the peace. Even in the newly crime-reduced city of the late nineties, Harry figured the real police had better things to do. The desk officer's response when Harry was finally driven to call the local precinct only confirmed Harry's guess that he wouldn't get any help there.

So all he had left were his fantasies. Sometimes they helped, sometimes they didn't.

'Your heart is beating so hard and so fast,' Vickie said one night. 'Are you sure you're all right?'

'I'll be fine,' he said. 'It's just the dogs are really getting to me.'

'I wish I understood that. But nobody does.'

That launched him on another series of fantasies – things he might do: Poisoned meat was one idea he'd had, with the advantage that he could plant it and leave. Or a high-power water gun with noxious fluid in it, or for that matter Mace or pepper spray – if he got caught spraying the dogs he could claim they'd attacked him.

He thought about more kinds of things like the thumbtacks in the grass that had been his first brainstorm: punji stakes or broken glass or barbed wire. The problem with all of those, and with the poisoned meat, too, was that there were kids in the park, and though most of them were well supervised, there was always the chance that something intended to make the area unappealing to dogs might harm a child frolicking on the hill. That was a risk Harry wasn't willing to take.

The idea of the self-defense sprays, which seemed too cruel to the dogs, even considering how cruel they were being to him, led Harry to think of spray paint. He could lurk at the bottom of the hill and spray them all silver or red or metallic blue as they came by. That wouldn't hurt the dogs, but it would be a nuisance to the owners. Only maybe not nuisance enough.

Running in the park for exercise and to clear his head no longer brought any tranquility. There'd always been people out walking dogs but never anywhere near this many and never dogs that barked as loudly or as much or as unrestrainedly. Dogs barking at each other or their owners or treed squirrels while the owners stood by chatting with each other, oblivious to the noise and the disruption it caused.

His one remaining pleasure was the time he spent with Vickie, though he was seeing signs of strain there, too. He couldn't blame her if her patience was running out.

They were in bed, taking things slowly, the heady sensations gradually driving away Harry's anxieties about his imminent return to Cleveland. Harry was getting into position when the night was ripped by a cacophony of dogs in conflict. Harry wanted to scream or cry. He collapsed onto the bed beside Vickie.

'I'm sorry,' he said.

She held him, crooned soothingly, rocked him like a

baby. He knew she wanted to help, but it was no good. He started to get out of bed.

'What are you going to do?'

'I'm going out there.'

'It's just going to make you feel worse.'

'I know. But I haven't been out there in so long. Maybe they've forgotten.'

'No one's come out in a while, so we thought it was okay,' Curt actually said to him.

Harry couldn't believe he was hearing it. 'It's not okay. It's worse, actually, but it's hard to keep coming out here time after time. I'm in bed usually, trying to sleep. You try to let it go by, you figure it's only going to be a few minutes. But it isn't and then by the time it's been a half hour you really figure what the hell. And coming out means getting up and getting dressed ...'

'I suppose I can see that would be a problem,' Curt said. 'Other people come out, you know, but you've been very understanding about it. We appreciate that.'

'I said it before. I just think this is a question of consideration.' Still feeling yessed and flattered without actually being heard. And what about the others who came out to complain?

'I tell you what,' Curt said, the picture of earnestness. 'I'll take it on myself to try to get everybody to move further into the park. I can't promise anything, but I will make it my responsibility.' He held out a hand. 'My name's Curt.'

Harry shook hands, said his name, feeling surreal. They'd already been through this. Had Curt just forgotten, or was his neighborliness so much an act that no part of it stuck with him once he'd said his lines?

Harry got back into bed with Vickie, but lovemaking was out of the question. He apologized again and she hugged him and said it was all right. She was trying to be good to him, but he wasn't convinced.

That night he knew he had to do something to gain control over the situation. To banish the dogs from his life for real.

Of all the ways to make the hillside seem unacceptable as a midnight dog run, scattering broken glass seemed the most practical. Better than thumbtacks.

To scatter broken glass he'd have to go out and buy a whole lot of glass dinnerware, handle it carefully, wearing gloves at all times to avoid fingerprints. Maybe wear a shower cap to keep his hair from falling unnoticed on it. Box up the fragments once he'd smashed the plates into appropriate shards. Rent a car maybe to transport it all in, again for purposes of anonymity. He couldn't be going in and out of the house with any of it, because the elevator men would see him. Maybe he could carry it in a knapsack, or his old duffel bag. Then, in the middle of the night he could go out and scatter it along the hillside, especially in the places most frequented by the dogs. He imagined wearing dark clothes and putting on a ski mask once he was in position so he wouldn't be identifiable as he sprinkled his private brand of dog repellent.

Harry's scheduled two days in Cleveland to make an interim report and fill in the blanks in what he'd learned that first week brought enough distraction to drive ideas of taking dramatic action to the back of Harry's mind. First on his agenda was his report to the executives. The COO glanced over his list of further subjects for investigation and clarification. Harry couldn't see approval in the nod the COO gave him, but he couldn't see disapproval, either.

The company president said, 'This is good. We hadn't thought of some of these, and I think they'll make a difference.'

The division chief said nothing.

Harry spent the rest of his time in Cleveland learning as much as he could. The division chief stayed out of his way.

Home again, Harry sat down to work on the new information from Cleveland with some hope that this was going to work out well for him. He worked as hard as he ever had and did everything he could to drown out the dogs – windows closed tight, earplugs, fan, and music all at once.

It made him crazy just to have to do all that, but he knew he had to endure it because he had to get this written. His whole career, his whole life depended on it, and his research materials were too bulky to be carrying them around.

Harry talked to Vickie on the phone once a day. They'd decided not to see each other this last week and a half of work on the report. Harry didn't say it, but he couldn't face the possibility that things might not work in bed again.

Harry worked almost nonstop, calling out for food, barely leaving his living room. The last full day and night before the report had to go out, he sat at his desk straight through until after one. By the end of it, he couldn't stand the noises he was creating to defend himself. He could barely breathe the stale air in the apartment, and his ears felt like noxious things were growing in the moist, airless space between the wax and his eardrums. The sheer indignity of being forced into this kind of discomfort by the rudeness of others was more than he could take anymore.

He looked out the window and didn't see the usual crowd. He took out the earplugs, turned off the rackety fan and the music. He was rewarded by the loudest, deepest barking he'd heard. He was up anyway, and dressed. He went out.

There was no crowd flirting with each other tonight, only Curt and a stout bald man Harry hadn't seen before, with a massive German shepherd on a chain leash.

'It's not me!' Curt was upset. 'Why do you always come to *me*, always accuse *me*? It's not my dogs.' One of his poodles came up the hill, green ball in mouth, barking at the top of her lungs. 'Look, it's true she barks,' Curt admitted, 'but she's got the ball in her mouth, it's all muted.'

The dog did have a saliva-soaked green tennis ball in her mouth, but far from quieting her barking, it didn't seem to impede the process in any way. Maybe the sound was muffled – that was beyond Harry's ability to judge. All he knew was that, muffled or not, it was disturbingly loud.

'There was another guy here tonight,' Curt insisted, looking to the shepherd owner for corroboration.

'Yeah. Boy, that dog was loud. Didn't stop. The guy just left before you got here.'

'I can't tell other people to go away,' Curt whined. 'Don't blame me for that.'

'No, I know you can't,' Harry said. 'All I'm asking, really, is if you can have some influence on your own group and your own dogs.'

'I see you're using an electric collar,' the shepherd owner remarked to Curt.

Sure enough there was a little box attached to the noisy poodle's collar – the kind that gave the dog an electric shock as a way to modify its behavior.

'Right,' Curt said, clearly not happy to have attention called to it. 'But it's not for barking.'

For what, then? Harry wondered, but some vestige of his up-bringing, operative even under this kind of pressure, kept him from asking the rude direct question. Still, it bothered him as he walked home and lay in bed waiting for sleep. How could it be that Curt was such a passionate defender of his dogs' need for exercise, yet if they did something he didn't like, the cure he chose was electric shocks?

After Harry sent the report to Cleveland he couldn't bear the thought of just sitting and waiting. He wasn't going to be hearing anything until at least after the weekend, and Vickie was away visiting family. There was no reason to stay put.

Harry had a friend from childhood who was a college teacher now and a part-time rural cop. They got together once a year if they were lucky. He called and invited himself.

'It's a great time to come up,' his friend said. 'We're having our local county fair. You can watch me pretend to be a marksman at the sharpshooters' contest.'

'Is it open to outsiders?'

'Sure. Anybody who pays a fee. You still have your old rifle? If not I'll see if I can borrow you one.'

Harry was pretty sure his old .22 was in the storage bin he and his brother had rented when their folks moved south and sold the house. The warehouse was right on the route he'd be taking anyway, so there was no reason not to stop.

The rifle felt surprisingly familiar, comfortable in his hands. He hadn't fired it in years. As a kid he hadn't even used it that much. But it would be fun to try it again, see if he had any skill. He wrapped it in a lap robe and put it in the back of the car.

They decided to go out in the woods for some target practice so Harry wouldn't make a total fool of himself at the contest. Harry thought it would be a great way to work out some of his anger and frustration. He'd set up a bunch of cans and shoot at them, or maybe something spectacular like a melon, imagining the targets to be the dogs that so tortured him.

Harry felt good being out in the woods. He liked hearing the crunch of pine needles underfoot and smelling the wood smoke and forest mold. He especially liked hearing the fall of water over rock. Even the occasional bark of a distant dog didn't bother him too much.

The target practice was everything he'd hoped for and more. It was as if his fury were exploding out of the end of the rifle barrel with each shot, as if all his tormentors were blowing apart like the rotten melons and water-filled cans he was hitting with more accuracy than he'd expected.

By the time they were done, Harry was feeling vibrant and relaxed. Saturday night he stayed up late with his friend, catching up on the year that had passed since they'd seen each other. Harry needed his sleep, but it would have been too rude just to turn in early and, besides, he was enjoying the conversation.

In the sharpshooters' contest on Sunday afternoon Harry

was no match for any of the rural hunters and police officers who were competing with him, but he didn't mind.

He wished he could stay and get a decent night's sleep Sunday night, but he needed to be home first thing Monday morning in case there was a call from Cleveland. He drove home late, hoping the dogs would have gone in by the time he arrived, but they started up just as he was brushing his teeth.

The call from Cleveland came late Monday morning. It was the division chief, not a good sign. He got right to the point.

'We read your report and all I can say about it is it's flat-out unacceptable.'

'What do you mean unacceptable?'

'Just what I said. It's no good to us, and we're not going to pay you another penny.'

'What are you talking about? I did what it said in the contract. I did what the president of the company told me to do.'

'Well, he had a talk with the board on Friday, and I hear he's taking early retirement, but that's not the point. The point is, we can't use what you did.'

'What about my expenses?'

'What about them? Take them out of the signing payment and be glad we don't sue you to get it back.'

Harry couldn't believe this was happening. He was sweating, his face was flushed, his heart was beating faster than it ever had.

He wasn't going to take it lying down. He started to call around for referrals to lawyers, being careful what he said. He couldn't let this get around. He talked to a few lawyers on the phone, made an afternoon appointment with the one who sounded most encouraging.

The consultation didn't go well. He had the feeling the lawyer was hustling him. It seemed possible that the lawyers who had been pessimistic about his chances might have been right.

The dogs were at it again. He tried to drink himself to sleep, but he'd always hated being drunk, and liquor stopped tasting good to him after the third drink or so.

He put in his earplugs and closed all the windows and tried to sleep. It helped that he was emotionally exhausted.

He woke up in the dark, sweating. It was after two.

He lay in bed. He couldn't fall back asleep. Even through the tightly closed double-pane windows and the earplugs, he could still hear the dogs barking. The actual sound wasn't that loud, but it was the psychic volume not the decibel count that mattered now.

He had to sleep. He couldn't stand this anymore. He hadn't slept through the night in so long, so long. He was frantic, waiting.

His eyes closed, waiting.

Waiting.

The dogs started barking again.

Harry got up in a kind of trance and went to the closet, took down the lap robe. He took an old duffel bag from the top shelf and put the lap robe in it and carried the heavy burden down the back stairs. When he emerged into the lobby, the elevator door was closed. The elevator man was in the basement.

Outside, he walked away from the park and around the

block so he would approach the park from farther north. As he walked, he could hear the barking – now raucous, now plaintive, quiet for those few deceptive minutes that even now caused him to let down his guard.

When he came out onto the avenue and looked south he could see that it was only Orange Slicker and Curt who were still out. They seemed to be saying good night. Harry watched, thinking he was too late. But Curt called the dogs to him and showed them the tennis ball and threw it off down the hill.

A path took Harry by a roundabout route to the bottom of the hill. There was a low stone wall there, no one in sight. Harry set down the duffel bag and took out the lap robe and rested it on the wall and waited.

He wished he had a dog whistle or some other way of calling them, but he thought if he was patient enough they'd come. The hardest part was having to endure the barking. Even that wasn't as bad as it might have been. He knew it was going to end, finally.

He was dozing in the cold night, his cheek against the hardness under the lap robe, when something brought him awake. He looked and there, black against the black hillside behind them, were Curt's two poodles. One of them had a ball in its mouth but they were both still, looking his way. The one with the ball barked tentatively. Orange Slicker's dog was nowhere around.

Moving slowly, Harry straightened up just enough to pull the lap robe carefully off the top of the rifle. Then he crouched behind it and worked the lever that brought a bullet into the chamber ready to fire. The dogs came closer, curious, their heads cocked slightly as if to say, 'Do we know you?'

Still kneeling behind the wall, Harry lowered his cheek to the smooth warmth of the rifle stock and sighted along the barrel. The dogs were standing still again. He watched them, gauging which one should be first, trying to imagine how the second one would react.

Another low, inquisitive bark from the one with the ball. The other one let out a low growl: Something was making him unhappy. That one, then.

Harry moved slightly so the barrel swung in the right direction without lifting from the wall. He let his forefinger slip into the trigger guard, curled it gently around the trigger. He could feel the coolness, the friction ridges on the front surface of the trigger. The dogs weren't moving.

Harry looked into the eyes of the dog beyond the rifle muzzle. The dog was looking back at him, still curious, but warier than his sister. Harry's finger tightened.

Harry saw motion out of the corner of his eye. He let up on the trigger and lifted his head from the stock only enough to see what was coming. A person.

Harry's heart was beating fast and his hands were cold. It was Curt coming to see what was keeping his dogs. They turned to him, newly alert, distracted from the strange-but-familiar man they'd been watching.

Harry felt a surge of frustration. He'd been so close.

The dog with the ball offered it to Curt, then pulled it back, frolicking in imitation of Curt's taunting game. The other dog, the suspicious one, crowded Curt's leg, panting up at him until he reached into his pocket for some kind of treat. The dog with the tennis ball dropped it into Curt's hand. He offered it back, but when the dog went for it Curt threw it the length of the hill's base. The dogs took off after it, barking.

Curt watched his dogs race into the darkness, then turned in the direction they'd been looking. He seemed curious to know what had kept them here.

Harry stood up. Curt was startled. He glanced over his shoulder for the dogs. They were just catching up to the ball, sparring for it. The familiar baritone-mixed-with-bass of their barking carried clearly over the ground.

Harry wondered if Curt recognized him. He thought he might.

Without thinking about it, Harry raised the rifle and shot Curt in the head.

By the time Harry had bent to put the lap robe back in the duffel bag, the dogs were back, circling their fallen owner. Harry slung the duffel bag over his shoulder and approached them carefully. They didn't seem to notice.

Harry watched for a while. Not long, because it wasn't a good idea to be standing here. He reached down and dug in Curt's pocket for some dog goodies. Gently, murmuring soothing words, Harry offered the dogs a nugget each.

While their rough tongues lapped at him, Harry ventured to pet the dogs with his free hand. Their curly hair tickled his palm. He could feel the smooth bones of their skulls when he scratched between their ears.

'It's way too late to be out like this,' he said as much to himself as to the dogs. He took the leashes from Curt's dead hand and clipped them to the poodles' collars. Then he led them up the hill. Home.

ELIZABETH GEORGE

....

There is no more authentically English detective fiction being written today than the splendid novels starring Scotland Yard's Inspector Thomas Lynley, eighth Earl of Asherton. The background, the characters, the feel of the books remind readers of the best of Dorothy L. Sayers. How surprising, then, that they are the work of a California writer.

The author explains that she chose to set her books in England because a writer ought to write about what she loves. She has a deep affection both for Great Britain and for detective stories (she once taught a course in the British detective novel), and so it seemed only natural to emulate the Sayers school of good old-fashioned stories populated by literate and witty people rather than using a grim and violent urban background.

As George's contemporary stories illustrate, an urban setting isn't needed for violence to erupt. As this historical tale demonstrates, wickedness is not new to this century.

I, RICHARD

By Elizabeth George

Malcolm Cousins groaned in spite of himself. Considering his circumstances, this was the last sound he wanted to make. A sigh of pleasure or a moan of satisfaction would have been more appropriate. But the truth was simple and he had to face it: No longer was he the performance artist he once had been in the sexual arena. Time was when he could bonk with the best of them. But that time had gone the way of his hair, and at forty-nine years old, he considered himself lucky to be able to get the appliance up and running twice a week.

He rolled off Betsy Perryman and thudded onto his back. His lower vertebrae were throbbing like drummers in a marching band, and the always-dubious pleasure he'd just taken from Betsy's corpulent, perfume-drenched charms was quickly transformed to a faint memory. Jesus God, he thought with a gasp. Forget justification altogether. Was the end even *worth* the bloody means?

Luckily, Betsy took the groan and the gasp the way Betsy took most everything. She heaved herself onto her side, propped her head upon the palm of her hand, and observed him with an expression that was meant to be coy. The last thing Betsy wanted him to know was how desperate she was for him to be her lifeboat out of her current marriage –

number four this one was – and Malcolm was only too happy to accommodate her in the fantasy. Sometimes it got a bit complicated, remembering what he was supposed to know and what he was supposed to be ignorant of, but he always found that if Betsy's suspicions about his sincerity became aroused, there was a simple and expedient, albeit back-troubling, way to assuage her doubts about him.

She reached for the tangled sheet, pulled it up, and extended a plump hand. She caressed his hairless pate and smiled at him lazily. 'Never did it with a baldy before. Have I told you that, Malc?'

Every single time the two of them – as she so poetically stated – did it, he recalled. He thought of Cora, the springer spaniel bitch he'd adored in childhood, and the memory of the dog brought suitable fondness to his face. He eased Betsy's fingers down his cheek and kissed each one of them.

'Can't get enough, naughty boy,' she said. 'I've never had a man like you, Malc Cousins.'

She scooted over to his side of the bed, closer and closer until her huge bosoms were less than an inch from his face. At this proximity, her cleavage resembled Cheddar Gorge and was just about as appealing a sexual object. God, another go round? he thought. He'd be dead before he was fifty if they went on like this. And not a step nearer to his objective.

He nuzzled within the suffocating depths of her mammaries, making the kinds of yearning noises that she wanted to hear. He did a bit of sucking and then made much of catching sight of his wrist-watch on the bedside table.

'Christ!' He grabbed the watch for a feigned better look. 'Jesus, Betsy, it's eleven o'clock. I told those Aussie

Ricardians I'd meet them at Bosworth Field at noon. I've got to get rolling.'

Which is what he did, right out of bed before she could protest. As he shrugged into his dressing gown, she struggled to transform his announcement into something comprehensible. Her face screwed up and she said, 'Those Ozzirecordians? What the hell's that?' She sat up, her blond hair matted and snarled and most of her makeup smeared from her face.

'Not Ozzirecordians,' Malcolm said. 'Aussie. Australian. Australian Ricardians. I told you about them last week, Betsy.'

'Oh, that.' She pouted. 'I thought we could have a picnic lunch today.'

'In this weather?' He headed for the bathroom. It wouldn't do to arrive for the tour reeking of sex and Shalimar. 'Where did you fancy having a picnic in January? Can't you hear that wind? It must be ten below outside.'

'A bed picnic,' she said. 'With honey and cream. You *said* that was your fantasy. Or don't you remember?'

He paused in the bedroom doorway. He didn't much like the tone of her question. It made a demand that reminded him of everything he hated about women. Of *course* he didn't remember what he'd claimed to be his fantasy about honey and cream. He'd said lots of things over the past two years of their liaison. But he'd forgotten most of them once it had become apparent that she was seeing him as he wished to be seen. Still, the only course was to play along. 'Honey and cream,' he sighed. 'You brought honey and cream? Oh Christ, Bets . . .' A quick dash back to the bed. A tonguely examination of her dental work. A frantic clutching between her legs. 'God, you're going to drive me mad, woman. I'll be walking around Bosworth with my prong like a poker all day.'

'Serves you right,' she said pertly, and reached for his groin. He caught her hand in his.

'You love it,' he said.

'No more'n you.'

He sucked her fingers again. 'Later,' he said. 'I'll trot those wretched Aussies round the battlefield and if you're still here then ... You know what happens next.'

'It'll be too late then. Bernie thinks I've only gone to the butcher.'

Malcolm favoured her with a pained look, the better to show that the thought of her hapless and ignorant husband – his old best friend Bernie – scored his soul. 'Then there'll be another time. There'll be hundreds of times. With honey and cream. With caviar. With oysters. Did I ever tell you what I'll do with the oysters?'

'What?' she asked.

He smiled. 'Just you wait.'

He retreated to the bathroom, where he turned on the shower. As usual, an inadequate spray of lukewarm water fizzled out of the pipe. Malcolm shed his dressing gown, shivered, and cursed his circumstances. Twenty-five years in the classroom, teaching history to spotty-faced hooligans who had no interest in anything beyond the immediate gratification of their sweaty-palmed needs, and what did he have to show for it? Two up and two down in an ancient terraced house down the street from Gloucester Grammar. An ageing Vauxhall with no spare tyre. A mistress with an agenda for marriage and a taste for kinky sex. And a passion for a long-dead king that – he was determined – would be the wellspring from which would flow his future. The means were so close, just tantalising centimetres from his eager grasp. And once his reputation was secured, the book contracts, the speaking engagements, and the offers of gainful employment would follow.

'Shit!' he bellowed as the shower water went from warm to scalding without a warning. 'Damn!' He fumbled for the taps.

'Serves you right,' Betsy said from the doorway. 'You're a naughty boy and naughty boys need punishing.'

He blinked water from his eyes and squinted at her. She'd put on his best flannel shirt – the very one he'd intended to wear on the tour of Bosworth Field, blast the woman – and she lounged against the doorjamb in her best attempt at a seductive pose. He ignored her and went about his showering. He could tell she was determined to have her way, and her way was another bonk before he left. Forget it, Bets, he said to her silently. Don't push your luck.

'I don't understand you, Malc Cousins,' she said. 'You're the only man in civilization who'd rather tramp round a soggy pasture with a bunch of tourists than cozy up in bed with the woman he says he loves.'

'Not says, does,' Malcolm said automatically. There was a dreary sameness to their post-coital conversations that was beginning to get him decidedly down.

'That so? I wouldn't've known. I'd've said you fancy whatsisname the King a far sight more'n you fancy me.'

Well, Richard was definitely more interesting a character, Malcolm thought. But he said, 'Don't be daft. It's money for our nest egg anyway.'

'We don't need a nest egg,' she said. 'I've told you that about a hundred times. We've got the—'

'Besides,' he cut in hastily. There couldn't be too little

said between them on the subject of Betsy's expectations. 'It's good experience. Once the book is finished, there'll be interviews, personal appearances, lectures. I need the practice. I need' – this with a winning smile in her direction – 'more than an audience of one, my darling. Just think what it'll be like, Bets. Cambridge, Oxford, Harvard, the Sorbonne. Will you like Massachusetts? What about France?'

'Bernie's heart's giving him trouble again, Malc,' Betsy said, running her finger up the doorjamb.

'Is it, now?' Malcolm said happily. 'Poor old Bernie. Poor bloke, Bets.'

The problem of Bernie had to be handled, of course. But Malcolm was confident that Betsy Perryman was up for the challenge. In the afterglow of sex and inexpensive champagne, she'd told him once that each one of her four marriages had been a step forward and upward from the marriage that had preceded it, and it didn't take a hell of a lot of brains to know that moving out of a marriage to a dedicated inebriate – no matter how affable – into a relationship with a schoolteacher on his way to unveiling a piece of mediaeval history that would set the country on its ear was a step in the right direction. So Betsy would definitely handle Bernie. It was only a matter of time.

Divorce was out of the question, of course. Malcolm had made certain that Betsy understood that while he was desperate mad hungry and all the etceteras for a life with her, he would no more ask her to come to him in his current impoverished circumstances than would he expect one of the Royals to take up life in a bed-sit on the south bank of the Thames. Not only would he not ask that of her, he wouldn't allow it. Betsy – his beloved – deserved so much more than he would be able to give her, such as he was. But when his ship came in, darling Bets . . . Or if, God forbid, anything should ever happen to Bernie . . . This, he hoped, was enough to light a fire inside the spongy grey mass that went for her brain.

Malcolm felt no guilt at the thought of Bernie Perryman's demise. True, they'd known each other in childhood as sons of mothers who'd been girlhood friends. But they'd parted ways at the end of adolescence, when poor Bernie's failure to pass more than one O-level had doomed him to life on the family farm while Malcolm had gone on to university. And after that . . . well, differing levels of education *did* take a toll on one's ability to communicate with one's erstwhile – and less educated – mates, didn't it? Besides, when Malcolm returned from university, he could see that his old friend had sold his soul to the Black Bush devil, and what would it profit him to renew a friendship with the district's most prominent drunk? Still, Malcolm liked to think he'd taken a modicum of pity on Bernie Perryman. Once a month for years, he'd gone to the farmhouse – under cover of darkness, of course – to play chess with his former friend and to listen to his inebriated musings about their childhood and the what-might-have-beens.

Which was how he first found out about The Legacy, as Bernie had called it. Which was what he'd spent the last two years bonking Bernie's wife in order to get his hands on. Betsy and Bernie had no children. Bernie was the last of his line. The Legacy was going to come to Betsy. And Betsy was going to give it to Malcolm.

She didn't know that yet. But she would soon enough. Malcolm smiled, thinking of what Bernie's legacy would do to further his career. For nearly ten years, he'd been writing furiously on what he'd nicknamed *Dickon Delivered* – his untarnishing of the reputation of Richard III – and once The Legacy was in his hands, his future was going to be assured. As he rolled towards Bosworth Field and the Australian Ricardians awaiting him there, he recited the first line of the penultimate chapter of his magnum opus. 'It is with the alleged disappearance of Edward the Lord Bastard, Earl of Pembroke and March, and Richard, Duke of York, that historians have traditionally begun to rely upon sources contaminated by their own self-interest.'

God, it was beautiful writing, he thought. And better than that, it was the truth as well.

The tour coach was already there when Malcolm roared into the car park at Bosworth Field. Its occupants had foolishly disembarked. All apparently female and of depressingly advanced years, they were huddled into a shivering pack, looking sheeplike and abandoned in the gale-force winds that were blowing. When Malcolm heaved himself out of his car, one of their number disengaged herself from their midst and strode towards him. She was sturdily built and much younger than the rest, which gave Malcolm hope of being able to grease his way through the moment with some generous dollops of charm. But then he noted her short clipped hair, elephantine ankles, and massive calves . . . not to mention the clipboard that she was smacking into her hand as she walked. An unhappy lesbian tour guide out for blood, he thought. God, what a deadly combination.

Nonetheless, he beamed a glittering smile in her direction. 'Sorry,' he sang out. 'Blasted car trouble.'

'See here, mate,' she said in the unmistakable discordant twang – all long *A*s becoming long *I*s – of a denizen of Deepest Down Under, 'when Romance of Great Britain pays for a tour at noon, Romance of Great Britain expects the bleeding tour to begin at noon. So why're you late? Christ, it's like Siberia out here. We could die of exposure. Jaysus, let's just get on with it.' She turned on her heel and waved her charges over towards the edge of the car park, where the footpath carved a trail round the circumference of the battlefield.

Malcolm dashed to catch up. His tips hanging in the balance, he would have to make up for his tardiness with a dazzling show of expertise.

'Yes, yes,' he said with insincere joviality as he reached her side. 'It's incredible that you should mention Siberia, Miss . . . ?'

'Sludgecur,' she said, and her expression dared him to react to the name.

'Ah. Yes. Miss Sludgecur. Of course. As I was saying, it's incredible that you should mention Siberia because this bit of England has the highest elevation west of the Urals. Which is why we have these rather Muscovian temperatures. You can imagine what it might have been like in the fifteenth century when—'

'We're not here for meteorology,' she barked. 'Get on with it before my ladies freeze their arses off.'

Her ladies tittered and clung to one another in the wind. They had the dried apple faces of octogenarians, and they watched Sludgecur with the devotion of children who'd seen their parent take on all comers and deck them unceremoniously.

'Yes, well,' Malcolm said. 'The weather's the principal

reason that the battlefield's closed in the winter. We made an exception for your group because they're fellow Ricardians. And when fellow Ricardians come calling at Bosworth, we like to accommodate them. It's the best way to see that the truth gets carried forward, as I'm sure you'll agree.'

'What the bloody hell are you yammering about?' Sludgecur asked. 'Fellow who? Fellow what?'

Which should have told Malcolm that the tour wasn't going to proceed as smoothly as he had hoped. 'Ricardians,' he said, and beamed at the elderly women surrounding Sludgecur. 'Believers in the innocence of Richard III.'

Sludgecur looked at him as if he'd sprouted wings. 'What? This is the Romance of Great Britain you're looking at, mate. Jane Bloody Eyre, Mr. Flaming Rochester, Heathcliff and Cathy, Maxim de Winter. Gabriel Oak. This is Love on the Battlefield Day, and we mean to have our money's worth. All right?'

Their money was what it was all about. The fact that they were paying was why Malcolm was here in the first place. But, Jesus, he thought, did these Seekers of Romance even know where they were? Did they know – much less care – that the last king to be killed in armed combat met his fate less than a mile from where they were standing? *And* that he'd met that same fate because of sedition, treachery, and betrayal? Obviously not. They weren't here in support of Richard. They were here because it was part of a package. Love Brooding, Love Hopeless, and Love Devoted had already been checked off the list. And now he was somehow supposed to cook up for them a version of Love Deadly that would make them part with a few quid apiece at the end of the afternoon. Well, all right. He could do that much.

Malcolm didn't think about Betsy until he'd paused at the first marker along the route, which showed King Richard's initial battle position. While his charges took snapshots of the White Boar standard that was whipping in the icy wind from the flagpole marking the King's encampment, Malcolm glanced beyond them to the tumbledown buildings of Windsong Farm, visible at the top of the next hill. He could see the house and he could see Betsy's car in the farmyard. He could imagine – and hope about – the rest.

Bernie wouldn't have noticed that it had taken his wife three and a half hours to purchase a package of minced beef in Market Bosworth. It was nearly half past noon, after all, and doubtless he'd be at the kitchen table where he usually was, attempting to work on yet another of his Formula One models. The pieces would be spread out in front of him, and he might have managed to glue one onto the car before the shakes came upon him and he had to have a dose of Black Bush to still them. One dose of whiskey would have led to another until he was too soused to handle a tube of glue.

Chances were good that he'd already passed out onto the model car. It was Saturday and he was supposed to work at St. James Church, preparing it for Sunday's service. But poor old Bernie'd have no idea of the day until Betsy returned, slammed the minced beef onto the table next to his car, and frightened him out of his sodden slumber.

When his head flew up, Betsy would see the imprint of the car's name on his flesh, and she'd be suitably disgusted. Malcolm fresh in her mind, she'd feel the injustice of her position.

'You been to the church yet?' she'd ask Bernie. It was his only job, as no Perryman had farmed the family's land in at least eight generations. 'Father Naughton's not like the others, Bernie. He's not about to put up with you just because you're a Perryman, you know. You got the church *and* the graveyard to see to today. And it's time you were about it.'

Bernie had never been a belligerent drunk, and he wouldn't be one now. He'd say, 'I'm going, Sweet Mama. But I got the most godawful thirst. Throat feels like a sandpit, Mama girl.'

He'd smile the same affable smile that had won Betsy's heart in Blackpool, where they'd met. And the smile would remind his wife of her duty, despite Malcolm's ministrations to her earlier. But that was fine, because the last thing that Malcolm Cousins wanted was Betsy Perryman forgetting her duty.

So she'd ask him if he'd taken his medicine, and since Bernie Perryman never did anything – save pour himself a Black Bush – without having been reminded a dozen times, the answer would be no. So Betsy would seek out the pills and shake the dosage into her palm. And Bernie would take it obediently and then stagger out of the house – sans jacket as usual – and head to St. James Church to do his duty.

Betsy would call after him to take his jacket, but Bernie would wave off the suggestion. His wife would shout, 'Bernie! You'll catch your death —' and then stop herself at the sudden thought that entered her mind. Bernie's death, after all, was what she needed in order to be with her Beloved.

So her glance would drop to the bottle of pills in her hand and she would read the label: *Digitoxin. Do not exceed one tablet per day without consulting physician.*

Perhaps at that point, she would also hear the doctor's

explanation to her: 'It's like digitalis. You've heard of that. An overdose would kill him, Mrs. Perryman, so you must be vigilant and see to it that he never takes more than one tablet.'

More than one tablet would ring in her ears. Her morning bonk with Malcolm would live in her memory. She'd shake a pill from the bottle and examine it. She'd finally start to think of a way that the future could be massaged into place.

Happily, Malcolm turned from the farmhouse to his budding Ricardians. All was going according to plan.

'From this location,' Malcolm told his audience of eager but elderly seekers of Love on the Battlefield, 'we can see the village of Sutton Cheney to our northeast.' All heads swiveled in that direction. They may have been freezing their antique pudenda, but at least they were a cooperative group. Save for Sludgecur who, if she had a pudendum, had no doubt swathed it in long underwear. Her expression challenged him to concoct a Romance out of the Battle of Bosworth. Very well, he thought, and picked up the gauntlet. He'd give them Romance. He'd also give them a piece of history that would change their lives. Perhaps this group of Aussie oldies hadn't been Ricardians when they'd arrived at Bosworth Field, but they'd damn well be neophyte Ricardians when they left. *And* they'd return Down Under and tell their grandchildren that it was Malcolm Cousins – *the* Malcolm Cousins, they would say – who had first made them aware of the gross injustice that had been perpetrated upon the memory of a decent king.

'It was there in the village of Sutton Cheney, in St. James Church, that King Richard prayed on the night before the battle,' Malcolm told them. 'Picture what the night must have been like.'

From there, he went onto automatic pilot. He'd told the story hundreds of times over the years that he'd served as Special Guide for Groups at Bosworth Field. All he had to do was to milk it for its Romantic Qualities, which wasn't a problem.

The King's forces – twelve thousand strong – were encamped on the summit of Ambion Hill, where Malcolm Cousins and his band of shivering neoRicardians were standing. The King knew that the morrow would decide his fate: whether he would continue to reign as Richard III or whether his crown would be taken by conquest and worn by an upstart who'd lived most of his life on the continent, safely tucked away and coddled by those whose ambitions had long been to destroy the York dynasty. The King would have been well aware that his fate rested in the hands of the Stanley brothers: Sir William and Thomas, Lord Stanley. They had arrived at Bosworth with a large army and were encamped to the north, not far from the King, but also – and ominously – not far from the King's pernicious adversary, Henry Tudor, Earl of Richmond, who also happened to be Lord Stanley's stepson. To secure the father's loyalty, King Richard had taken one of Lord Stanley's blood sons as a hostage, the young man's life being the forfeit if his father betrayed England's anointed King by joining Tudor's forces in the upcoming battle. The Stanleys, however, were a wily lot and had shown themselves dedicated to nothing but their own self-interest, so – holding George Stanley hostage or not – the King must have known how great was the risk of entrusting the security of his throne to the whimsies of men whose devotion to self was their most notable quality.

The night before the battle, Richard would have seen the

Stanleys camped to the north, in the direction of Market Bosworth. He would have sent a messenger to remind them that, as George Stanley was still being held hostage and as he was being held hostage right there in the King's encampment, the wise course would be to throw their lot in with the King on the morrow.

He would have been restless, Richard. He would have been torn. Having lost first his son and heir and then his wife during his brief reign, having been faced with the treachery of once-close friends, can there be any doubt that he would have wondered – if only fleetingly – how much longer he was meant to go on? And, schooled in the religion of his time, can there be any doubt that he knew how great a sin was despair? And, having established this fact, can there be any question about what the King would have chosen to do on the night before the battle?

Malcolm glanced over his group. Yes, there was a satisfactorily misty eye or two among them. They saw the inherent Romance in a widowed king who'd lost not only his wife but his heir and was hours away from losing his life as well.

Malcolm directed a victorious glance at Sludgecur. Her expression said, Don't press your luck.

It wasn't luck at all, Malcolm wanted to tell her. It was the Great Romance of Hearing the Truth. The wind had picked up velocity and lost another three or four degrees of temperature, but his little band of Antique Aussies was caught in the thrall of that August night in 1485.

The night before the battle, Malcolm told them, knowing that if he lost, he would die, Richard would have sought to be shriven. History tells us that there were no priests or chaplains available among Richard's forces, so what better place to find a confessor than in St. James Church. The church would have been quiet as Richard entered. A votive candle or rushlight would have burned in the nave, but nothing more. The only sound inside the building would have come from Richard himself as he moved from the doorway to kneel before the altar: the rustle of his fustian doublet (satin-lined, Malcolm informed his scholars, knowing the importance of detail to the Romantic Minded), the creak of leather from his heavy-soled battle shoes and from his scabbard, the clank of his sword and dagger as he—

'Oh my goodness,' a Romantic neoRicardian chirruped. 'What sort of man would take swords and daggers into a church?'

Malcolm smiled winsomely. He thought, A man who had a bloody good use for them, just the very things needed for a bloke who wanted to prise loose a stone. But what he said was, 'Unusual, of course. One doesn't think of someone carrying weapons into a church, does one? But this was the night before the battle. Richard's enemies were everywhere. He wouldn't have walked into the darkness unprotected.'

Whether the King wore his crown that night into the church, no one can say, Malcolm continued. But if there was a priest in the church to hear his confession, that same priest left Richard to his prayers soon after giving him absolution. And there in the darkness, lit only by the small rushlight in the nave, Richard made peace with his Lord God and prepared to meet the fate that the next day's battle promised him.

Malcolm eyed his audience, gauging their reactions and their attentiveness. They were entirely with him. They were, he hoped, thinking about how much they should tip him for giving a bravura performance in the deadly wind.

His prayers finished, Malcolm informed them, the King unsheathed his sword and dagger, set them on the rough wooden bench, and sat next to them. And there in the church, King Richard laid his plans to ruin Henry Tudor should the upstart be the victor in the morrow's battle. Because Richard knew that he held – and had always held – the whip hand over Henry Tudor. He held it in life as a proven and victorious battle commander. He would hold it in death as the single force who could destroy the usurper.

'Goodness me,' someone murmured appreciatively. Yes, Malcolm's listeners were fully attuned to the Romance of the Moment. Thank God.

Richard, he told them, wasn't oblivious of the scheming that had been going on between Henry Tudor and Elizabeth Woodville – widow of his brother Edward IV and mother of the two young princes whom he had earlier placed in the Tower of London.

'The princes in the Tower,' another voice remarked. 'That's the two little boys who—'

'The very ones,' Malcolm said solemnly. 'Richard's own nephews.'

The King would have known that, holding true to her propensity for buttering her bread not only on both sides but along the crust as well, Elizabeth Woodville had promised the hand of her eldest daughter to Tudor should he obtain the crown of England. But should Tudor obtain the crown of England on the morrow, Richard also knew that every man, woman, and child with a drop of York blood in his body stood in grave danger of being eliminated – permanently – as a claimant to the throne. And this included Elizabeth Woodville's children.

He himself ruled by right of succession and by law.

Descended directly – and more important legitimately –
from Edward III, he had come to the throne after the death
of his brother Edward IV, upon the revelation of the
licentious Edward's secret pledge of marriage to another
woman long before his marriage to Elizabeth Woodville.
This pledged contract of marriage had been made before a
bishop of the church. As such, it was as good as a marriage
performed with pomp and circumstance before a thousand
onlookers, and it effectively made Edward's later marriage
to Elizabeth Woodville bigamous at the same time as it
bastardised all of their children.

Henry Tudor would have known that the children had
been declared illegitimate by an Act of Parliament. He
would also have known that, should he be victorious in his
confrontation with Richard III, his tenuous claim to the
throne of England would not be shored up by marriage to
the bastard daughter of a dead king. So he would have to do
something about her illegitimacy.

King Richard would have concluded this once he heard
the news that Tudor had pledged to marry the girl. He
would also have known that to legitimatise Elizabeth of
York was also to legitimatise all her sisters ... and her
brothers. One could not declare the eldest child of a dead
king legitimate while simultaneously claiming her siblings
were not.

Malcolm paused meaningfully in his narrative. He waited
to see if the eager Romantics gathered round him would
twig the implication. They smiled and nodded and looked
at him fondly, but no one said anything. So Malcolm did
their twigging for them.

'Her brothers,' he said patiently, and slowly to make sure
they absorbed each Romantic detail. 'If Henry Tudor

legitimatised Elizabeth of York prior to marrying her, he would have been legitimatising her brothers as well. And if he did that, the elder of the boys—'

'Gracious me,' one of the group sang out. '*He* would've been the true king once Richard died.'

Bless you, my child, Malcolm thought. 'That,' he cried, 'is exactly spot on.'

'See here, mate,' Sludgecur interrupted, some sort of light dawning in the cobwebbed reaches of her brain. 'I've heard this story, and Richard killed those little blighters himself while they were in the Tower.'

Another fish biting the Tudor bait, Malcolm realised. Five hundred years later and that scheming Welsh upstart was still successfully reeling them in. He could hardly wait until the day when his book came out, when his history of Richard was heralded as the triumph of truth over Tudor casuistry.

He was Patience itself as he explained. The princes in the Tower – Edward IV's two sons – had indeed been long reputed by tradition to have been murdered by their uncle Richard III to shore up his position as King. But there were no witnesses to any murder and as Richard was King through an Act of Parliament, he had no motive to kill them. And since he had no direct heir to the throne – his own son having died, as you heard moments ago – what better way to ensure the Yorks' continued possession of the throne of England than to designate the two princes legitimate . . . after his own death? Such designation could be made only by papal decree at this point, but Richard had sent two emissaries to Rome, and why send them such a distance unless it was to arrange for the legitimatising of the very boys whose rights had been wrested from them by their father's lascivious conduct?

'The boys were indeed rumoured to be dead.' Malcolm aimed for kindness in his tone. 'But that rumour, interestingly enough, never saw the light of day until just before Henry Tudor's invasion of England. He wanted to be King, but he had no rights to kingship. So he had to discredit the reigning monarch. Could there possibly be a more efficacious way to do it than by spreading the word that the princes – who were gone from the Tower – were actually dead? But this is the question I pose to you, ladies: What if they weren't?'

An appreciative murmur went through the group. Malcolm heard one of the ancients commenting, 'Lovely eyes, he has,' and he turned them towards the sound of her voice. She looked like his grandmother. She also looked rich. He increased the wattage of his charm.

'What if the two boys had been removed from the Tower by Richard's own hand, sent into safekeeping against a possible uprising? Should Henry Tudor prevail at Bosworth Field, those two boys would be in grave danger and King Richard knew it. Tudor was pledged to their sister. To marry her, he had to declare her legitimate. Declaring her legitimate made them legitimate. Making them legitimate made one of them – young Edward – the true and rightful King of England. The only way for Tudor to prevent this was to get rid of them. Permanently.'

Malcolm waited a moment to let this sink in. He noted the collection of grey heads turning towards Sutton Cheney. Then towards the north valley, where a flagpole flew the seditious Stanleys' standard. Then over towards the peak of Ambion Hill, where the unforgiving wind whipped

Richard's White Boar briskly. Then down the slope in the direction of the railway tracks, where the Tudor mercenaries had once formed their meagre front line. Vastly outnumbered, outgunned, and outarmed, they would have been waiting for the Stanleys to make their move: for King Richard or against him. Without the Stanleys throwing their lot in with Tudor's, the day would be lost.

The Grey Ones were clearly with him, Malcolm noted. But Sludgecur was not so easily drawn in. 'How was Tudor supposed to kill them if they were gone from the Tower?' She'd taken to beating her hands against her arms, doubtless wishing she were pummeling his face.

'He didn't kill them,' Malcolm said pleasantly, 'although his Machiavellian fingerprints are all over the crime. No. Tudor wasn't directly involved. I'm afraid the situation's a little nastier than that. Shall we walk on and discuss it, ladies?'

'Lovely little bum as well,' one of the group murmured. 'Quite a crumpet, that bloke.'

Ah, they were in his palm. Malcolm felt himself warm to his own seductive talents.

He knew that Betsy was watching from the farmhouse, from the first-floor bedroom from which she could see the battlefield. How could she possibly keep herself from doing so after their morning together? She'd see Malcolm shepherding his little band from site to site, she'd note that they were hanging on to his every word, and she'd think about how she herself had hung upon him less than two hours earlier. And the contrast between her drunken sot of a husband and her virile lover would be painfully and mightily on her mind.

This would make her realise how wasted she was on Bernie Perryman. She was, she would think, forty years old and at the prime of her life. She deserved better than Bernie. She deserved, in fact, a man who understood God's plan when He'd created the first man and woman. He'd used the man's rib, hadn't He? In doing that, He'd illustrated for all time that women and men were bound together, women taking their form and substance from their men, living their lives in the service of their men, for which their reward was to be sheltered and protected by their men's superior strength. But Bernie Perryman only ever saw one half of the man–woman equation. She – Betsy – was to work in his service, care for him, feed him, see to his well-being. He – Bernie – was to do nothing. Oh, he'd make a feeble attempt to give her a length now and again if the mood was upon him and he could keep it up long enough. But whiskey had long since robbed him of whatever ability he'd once had to be pleasing to a woman. And as for understanding her subtler needs and his responsibility in meeting them ... forget that area of life altogether.

Malcolm liked to think of Betsy in these terms: up in her barren bedroom in the farmhouse, nursing a righteous grievance against her husband. She would proceed from that grievance to the realisation that he, Malcolm Cousins, was the man she'd been intended for, and she would see how every other relationship in her life had been but a prologue to the connection she now had with him. She and Malcolm, she would conclude, were suited for each other in every way.

Watching him on the battlefield, she would recall their initial meeting and the fire that had existed between them from the first day when Betsy had begun to work at Gloucester Grammar as the headmaster's secretary. She'd recall the spark she'd felt when Malcolm had said, 'Bernie Perryman's wife?' and admired her openly. 'Old Bernie's been holding back on me, and I thought we shared every secret of our souls.' She would remember how she'd asked, 'You know Bernie?' still in the blush of her newlywed bliss and not yet aware of how Bernie's drinking was going to impair his ability to care for her. And she'd well remember Malcolm's response:

'Have done for years. We grew up together, went to school together, spent holidays roaming the countryside. We even shared our first woman' – and she'd remember his smile – 'so we're practically blood brothers if it comes to that. But I can see there might be a decided impediment to our future relationship, Betsy.' And his eyes had held hers just long enough for her to realise that her newlywed bliss wasn't nearly as hot as the look he was giving her.

From that upstairs bedroom, she'd see that the group Malcolm was squiring round the field comprised women, and she'd begin to worry. The distance from the farmhouse to the field would prevent her from seeing that Malcolm's antiquated audience had one collective foot in the collective grave, so her thoughts would turn ineluctably to the possibilities implied by his current circumstances. What was to prevent one of those women from becoming captivated by the enchantment he offered?

These thoughts would lead to her desperation, which was what Malcolm had been assiduously massaging for months, whispering at the most tender of moments, 'Oh God, if I'd only known what it was going to be like to have you, finally. And now to want you completely . . .' And then the tears, wept into her hair, and the revelation of the agonies of guilt and despair he experienced each time he rolled deliciously within the arms of his old friend's wife. 'I can't bear to hurt him, darling Bets. If you and he were to divorce . . . How could I live with myself if he ever knew how I've betrayed our friendship?'

She'd remember this, in the farmhouse bedroom with her hot forehead pressed to the cold windowpane. They'd been together for three hours that morning, but she'd realise that it was not enough. It would never be enough to sneak round as they were doing, to pretend indifference to each other when they met at Gloucester Grammar. Until they were a couple – legally, as much as they were already a couple spiritually, mentally, emotionally, and physically – she could never have peace.

But Bernie stood between her and happiness, she would think. Bernie Perryman, driven to alcohol by the demon of fear that the congenital abnormality that had taken his grandfather, his father, and both of his brothers before their forty-fifth birthdays would claim him as well. 'Weak heart,' Bernie had doubtless told her, since he'd used it as an excuse for everything he'd done – and not done – for the last thirty years. 'It don't ever pump like it ought. Just a little flutter when it oughter be a thud. Got to be careful. Got to take m' pills.'

But if Betsy didn't remind her husband to take his pills daily, he was likely to forget there were pills altogether, let alone a reason for taking them. It was almost as if he had a death wish, Bernie Perryman. It was almost as if he was only waiting for the appropriate moment to set her free.

And once she was free, Betsy would think, The Legacy would be hers. And The Legacy was the key to her future with Malcolm. Because with The Legacy in hand at last, she and Malcolm could marry and Malcolm could leave his ill-paying job at Gloucester Grammar. Content with his research, his writing, and his lecturing, he would be filled with gratitude for her having made his new lifestyle possible. Grateful, he would be eager to meet her needs.

Which is, she would think, certainly how it was meant to be.

In the Plantagenet Pub in Sutton Cheney, Malcolm counted the tip money from his morning's labour. He'd given his all, but the Aussie Oldies had proved to be a niggardly lot. He'd ended up with forty pounds for the tour and lecture – which was an awesomely cheap price considering the depth of information he imparted – and twenty-five pounds in tips. Thank God for the pound coin, he concluded morosely. Without it, the tightfisted old slags would probably have parted with nothing more than fifty pence apiece.

He pocketed the money as the pub door opened and a gust of icy air whooshed into the room. The flames of the fire next to him bobbled. Ash from the fireplace blew onto the hearth. Malcolm looked up. Bernie Perryman – clad only in cowboy boots, blue jeans, and a T-shirt with the words *Team Ferrari* printed on it – staggered drunkenly into the pub. Malcolm tried to shrink out of view, but it was impossible. After the prolonged exposure to the wind on Bosworth Field, his need for warmth had taken him to the blazing beech-wood fire. This put him directly in Bernie's sight line.

'Malkie!' Bernie cried out joyfully, and went on as he always did whenever they met. 'Malkie ol' mate! How 'bout a chess game? I miss our matches, I surely do.' He shivered and beat his hands against his arms. His lips were practically blue. 'Shit on toast. It's blowing a cold one out there. Pour me a Blackie,' he called out to the publican. 'Make it a double and make it double quick.' He grinned and dropped onto the stool at Malcolm's table. 'So. How's the book comin', Malkie? Gotcher name in lights? Found a publisher yet?' He giggled.

Malcolm put aside whatever guilt he may have felt at the fact that he was industriously stuffing this inebriate's wife whenever his middle-aged body was up to the challenge. Bernie Perryman deserved to be a cuckold, his punishment for the torment he'd been dishing out to Malcolm for the last ten years.

'Never got over that last game, did you?' Bernie grinned again. He was served his Black Bush, which he tossed back in a single gulp. He blubbered air out between his lips. He said, 'Did me right, that,' and called for another. 'Now, what was the full-on tale again, Malkie? You get to the good part of the story yet? Course, it'll be a tough one to prove, won't it, mate?'

Malcolm counted to ten. Bernie was presented with his second double whiskey. It went the way of the first.

'But I'm givin' you a bad time for nothing,' Bernie said, suddenly repentant in the way of all drunks. 'You never did me a bad turn – 'cept that time with the O-levels, 'course – and I shouldn't do you one. I wish you the best. Truly, I do. It's just that things never work out the way they're s'posed to, do they?'

Which, Malcolm thought, was the whole bloody point. Things – as Bernie liked to call them – hadn't worked out for Richard, either, that fatal morning on Bosworth Field.

The Earl of Northumberland had let him down, the Stanleys had out-and-out betrayed him, and an untried upstart who had neither the skill nor the courage to face the King personally in decisive combat had won the day.

'So tell Bern your theory another time. I love the story, I do, I do. I just wish there was a way for you to prove it. It'd be the making of you, that book would. How long you been working on the manuscript?' Bernie swiped the interior of his whiskey glass with a dirty finger and licked off the residue. He wiped his mouth on the back of his hand. He hadn't shaved that morning. He hadn't bathed. For a moment, Malcolm almost felt sorry for Betsy, having to live in the same house with the odious man.

'I've come to Elizabeth of York,' Malcolm said as pleasantly as he could manage considering the antipathy he was feeling for Bernie. 'Edward the Fourth's daughter. Future wife to the King of England.'

Bernie cocked his head. 'Cor, I always forget that bird, Malkie. Why's that, d'you think?'

Because everyone always forgot Elizabeth, Malcolm said silently. The eldest daughter of Edward IV, she was generally consigned to a footnote in history as the oldest sister of the princes in the Tower, the dutiful daughter of Elizabeth Woodville, a pawn in the political power game, the later wife of that Tudor usurper Henry VII. Her job was to carry the seed of the dynasty, to deliver the heirs, and to fade into obscurity.

But here was a woman who was one-half Woodville, with the thick blood of that scheming and ambitious clan coursing through her veins. That she wanted to be Queen of England like her mother before her had been established in the seventeenth century when Sir George Buck had written – in his *History of the Life and Reigne of Richard III* – of young Elizabeth's letter asking the Duke of Norfolk to be the mediator between herself and King Richard on the subject of their marriage, telling him that she was the King's in heart and in thought. That she was as ruthless as her two parents was made evident in the fact that her letter to Norfolk was written prior to the death of Richard's wife, Queen Anne.

Young Elizabeth had been bundled out of London and up to Yorkshire, ostensibly for safety's sake, prior to Henry Tudor's invasion. There she resided at Sheriff Hutton, a stronghold deep in the countryside where loyalty to King Richard was a constant of life. Elizabeth would be well protected – not to mention well guarded – in Yorkshire. As would be her siblings.

'You still hot for Lizzie?' Bernic asked with a chuckle. 'Cor, how you used to go on about that girl.'

Malcolm suppressed his rage but did not forbid himself from silently cursing the other man into eternal torment. Bernie had a deep aversion for anyone who tried to make something of his life. That sort of person served to remind him of what a waste he'd made of his own.

Bernie must have read something on Malcolm's face because, as he called for his third double whiskey, he said, 'No, no, get on with you. I 'as only kidding. What's you doing out here today anyway? Was that you in the battlefield when I drove by?'

Bernie knew it was he, Malcolm realised. But mentioning the fact served to remind them both of Malcolm's passion and the hold that Bernie Perryman had upon it. God, how he wanted to stand on the table and shout, 'I'm bonking this idiot's wife twice a week, three or four times if I can manage it. They'd been married two months when I bonked her the first time, six days after we were introduced.'

But losing control like that was exactly what Bernie Ferryman wanted of his old friend Malcolm Cousins: payback time for having once refused to help Bernie cheat his way through his O-levels. The man had an elephantine memory and a grudge-bearing spirit. But so did Malcolm.

'I don't know, Malkie,' Bernie said, shaking his head as he was presented with his whiskey. He reached unsteadily for it, his bloodless tongue wetting his lower lip. 'Don't seem natural that Lizzie'd hand those lads over to be given the chop. Not her own brothers. Not even to be Queen of England. 'Sides, they weren't even anywheres near her, were they? All speculation, 'f you ask me. All speculation and not a speck of proof.'

Never, Malcolm thought for the thousandth time, never tell a drunkard your secrets or your dreams.

'It was Elizabeth of York,' he said again. 'She was ultimately responsible.'

Sheriff Hutton was not an insurmountable distance from Rievaulx, Jervaulx, and Fountains Abbeys. And tucking individuals away in abbeys, convents, monasteries, and priories was a great tradition at that time. Women were the usual recipients of a one-way ticket to the ascetic life. But two young boys – disguised as youthful entrants into a novitiate – would have been safe there from the arm of Henry Tudor should he take the throne of England by means of conquest.

'Tudor would have known the boys were alive,' Malcolm said. 'When he pledged himself to marry Elizabeth, he would have known the boys were alive.'

Bernie nodded. 'Poor little tykes,' he said with factitious sorrow. 'And poor old Richard, who took the blame. How'd she get her mitts on them, Malkie? What d'you think? Think she cooked up a deal with Tudor?'

'She wanted to be a queen more than she wanted to be merely the sister to a king. There was only one way to make that happen. And Henry had been looking elsewhere for a wife at the same time that he was bargaining with Elizabeth Woodville. The girl would have known that. And what it meant.'

Bernie nodded solemnly, as if he cared a half fig for what had happened more than five hundred years ago on an August night not two hundred yards from the pub in which they sat. He shot back his third double whiskey and slapped his stomach like a man at the end of a hearty meal.

'Got the church all prettied up for tomorrow,' he informed Malcolm. ''Mazing when you think of it, Malkie. Perrymans been tinkering round St. James Church for two hundred years. Like a family pedigree, that. Don't you think? Remarkable, I'd say.'

Malcolm regarded him evenly. 'Utterly remarkable, Bernie,' he said.

'Ever think how different life might've been if your dad and granddad and his granddad before him were the ones who tinkered round St. James Church? P'rhaps I'd be you and you'd be me. What d'you think of that?'

What Malcolm thought of that couldn't be spoken to the man sitting opposite him at the table. Die, he thought. Die before I kill you myself.

'Do you want to be together, darling?' Betsy breathed the question wetly into his ear. Another Saturday. Another three hours of bonking Betsy. Malcolm wondered how much longer he'd have to continue with the charade.

He wanted to ask her to move over – the woman was capable of inducing claustrophobia with more efficacy than a plastic bag – but at this point in their relationship he knew that a demonstration of post-coital togetherness was as important to his ultimate objective as was a top-notch performance between the sheets. And since his age, his inclinations, and his energy were all combining to take his performances down a notch each time he sank between Betsy's well-padded thighs, he realised the wisdom of allowing her to cling, coo, and cuddle for as long as he could endure it without screaming once the primal act was completed between them.

'We *are* together,' he said, stroking her hair. It was wire-like to the touch, the result of too much bleaching and even more hair spray. 'Unless you mean that you want another go. And I'll need some recovery time for that.' He turned his head and pressed his lips to her forehead. 'You take it out of me and that's the truth of it, darling Bets. You're woman enough for a dozen men.'

She giggled. 'You love it.'

'Not it. You. Love, want, and can't be without.' He sometimes pondered where he came up with the nonsense he told her. It was as if a primitive part of his brain reserved for female seduction went onto auto-pilot whenever Betsy climbed into his bed.

She buried her fingers in his ample chest hair. 'I mean really be together, darling. Do you want it? The two of us? Like this? Forever? Do you want it more than anything on earth?'

The thought alone was like being imprisoned in concrete.

But he said, 'Darling Bets,' by way of answer and he trembled his voice appropriately. 'Don't. Please. We can't go through this again.' And he pulled her roughly to him because he knew that was the move she desired. He sank his face into the curve of her shoulder and neck. He breathed through his mouth to avoid inhaling the day's litre of Shalimar that she'd doused herself with. He made the whimpering noises of a man in extremis. God, what he wouldn't do for King Richard.

'I was on the Internet,' she whispered, fingers caressing the back of his neck. 'In the school library. All Thursday and Friday lunch, darling.'

He stopped his whimpering, sifting through this declaration for deeper meaning. 'Were you?' He temporised by nibbling at her earlobe, waiting for more information. It came obliquely.

'You *do* love me, don't you, Malcolm dearest?'

'What do you think?'

'And you do want me, don't you?'

'That's obvious, isn't it?'

'Forever and ever?'

Whatever it takes, he thought. And he did his best to prove it to her, although his body wasn't up to a full performance.

Afterwards, while she was dressing, she said, 'I was so surprised to see all the topics. You c'n look up anything on the Internet. Fancy that, Malcolm. Anything at all. Bernie's playing in the chess night at the Plantagenet, dearest. Tonight, that is.'

Malcolm furrowed his brow, automatically seeking the connection between these apparently unrelated topics. She went on.

'He misses your games, Bernie does. He always wishes you'd come by on chess night and give it another go with him, darling.' She padded to the chest of drawers, where she began repairing her makeup. 'Course, he doesn't play well. Just uses chess as an extra excuse to go to the pub.'

Malcolm watched her, eyes narrowed, waiting for a sign.

She gave it to him. 'I worry about him, Malcolm dear. His poor heart's going to give out someday. I'm going with him tonight. Perhaps we'll see you there? Malcolm, dearest, do you love me? Do you want to be together more than anything on earth?'

He saw that she was watching him closely in the mirror even as she repaired the damage he'd done to her makeup. She was painting her lips into bee-sting bows. She was brushing her cheeks with blusher. But all the time she was observing him.

'More than life itself,' he said.

And when she smiled, he knew he'd given her the correct answer.

That night at the Plantagenet Pub, Malcolm joined the Sutton Cheney Chessmen, of whose society he'd once been a regular member. Bernie Perryman was delighted to see him. He deserted his regular opponent – seventy-year-old Angus Ferguson, who used the excuse of playing chess at the Plantagenet to get as sloshed as Bernie – and pressed Malcolm into a game at a table in the smoky corner of the pub. Betsy was right, naturally: Bernie drank far more than he played, and the Black Bush served to oil the mechanism of his conversation. So he also talked incessantly.

He talked to Betsy, who was playing the role of serving wench for her husband that evening. From half past seven until half past ten, she trotted back and forth from the bar, bringing Bernie one double Black Bush after another, saying, 'You're drinking too much,' and 'This is the last one, Bernie,' in a monitory fashion. But he always managed to talk her into 'just one more wet one. Mama girl,' and he patted her bum, winked at Malcolm, and whispered loudly what he intended to do to her once he got her home. Malcolm was at the point of thinking he'd utterly misunderstood Betsy's implied message to him in bed that morning when she finally made her move.

It came at half past ten, one hour before George the Publican called for last orders. The pub was packed, and Malcolm might have missed her manoeuvre altogether had he not anticipated that something was going to happen that night. As Bernie nodded over the chessboard, contemplating his next move eternally, Betsy went to the bar for yet another 'double Blackie.' To do this, she had to shoulder her way through the Sutton Cheney Dartsmen, the Wardens of the Church, a women's support group from Dadlington, and a group of teenagers intent upon success with a fruit machine. She paused in conversation with a balding woman who seemed to be admiring Betsy's hair with that sort of artificial enthusiasm women reserve for other women whom they particularly hate, and it was while she and the other woman chatted that Malcolm saw her empty the vial into Bernie's tumbler.

He was awestruck at the ease with which she did it. She must have been practising the move for days, he realised. She was so adept that she did it with one hand as she chatted: slipping the vial out of her sweater sleeve, uncapping it, dumping it, returning it to her sweater. She finished her conversation, and she continued on her way.

And no one save Malcolm was wise to the fact that she'd done something more than merely fetch another whiskey for her husband. Malcolm eyed her with new respect when she set the glass in front of Bernie. He was glad he had no intention of hooking himself up with the murderous bitch.

He knew what was in the glass: the results of Betsy's few hours surfing the Internet. She'd crushed at least ten tablets of digitoxin into a lethal powder. An hour after Bernie ingested the mixture, he'd be a dead man.

Ingest it Bernie did. He drank it down the way he drank down every double Black Bush he encountered: He poured it directly down his throat and wiped his mouth on the back of his hand. Malcolm had lost count of the number of whiskeys Bernie had imbibed that evening, but it seemed to him that if the drug didn't kill him, the alcohol certainly would.

'Bernie,' Betsy said mournfully, 'let's go home.'

'Can't just yet,' Bernie said. 'Got to finish my bit with Malkie boy here. We haven't had us a chess-up in years. Not since ...' He smiled at Malcolm blearily. 'Why, I 'member that night up the farm, doanchew, Malkie? Ten years back? Longer, was it? When we played that last game, you and me?'

Malcolm didn't want to get onto that subject. He said, 'Your move, Bernie. Or do you want to call it a draw?'

'No way, Joe-zay.' Bernie swayed on his stool and studied the board.

'Bernie ...' Betsy said coaxingly.

He patted her hand, which she'd laid on his shoulder. 'You g'wan, Bets. I c'n find my way home. Malkie'll drive me, woanchew, Malkie?' He dug his car keys out of his pocket and pressed them into his wife's palm. 'But doanchew fall asleep, sweet Mama. We got business together when I get home.'

Betsy made a show of reluctance and a secondary show of her concern that Malcolm might have had too much to drink himself and thereby be an unsafe driver for her precious Bernie to ride along with. Bernie said, ' 'F he can't do a straight line in the car park, I'll walk. Promise, Mama. Cross m' heart.'

Betsy leveled a meaningful look at Malcolm. She said, 'See that you keep him safe, then.'

Malcolm nodded. Betsy departed. And all that was left was the waiting.

For someone who was supposed to be suffering from congenital heart problems, Bernie Perryman seemed to have the constitution of a mule. An hour later, Malcolm had him in the car and was driving him home, and Bernie was still talking like a man with a new lease on life. He was just itching to get up those farmhouse stairs and rip off his wife's knickers, to hear him tell it. Nothing but the Day of Judgement was going to stop Bernie from showing his Sweet Mama the time of her life.

By the time Malcolm had taken the longest route possible to get to the farm without raising Bernie's suspicions, he'd begun to believe that his paramour hadn't slipped her husband an overdose of his medication at all. It was only when Bernie got out of the car at the edge of the drive that Malcolm had his hopes renewed. Bernie said, 'Feel peaked a bit, Malkie. Whew. Nice lie down. That's just the ticket,' and staggered in the direction of the distant house. Malcolm watched him until he toppled into the hedgerow at the side of the drive. When he didn't move after the fall, Malcolm knew that the deed had finally been done.

He drove off happily. If Bernie hadn't been dead when he hit the ground, Malcolm knew that he'd be dead by the morning.

Wonderful, he thought. It may have been ages in the execution, but his well-laid plan was going to pay off.

Malcolm had worried a bit that Betsy might muff her role in the ensuing drama. But during the next few days, she proved herself to be an actress of formidable talents. Having awakened in the morning to discover herself alone in the bed, she'd done what any sensible wife-of-a-drunk would do: She went looking for her husband. She didn't find him anywhere in the house or in the other farm buildings, so she placed a few phone calls. She checked the pub; she checked the church; she checked with Malcolm. Had Malcolm not seen her poison her husband with his own eyes, he would have been convinced that on the other end of the line was a woman anxious for the welfare of her man. But then, she *was* anxious, wasn't she? She needed a corpse to prove Bernie was dead.

'I dropped him at the end of the drive,' Malcolm told her, help and concern personified. 'He was heading up to the house the last I saw him, Bets.'

So out she went and found Bernie exactly where he'd fallen on the previous night. And her discovery of his body set the necessary events in motion.

An inquest was called, of course. But it proved to be a mere formality. Bernie's history of heart problems and his 'difficulty with the drink,' as the authorities put it, combined with the fiercely inclement weather they'd been having were enough to provide the coroner's jury with a most reasonable conclusion. Bernie Perryman was declared dead of exposure, having passed out on the coldest night of the year, teetering up the lengthy drive to the farmhouse after a full night of drink at the Plantagenet Pub, where sixteen witnesses called to testify had seen him down at least eleven double whiskeys in less than three hours.

There was no reason to check for toxicity in his blood. Especially once his doctor said that it was a miracle the man had lived to forty-nine, considering the medical history of his family, not to mention his 'problem with the drink.'

So Bernie was buried at the side of his forebears, in the graveyard of St. James Church, where his father and all the fathers before him for at least the past two hundred years had toiled in the cause of a neat and tidy house of worship.

Malcolm soothed what few pangs of guilt he had over Bernie's passing by ignoring them. Bernie'd had a history of heart disease. Bernie had been a notorious drunk. If Bernie, in his cups, had passed out on the driveway a mere fifty yards from his house and died from exposure as a result . . . well, who could possibly hold himself responsible?

And while it was sad that Bernie Perryman had had to give his life for the cause of Malcolm's search for the truth, it was also the truth that he'd brought his premature death upon himself.

After the funeral, Malcolm knew that all he needed to employ was patience. He hadn't spent the last two years industriously ploughing Betsy's field, only to be thwarted by a display of unseemly haste at the moment of harvest. Besides, Betsy was doing enough bit-chomping for both of them, so he knew it was only a matter of days – perhaps hours – before she took herself off to the Perrymans' longtime solicitor for an accounting of the inheritance that was coming her way.

Malcolm had pictured the moment enough times during his liaison with Betsy. Sometimes picturing the moment when Betsy learned the truth was the only fantasy that got him through his interminable lovemaking sessions with the woman.

Howard Smythe-Thomas would open his Nuneaton office to her and break the news in a suitably funereal fashion, no doubt. And perhaps at first, Betsy would think his sombre demeanour was an air adopted for the occasion. He'd begin by calling her 'My dear Mrs. Perryman,' which should give her an idea that bad news was in the offing, but she wouldn't have an inkling of how bad the news was until he spelled out the bitter reality for her.

Bernie had no money. The farm had been mortgaged three times; there were no savings worth speaking of and no investments. The contents of the house and the outbuildings were hers, of course, but only by selling off every possession – and the farm itself – would Betsy be able to avoid bankruptcy. And even then, it would be touch and go. The only reason the bank hadn't foreclosed on the property before now was that the Perrymans had been doing business with that same financial institution for more than two hundred years. 'Loyalty,' Mr. Smythe-Thomas would no doubt intone. 'Bernard may have had his difficulties, Mrs. Perryman, but the bank had respect for his lineage. When one's father and one's father's father and his father before him have done business with a banking establishment, there is a certain leeway given that might not be given to a personage less well known to that bank.'

Which would be legal doublespeak for the fact that since there were no other Perrymans at Windsong Farm – and Mr. Smythe-Thomas would be good about gently explaining that a short-term wife of a long-term alcoholic Perryman didn't count – the bank would probably be calling in Bernie's debts. She would be wise to prepare herself for that eventuality.

But what about The Legacy? Betsy would ask. 'Bernie always nattered on about a legacy.' And she would be stunned to think of the depth of her husband's deception.

Mr. Smythe-Thomas, naturally, would know nothing about a legacy. And considering the Perryman history of ne'er-do-wells earning their keep by doing nothing more than working round the church in Sutton Cheney ... He would kindly point out that it wasn't very likely that anyone had managed to amass a fortune doing handywork, was it?

It would take some hours – perhaps even days – for the news to sink into Betsy's skull. She'd think at first that there had to be some sort of mistake. Surely there were jewels hidden somewhere, cash tucked away, silver or gold or deeds to property heretofore unknown packed in the attic. And thinking this, she would begin her search. Which was exactly what Malcolm intended her to do: Search first and come weeping to Malcolm second. And Malcolm himself would take it from there.

In the meantime, he happily worked on his magnum opus. The pages to the left of his typewriter piled up satisfactorily as he redeemed the reputation of England's most maligned king.

Many of the righteous fell that morning of 22 August 1485, and among them was the Duke of Norfolk, who commanded the vanguard at the front of Richard's army.

When the Earl of Northumberland refused to engage his forces to come to the aid of Norfolk's leaderless men, the psychological tide of the battle shifted.

Those were the days of mass desertions, of switching loyalties, of outright betrayals on the field of battle. And both the King and his Tudor foe would have known that. Which went far to explain why both men simultaneously needed and doubted the Stanleys. Which also went far to explain why – in the midst of the battle – Henry Tudor made a run for the Stanleys, who had so far refused to enter the fray. Outnumbered as he was, Henry Tudor's cause would be lost without the Stanleys' intervention. And he wasn't above begging for it, which is why he made that desperate ride across the plain towards the Stanley forces.

King Richard intercepted him, thundering down Ambion Hill with his Knights and Esquires of the Body. The two small forces engaged each other a bare half mile from the Stanleys' men. Tudor's knights began falling quickly under the King's attack: William Brandon and the banner of Cadwallader plummeted to the ground; the enormous Sir John Cheyney fell beneath the King's own ax. It was only a matter of moments before Richard might fight his way to Henry Tudor himself, which was what the Stanleys realised when they made their decision to attack the King's small force.

In the ensuing battle, King Richard was unhorsed and could have fled the field. But declaring that he would 'die King of England,' he continued to fight even when grievously wounded. It took more than one man to bring him down. And he died like the Royal Prince that he was.

The King's army fled, pursued hotly by the Earl of Oxford, whose intent it would have been to kill as many of them as possible. They shot off towards the village of Stoke Golding, in the opposite direction from Sutton Cheney.

This fact was the crux of the events that followed. When one's life is hanging in the balance, when one is a blood relative of the defeated King of England, one's thoughts turn inexorably towards self-preservation. John de la Pole, Earl of Lincoln and nephew to King Richard, was among the fleeing forces. To ride towards Sutton Cheney would have put him directly into the clutches of the Earl of Northumberland, who had refused to come to the King's aid and would have been only too happy to cement his position in Henry Tudor's affections – such as they were – by handing over the dead King's nephew. So he rode to the south instead of to the north. And in doing so, he condemned his uncle to five hundred years of Tudor propaganda.

Because history is written by the winners, Malcolm thought.

Only sometimes history gets to be rewritten.

And as he rewrote it, in the back of his mind was the picture of Betsy and her growing desperation. In the two weeks following Bernie's death, she hadn't returned to work. Gloucester Grammar's headmaster – the sniveling Samuel, as Malcolm liked to call him – reported that Betsy was prostrate over her husband's sudden death. She needed time to deal with and to heal from her grief, he told the staff sorrowfully.

Malcolm knew that what she had to deal with was finding something that she could pass off as The Legacy so as to bind him to her despite the fact that her expectations of inheritance had come to nothing. Tearing through the old farmhouse like a wild thing, she would probably go through Bernie's wardrobe one thread at a time in an attempt to unearth some item of value. She'd shake open books, seeking everything from treasure maps to deeds. She'd sift through the contents of the half dozen trunks in the attic. She'd knock about the outbuildings with her lips turning blue from the cold. And if she was assiduous, she would find the key.

And the key would take her to the safe-deposit box at that very same bank in which the Perrymans had transacted business for two hundred years. Widow of Bernard Perryman, with his will in one hand and his death certificate in the other, she would be given access. And there, she'd come to the end of her hopes.

Malcolm wondered what she would think when she saw the single grubby piece of paper that was the long-heralded Legacy of the Perrymans. Filled with handwriting so cramped as to be virtually illegible, it looked like nothing to the untrained eye. And that's what Betsy would think she had in her possession when she finally threw herself upon Malcolm's mercy.

Bernie Perryman had known otherwise, however, on that long-ago night when he'd shown Malcolm the letter.

'Have a lookit this here, Malkie,' Bernie had said. 'Tell ol' Bern whatchoo think of this.'

He was in his cups, as usual, but he wasn't yet entirely blotto. And Malcolm, having just obliterated him at chess, was feeling expansive and willing to put up with his childhood friend's inebriated ramblings.

At first he thought that Bernie was taking a page from out of a large old Bible, but he quickly saw that the Bible was really an antique leather album of some sort and the page was a document, a letter in fact. Although it had no salutation, it was signed at the bottom, and next to the signature were the remains of a wax imprint from a signet ring.

Bernie was watching him in that sly way drunks have: gauging his reaction. So Malcolm knew that Bernie knew what it was that he had in his possession. Which made him curious, but wary as well.

The wary part of him glanced at the document, saying, 'I don't know, Bernie. I can't make much of it.' While the curious part of him added, 'Where'd it come from?'

Bernie played coy. 'That ol' floor always gave them trouble, di'n't it, Malkie? Too low it was, stones too rough, never a decent job of building. But what else c'n you expect when a structure's donkey's ears old?'

Malcolm mined through this non sequitur for meaning. The old buildings in the area were Gloucester Grammar School, the Plantagenet Pub, Market Bosworth Hall, the timbered cottages in Rectory Lane, St. James Church in—

His gaze sharpened, first on Bernie and then on his document. St. James Church in Sutton Cheney, he thought. And he gave the document a closer look.

Which was when he deciphered the first line of it – I, *Richard, by the Grace of God Kyng of England and France and Lord of Ireland* – which was when his glance dropped to the hastily scrawled signature, which he also deciphered. *Richard R.*

Holy Jesus God, he thought. What had Bernie got his drunken little hands on?

He knew the importance of staying cool. One indication of his interest and he'd be Bernie's breakfast. So he said,

'Can't tell much in this light, Bernie. Mind if I have a closer look at home?'

But Bernie wasn't about to buy that proposal. He said, 'Can't let it out of m' sight, Malkie. Family legacy, that. Been our goods for donkey's years, that has, and every one of us swore to keep it safe.'

'How did you . . .?' But Malcolm knew better than to ask how Bernie had come to have a letter written by Richard III among his family belongings. Bernie would tell him only what Bernie deemed necessary for Malcolm to know. So he said, 'Let's have a look in the kitchen, then. That all right with you?'

That was just fine with Bernie Perryman. He, after all, wanted his old mate to see what the document was. So they went into the kitchen and sat at the table and Malcolm pored over the thick piece of paper.

The writing was terrible, not the neat hand of the professional scribe who would have attended the King and written his correspondence for him, but the hand of a man in agitated spirits. Malcolm had spent nearly twenty years consuming every scrap of information on Richard Plantagenet, Duke of Gloucester, later Richard III, called the Usurper, called England's Black Legend, called the Hunch-Backed Toad and every other foul sobriquet imaginable. So he knew how possible it actually was that here in this farmhouse, not two hundred yards from Bosworth Field and little over a mile from St. James Church, he was looking at the genuine article. Richard had lived his last night in this vicinity. Richard had fought here. Richard had died here. How unimaginable a circumstance was it that Richard had also written a letter somewhere nearby, in a building where it lay hidden until . . .

Malcolm thought about everything he knew of the area's history. He came up with the fact he needed. 'The floor of St. James Church,' he said. 'It was raised two hundred years ago, wasn't it?' And one of the countless ne'er-do-well Perrymans had been there, had probably helped with the work, and had found this letter.

Bernie was watching him, a sly smile tweaking the corners of his mouth. 'Whatchoo think it says, Malkie?' he asked. 'Think it might be worth a bob or two?'

Malcolm wanted to strangle him, but instead he studied the priceless document. It wasn't long, just a few lines that, he saw, could have altered the course of history and that would – when finally made public through the historical discourse he instantaneously decided to write – finally redeem the King who for five hundred years had been maligned by an accusation of butchery for which there had never been a shred of proof.

> I, Richard, by the Grace of God Kyng of England and France and Lord of Ireland, on thys daye of 21 August 1485 do with thys document hereby enstruct the good fadres of Jervaulx to gyve unto the protection of the beerrer Edward hytherto called Lord Bastarde and hys brother Richard, called Duke of Yrk. Possession of thys document wyll suffyce to identyfie the beerrer as John de la Pole, Earl of Lyncoln, beloved nephew of the Kyng. Wrytten in hast at Suton Chene. Richard R.

Two sentences and a phrase only, but enough to redeem a man's reputation. When the King had died on the field of battle that 22 of August 1485, his two young nephews had been alive.

Malcolm looked at Bernie steadily. 'You know what this is, don't you, Bernie?' he asked his old friend.

'Numbskull like me?' Bernie asked. 'Him what couldn't even pass his O-levels? How'd I know what that bit of trash is? But what d'you think? Worth something if I flog it?'

'You can't sell this, Bernie.' Malcolm spoke before he thought and much too hastily. Doing so, he inadvertently revealed himself.

Bernie scooped the paper up and manhandled it to his chest. Malcolm winced. God only knew the damage the fool was capable of doing when he was drunk.

'Go easy with that,' Malcolm said. 'It's fragile, Bernie.'

'Like friendship, isn't it?' Bernie said. He tottered from the kitchen.

It would have been shortly after that that Bernie had moved the document to another location, for Malcolm had never seen it again. But the knowledge of its existence had festered inside him for years. And only with the advent of Betsy had he finally seen a way to make that precious piece of paper his.

And it would be, soon. Just as soon as Betsy got up her nerve to phone him with the terrible news that what she'd thought was a legacy was only – to her utterly unschooled eyes – a bit of old paper suitable for lining the bottom of a parakeet cage.

While awaiting her call, Malcolm put the finishing touches on his *The Truth About Richard and Bosworth Field*, ten years in the writing and wanting only a single, final, and previously unseen historical document to serve as witness to the veracity of his theory about what happened to the two young princes. The hours that he spent at his typewriter flew by like leaves blown off the trees in Ambion Forest, where once a marsh had protected Richard's south flank from attack by Henry Tudor's mercenary army.

The letter gave credence to Malcolm's surmise that Richard would have told someone of the boys' whereabouts. Should the battle favour Henry Tudor, the princes would be in deadly danger, so the night before the battle Richard would finally have had to tell someone his most closely guarded secret: where the two boys were. In that way, if the day went to Tudor, the boys could be fetched from the monastery and spirited out of the country and out of the reach of harm.

John de la Pole, Earl of Lincoln, and beloved nephew to Richard III, would have been the likeliest candidate. He would have been instructed to ride to Yorkshire if the King fell, to safeguard the lives of the boys who would be made legitimate – and hence the biggest threat to the usurper – the moment Henry Tudor married their sister.

John de la Pole would have known the gravity of the boys' danger. But despite the fact that his uncle would have told him where the princes were hidden, he would never have been given access to them, much less had them handed over to him, without express direction to the monks from the King himself.

The letter would have given him that access. But he'd had to flee to the south instead of to the north. So he couldn't pull it from the stones in St. James Church where his uncle had hidden it the night before the battle.

And yet the boys disappeared, never to be heard of again. So who took them?

There could be only one answer to that question: Elizabeth of York, sister to the princes but also affianced wife of the newly crowned-right-there-on-the-battlefield King.

Hearing the news that her uncle had been defeated, Elizabeth would have seen her options clearly: Queen of England should Henry Tudor retain his throne, or sister to a mere youthful king should her brother Edward claim his own legitimacy the moment Henry legitimatised her or suppressed the Act by which she'd been made illegitimate in the first place. Thus, she could be the matriarch of a royal dynasty or a political pawn to be given in marriage to anyone with whom her brother wished to form an alliance.

Sheriff Hutton, her temporary residence, was no great distance from any of the abbeys. Ever her uncle's favourite niece and knowing his bent for things religious, she would have guessed – if Richard hadn't told her directly – where he'd hidden her brothers. And the boys would have gone with her willingly. She was their sister, after all.

'I am Elizabeth of York,' she would have told the abbot in that imperious voice she'd heard used so often by her cunning mother. 'I shall see my brothers alive and well. And instantly.'

How easily it would have been accomplished. The two young princes seeing their older sister for the first time in who knew how long, running to her, embracing her, eagerly turning to the abbot when she informed them that she'd come for them at last . . . And who was the abbot to deny a royal princess – clearly recognised by the boys themselves – her own brothers? Especially in the current situation, with King Richard dead and sitting on the throne a man who'd illustrated his bloodthirst by making one of his first acts as King a declaration of treason against all who had fought on the side of Richard at Bosworth Field? Tudor wouldn't look kindly on the abbey that was found to be sheltering the two boys. God only knew what his revenge would be should he find them.

Thus it made sense for the abbot to deliver Edward the Lord Bastard and his brother Richard the Duke of York into the hands of their sister. And Elizabeth, with her brothers in her possession, handed them over to someone. One of the Stanleys? The duplicitous Earl of Northumberland, who went on to serve Henry Tudor in the North? Sir James Tyrell, one-time follower of Richard, who was the recipient of two general pardons from Tudor not a year after he took the throne?

Whoever it was, once the princes were in his hands, their fates were sealed. And no one wishing to preserve his life afterwards would have thought about leveling an accusation against the wife of a reigning monarch who had already shown his inclination for attainting subjects and confiscating their land.

It was, Malcolm thought, such a brilliant plan on Elizabeth's part. She was her mother's own daughter, after all. She knew the value of placing self-interest above everything else. Besides, she would have told herself that keeping the boys alive would only prolong a struggle for the throne that had been going on for thirty years. She could put an end to the bloodshed by shedding just a little more blood. What woman in her position would have done otherwise?

The fact that it took Betsy more than three months to develop the courage to break the sorrowful news to Malcolm did cause him a twinge of concern now and then. In the timeline he'd long ago written in his mind, she'd have come to him in hysterics not twenty-four hours after discovering that her Legacy was a scribbled-up scrap of dirty paper. She'd have thrown herself into his arms and wept and waited for rescue. To emphasise the dire straits she was in, she'd have brought the paper with her to show him how ill Bernie Perryman had used his loving wife. And he – Malcolm – would have taken the paper from her shaking fingers, would have given it a glance, would have tossed it to the floor and joined in her weeping, mourning the death of their dearly held dreams. For she was ruined financially and he, on a mere paltry salary from Gloucester Grammar, could not offer her the life she deserved. Then, after a vigorous and memorable round of mattress poker, she would leave, the scorned bit of paper still lying on the floor. And the letter would be his. And when his tome was published and the lectures, television interviews, chat shows and book tours began cluttering up his calendar, he would have no time for a bumpkin housewife who'd been too dim to know what she'd had in her fingers.

That was the plan. Malcolm felt the occasional pinch of worry when it didn't come off quickly and without a hitch. But he told himself that Betsy's reluctance to reveal the truth to him was all part of God's Great Plan. This gave him time to complete his manuscript. And he used the time well.

Since he and Betsy had decided that discretion was in order following Bernie's death, they saw each other only in the corridors of Gloucester Grammar when she returned to work. During this time, Malcolm phoned her nightly for telesex once he realised that he could keep her oiled and proofread the earlier chapters of his opus simultaneously.

Then finally, three months and four days after Bernie's

unfortunate demise, Betsy whispered a request to him in the corridor just outside the headmaster's office. Could he come to the farm for dinner that night? She didn't look as solemn-faced as Malcolm would have liked, considering her impoverished circumstances and the death of her dreams, but he didn't worry much about this. Betsy had already proved herself a stunning actress. She wouldn't want to break down at the school.

Prior to leaving that afternoon, swollen with anticipation that his fantasy was about to be realised, Malcolm handed in his notice to the headmaster. Samuel Montgomery accepted it with a rather disturbing alacrity that Malcolm didn't much like, and although the headmaster covered his surprise and delight with a spurious show of regret at losing 'a veritable institution here at GG,' Malcolm could see him savouring the triumph of being rid of someone he'd decided was an educational dinosaur. So it gave him more satisfaction than he would have thought possible, knowing how great his own triumph was going to be when he made his mark upon the face of English history.

Malcolm couldn't have been happier as he drove to Windsong Farm that evening. The long winter of his discontent had segued into a beautiful spring, and he was minutes away from being able to right a five-hundred-year-old wrong at the same time as he carved a place for himself in the pantheon of the Historical Greats. God is good, he thought as he made the turn into the farm's long driveway. It was unfortunate that Bernie Perryman had had to die, but as his death was in the interest of historical redemption, it would have to be said that the end richly justified the means.

As he got out of the car, Betsy opened the farmhouse

door. Malcolm blinked at her, puzzled at her manner of dress. It took him a moment to digest the fact that she was wearing a full-length fur coat. Silver mink by the look of it, or possibly ermine. It wasn't the wisest get-up to don in these days of animal-rights activists, but Betsy had never been a woman to think very far beyond her own desires.

Before Malcolm had a moment to wonder how Betsy had managed to finance the purchase of a fur coat, she had thrown it open and was standing in the doorway, naked to her toes.

'Darling!' she cried. 'We're rich, rich, rich. And you'll never guess what I sold to make us so!'

JAMES W. HALL

....

Sometimes, you get to go full circle in life. James W. Hall started out as a poet and a short-story writer before becoming a best-selling novelist of some of the finest contemporary American crime fiction produced in the past decade, so he is back on familiar turf with this tale.

No story in this book captures the concept of obsession as well as this one. It is a bizarre story, certainly, but it resonates because it all seems so possible. What man, walking past a wall with a crack in it, could resist having a peek at the pretty and sexy young woman next door? Especially if she happens to be taking her clothes off. Yes, yes, I know it's bad form and juvenile and ill-mannered. But what I asked is, what man could resist? Hall's character didn't resist. Nor did he resist the next day, nor the next.

Perhaps what is so disturbing is that none of us (this applies only to men, of course, because women would never do anything as degrading as surreptitiously invade another person's privacy) knows when we would stop looking, either.

CRACK

By James W. Hall

When I first saw the slit of light coming through the wall, I
halted abruptly on the stairway, and instantly my heart
began to thrash with a giddy blend of dread and craving.

At the time, I was living in Spain, a section named Puerto
Viejo, or the Old Port, in the small village of Algorta just
outside the industrial city of Bilbao. It was a filthy town, a
dirty region, with a taste in the air of old pennies and a
patina of grime dulling every bright surface. The sunlight
strained through perpetual clouds that had the density and
monotonous luster of lead. It was to have been my year of
flamenco y sol, but instead I was picked to be the Fulbright
fellow of a dour Jesuit university in Bilbao on the northern
coast where the umbrellas were pocked by ceaseless acid
rain and the customary dress was black – shawls, dresses,
berets, raincoats, shirts, and trousers. It was as if the entire
Basque nation was in perpetual mourning.

The night I first saw the light I was drunk. All afternoon I
had been swilling Rioja on the balcony overlooking the
harbor, celebrating the first sunny day in a month. It was
October and despite the brightness and clarity of the light,
my wife had been darkly unhappy all day, even unhappier
than usual. At nine o'clock she was already in bed paging
aimlessly through month-old magazines and sipping her

sherry. I finished with the dishes and double-checked all the locks and began to stumble up the stairs of our two-hundred-fifty-year-old stone house that only a few weeks before our arrival in Spain had been subdivided into three apartments.

I was midway up the stairs to the second floor when I saw the slim line of light shining through a chink in the new mortar. There was no debate, not even a millisecond of equivocation about the propriety of my actions. In most matters I considered myself a scrupulously moral man. I had always been one who could be trusted with other people's money or their most damning secrets. But like so many of my fellow Puritans I long ago had discovered that when it came to certain libidinous temptations I was all too easily swept off my safe moorings into the raging currents of erotic gluttony.

I immediately pressed my eye to the crack.

It took me a moment to get my bearings, to find the focus. And when I did, my knees softened and my breath deserted me. The view was beyond anything I might have hoped for. The small slit provided a full panorama of my neighbors' second story. At knee-high level I could see their master bathroom and a few feet to the left their king-size brass bed.

That first night the young daughter was in the bathroom with the door swung open. If the lights had been off in their apartment or the bathroom door had been closed I might never have given the peephole another look. But that girl was standing before the full-length mirror and she was lifting her fifteen-year-old breasts that had already developed quite satisfactorily, lifting them both at once and reshaping them with her hands to meet some standard that only she could see. After a while she released them from her grip, then lifted them on her flat palms as though offering them to her image in the mirror. They were beautiful breasts, with small nipples that protruded nearly an inch from the aureole, and she handled them beautifully, in a fashion that was far more mature and knowing than one would expect from any ordinary fifteen-year-old.

I did not know her name. I still don't, though certainly she is the most important female who ever crossed my path. Far more crucial in my life's trajectory than my mother or either of my wives. Yet it seems appropriate that I should remain unaware of her name. That I should not personalize her in any way. That she should remain simply an abstraction – simply the girl who destroyed me.

In the vernacular of that year in Spain, she was known as a *niña pera*, or pear girl. One of hundreds of shapely and succulent creatures who cruised about the narrow, serpentine roads of Algorta and Bilbao on loud mopeds, their hair streaming in their wake. She was as juicy as any of them. More succulent than most, as I had already noticed from several brief encounters as we exited from adjacent doors onto the narrow alley-streets of the Old Port. On these two or three occasions, I remember fumbling through my Spanish greetings and taking a stab at small talk while she, with a patient but faintly disdainful smile, suffered my clumsy attempts at courtesy. Although she wore the white blouse and green plaid skirts of all the other Catholic schoolgirls, such prosaic dress failed to disguise her pearness. She was achingly succulent, blindingly juicy. At the time I was twice her age. Double the fool and half the man I believed I was.

That first night, after a long, hungering look, I pulled

away from the crack of light and with equal measures of reluctance and urgency, I marched back down the stairs and went immediately to the kitchen and found the longest and flattest knife in the drawer and brought it back to the stairway, and with surgical precision I inserted the blade into the soft mortar and as my pulse throbbed, I painstakingly doubled the size of my peephole.

When I withdrew the blade and applied my eye again to the slit, I now could see my *niña pera* from her thick black waist-length hair to her bright pink toenails. While at the same time I calculated that if my neighbors ever detected the lighted slit from their side and dared to press an eye to the breach, they would be rewarded with nothing more than a static view of the two-hundred-fifty-year-old stones of my rented stairwell.

I knew little about my neighbors except that the father of my pear girl was a vice-consul for that South American country whose major role in international affairs seemed to be to supply America with her daily dose of granulated ecstasy.

He didn't look like a gangster. He was tall and elegant, with wavy black hair that touched his shoulders and an exquisitely precise beard. He might have been a maestro of a European symphony or a painter of romantic landscapes. And his young wife could easily have been a slightly older sister to my succulent one. She was in her middle thirties and had the wide and graceful hips, the bold, uplifting breasts, the gypsy features and black unfathomable eyes that seemed to spring directly from the archetypal pool of my carnality. In the Jungian parlance of my age, the wife was my anima, while the daughter was the anima of my adolescent self. They were perfect echoes of the dark secret female who glowed like uranium in the bowels of my psyche.

That first night when the bedsprings squeaked behind me, and my wife padded across the bedroom floor for her final visit to the bathroom, I allowed myself one last draught of the amazing sight before me. The *niña* was now stooped forward and was holding a small hand mirror to her thicket of pubic hair, poking and searching with her free hand through the dense snarl as if she were seeking that tender part of herself she had discovered by touch but not yet by sight.

Trembling and breathless, I pressed my two hands flat against the stone wall and shoved myself away and with my heart in utter disarray, I carried my lechery up the stairs to bed.

The next day I set about learning my neighbors' schedule and altering mine accordingly. My wife had taken a job as an English teacher in a nearby *instituto* and was occupied every afternoon and through the early evening. My duties at the university occupied me Monday, Wednesday and Friday. I was expected to offer office hours before and after my classes on those days. However, I immediately began to curtail these sessions because I discovered that my *niña pera* returned from school around three o'clock, and on many days she showered and changed into casual clothes, leaving her school garb in a heap on the bathroom floor as she fled the apartment for an afternoon of boy-watching in the Algorta pubs.

To my department chairman's dismay, I began to absent myself from the university hallways immediately after my last class of the day, hurrying with my umbrella along the five blocks to the train station so I could be home by 2:55. In the silence of my apartment, hunched breathless at my hole, I watched her undress. I watched the steam rise from her shower, and I watched her towel herself dry. I watched her on the toilet and I watched her using the sanitary products she preferred. I watched her touch the flawless skin of her face with her fingertips, applying makeup or wiping it away. On many afternoons I watched her examine herself in the full-length mirror. Running her hands over that seamless flesh, trying out various seductive poses while an expression played on her face that was equal parts exultation and shame – that peculiar adolescent emotion I so vividly recalled.

These were the times when I would have touched myself were I going to do so. But these moments at the peephole, while they were intensely sexual, were not the least masturbatory. Instead, they had an almost spiritual component. As though I were worshiping at the shrine of hidden mysteries, allowed by divine privilege to see beyond the walls of my own paltry life. In exchange for this gift I was cursed to suffer a brand of reverential horniness I had not imagined possible. I lusted for a vision that was forever intangible, a girl I could not touch, nor smell, nor taste. A girl who was no more than a scattering of light across my retina.

Although I never managed to establish a definite pattern to her mother's schedule, I did my best to watch her as well. At odd unpredictable hours, she appeared in my viewfinder and I watched the elder *niña pera* bathe in a tub of bubbles, and even when her house was empty, I watched her chastely close the bathroom door whenever she performed her toilette. I watched her nap on the large brass bed. And three times that fall in the late afternoons, I watched her slide her hand inside her green silk robe and touch herself between the legs, hardly moving the hand at all, giving herself the subtlest of touches until she rocked her head back into the pillow and wept.

I kept my eye to the wall during the hours when I should have been preparing for my classes and grading my students' papers and writing up their weekly exams. Instead, I stationed myself at the peephole, propping myself up with pillows, finding the best alignment for nose and cheek against the rough cool rock. I breathed in the sweet grit of mortar, trained my good right eye on the bathroom door and the bed, scanning the floor for shadows, primed for any flick of movement, always dreadfully alert for the sound of my wife's key in the front door.

After careful study, I had memorized her homecoming ritual. Whenever she entered our apartment, it took her two steps to reach the foyer and put down her bag. She could then choose to turn right into the kitchen or take another step toward the stairway. If she chose the latter, almost instantly she would be able to witness me perched at the peephole, and my clandestine life would be exposed. In my leisure, I clocked a normal entry and found that on average I had almost a full twenty seconds from the moment her key turned the tumblers till she reached the bottom of the stairs, twenty seconds to toss the pillows back into the bedroom and absent myself from the hole.

I briefly toyed with the idea of revealing the peephole to her. But I knew her sense of the perverse was far short of my own. She was constitutionally gloomy, probably a clinical depressive. Certainly a passive-aggressive, who reveled in bitter non-response, bland effect, withdrawing into maddening hours of silence whenever I blundered across another invisible foul line she had drawn.

I watched the father too, the vice-consul. On many occasions I saw him strip off his underwear and climb into the shower, and I saw him dry himself and urinate and brush his teeth. Once I saw him reach down and retrieve a pair of discarded briefs and bring the crotch to his nose before deciding they were indeed fresh enough to wear again. He had the slender and muscular build of a long-distance runner. Even in its slackened state his penis was formidable.

On one particular Sunday morning, I watched with grim fascination as he worked his organ to an erection, all the while gazing at the reflection of his face. And a few moments later as the spasms of his pleasure shook him and he was bending forward to ejaculate into the sink, the *niña pera* appeared at the doorway of the bathroom. She paused briefly to watch the vice-consul's last strokes, then passed behind him and stepped into the shower with a nonchalance that I found more shocking than anything I had witnessed to that point.

Late in November, the chairman of my department called me into his office and asked me if I was happy in Spain, and I assured him that I most certainly was. He smiled uncomfortably and offered me a glass of scotch and as we sipped, he told me that the students had been complaining that I was not making myself sufficiently available to them. I feigned shock, but he simply shook his head and waved off my pretense. Not only had I taken to missing office house, I had failed to return a single set of papers or tests. The students were directionless and confused and in a unified uproar. And because of their protests, much to his regret, the chairman was going to have to insist that I begin holding my regular office hours immediately. If I failed to comply, he would have no choice but to act in his students' best interest by calling the Fulbright offices in Madrid and having my visiting professorship withdrawn for the second semester. I would be shipped home in disgrace.

I assured him that I would not disappoint him again.

Two days later after my last class of the day as I walked back to my office, all I could think of was my *niña pera* stripping away her Catholic uniform and stepping into the shower, then stepping out again wet and naked and perfectly succulent. I turned from my office door and the five scowling students waiting there and hurried out of the building. I caught the train just in time and was home only seconds before she arrived.

And this was the day it happened.

Breathless from my jog from the train station, I clambered up the stairs and quickly assumed my position at the slit, but was startled to see that it was not my *niña pera* beyond the wall, but her father, the diplomat in his dark suit, home at that unaccustomed hour. He was pacing back and forth in front of the bathroom, where a much shorter and much less elegant man was holding the head of a teenage boy over the open toilet bowl. The young man had long stringy hair and was dressed in a black T-shirt and blue jeans. The thug who was gripping him by the ears above the bowl was also dressed in black, a bulky black sweatshirt with the sleeves torn away and dark jeans and a black Basque beret. His arms were as gnarled as oak limbs, and the boy he held was unable to manage even a squirm.

The vice-consul stopped his pacing and spat out a quick, indecent bit of Spanish. Even though the wall muffled most conversation, I heard and recognized the phrase. While my conversation skills were limited, I had mastered a dozen or so of the more useful and colorful Spanish curses. The vice-consul had chosen to brand the boy as a pig's bastard child. Furthermore, a pig covered in its own excrement.

Though my disappointment at missing my daily appointment with the *niña pera* deflated my spirits, witnessing such violence and drama was almost fair compensation. My assumption was that my neighbor was disciplining the young man for some botched assignment – the most natural guess being that he was a courier who transported certain highly valued pharmaceutical products that happened also to be the leading export of the vice-consul's country. The other possibility, of course, and one that gave me a particularly nasty thrill, was that the boy was guilty of some impropriety with the diplomat's daughter, my own *niña pera*, and now was suffering the dire consequences of his effrontery.

I watched as the vice-consul came close to the boy and bent to whisper something to him, then tipped his head up by the chin and gave some command to the thug. The squat man let go of the boy's right ear, and with a gesture so quick I only caught the end of it, he produced a knife and slashed the boy's right ear away from his head.

I reeled back from the slit in the wall and pressed my back against the banister and tried to force the air into my lungs.

At that moment I should have rushed downstairs, gotten on the phone, and called the militia to report the outrage beyond my wall. And I honestly considered doing so. For surely it would have been the moral, virtuous path. But I could not move. And as I considered my paralysis, the utter selfishness of my inaction filled me with acid self-contempt. I reviled myself even as I kept my place. I could not call for help because I did not dare to upset the delicate equipoise of my neighbors' lives. The thought of losing my *niña pera* to the judicial process, or even worse to extradition, left me lifeless on the stairway. Almost as terrifying was the possibility that if I called for the militia, a further investigation would expose the slit in the wall and I would be hauled out into the streets for a public thrashing.

For a very long while I did not move.

Finally, when I found the courage to bring my eye back to the crack in the wall, I saw that the thug had lifted the boy to a standing position before the toilet, and the vice-consul had unzipped him and was gripping the tip of his penis, holding it out above the bloody porcelain bowl, a long steak knife poised a few inches above the pale finger of flesh.

The vice-consul's arm quivered and began its downward slash.

'No!' I cried out, then louder, 'No!'

My neighbor aborted his savage swipe and spun around. I watched him take a hesitant step my way, then another. His patent-leather shoes glowed in the eerie light beyond the wall. Then in an unerring path he marched directly to the wall where I was perched.

I pulled away, scooted backward up the stairs, and held my breath.

I waited.

I heard nothing but the distant siren wail of another supertanker coming into port.

I was just turning to tiptoe up to the bedroom when the blade appeared. It slid through the wall and glittered in the late-afternoon light, protruding a full five inches into my apartment. He slipped it back and forth as if he, too, were trying to widen the viewing hole, then drew it slowly out of sight. For a second I was in real danger of toppling forward down the flight of stairs, but I found a grip on the handrail and restrained myself on the precarious landing.

Though it was no longer visible, the knife blade continued to vibrate in my inner sight. I realized it was not a steak knife at all, but a very long fillet knife with a venomous tapered blade that shone with the brilliance of a surgical tool. I had seen similar knives many times along the Algorta docks, for this was the sort of cutlery that saw service gutting the abundant local cod.

And while I held my place on the stairs, the point of the knife shot through the wall again and remained there, very still, as eloquent and vile a threat as I had ever experienced. And a moment later in the vice-consul's apartment I heard a wet, piercing noise followed by a heavy thunk, as if a sack of cement had been broken open with the point of a shovel.

A second later my wife's key turned in the front-door lock and she entered the apartment, shook her umbrella, stripped off her rain gear and took her standard fifteen seconds to reach the bottom of the stairs. She gazed up and saw me frozen on the landing and the knife blade still shimmering through the wall of this house she had come to despise. For it was there in those four walls that I had fatally withdrawn from her as well as my students, where I had begun to match her obdurate silences with my own. In these last few months I had become so devoted to my *niña pera* that I had established a bond with this unknown juvenile beyond the wall that was more committed and passionate than any feelings I had ever shown my wife.

And when she saw the knife blade protruding from the wall, she knew all this and more. More than I could have told her if I had fallen to my knees and wallowed in confession. Everything was explained to her, my vast guilt, my repellent preoccupation, the death of our life together. Our eyes interlocked, and whatever final molecules of adhesion still existed between us dissolved in those silent seconds.

She turned and strode to the foyer. As I came quickly down the stairs, she picked up her raincoat and umbrella and opened the heavy door of our apartment and stepped out into the narrow alley-street of the Old Port. I hurried after her, calling out her name, pleading with her, but she shut the door behind her with brutal finality.

As I rushed to catch her, pushing open the door, I nearly collided with my succulent young neighbor coming home late from school. She graced me with a two-second smile and entered her door, and I stood on the stoop for a moment looking down the winding, rain-slicked street after my wife. Wretched and elated, I swung around and shut myself in once more with my utter depravity.

I mounted the stairs.

There was nothing in my heart, nothing in my head. Simply the raging current of blood that powered my flesh. I knelt at the wall and felt the magnetic throb of an act committed a thousand times and rewarded almost as often, the Pavlovian allure, a need beyond need, a death-hungering wish to see, to know, to live among that nefarious family who resided only a knife blade away.

I pressed my eye to the hole and she was there, framed in the bathroom doorway wearing her white blouse, her green plaid skirt. Behind her I could see that the toilet bowl had been wiped clean of blood. My *niña pera*'s hands hung uneasily at her sides and she was staring across the room at the wall we shared, her head canted to the side, her eyes focused on the exact spot where I pressed my face into the stone and drank her in. My pear girl, my succulent child, daughter of the Devil.

And though I was certain that the glimmer of my eye was plainly visible to her and anyone else who stood on that side of the wall, I could not pull myself from the crack, for my *niña pera* had begun to lift her skirt, inch by excruciating inch, exposing those immaculate white thighs. And though there was no doubt she was performing under duress and on instructions from her father, I pressed my face still harder against the wall and drank deep of the vision before me.

Even when my succulent one cringed and averted her face, giving me a second or two of ample warning of what her father was about to do, I could not draw my eye away from the lush expanse of her thighs.

A half second later her body disappeared and a wondrous flash of darkness swelled inside me and exploded. I was launched into utter blankness, riding swiftly out beyond the edges of the visible world, flying headlong into a bright galaxy of pain.

And yet, if I had not passed out on the stairway, bleeding profusely from my ruined eye, if somehow I had managed to stay conscious for only a few seconds more, I am absolutely certain that after I suffered the loss of sight in my right eye, I would have used the last strength I had to reposition myself on the stairway and resume my vigil with my left.

In the following months of recuperation and repair, I came to discover that a man can subsist with one eye as readily as with one hand or leg. For apparently nature anticipated that some of us would commit acts of such extreme folly and self-destructiveness that we would require such anatomical redundancy if we were to survive. And in her wisdom, she created us to be two halves co-joined. So that even with one eye, a man can still see, just as with only a single hand he may still reach out and beckon for his needs. And yes, even half-heartedly, he may once again know love.

DENNIS LEHANE

....

If there is a more talented young writer in America than Dennis Lehane, I haven't read his book yet. A Drink Before the War *and* Darkness Take My Hand *had been published when I asked him to write a story for this book, and then* Sacred *came out, to be followed by* Gone, Baby, Gone, Prayers for Rain, *and* Mystic River. *Each book was a joy and had a very distinctive style that spoke directly to me.*

Imagine how my heart sank when the envelope bearing this story arrived with a covering note that said something like 'This is entirely different from my other stuff.' No, no, no, no, no. I wanted the other stuff; that's why I asked for a story. So I read it and, you know what? It is entirely unlike anything else he's ever written. It's a great stretch of the imagination to even consider the possibility that the same man who wrote the novels about Boston private detectives Patrick Kenzie and Angela Gennaro could have written this.

But ... you know what else? It should be no surprise to learn that it, too, is brilliant. Read a Lehane novel if you haven't already. Can you believe it's the same author of this wonderful tale? Oh, and between books he also made (wrote and directed) his own feature film, Neighbors. *This is a career worth watching.*

RUNNING OUT OF DOG

By Dennis Lehane

This thing with Blue and the dogs and Elgin Bern happened a while back, a few years after some of our boys – like Elgin Bern and Cal Sears – came back from Vietnam, and a lot of others – like Eddie Vorcy and Carl Joe Carol, the Stewart cousins – didn't. We don't know how it worked in other towns, but that war put something secret in our boys who returned. Something quiet and untouchable. You sensed they knew things they'd never say, did things on the sly you'd never discover. Great card players, those boys, able to bluff with the best, let no joy show in their face no matter what they were holding.

A small town is a hard place to keep a secret, and a small Southern town with all that heat and all those open windows is an even harder place than most. But those boys who came back from overseas, they seemed to have mastered the trick of privacy. And the way it's always been in this town, you get a sizable crop of young, hard men coming up at the same time, they sort of set the tone.

So, not long after the war, we were a quieter town, a less trusting one (or so some of us seemed to think), and that's right when tobacco money and textile money reached a sort of critical mass and created construction money and pretty soon there was talk that our small town should maybe get a little bigger, maybe build something that would bring in more tourist dollars than we'd been getting from fireworks and pecans.

That's when some folks came up with this Eden Falls idea — a big carnival-type park with roller coasters and water slides and such. Why should all those Yankees spend all their money in Florida? South Carolina had sun too. Had golf courses and grapefruit and no end of KOA campgrounds.

So now a little town called Eden was going to have Eden Falls. We were going to be on the map, people said. We were going to be in all the brochures. We were small now, people said, but just you wait. Just you wait.

And that's how things stood back then, the year Perkin and Jewel Lut's marriage hit a few bumps and Elgin Bern took up with Shelley Briggs and no one seemed able to hold on to their dogs.

The problem with dogs in Eden, South Carolina, was that the owners who bred them bred a lot of them. Or they allowed them to run free where they met up with other dogs of opposite gender and achieved the same result. This wouldn't have been so bad if Eden weren't so close to 1–95, and if the dogs weren't in the habit of bolting into traffic and fucking up the bumpers of potential tourists.

The mayor, Big Bobby Vargas, went to a mayoral conference up in Beaufort, where the governor made a surprise appearance to tell everyone how pissed off he was about this dog thing. Lot of money being poured into Eden these days, the governor said, lot of steps being taken to change her image, and he for one would be goddamned if a bunch of misbehaving canines was going to mess all that up.

'Boys,' he'd said, looking Big Bobby Vargas dead in the eye, 'they're starting to call this state the Devil's Kennel 'cause of all them pooch corpses along the interstate. And I don't know about you all, but I don't think that's a real pretty name.'

Big Bobby told Elgin and Blue he'd never heard anyone call it the Devil's Kennel in his life. Heard a lot worse, sure, but never that. Big Bobby said the governor was full of shit. But, being the governor and all, he was sort of entitled.

The dogs in Eden had been a problem going back to the twenties and a part-time breeder named J. Mallon Ellenburg who, if his arms weren't up to their elbows in the guts of the tractors and combines he repaired for a living, was usually lashing out at something – his family when they weren't quick enough, his dogs when the family was. J. Mallon Ellenburg's dogs were mixed breeds and mongrels and they ran in packs, as did their offspring, and several generations later, those packs still moved through the Eden night like wolves, their bodies stripped to muscle and gristle, tense and angry, growling in the dark at J. Mallon Ellenburg's ghost.

Big Bobby went to the trouble of measuring exactly how much of 95 crossed through Eden, and he came up with 2.8 miles. Not much really, but still an average of .74 dog a day or 4.9 dogs a week. Big Bobby wanted the rest of the state funds the governor was going to be doling out at year's end, and if that meant getting rid of five dogs a week, give or take, then that's what was going to get done.

'On the QT,' he said to Elgin and Blue, 'on the QT, what we going to do, boys, is set up in some trees and shoot every canine who gets within barking distance of that interstate.'

Elgin didn't much like this 'we' stuff. First place, Big Bobby'd said 'we' that time in Double O's four years ago. This was before he'd become mayor, when he was nothing

more than a county tax assessor who shot pool at Double
O's every other night, same as Elgin and Blue. But one
night, after Harlan and Chub Uke had roughed him up over
a matter of some pocket change, and knowing that neither
Elgin nor Blue was too fond of the Uke family either, Big
Bobby'd said, 'We going to settle those boys' asses tonight,'
and started running his mouth the minute the brothers
entered the bar.

Time the smoke cleared, Blue had a broken hand, Harlan
and Chub were curled up on the floor, and Elgin's lip was
busted. Big Bobby, meanwhile, was hiding under the pool
table, and Cal Sears was asking who was going to pay for the
pool stick Elgin had snapped across the back of Chub's head.

So Elgin heard Mayor Big Bobby saying 'we' and
remembered the ten dollars it had cost him for that pool
stick, and he said, 'No, sir, you can count me out this
particular enterprise.'

Big Bobby looked disappointed. Elgin was a veteran of a
foreign war, former Marine, a marksman. 'Shit,' Big Bobby
said, 'what good are you, you don't use the skills Uncle Sam
spent good money teaching you?'

Elgin shrugged. 'Damn, Bobby. I guess not much.'

But Blue kept his hand in, as both Big Bobby and Elgin
knew he would. All the job required was a guy didn't mind
sitting in a tree who liked to shoot things. Hell, Blue was home.

Elgin didn't have the time to be sitting up in a tree anyway.
The past few months, he'd been working like crazy after
they'd broke ground at Eden Falls – mixing cement, digging
postholes, draining swamp water to shore up the foundation – with the real work still to come. There'd be several
more months of drilling and bilging, spreading cement like
cake icing, and erecting scaffolding to build walls and

facades. There'd be the hump-and-grind of rolling along in the dump trucks and drill trucks, the forklifts and cranes and industrial diggers, until the constant heave and jerk of them drove up his spine or into his kidneys like a corkscrew.

Time to sit up in a tree shooting dogs? Shit. Elgin didn't have time to take a piss some days.

And then on top of all the work, he'd been seeing Drew Briggs's ex-wife, Shelley, lately. Shelley was the receptionist at Perkin Lut's Auto Emporium, and one day Elgin had brought his Impala in for a tire rotation and they'd got to talking. She'd been divorced from Drew over a year, and they waited a couple of months to show respect, but after a while they began showing up at Double O's and down at the IHOP together.

Once they drove clear to Myrtle Beach together for the weekend. People asked them what it was like, and they said, 'Just like the postcards.' Since the postcards never mentioned the price of a room at the Hilton, Elgin and Shelley didn't mention that all they'd done was drive up and down the beach twice before settling in a motel a bit west in Conway. Nice, though; had a color TV and one of those switches turned the bathroom into a sauna if you let the shower run. They'd started making love in the sauna, finished up on the bed with the steam coiling out from the bathroom and brushing their heels. Afterward, he pushed her hair back off her forehead and looked in her eyes and told her he could get used to this.

She said, 'But wouldn't it cost a lot to install a sauna in your trailer?' then waited a full thirty seconds before she smiled.

Elgin liked that about her, the way she let him know he was still just a man after all, always would take himself too seriously, part of his nature. Letting him know she might be around to keep him apprised of that fact every time he did.

Keep him from pushing a bullet into the breech of a thirty-eight-six, slamming the bolt home, firing into the flank of some wild dog.

Sometimes, when they'd shut down the site early for the day – if it had rained real heavy and the soil loosened near a foundation, or if supplies were running late – he'd drop by Lut's to see her. She'd smile as if he'd brought her flowers, say, 'Caught boozing on the job again?' or some other smartass thing, but it made him feel good, as if something in his chest suddenly realized it was free to breathe.

Before Shelley, Elgin had spent a long time without a woman he could publicly acknowledge as his. He'd gone with Mac Shiller from fifteen to nineteen, but she'd gotten lonely while he was overseas, and he'd returned to find her gone from Eden, married to a boy up in South of the Border, the two of them working a corn-dog concession stand, making a tidy profit, folks said. Elgin dated some, but it took him a while to get over Mac, to get over the loss of something he'd always expected to have, the sound of her laugh and an image of her stepping naked from Cooper's Lake, her pale flesh beaded with water, having been the things that got Elgin through the jungle, through the heat, through the ticking of his own death he'd heard in his ears every night he'd been over there.

About a year after he'd come home, Jewel Lut had come to visit her mother, who still lived in the trailer park where Jewel had grown up with Elgin and Blue, where Elgin still lived. On her way out, she'd dropped by Elgin's and they'd sat out front of his trailer in some folding chairs, had a few drinks, talked about old times. He told her a bit about Vietnam, and she told him a bit about marriage. How it wasn't what you expected, how Perkin Lut might know a lot of things but he didn't know a damn sight about having fun.

There was something about Jewel Lut that sank into men's flesh the way heat did. It wasn't just that she was pretty, had a beautiful body, moved in a loose, languid way that made you picture her naked no matter what she was wearing. No, there was more to it. Jewel, never the brightest girl in town and not even the most charming, had something in her eyes that none of the women Elgin had ever met had; it was a capacity for living, for taking moments – no matter how small or inconsequential – and squeezing every last thing you could out of them. Jewel gobbled up life, dove into it like it was a cool pond cut in the shade of a mountain on the hottest day of the year.

That look in her eyes – the one that never left – said, Let's have fun, goddammit. Let's eat. Now.

She and Elgin hadn't been stupid enough to do anything that night, not even after Elgin caught that look in her eyes, saw it was directed at him, saw she wanted to eat.

Elgin knew how small Eden was, how its people loved to insinuate and pry and talk. So he and Jewel worked it out, a once-a-week thing mostly that happened down in Carlyle, at a small cabin had been in Elgin's family since before the War Between the States. There, Elgin and Jewel were free to partake of each other, squeeze and bite and swallow and inhale each other, to make love in the lake, on the porch, in the tiny kitchen.

They hardly ever talked, and when they did it was about nothing at all, really – the decline in quality of the meat at Billy's Butcher Shop, rumors that parking meters were going to be installed in front of the courthouse, if McGarrett and the rest of Five-O would ever put the cuffs on Wo Fat.

There was an unspoken understanding that he was free to date any woman he chose and that she'd never leave

Perkin Lut. And that was just fine. This wasn't about love; it was about appetite.

Sometimes, Elgin would see her in town or hear Blue speak about her in that puppy-dog-love way he'd been speaking about her since high school, and he'd find himself surprised by the realization that he slept with this woman. That no one knew. That it could go on forever, if both of them remained careful, vigilant against the wrong look, the wrong tone in their voices when they spoke in public.

He couldn't entirely put his finger on what need she satisfied, only that he needed her in that lakefront cabin once a week, that it had something to do with walking out of the jungle alive, with the ticking of his own death he'd heard for a full year. Jewel was somehow reward for that, a fringe benefit. To be naked and spent with her lying atop him and seeing that look in her eyes that said she was ready to go again, ready to gobble him up like oxygen. He'd earned that by shooting at shapes in the night, pressed against those damp foxhole walls that never stayed shored up for long, only to come home to a woman who couldn't wait, who'd discarded him as easily as she would a once-favored doll she'd grown beyond, looked back upon with a wistful mix of nostalgia and disdain.

He'd always told himself that when he found the right woman, his passion for Jewel, his need for those nights at the lake, would disappear. And, truth was, since he'd been with Shelley Briggs, he and Jewel had cooled it. Shelley wasn't Perkin, he told Jewel; she'd figure it out soon enough if he left town once a week, came back with bite marks on his abdomen.

Jewel said, 'Fine. We'll get back to it whenever you're ready.'

Knowing there'd be a next time, even if Elgin wouldn't admit it to himself.

So Elgin, who'd been so lonely in the year after his discharge, now had two women. Sometimes, he didn't know what to think of that. When you were alone, the happiness of others boiled your insides. Beauty seemed ugly. Laughter seemed evil. The casual grazing of one lover's hand into another was enough to make you want to cut them off at the wrist. *I will never be loved*, you said. *I will never know joy.*

He wondered sometimes how Blue made it through. Blue, who'd never had a girlfriend he hadn't rented by the half hour. Who was too ugly and small and just plain weird to evoke anything in women but fear or pity. Blue, who'd been carrying a torch for Jewel Lut since long before she married Perkin and kept carrying it with a quiet fever Elgin could only occasionally identify with. Blue, he knew, saw Jewel Lut as a queen, as the only woman who existed for him in Eden, South Carolina. All because she'd been nice to him, pals with him and Elgin, back about a thousand years ago, before sex, before breasts, before Elgin or Blue had even the smallest clue what that thing between their legs was for, before Perkin Lut had come along with his daddy's money and his nice smile and his bullshit stories about how many men he'd have killed in the war if only the draft board had seen fit to let him go.

Blue figured if he was nice enough, kind enough, waited long enough – then one day Jewel would see his decency, need to cling to it.

Elgin never bothered telling Blue that some women didn't want decency. Some women didn't want a nice guy. Some women, and some men too, wanted to get into a bed, turn out the lights, and feast on each other like animals until it hurt to move.

Blue would never guess that Jewel was that kind of

woman, because she was always so sweet to him, treated
him like a child really, and with every friendly hello she gave
him, every pat on the shoulder, every 'What you been up to,
old bud?' Blue pushed her further and further up the
pedestal he'd built in his mind.

'I seen him at the Emporium one time,' Shelley told
Elgin. 'He just come in for no reason anyone understood
and sat reading magazines until Jewel came in to see Perkin
about something. And Blue, he just stared at her. Just stared
at her talking to Perkin in the showroom. When she finally
looked back, he stood up and left.'

Elgin hated hearing about, talking about, or thinking
about Jewel when he was with Shelley. It made him feel
unclean and unworthy.

'Crazy love,' he said to end the subject.

'Crazy something, babe.'

Nights sometimes, Elgin would sit with Shelley in front
of his trailer, listen to the cicadas hum through the scrawny
pine, smell the night and the rock salt mixed with gravel;
the piña colada shampoo Shelley used made him think of
Hawaii, though he'd never been, and he'd think how their
love wasn't crazy love, wasn't burning so fast and furious
it'd burn itself out they weren't careful. And that was fine
with him. If he could just get his head around this Jewel Lut
thing, stop seeing her naked and waiting and looking back
over her shoulder at him in the cabin, then he could make
something with Shelley. She was worth it. She might not be
able to fuck like Jewel, and, truth be told, he didn't laugh as
much with her, but Shelley was what you aspired to. A good
woman, who'd be a good mother, who'd stick by you when
times got tough. Sometimes he'd take her hand in his and
hold it for no other reason but the doing of it. She caught

him one night, some look in his eyes, maybe the way he tilted his head to look at her small white hand in his big brown one.

She said, 'Damn, Elgin, if you ain't simple sometimes.' Then she came out of her chair in a rush and straddled him, kissed him as if she were trying to take a piece of him back with her. She said, 'Baby, we ain't getting any younger. You know?'

And he knew, somehow, at that moment why some men build families and others shoot dogs. He just wasn't sure where he fit in the equation.

He said, 'We ain't, are we?'

Blue had been Elgin's best buddy since either of them could remember, but Elgin had been wondering about it lately. Blue'd always been a little different, something Elgin liked, sure, but there was more to it now. Blue was the kind of guy you never knew if he was quiet because he didn't have anything to say or, because what he had to say was so horrible, he knew enough not to send it out into the atmosphere.

When they'd been kids, growing up in the trailer park, Blue used to be out at all hours because his mother was either entertaining a man or had gone out and forgotten to leave him the key. Back then, Blue had this thing for cockroaches. He'd collect them in a jar, then drop bricks on them to test their resiliency. He told Elgin once, 'That's what they are – resilient. Every generation, we have to come up with new ways to kill 'em because they get immune to the poisons we had before.' After a while, Blue took to dousing them in gasoline, lighting them up, seeing how resilient they were then.

Elgin's folks told him to stay away from the strange, dirty kid with the white-trash mother, but Elgin felt sorry for Blue. He was half Elgin's size even though they were the same age; you could place your thumb and forefinger around Blue's biceps and meet them on the other side. Elgin hated how Blue seemed to have only two pairs of clothes, both usually dirty, and how sometimes they'd pass his trailer together and hear the animal sounds coming from inside, the grunts and moans, the slapping of flesh. Half the time you couldn't tell if Blue's old lady was in there fucking or fighting. And always the sound of country music mingled in with all that animal noise, Blue's mother and her man of the moment listening to it on the transistor radio she'd given Blue one Christmas.

'*My* fucking radio,' Blue said once and shook his small head, the only time Elgin ever saw him react to what went on in that trailer.

Blue was a reader – knew more about science and ecology, about anatomy and blue whales and conversion tables than anyone Elgin knew. Most everyone figured the kid for a mute – hell, he'd been held back twice in fourth grade – but with Elgin he'd sometimes chat up a storm while they puffed smokes together down at the drainage ditch behind the park. He'd talk about whales, how they bore only one child, whom they were fiercely protective of, but how if another child was orphaned, a mother whale would take it as her own, protect it as fiercely as she did the one she gave birth to. He told Elgin how sharks never slept, how electrical currents worked, what a depth charge was. Elgin, never much of a talker, just sat and listened, ate it up and waited for more.

The older they got, the more Elgin became Blue's

protector, till finally, the year Blue's face exploded with acne, Elgin got in about two fights a day until there was no one left to fight. Everyone knew – they were brothers. And if Elgin didn't get you from the front, Blue was sure to take care of you from behind, like that time a can of acid fell on Roy Hubrist's arm in shop, or the time someone hit Carnell Lewis from behind with a brick, then cut his Achilles tendon with a razor while he lay out cold. Everyone knew it was Blue, even if no one actually saw him do it.

Elgin figured with Roy and Carnell, they'd had it coming. No great loss. It was since Elgin'd come back from Vietnam, though, that he'd noticed some things and kept them to himself, wondered what he was going to do the day he'd know he had to do something.

There was the owl someone had set afire and hung upside down from a telephone wire, the cats who turned up missing in the blocks that surrounded Blue's shack off Route 11. There were the small pink panties Elgin had seen sticking out from under Blue's bed one morning when he'd come to get him for some cleanup work at a site. He'd checked the missing-persons reports for days, but it hadn't come to anything, so he'd just decided Blue had picked them up himself, fed a fantasy or two. He didn't forget, though, couldn't shake the way those panties had curled upward out of the brown dust under Blue's bed, seemed to be pleading for something.

He'd never bothered asking Blue about any of this. That never worked. Blue just shut down at times like that, stared off somewhere as if something you couldn't hear was drowning out your words, something you couldn't see was taking up his line of vision. Blue, floating away on you, until you stopped cluttering up his mind with useless talk.

*

One Saturday, Elgin went into town with Shelley so she could get her hair done at Martha's Unisex on Main. In Martha's, as Dottie Leeds gave Shelley a shampoo and rinse, Elgin felt like he'd stumbled into a chapel of womanhood. There was Jim Hayder's teenage daughter, Sonny, getting one of those feathered cuts was growing popular these days and several older women who still wore beehives, getting them reset or plastered or whatever they did to keep them up like that. There was Joylene Covens and Lila Sims having their nails done while their husbands golfed and the black maids watched their kids, and Martha and Dottie and Esther and Gertrude and Hayley dancing and flirting, laughing and chattering among the chairs, calling everyone 'Honey,' and all of them – the young, the old, the rich, and Shelley – kicking back like they did this every day, knew each other more intimately than they did their husbands or children or boyfriends.

When Dottie Leeds looked up from Shelley's head and said, 'Elgin, honey, can we get you a sports page or something?' the whole place burst out laughing, Shelley included. Elgin smiled though he didn't feel like it and gave them all a sheepish wave that got a bigger laugh, and he told Shelley he'd be back in a bit and left.

He headed up Main toward the town square, wondering what it was those women seemed to know so effortlessly that completely escaped him, and saw Perkin Lut walking in a circle outside Dexter Isley's Five & Dime. It was one of those days when the wet, white heat was so overpowering that unless you were in Martha's, the one place in town with central air-conditioning, most people stayed inside with their shades down and tried not to move much.

And there was Perkin Lut walking the soles of his shoes

into the ground, turning in circles like a little kid trying to make himself dizzy.

Perkin and Elgin had known each other since kindergarten, but Elgin could never remember liking the man much. Perkin's old man, Mance Lut, had pretty much built Eden, and he'd spent a lot of money keeping Perkin out of the war, hid his son up in Chapel Hill, North Carolina, for so many semesters even Perkin couldn't remember what he'd majored in. A lot of men who'd gone overseas and come back hated Perkin for that, as did the families of most of the men who hadn't come back, but that wasn't Elgin's problem with Perkin. Hell, if Elgin'd had the money, he'd have stayed out of that shitty war too.

What Elgin couldn't abide was that there was something in Perkin that protected him from consequence. Something that made him look down on people who paid for their sins, who fell without a safety net to catch them.

It had happened more than once that Elgin had found himself thrusting in and out of Perkin's wife and thinking, Take that, Perkin. Take that.

But this afternoon, Perkin didn't have his salesman's smile or aloof glance. When Elgin stopped by him and said, 'Hey, Perkin, how you?' Perkin looked up at him with eyes so wild they seemed about to jump out of their sockets.

'I'm not good, Elgin. Not good.'

'What's the matter?'

Perkin nodded to himself several times, looked over Elgin's shoulder. 'I'm fixing to do something about that.'

'About what?'

'About that.' Perkin's jaw gestured over Elgin's shoulder.

Elgin turned around, looked across Main and through the windows of Miller's Laundromat saw Jewel Lut pulling

245

her clothes from the dryer, saw Blue standing beside her, taking a pair of jeans from the pile and starting to fold. If either of them had looked up and over, they'd have seen Elgin and Perkin Lut easily enough, but Elgin knew they wouldn't. There was an air to the two of them that seemed to block out the rest of the world in that bright Laundromat as easily as it would in a dark bedroom. Blue's lips moved and Jewel laughed, flipped a T-shirt on his head.

'I'm fixing to do something right now,' Perkin said.

Elgin looked at him, could see that was a lie, something Perkin was repeating to himself in hopes it would come true. Perkin was successful in business, and for more reasons than just his daddy's money, but he wasn't the kind of man who did things; he was the kind of man who had things done.

Elgin looked across the street again. Blue still had the T-shirt sitting atop his head. He said something else and Jewel covered her mouth with her hand when she laughed.

'Don't you have a washer and dryer at your house, Perkin?'

Perkin rocked back on his heels. 'Washer broke. Jewel decides to come in town.' He looked at Elgin. 'We ain't getting along so well these days. She keeps reading those magazines, Elgin. You know the ones? Talking about liberation, leaving your bra at home, shit like that.' He pointed across the street. 'Your friend's a problem.'

Your friend.

Elgin looked at Perkin, felt a sudden anger he couldn't completely understand, and with it a desire to say, 'That's my friend and he's talking to my fuck-buddy.' Get it, Perkin?

Instead, he just shook his head and left Perkin there, walked across the street to the Laundromat.

Blue took the T-shirt off his head when he saw Elgin enter. A smile, half frozen on his pitted face, died as he blinked into the sunlight blaring through the windows.

Jewel said, 'Hey, we got another helper!' She tossed a pair of men's briefs over Blue's head, hit Elgin in the chest with them.

'Hey, Jewel.'

'Hey, Elgin. Long time.' Her eyes dropped from his, settled on a towel.

Didn't seem like it at the moment to Elgin. Seemed almost as if he'd been out at the lake with her as recently as last night. He could taste her in his mouth, smell her skin damp with a light sweat.

And standing there with Blue, it also seemed like they were all three back in that trailer park, and Jewel hadn't aged a bit. Still wore her red hair long and messy, still dressed in clothes seemed to have been picked up, wrinkled, off her closet floor and nothing fancy about them in the first place, but draped over her body, they were sexier than clothes other rich women bought in New York once a year.

This afternoon, she wore a crinkly, paisley dress that might have been on the pink side once but had faded to a pasty newspaper color after years of washing. Nothing special about it, not too high up her thigh or down her chest, and loose – but something about her body made it appear like she might just ripen right out of it any second.

Elgin handed the briefs to Blue as he joined them at the folding table. For a while, none of them said anything. They picked clothes from the large pile and folded, and the only sound was Jewel whistling.

Then Jewel laughed.

'What?' Blue said.

'Aw, nothing.' She shook her head. 'Seems like we're just one happy family here, though, don't it?'

Blue looked stunned. He looked at Elgin. He looked at Jewel. He looked at the pair of small, light-blue socks he held in his hands, the monogram *JL* stitched in the cotton. He looked at Jewel again.

'Yeah,' he said eventually, and Elgin heard a tremor in his voice he'd never heard before. 'Yeah, it does.'

Elgin looked up at one of the upper dryer doors. It had been swung out at eye level when the dryer had been emptied. The center of the door was a circle of glass, and Elgin could see Main Street reflected in it, the white posts that supported the wood awning over the Five & Dime, Perkin Lut walking in circles, his head down, heat shimmering in waves up and down Main.

The dog was green.

Blue had used some of the money Big Bobby'd paid him over the past few weeks to upgrade his target scope. The new scope was huge, twice the width of the rifle barrel, and because the days were getting shorter, it was outfitted with a light-amplification device. Elgin had used similar scopes in the jungle, and he'd never liked them, even when they'd saved his life and those of his platoon, picked up Charlie coming through the dense flora like icy gray ghosts. Night scopes – or LADs as they'd called them over there – were just plain unnatural, and Elgin always felt like he was looking through a telescope from the bottom of a lake. He had no idea where Blue would have gotten one, but hunters in Eden had been showing up with all sorts of weird Marine or army surplus shit these last few years; Elgin had even heard of a hunting party using grenades to scare up fish – blowing 'em up into the boat already half cooked, all you had to do was scale 'em.

The dog was green, the highway was beige, the top of the tree line was yellow, and the trunks were the color of army fatigues.

Blue said, 'What you think?'

They were up in the tree house Blue'd built. Nice wood, two lawn chairs, a tarp hanging from the branch overhead, a cooler filled with Coors. Blue'd built a railing across the front, perfect for resting your elbows when you took aim. Along the tree trunk, he'd mounted a huge klieg light plugged to a portable generator, because while it was illegal to 'shine' deer, nobody'd ever said anything about shining wild dogs. Blue was definitely home.

Elgin shrugged. Just like in the jungle, he wasn't sure he was meant to see the world this way – faded to the shades and textures of old photographs. The dog, too, seemed to sense that it had stepped out of time somehow, into this seaweed circle punched through the landscape. It sniffed the air with a misshapen snout, but the rest of its body was tensed into one tight muscle, leaning forward as if it smelled prey.

Blue said, 'You wanna do it?'

The stock felt hard against Elgin's shoulder. The trigger, curled under his index finger, was cold and thick, something about it that itched his finger and the back of his head simultaneously, a voice back there with the itch in his head saying, 'Fire.'

What you could never talk about down at the bar to people who hadn't been there, to people who wanted to

Dennis Lehane

know, was what it had been like firing on human beings, on those icy gray ghosts in the dark jungle. Elgin had been in fourteen battles over the course of his twelve-month tour, and he couldn't say with certainty that he'd ever killed anyone. He'd shot some of those shapes, seen them go down, but never the blood, never their eyes when the bullets hit. It had all been a cluster-fuck of swift and sudden noise and color, an explosion of white lights and tracers, green bush, red fire, screams in the night. And afterward, if it was clear, you walked into the jungle and saw the corpses, wondered if you'd hit this body or that one or any at all.

And the only thing you were sure of was that you were too fucking hot and still – this was the terrible thing, but oddly exhilarating too – deeply afraid.

Elgin lowered Blue's rifle, stared across the interstate, now the color of seashell, at the dark mint tree line. The dog was barely noticeable, a soft dark shape amid other soft dark shapes.

He said, 'No, Blue, thanks,' and handed him the rifle.

Blue said, 'Suit yourself, buddy.' He reached behind them and pulled the beaded string on the klieg light. As the white light erupted across the highway and the dog froze, blinking in the brightness, Elgin found himself wondering what the fucking point of a LAD scope was when you were just going to shine the animal anyway.

Blue swung the rifle around, leaned into the railing, and put a round in the center of the animal, right by its rib cage. The dog jerked inward, as if someone had whacked it with a bat, and as it teetered on wobbly legs, Blue pulled back on the bolt, drove it home again, and shot the dog in the head. The dog flipped over on its side, most of its skull gone, back leg kicking at the road like it was trying to ride a bicycle.

'You think Jewel Lut might, I dunno, like me?' Blue said.

Elgin cleared his throat. 'Sure. She's always liked you.'

'But I mean ...' Blue shrugged, seemed embarrassed suddenly. 'How about this: You think a girl like that could take to Australia?'

'Australia?'

Blue smiled at Elgin. 'Australia.'

'Australia?' he said again.

Blue reached back and shut off the light. 'Australia. They got some wild dingoes there, buddy. Could make some real money. Jewel told me the other day how they got real nice beaches. But dingoes, too. Big Bobby said people're starting to bitch about what's happening here, asking where Rover is and such, and anyway, ain't too many dogs left dumb enough to come this way anymore. Australia,' he said, 'they never run out of dog. Sooner or later, here, I'm gonna run out of dog.'

Elgin nodded. Sooner or later, Blue would run out of dog. He wondered if Big Bobby'd thought that one through, if he had a contingency plan, if he had access to the National Guard.

'The boy's just, what you call it, zealous,' Big Bobby told Elgin.

They were sitting in Phil's Barbershop on Main. Phil had gone to lunch, and Big Bobby'd drawn the shades so people'd think he was making some important decision of state.

Elgin said, 'He ain't zealous, Big Bobby. He's losing it. Thinks he's in love with Jewel Lut.'

'He's always thought that.'

'Yeah, but now maybe he's thinking she might like him a bit, too.'

Big Bobby said, 'How come you never call me Mayor?'

Elgin sighed.

'All right, all right. Look,' Big Bobby said, picking up one of the hair-tonic bottles on Phil's counter and sniffing it, 'so Blue likes his job a little bit.'

Elgin said, 'There's more to it and you know it.'

Playing with combs now. 'I do?'

'Bobby, he's got a taste for shooting things now.'

'Wait.' He held up a pair of fat, stubby hands. 'Blue always liked to shoot things. Everyone knows that. Shit, if he wasn't so short and didn't have six or seven million little health problems, he'd a been the first guy in this town to go to The 'Nam. 'Stead, he had to sit back here while you boys had all the fun.'

Calling it The 'Nam. Like Big Bobby had any idea. Calling it fun. Shit.

'Dingoes,' Elgin said.

'Dingoes?'

'Dingoes. He's saying he's going to Australia to shoot dingoes.'

'Do him a world of good, too.' Big Bobby sat back down in the barber's chair beside Elgin. 'He can see the sights, that sort of thing.'

'Bobby, he ain't going to Australia and you know it. Hell, Blue ain't never stepped over the county line in his life.'

Big Bobby polished his belt buckle with the cuff of his sleeve. 'Well, what you want me to do about it?'

'I don't know. I'm just telling you. Next time you see him, Bobby, you look in his fucking eyes.'

'Yeah. What'll I see?'

Elgin turned his head, looked at him. 'Nothing.'

Bobby said, 'He's your buddy.'

Elgin thought of the small panties curling out of the dust under Blue's bed. 'Yeah, but he's your problem.'

Big Bobby put his hands behind his head, stretched in the chair. 'Well, people getting suspicious about all the dogs disappearing, so I'm going to have to shut this operation down immediately anyway.'

He wasn't getting it. 'Bobby, you shut this operation down, someone's gonna get a world's worth of that nothing in Blue's eyes.'

Big Bobby shrugged, a man who'd made a career out of knowing what was beyond him.

The first time Perkin Lut struck Jewel in public was at Chuck's Diner.

Elgin and Shelley were sitting just three booths away when they heard a racket of falling glasses and plates, and by the time they came out of their booth, Jewel was lying on the tile floor with shattered glass and chunks of bone china by her elbows and Perkin standing over her, his arms shaking, a look in his eyes that said he'd surprised himself as much as anyone else.

Elgin looked at Jewel, on her knees, the hem of her dress getting stained by the spilled food, and he looked away before she caught his eye, because if that happened he just might do something stupid, fuck Perkin up a couple-three ways.

'Aw, Perkin,' Chuck Blade said, coming from behind the counter to help Jewel up, wiping gravy off his hands against his apron.

Dennis Lehane

'We don't respect that kind of behavior 'round here, Mr. Lut,' Clara Blade said. 'Won't have it neither.'

Chuck Blade helped Jewel to her feet, his eyes cast down at his broken plates, the half a steak lying in a soup of beans by his shoe. Jewel had a welt growing on her right check, turning a bright red as she placed her hand on the table for support.

'I didn't mean it,' Perkin said.

Clara Blade snorted and pulled the pen from behind her ear, began itemizing the damage on a cocktail napkin.

'I didn't.' Perkin noticed Elgin and Shelley. He locked eyes with Elgin, held out his hands. 'I swear.'

Elgin turned away and that's when he saw Blue coming through the door. He had no idea where he'd come from, though it ran through his head that Blue could have just been standing outside looking in, could have been standing there for an hour.

Like a lot of small guys, Blue had speed, and he never seemed to walk in a straight line. He moved as if he were constantly sidestepping tackles or land mines – with sudden, unpredictable pivots that left you watching the space where he'd been, instead of the place he'd ended up.

Blue didn't say anything, but Elgin could see the determination for homicide in his eyes and Perkin saw it too, backed up, and slipped on the mess on the floor and stumbled back, trying to regain his balance as Blue came past Shelley and tried to lunge past Elgin.

Elgin caught him at the waist, lifted him off the ground, and held on tight because he knew how slippery Blue could be in these situations. You'd think you had him and he'd just squirm away from you, hit somebody with a glass.

Elgin tucked his head down and headed for the door,

Blue flopped over his shoulder like a bag of cement mix, Blue screaming,

'You see me, Perkin? You see me? I'm a last face you see, Perkin! Real soon.'

Elgin hit the open doorway, felt the night heat on his face as Blue screamed, 'Jewel! You all right? Jewel?'

Blue didn't say much back at Elgin's trailer.

He tried to explain to Shelley how pure Jewel was, how hitting something that innocent was like spitting on the Bible.

Shelley didn't say anything, and after a while Blue shut up, too.

Elgin just kept plying him with Beam, knowing Blue's lack of tolerance for it, and pretty soon Blue passed out on the couch, his pitted face still red with rage.

'He's never been exactly right in the head, has he?' Shelley said.

Elgin ran his hand down her bare arm, pulled her shoulder in tighter against his chest, heard Blue snoring from the front of the trailer. 'No, ma'am.'

She rose above him, her dark hair falling to his face, tickling the corners of his eyes. 'But you've been his friend.'

Elgin nodded.

She touched his cheek with her hand. 'Why?'

Elgin thought about it a bit, started talking to her about the little, dirty kid and his cockroach flambés, of the animal sounds that came from his mother's trailer. The way Blue used to sit by the drainage ditch, all pulled into himself, his body tight. Elgin thought of all those roaches and cats and rabbits and dogs, and he told Shelley that he'd always thought Blue was dying, ever since he'd met him, leaking away in front of his eyes.

'Everyone dies,' she said.

'Yeah.' He rose up on his elbow, rested his free hand on her warm hip. 'Yeah, but with most of us it's like we're growing toward something and then we die. But with Blue, it's like he ain't never grown toward nothing. He's just been dying real slowly since he was born.'

She shook her head. 'I'm not getting you.'

He thought of the mildew that used to soak the walls in Blue's mother's trailer, of the mold and dust in Blue's shack off Route 11, of the rotting smell that had grown out of the drainage ditch when they were kids. The way Blue looked at it all – seemed to be at one with it – as if he felt a bond.

Shelley said, 'Babe, what do you think about getting out of here?'

'Where?'

'I dunno. Florida. Georgia. Someplace else.'

'I got a job. You too.'

'You can always get construction jobs other places. Receptionist jobs too.'

'We grew up here.'

She nodded. 'But maybe it's time to start our life somewhere else.'

He said, 'Let me think about it.'

She tilted his chin so she was looking in his eyes. 'You've *been* thinking about it.'

He nodded. 'Maybe I want to think about it some more.'

In the morning, when they woke up, Blue was gone.

Shelley looked at the rumpled couch, over at Elgin. For a

good minute they just stood there, looking from the couch to each other, the couch to each other.

An hour later, Shelley called from work, told Elgin that Perkin Lut was in his office as always, no signs of physical damage.

Elgin said, 'If you see Blue . . .'

'Yeah?'

Elgin thought about it. 'I dunno. Call the cops. Tell Perkin to bail out a back door. That sound right?'

'Sure.'

Big Bobby came to the site later that morning, said, 'I go over to Blue's place to tell him we got to end this dog thing and—'

'Did you tell him it was over?' Elgin asked.

'Let me finish. Let me explain.'

'Did you tell him?'

'Let me finish.' Bobby wiped his face with a handkerchief. 'I was gonna tell him, but—'

'You didn't tell him.'

'But Jewel Lut was there.'

'What?'

Big Bobby put his hand on Elgin's elbow, led him away from the other workers. 'I said Jewel was there. The two of them sitting at the kitchen table, having breakfast.'

'In Blue's place?'

Big Bobby nodded. 'Biggest dump I ever seen. Smells like something I-don't-know-what. But bad. And there's Jewel, pretty as can be in her summer dress and soft skin and make-up, eating Eggos and grits with Blue, big brown shiner under her eye. She smiles at me, says, 'Hey, Big Bobby,' and goes back to eating.'

'And that was it?'

'How come no one ever calls me Mayor?'

'And that was it?' Elgin repeated.

'Yeah. Blue asks me to take a seat, I say I got business. He says him, too.'

'What's that mean?' Elgin heard his own voice, hard and sharp.

Big Bobby took a step back from it. 'Hell do I know? Could mean he's going out to shoot more dog.'

'So you never told him you were shutting down the operation.'

Big Bobby's eyes were wide and confused. 'You hear what I told you? He was in there with Jewel. Her all doll-pretty and him looking, well, ugly as usual. Whole situation was too weird. I got out.'

'Blue said he had business, too.'

'He said he had business, too,' Bobby said, and walked away.

The next week, they showed up in town together a couple of times, buying some groceries, toiletries for Jewel, boxes of shells for Blue.

They never held hands or kissed or did anything romantic, but they were together, and people talked. Said, 'Well, of all things. And I never thought I'd see the day. How do you like that? I guess this is the day the cows actually come home.'

Blue called and invited Shelley and Elgin to join them one Sunday afternoon for a late breakfast at the IHOP. Shelley begged off, said something about coming down with the flu, but Elgin went. He was curious to see where this was going, what Jewel was thinking, how she thought her hanging around Blue was going to come to anything but bad.

He could feel the eyes of the whole place on them as they ate.

'See where he hit me?' Jewel tilted her head, tucked her beautiful red hair back behind her ear. The mark on her cheekbone, in the shape of a small rain puddle, was faded yellow now, its edges roped by a sallow beige.

Elgin nodded.

'Still can't believe the son of a bitch hit me,' she said, but there was no rage in her voice anymore, just a mild sense of drama, as if she'd pushed the words out of her mouth the way she believed she should say them. But the emotion she must have felt when Perkin's hand hit her face, when she fell to the floor in front of people she'd known all her life – that seemed to have faded with the mark on her cheekbone.

'Perkin Lut,' she said with a snort, then laughed.

Elgin looked at Blue. He'd never seemed so . . . fluid in all the time Elgin had known him. The way he cut into his pancakes, swept them off his plate with a smooth dip of the fork tines; the swift dab of the napkin against his lips after every bite; the attentive swivel of his head whenever Jewel spoke, usually in tandem with the lifting of his coffee mug to his mouth.

This was not a Blue Elgin recognized. Except when he was handling weapons, Blue moved in jerks and spasms. Tremors rippled through his limbs and caused his fingers to drop things, his elbows and knees to move too fast, crack against solid objects. Blue's blood seemed to move too quickly through his veins, made his muscles obey his brain after a quarter-second delay and then too rapidly, as if to catch up on lost time.

But now he moved in concert, like an athlete or a jungle cat.

That's what you do to men, Jewel: You give them a confidence so total it finds their limbs.

'Perkin,' Blue said, and rolled his eyes at Jewel and they both laughed.

She not as hard as he did, though.

Elgin could see the root of doubt in her eyes, could feel her loneliness in the way she fiddled with the menu, touched her cheekbone, spoke too loudly, as if she wasn't just telling Elgin and Blue how Perkin had mistreated her, but the whole IHOP as well, so people could get it straight that she wasn't the villain, and if after she returned to Perkin she had to leave him again, they'd know why.

Of course she was going back to Perkin.

Elgin could tell by the glances she gave Blue – unsure, slightly embarrassed, maybe a bit repulsed. What had begun as a nighttime ride into the unknown had turned cold and stale during the hard yellow lurch into morning.

Blue wiped his mouth, said, 'Be right back,' and walked to the bathroom with surer strides than Elgin had ever seen on the man.

Elgin looked at Jewel.

She gripped the handle of her coffee cup between the tips of her thumb and index finger and turned the cup in slow revolutions around the saucer, made a soft scraping noise that climbed up Elgin's spine like a termite trapped under the skin.

'You ain't sleeping with him, are you?' Elgin said quietly.

Jewel's head jerked up and she looked over her shoulder, then back at Elgin. 'What? God, no. We're just . . . He's my pal. That's all. Like when we were kids.'

'We ain't kids.'

'I know. Don't you think I know?' She fingered the coffee cup again. 'I miss you,' she said softly. 'I miss you. When you coming back?'

Elgin kept his voice low. 'Me and Shelley, we're getting pretty serious.'

She gave him a small smile that he instantly hated. It seemed to know him; it seemed like everything he was and everything he wasn't was caught in the curl of her lips. 'You miss the lake, Elgin. Don't lie.'

He shrugged.

'You ain't ever going to marry Shelley Briggs, have babies, be an upstanding citizen.'

'Yeah? Why's that?'

'Because you got too many demons in you, boy. And they need me. They need the lake. They need to cry out every now and then.'

Elgin looked down at his own coffee cup. 'You going back to Perkin?'

She shook her head hard. 'No way. Uh-uh. No way.'

Elgin nodded, even though he knew she was lying. If Elgin's demons needed the lake, needed to be unbridled, Jewel's needed Perkin. They needed security. They needed to know the money'd never run out, that she'd never go two full days without a solid meal, like she had so many times as a child in the trailer park.

Perkin was what she saw when she looked down at her empty coffee cup, when she touched her cheek. Perkin was at their nice home with his feet up, watching a game, petting the dog, and she was in the IHOP in the middle of a Sunday when the food was at its oldest and coldest, with one guy who loved her and one who fucked her, wondering how she got there.

Blue came back to the table, moving with that new sure stride, a broad smile in the wide swing of his arms.

'How we doing?' Blue said. 'Huh? How we doing?' And his lips burst into a grin so huge Elgin expected it to keep going right off the sides of his face.

Jewel left Blue's place two days later, walked into Perkin Lut's Auto Emporium and into Perkin's office, and by the time anyone went to check, they'd left through the back door, gone home for the day.

Elgin tried to get a hold of Blue for three days – called constantly, went by his shack and knocked on the door, even staked out the tree house along 1–95 where he fired on the dogs.

He'd decided to break into Blue's place, was fixing to do just that, when he tried one last call from his trailer that third night and Blue answered with a strangled 'Hello.'

'It's me. How you doing?'

'Can't talk now.'

'Come on, Blue. It's me. You okay?'

'All alone,' Blue said.

'I know. I'll come by.'

'You do, I'll leave.'

'Blue.'

'Leave me alone for a spell, Elgin. Okay?'

That night Elgin sat alone in his trailer, smoking cigarettes, staring at the walls.

Blue'd never had much of anything his whole life – not a job he enjoyed, not a woman he could consider his – and then between the dogs and Jewel Lut he'd probably thought he'd got it all at once. Hit pay dirt.

Elgin remembered the dirty little kid sitting down by the drainage ditch, hugging himself. Six, maybe seven years old, waiting to die.

You had to wonder sometimes why some people were even born. You had to wonder what kind of creature threw bodies into the world, expected them to get along when they'd been given no tools, no capacity to get any either.

In Vietnam, this fat boy, name of Woodson from South Dakota, had been the least popular guy in the platoon. He wasn't smart, he wasn't athletic, he wasn't funny, he wasn't even personable. He just was. Elgin had been running beside him one day through a sea of rice paddies, their boots making sucking sounds every step they took, and someone fired a hell of a round from the other side of the paddies, ripped Woodson's head in half so completely all Elgin saw running beside him for a few seconds was the lower half of Woodson's face. No hair, no forehead, no eyes. Just half the nose, a mouth, a chin.

Thing was, Woodson kept running, kept plunging his feet in and out of the water, making those sucking sounds, M-15 hugged to his chest, for a good eight or ten steps. Kid was dead, he's still running. Kid had no reason to hold on, but he don't know it, he keeps running.

What spark of memory, hope, or dream had kept him going?

You had to wonder.

In Elgin's dream that night, a platoon of ice-gray Vietcong rose in a straight line from the center of Cooper's Lake while Elgin was inside the cabin with Shelley and Jewel. He penetrated them both somehow, their separate torsos branching out from the same pair of hips, their four legs clamping at the small of his back, this Shelley–Jewel creature crying out for more, more, more.

And Elgin could see the VC platoon drifting in formation toward the shore, their guns pointed, their faces hidden behind thin wisps of green fog.

The Shelley–Jewel creature arched her backs on the bed below him, and Woodson and Blue stood in the corner of the room watching as their dogs padded across the floor, letting out low growls and drooling.

Shelley dissolved into Jewel as the VC platoon reached the porch steps and released their safeties all at once, the sound like the ratcheting of a thousand shotguns. Sweat exploded in Elgin's hair, poured down his body like warm rain, and the VC fired in concert, the bullets shearing the walls of the cabin, lifting the roof off into the night. Elgin looked above him at the naked night sky, the stars zipping by like tracers, the yellow moon full and mean, the shivering branches of birch trees. Jewel rose and straddled him, bit his lip, and dug her nails into his back, and the bullets danced through his hair, and then Jewel was gone, her writhing flesh having dissolved into his own.

Elgin sat naked on the bed, his arms stretched wide, waiting for the bullets to find his back, to shear his head from his body the way they'd sheared the roof from the cabin, and the yellow moon burned above him as the dogs howled and Blue and Woodson held each other in the corner of the room and wept like children as the bullets drilled holes in their faces.

Big Bobby came by the trailer late the next morning, a Sunday, and said, 'Blue's a bit put out about losing his job.'

'What?' Elgin sat on the edge of his bed, pulled on his socks. 'You picked now – now, Bobby – to fire him?'

'It's in his eyes,' Big Bobby said. 'Like you said. You can see it.'

Elgin had seen Big Bobby scared before, plenty of times, but now the man was trembling.

Elgin said, 'Where is he?'

Blue's front door was open, hanging half down the steps from a busted hinge. Elgin said, 'Blue.'

'Kitchen.'

He sat in his Jockeys at the table, cleaning his rifle, each shiny black piece spread in front of him on the table. Elgin's eyes watered a bit because there was a stench coming from the back of the house that he felt might strip his nostrils bare. He realized then that he'd never asked Big Bobby or Blue what they'd done with all those dead dogs.

Blue said, 'Have a seat, bud. Beer in the fridge if you're thirsty.'

Elgin wasn't looking in that fridge. 'Lost your job, huh?'

Blue wiped the bolt with a shammy cloth. 'Happens.' He looked at Elgin. 'Where you been lately?'

'I called you last night.'

'I mean in general.'

'Working.'

'No, I mean at night.'

'Blue, you been' – he almost said 'playing house with Jewel Lut' but caught himself – 'up in a fucking tree, how do you know where I been at night?'

'I don't,' Blue said. 'Why I'm asking.'

Elgin said, 'I've been at my trailer or down at Doubles, same as usual.'

'With Shelley Briggs, right?'

Slowly, Elgin said, 'Yeah.'

'I'm just asking, buddy. I mean, when we all going to go out? You, me, your new girl.'

The pits that covered Blue's face like a layer of bad meat had faded some from all those nights in the tree.

Elgin said, 'Anytime you want.'

Blue put down the bolt. 'How 'bout right now?' He stood and walked into the bedroom just off the kitchen. 'Let me just throw on some duds.'

'She's working now, Blue.'

'At Perkin Lut's? Hell, it's almost noon. I'll talk to Perkin about that Dodge he sold me last year, and when she's ready we'll take her out someplace nice.' He came back into the kitchen wearing a soiled brown T-shirt and jeans.

'Hell,' Elgin said, 'I don't want the girl thinking I've got some serious love for her or something. We come by for lunch, next thing she'll expect me to drop her off in the mornings, pick her up at night.'

Blue was reassembling the rifle, snapping all those shiny pieces together so fast, Elgin figured he could do it blind. He said, 'Elgin, you got to show them some affection sometimes. I mean, Jesus.' He pulled a thin brass bullet from his T-shirt pocket and slipped it in the breech, followed it with four more, then slid the bolt home.

'Yeah, but you know what I'm saying, bud?' Elgin watched Blue nestle the stock in the space between his left hip and ribs, let the barrel point out into the kitchen.

'I know what you're saying,' Blue said. 'I know. But I got to talk to Perkin about my Dodge.'

'What's wrong with it?'

'What's wrong with it?' Blue turned to look at him, and the barrel swung level with Elgin's belt buckle. 'What's wrong with it, it's a piece of shit, what's wrong with it, Elgin. Hell, you know that. Perkin sold me a lemon. This is the situation.' He blinked. 'Beer for the ride?'

Elgin had a pistol in his glove compartment. A .32. He considered it.

'Elgin?'

'Yeah?'

'Why you looking at me funny?'

'You got a rifle pointed at me, Blue. You realize that?'

Blue looked at the rifle, and its presence seemed to surprise him. He dipped it toward the floor. 'Shit, man, I'm sorry. I wasn't even thinking. It feels like my arm sometimes. I forget. Man, I am sorry.' He held his arms out wide, the rifle rising with them.

'Lotta things deserve to die, don't they?'

Blue smiled. 'Well, I wasn't quite thinking along those lines, but now you bring it up ...'

Elgin said, 'Who deserves to die, buddy?'

Blue laughed. 'You got something on your mind, don't you?' He hoisted himself up on the table, cradled the rifle in his lap. 'Hell, boy, who you got? Let's start with people who take two parking spaces.'

'Okay.' Elgin moved the chair by the table to a position slightly behind Blue, sat in it. 'Let's.'

'Then there's DJs talk through the first minute of a song. Fucking Guatos coming down here these days to pick tobacco, showing no respect. Women wearing all those tight clothes, look at you like you're a pervert when you stare at what they're advertising.' He wiped his forehead with his arm. 'Shit.'

'Who else?' Elgin said quietly.

'Okay. Okay. You got people like the ones let their dogs run wild into the highway, get themselves killed. And you got dishonest people, people who lie and sell insurance and cars and bad food. You got a lot of things. Jane Fonda.'

'Sure.' Elgin nodded.

Blue's face was drawn, gray. He crossed his legs over each other like he used to down at the drainage ditch. 'It's all out there.' He nodded and his eyelids drooped.

'Perkin Lut?' Elgin said. 'He deserve to die?'

'Not just Perkin,' Blue said. 'Not just. Lots of people. I mean, how many you kill over in the war?'

Elgin shrugged. 'I don't know.'

'But some. Some. Right? Had to. I mean, that's war – someone gets on your bad side, you kill them and all their friends till they stop bothering you.' His eyelids drooped again, and he yawned so deeply he shuddered when he finished.

'Maybe you should get some sleep.'

Blue looked over his shoulder at him. 'You think? It's been a while.'

A breeze rattled the thin walls at the back of the house, pushed that thick dank smell into the kitchen again, a rotting stench that found the back of Elgin's throat and stuck there. He said, 'When's the last time?'

'I slept? Hell, a while. Days maybe.' Blue twisted his body so he was facing Elgin. 'You ever feel like you spend your whole life waiting for it to get going?'

Elgin nodded, not positive what Blue was saying, but knowing he should agree with him. 'Sure.'

'It's hard,' Blue said. 'Hard.' He leaned back on the table, stared at the brown water marks in his ceiling.

Elgin took in a long stream of that stench through his nostrils. He kept his eyes open, felt that air entering his nostrils creep past into his corneas, tear at them. The urge to close his eyes and wish it all away was as strong an urge as he'd ever felt, but he knew now was that time he'd always known was coming.

He leaned in toward Blue, reached across him, and pulled the rifle off his lap.

Blue turned his head, looked at him.

'Go to sleep,' Elgin said. 'I'll take care of this a while. We'll go see Shelley tomorrow. Perkin Lut, too.'

Blue blinked. 'What if I can't sleep? Huh? I've been having that problem, you know. I put my head on the pillow and I try to sleep and it won't come and soon I'm just bawling like a fucking child till I got to get up and do something.'

Elgin looked at the tears that had just then sprung into Blue's eyes, the red veins split across the whites, the desperate, savage need in his face that had always been there if anyone had looked close enough, and would never, Elgin knew, be satisfied.

'I'll stick right here, buddy. I'll sit here in the kitchen and you go in and sleep.'

Blue turned his head and stared up at the ceiling again. Then he slid off the table, peeled off his T-shirt, and tossed it on top of the fridge. 'All right. All right. I'm gonna try.' He stopped at the bedroom doorway. ' 'Member – there's beer in the fridge. You be here when I wake up?'

Elgin looked at him. He was still so small, probably so thin you could still wrap your hand around his biceps, meet the fingers on the other side. He was still ugly and stupid-looking, still dying right in front of Elgin's eyes.

'I'll be here, Blue. Don't you worry.'

'Good enough. Yes, sir.'

Blue shut the door and Elgin heard the bedsprings grind, the rustle of pillows being arranged. He sat in the chair, with the smell of whatever decayed in the back of the house swirling around his head. The sun had hit the cheap tin roof now, heating the small house, and after a while he realized the buzzing he'd thought was in his head came from somewhere back in the house too.

He wondered if he had the strength to open the fridge. He wondered if he should call Perkin Lut's and tell Perkin to get the hell out of Eden for a bit. Maybe he'd just ask for Shelley, tell her to meet him tonight with her suitcases. They'd drive down 95 where the dogs wouldn't disturb them, drive clear to Jacksonville, Florida, before the sun came up again. See if they could outrun Blue and his tiny, dangerous wants, his dog corpses, and his smell; outrun people who took two parking spaces and telephone solicitors and Jane Fonda,

Jewel flashed through his mind then, an image of her sitting atop him, arching her back and shaking that long red hair, a look in her green eyes that said this was it, this was why we live.

He could stand up right now with this rifle in his hands, scratch the itch in the back of his head, and fire straight through the door, end what should never have been started.

He sat there staring at the door for quite a while, until he knew the exact number of places the paint had peeled in teardrop spots, and eventually he stood, went to the phone on the wall by the fridge, and dialed Perkin Lut's.

'Auto Emporium,' Shelley said, and Elgin thanked God that in his present mood he hadn't gotten Glynnis Verdon, who snapped her gum and always placed him on hold, left him listening to Muzak versions of The Shirelles.

'Shelley?'

'People gonna talk, you keep calling me at work, boy.'

He smiled, cradled the rifle like a baby, leaned against the wall. 'How you doing?'

'Just fine, handsome. How 'bout yourself?'

Elgin turned his head, looked at the bedroom door. 'I'm okay.'

'Still like me?'

Elgin heard the springs creak in the bedroom, heard weight drop on the old floorboards. 'Still like you.'

'Well, then, it's all fine then, isn't it?'

Blue's footfalls crossed toward the bedroom door, and Elgin used his hip to push himself off the wall.

'It's all fine,' he said. 'I gotta go. I'll talk to you soon.'

He hung up and stepped away from the wall.

'Elgin,' Blue said from the other side of the door.

'Yeah, Blue?'

'I can't sleep. I just can't.'

Elgin saw Woodson sloshing through the paddy, the top of his head gone. He saw the pink panties curling up from underneath Blue's bed and a shaft of sunlight hitting Shelley's face as she looked up from behind her desk at Perkin Lut's and smiled. He saw Jewel Lut dancing in the night rain by the lake and that dog lying dead on the shoulder of the interstate, kicking its leg like it was trying to ride a bicycle.

'Elgin,' Blue said. 'I just can't sleep. I got to do something.'

'Try,' Elgin said and cleared his throat.

'I just can't. I got to . . . do something. I got to go . . .' His voice cracked, and he cleared his throat. 'I can't sleep.'

The doorknob turned and Elgin raised the rifle, stared down the barrel.

'Sure, you can, Blue.' He curled his finger around the trigger as the door opened. 'Sure you can,' he repeated and took a breath, held it in.

The skeleton of Eden Falls still sits on twenty-two acres of land just east of Brimmer's Point, covered in rust thick as flesh. Some say it was the levels of iodine an environmental inspector found in the ground-water that scared off the original investors. Others said it was the downswing of the state economy or the governor's failed reelection bid. Some say Eden Falls was just plain a dumb name, too Biblical. And then, of course, there were plenty who claimed it was Jewel Lut's ghost scared off all the workers.

They found her body hanging from the scaffolding they'd erected by the shell of the roller coaster. She was naked and hung upside down from a rope tied around her ankles. Her throat had been cut so deep the coroner said it was a miracle her head was still attached when they found her. The coroner's assistant, man by the name of Chris Gleason, would claim when he was in his cups that the head had fallen off in the hearse as they drove down Main toward the morgue. Said he heard it cry out.

This was the same day Elgin Bern called the sheriff's office, told them he'd shot his buddy Blue, fired two rounds into him at close range, the little guy dead before he hit his kitchen floor. Elgin told the deputy he was still sitting in the kitchen, right where he'd done it a few hours before. Said to send the hearse.

Due to the fact that Perkin Lut had no real alibi for his whereabouts when Jewel passed on and owing even more to the fact there'd been some very recent and very public discord in their marriage, Perkin was arrested and brought before a grand jury, but that jury decided not to indict. Perkin and Jewel had been patching things up, after all; he'd bought her a car (at cost, but still . . .).

Besides, we all knew it was Blue had killed Jewel. Hell, the Simmons boy, a retard ate paint and tree bark, could have told you that. Once all that stuff came out about what Blue and Big Bobby'd been doing with the dogs around here, well, that just sealed it. And everyone remembered how that week she'd been separated from Perkin, you could see the dream come alive in Blue's eyes, see him allow hope into his heart for the first time in his sorry life.

And when hope comes late to a man, it's quite a dangerous thing. Hope is for the young, the children. Hope in a full-grown man – particularly one with as little acquaintanceship with it or prospect for it as Blue – well, that kind of hope burns as it dies, boils blood white, and leaves something mean behind when it's done.

Blue killed Jewel Lut.

And Elgin Bern killed Blue. And ended up doing time. Not much, due to his war record and the circumstances of who Blue was, but time just the same. Everyone knew Blue probably had it coming, was probably on his way back into town to do to Perkin or some other poor soul what he'd done to Jewel. Once a man gets that look in his eyes – that boiled look, like a dog searching out a bone who's not going to stop until he finds it – well, sometimes he has to be put down like a dog. Don't he?

And it was sad how Elgin came out of prison to find Shelley Briggs gone, moved up North with Perkin Lut of all people, who'd lost his heart for the car business after Jewel died, took to selling home electronics imported from Japan and Germany, made himself a fortune. Not long after he got out of prison, Elgin left too, no one knows where, just gone, drifting.

See, the thing is – no one wanted to convict Elgin. We all understood. We did. Blue had to go. But he'd had no weapon in his hand when Elgin, standing just nine feet away, pullèd that trigger. Twice. Once we might been able to overlook, but twice, that's something else again. Elgin offered no defense, even refused a fancy lawyer's attempt to get him to claim he'd suffered something called Post Traumatic Stress Disorder, which we're hearing a lot more about these days.

'I don't have that,' Elgin said. 'I shot a defenseless man. That's the long and the short of it, and that's a sin.'

And he was right:

In the world, 'case you haven't noticed, you usually pay for your sins.

And in the South, always.

ELMORE LEONARD

Can there be any doubt that the *voice of American crime fiction over the past quarter century has belonged to 'Dutch' Leonard? He speaks to his contemporaries but, astonishingly, he also speaks to people who are the same age as his grandchildren.*

He was recently booked into one of New York City's hippest clubs, down in the East Village, where hipness is next to godliness. He was booked with one of the hippest rock bands in America, The Stone Coyotes. And you knew the crowd was hip, because they were all in their twenties, all wore black, and body piercing was as common in that room as long-necked beer bottles. The band played and sang, and Leonard read from his latest Chili Palmer adventure. And what was extraordinary (at least to a stodgy old guy like me) is that it soon was apparent that the crowd had come to hear Leonard – not the band. And they got it. Every joke, however subtle, caused ripples of laughter. And Leonard loved every minute of it – including the very loud band.

When Leonard wrote a story for Murder for Love *a few years ago, he liked the character so much that he put her in a book. The book was so good that it was filmed.* Out of Sight, *if you haven't followed the movements of Karen Sisco. He likes the characters in this story, too, he says, so let's see if they show up again.*

SPARKS

By Elmore Leonard

They sat close to each other on the sofa, Canavan aware of Mrs. Harris's scent and her dark hair, parted to one side, she would hold away from her face to look at the map spread open on the coffee table.

Canavan was showing her the areas destroyed by fire, explaining how the hot Santa Ana wind swept the flames through these canyons and on down toward the Pacific Coast Highway. Close to four thousand acres destroyed but only nine homes this time, including Mrs. Harris's Mediterranean villa, here, at the top of Arroyo Verde. Nothing like five years ago when over two hundred homes were lost. He showed her photographs, too, fires raging against the night sky.

Robin Harris said, 'Yeah . . . ?' looking at the photos but not showing any real interest.

Canavan kept glancing at her, Robin a slim turn-on in a trendy kind of way: pale skin and heavy eyeliner, silver rings, designer-ripped jeans, barefoot, a black sleeveless top that showed the chain, tattooed blue steel, around her upper left arm, the one close to Canavan.

The profile he had in his case file described her as the former Robin Marino: sang with a rock band that played L.A. clubs, produced one album, gave it up five years ago to marry Sid Harris: the legendary Sid Harris, lawyer to platinum-selling recording artists. Now a widow at thirty-seven, Robin was estimated to be worth around ten million. She had lost Sid to a coronary thrombosis, at home, only three months ago, Sid sixty-three when he died. And had lost the house in the Malibu hills three weeks ago, close to a million dollars' worth of furniture and contents destroyed. But she had bought the Wilshire apartment, where she was living now, right after Sid's death. Why? It was on Canavan's checklist, one of the things he'd ask her about.

She said, 'What's the point?' Meaning the map and the pictures. 'I saw the fire, Joe. I was there.'

Arriving, he had introduced himself and handed Robin his business card that said *Joseph Canavan Associates, Insurance Investigations.* She had looked at it and said, 'Are you a Joe or a Joseph?' He told her either, but usually Joe. She said, 'Well, come in and sit down, Joe, anywhere you like,' picking up on his name in a way that sounded natural and gave him a glimpse of her personality. She looked at his business card again and said, 'You're not with the insurance company, like the ones before.' He told her they called him in when they red-flagged a claim, had questions about it. All it meant, certain conditions existed the company felt should be investigated. Canavan said they wanted to know in their hearts the fire was either accidental or providential before paying the claim. Robin said, 'Well, I can tell you the same thing I told the fire department, sheriff's deputies, the state fire marshal's office, the California Forestry Department, and a guy from Alcohol, Tobacco, and Firearms. The fire marshal's guy brought a dog that sniffed around. He said when the dog was working it ate seventy kibbles a day. What would you like to know?'

This was when Canavan first arrived.

Now he turned from the map to look at Robin sitting back in the sofa. She resembled a girl in the movies he liked a lot, Linda ... very sexy, had an Italian name. He said, 'I wanted to show you the path of the main fire, where it came down west of your place, on the other side of the ridge.'

'So how did my house catch fire,' Robin said. 'Is that the question? How about sparks, Joe? The wind blows sparks over the ridge from the brush fires in Boca Chica and they land by my house. You buy that? Or a rabbit or a coyote caught fire and ran like hell right through my yard. They said on the news, look out for animals that catch fire and spread it around. Otherwise, I have no idea. Joe, I watched my house go up in flames. I might've stayed till it burned down, I don't know, maybe not. A deputy came up the road and made me leave.'

Linda Fiorentino.

That was who Robin looked like, in that movie – he couldn't remember the name of it – where she goes into a bar called Ray's, remembering that because of the sign, the Y in RAY's shaped like a martini glass. Linda goes in and asks for a Manhattan. The bartender ignores her and she asks him who you have to blow to get a drink around here. Those weren't the exact words, but that was the idea. Robin had that same effortless way about her, confident, with the New York sound like Linda's, a cool chick, tough. Watch your step with her.

'So you weren't living in the house at the time.'

'I was here. I happened to see it on TV – fire trucks, people loading their cars, coming out of the house with their insurance policies, running around looking for pets.

One guy had all their good china in a basket and was lowering it into the swimming pool. I thought, I better get up there, quick.'

'Load your car,' Canavan said, 'with anything of value, huh? But I understand the house was already on fire. I think that's in the statement you made.'

'By the time I got there, yeah.' Linda waved her hand in the air. 'The back of the house, by a brush thicket. Sid was supposed to have it cut back but never got around to it. The sky by that time was thick with smoke.'

'See, what the company wonders about, why your house was the only one on Arroyo that caught fire.'

'I guess 'cause there aren't any close by. I'm at the very top of the road. Have you been up there?'

'I had a look at your place,' Canavan said, 'the chimney and some of the walls. What's hard to tell is where the fire started.'

'I told you, in the brush thicket.'

'Maybe, except it looks like the direction of the fire in the thicket was away from the house. I'm told the wind shifted that afternoon and came off the ocean.'

'I don't know,' Robin said, 'it's always windy up there.'

Canavan gathered the map from the coffee table. 'You bought this place a few months ago?'

An easy question, but she paused before telling him, 'Not long after Sid died. But I haven't bought it. I'm leasing it furnished, nine grand a month with an option to buy.'

Canavan looked around the formal living room, white and cream, touches of color, landscapes framed in gold tint, a garden terrace through the French doors, poppies and ficus trees fifteen stories above Wilshire Boulevard. A nine-thousand-a-month penthouse she might or might not buy. He said, 'This place is worth as much as your house?'

'They'd go for about the same price,' Robin said, 'two and a half million. Sidney said the house was underinsured. That's why, just before he died, he had the value of the policy increased.'

'And when that happened,' Canavan said, 'and the house burns down soon after, the claim gets a red flag.'

Looking right at him Robin said, 'Well, you know Sid didn't do it. And I'd have nothing to gain, would I? I'd already made up my mind to sell the house.'

'That's why you moved out?'

'It's too lonely up there. Just me and the coyotes. Once they ate my cats, both of them, Puddin and Mr. Piper. I bought a shotgun, see if I could even the score, a 20-gauge Remington. But then a couple of deputies came by to tell me I had to stop shooting. A neighbor had complained. Some woman said I was shooting toward her house. I go, "What neighbor? I don't have any neighbors. She might've heard shots, but how does she know I'm the one shooting?" They said she saw me.'

'Mrs. Montaigne,' Canavan said. 'She uses binoculars.'

It caused Robin to pause, and he felt her looking at him with new interest.

'How do you know that?'

'I spoke to her. Mrs. Montaigne's a self-appointed fire warden. Twice a day she drives to a spot up on Piuma Road, near Rambla Pacífico, and looks for smoke. She lost a house in '93 and had it rebuilt.'

'She actually saw me shooting coyotes? I'm a good mile below Piuma Road.'

'Not as the crow flies. I went to see her, talk to her about spotting fires, and she surprised me. Said she saw you the day your house burned down.'

'Saw me where?'

'At the house. She spotted the main fire and called the county fire camp. They were already on it. Still, eight houses burned to the ground.'

'Nine,' Robin said.

'She saw your car, too, the Mercedes convertible?'

'Yeah, as soon as it came on the news I got dressed, jumped in the car—'

'But why the convertible?'

'Why not?'

'If you were going there to save some more of your stuff, and it might be your only chance ... Don't you have a Range Rover?'

'I was thinking about the *house*,' Robin said. 'I wanted to find out if it was still there. I'd already picked up my jewelry, moved out most of my clothes.'

'There wasn't anything else of value?'

'You have a list, don't you, on the claim?'

'In my file. I haven't really looked at it.'

'It's all Asian art, Chinese, some authentic, some copies. But even if I'd brought the Rover there wouldn't have been room for the big pieces.'

'So for about three months the house was locked up, nobody there?'

'I'd spend a weekend.'

'Alone?'

She smiled, just a little. 'Where're you going with that, Joe?' And said, 'No, I wasn't always alone.'

He smiled the same way she did, just barely. He said, 'You got up there and the house is on fire.'

'Yeah, but I didn't see the flames right away. I told you, the fire started on the other side of the house, away from the road.'

'You say in that thicket.'

'Yeah. You have a problem with that?'

'I might,' Canavan said. 'According to Mrs. Montaigne, you were there a good twenty minutes to a half hour before there was smoke or any sign of a fire. And she had a pretty good view of the back side of the property.'

There was a silence.

'In fact, she said she saw you go in the house.'

Robin took her time getting up from the sofa. She said, 'Joseph,' walking across the room to a bar with a rose-tinted mirror behind it, 'what would you like to drink?'

'Whatever you're having,' Canavan said.

Straight-up martinis. He sipped his watching Robin roll a perfect joint, tips of her fingers working but not looking at it, Robin asking in her Linda Fiorentino voice why he would want to be an insurance-company stooge, Jesus, or why anyone would – Canavan letting it happen, giving Robin time to make her play. She said, 'No, first let me guess where you're from. The Midwest, right?' He saw this could take time, so he told her he was from Detroit, born and raised. Came out to sunny California six years ago. She wanted to know what he did in Detroit and Canavan said:

'I was a police officer.'

She said, 'Jesus, really? What kind?'

Radio cars and then ten years on the bomb squad. Offered a job out here with an insurance company, investigating claims, before setting up his own company. He said he'd learned to recognize arson from working on the bomb squad. See what Robin thought of that.

She was cool. Handing him the joint she said, 'You left out your wife.'

'I don't have one,' Canavan said, hoping this was a variety of weed that inspired wit and not the kind that put you to sleep. He took a pretty good hit and passed the joint back to Robin.

She said, 'You don't have to tell me if you don't want to, but I'll bet anything you had a wife at one time.'

He told her yeah, he got married while he was a cop. They came out here, he happened to get involved with a girl at the insurance company, and his wife found out about it.

'She divorced you for *that*?'

'You'd have to know her,' Canavan said.

'So it wasn't the first time.'

He told her it was, as a matter of fact, the first and only time he ever fooled around.

She didn't believe him. Lying back among little pastel pillows on the white sofa, Robin raised her eyebrows. She said, 'Really? You look to me, Joe, like the kind of guy, if it's there you don't pass it up. You still see her?'

'Who?'

'The girlfriend.'

'That was over before it went anywhere. I see my ex-wife now and then, we go out to dinner. Sometimes she does jobs for me. Chris's a photographer.' He picked up the raging-fire shots from the coffee table. 'She took these. Chris takes long-lens shots of people walking around who claim they can't walk. A guy shooting hoops in the backyard who's supposed to be in a wheelchair. Insurance-fraud situations, all kinds, including arson,' Canavan said, bringing it back to Robin.

No reaction. Ducked that one like she didn't even hear it, saying, 'You go to bed with her?'

'What's between Chris and me,' Canavan said, 'stays between us. Okay?'

'That means you do,' Robin said. 'You keep Chris for backup, right? Call her when you haven't scored in a while.' Robin pushed up from the sofa with her empty glass. 'You ready? One more – I have to go out tonight.'

Her husband dies and three months later fire destroys the house. Canavan wondered if there was a connection. He had no reason to believe there was; still, he didn't rule it out. He watched Robin sipping her martini. The only apparent effect the gin had on her, she spoke in a quieter voice and stared at him. Canavan could feel a buzz; combined with the weed it allowed him to stare back at Robin, time suspended, and ask her whatever he felt like asking.

'When you got married, did you have to sign a prenuptial agreement?'

She said, 'Don't worry about it.'

So he tried another tack. 'How'd you and Sid meet?'

'He saw me perform and we talked after. He asked me out. He knew who I was. But basically, Joe, we got together the way people usually do, and fall in love.'

'He was a lot older than you.'

'What you're asking now, did I marry him for his money. Sure, that had a lot to do with it, but I liked him. Sid was full of energy, played tennis – he'd sit down and cross his legs you'd see his foot going a mile a minute. You want to know how he was in bed? Not bad, though we had to get almost perpendicular – you know what I mean? – to do it.'

'Wasn't he kind of heavy?'

'That's what I'm talking about. But then toward the end he lost a lot of weight, like thirty pounds. No, Sid was tender, very gentle, till Viagra came along and he turned into Attila the fucking Hun. If you can picture that.'

'I thought he had a heart condition.'

'It wasn't serious. He took something for it. His blood pressure was a little high.'

'And his doctor let him have Viagra?'

'Sid got it over the Internet.'

'But he must've known the combination was dangerous, Viagra and heart medication?'

She said, 'Joe, Sid was a shooter. He didn't get where he was being cautious. It helped he was a genius.'

'You were happily married.'

'Yeah, very.'

'But you fooled around a little.'

'Once in a while I'd find myself in a situation. You know, but it was never serious. Like you and the chick from the insurance company.' She sipped her drink and then finished it. 'I'll tell you the truth, Joe, I miss him. Sid was good to me.' She got up with her empty glass, saying, 'You're ready, aren't you?'

'I thought you were going out.'

'I changed my mind.'

Watching her cross to the bar he said, 'Tell me something,' and watched her looking in the mirror, staring at her image, her pale skin tan in the tinted glass.

'What do you want to know?'

'Why you burned your house down.'

Robin didn't answer until she was coming back with the martinis, her raccoon eyes in the dark liner holding on Canavan.

'Why would I?'

'That's what I'd like to know.'

She gave him his drink and placed a hand on his shoulder as she edged past the coffee table and sat down again.

'You tell me,' Canavan said, 'you'd have nothing to gain, you were gonna sell the house. Now you don't have it to sell, but you get two and a half million when they pay the claim, plus the value of the contents.'

'I could've sold the house for more, easy.' Robin sipped her drink and said, 'But what if . . . This is hypothetical, okay? What if a person does actually burn down her house? She owns the property, she can rebuild if she wants. She might even tell the insurance company to forget the claim.'

'They'd want to know why.'

'Because they piss her off acting so suspicious, dragging their feet, sending out adjusters and investigators instead of paying the claim. She's above dealing with people with small minds.'

This was one Canavan hadn't heard before. He said, 'Tell me how she starts the fire.'

'She rolls up the *Wall Street Journal* and lights it with a match. The point I'm making, Joe—'

'She starts the fire inside the house or outside?'

'Inside. The point I'm making, they can pay the claim or not. If they choose to, fine. If they don't, who's out anything?'

'She's already out the Mediterranean villa.'

'And doesn't care.'

'What makes it Mediterranean, looking down at the Pacific Ocean?'

'Tile roof, big oval windows and doors. The outside wasn't bad, even though pink's not one of her favorite colors. It's the inside of the house she can't stand. The decor throughout, the furniture, the art, floor to ceiling everything's Chinese. And she doesn't even like Chinese food. Listen, I can roll us another one if you want.'

'Not for me.'

'It's local, Malibu Gold, but pretty good, huh?'

Canavan said, 'Yeah, great,' and asked Robin, 'Why didn't this hypothetical woman change the decor?'

'Her husband loved it. He knew what everything was and where it came from. It was like a culture thing with him. He becomes an expert on something besides picking hits. Incidentally, not one of the artists he represented ever made a record that stiffed.'

'He bought all the Chinese stuff?'

'His previous wife, the second one. They redecorated completely after a trip to China.'

Canavan said, 'You couldn't—' caught himself and said, 'She couldn't get used to it?'

'Joe, it was like living in a fucking pagoda. Jade figurines, Tang horses and tomb figures, that honey-colored *huanghali* furniture, blue and white Ming garnitures – they're vases – Ming *kesi* panels on the walls, ink paintings, opium beds, snuff bottles, ivory carvings, coromandel screens, Quing dynasty court rugs ...'

'She could've sold it.'

'Cloisonné enamel incense burners, Sung dynasty Buddhas. Five years,' Robin said, 'she lives with all this

Chinese shit cluttering up the house. Big, heavy pieces, the tomb figures almost life-size. Five years, Joe. She begs her husband, "Please, can't we try something else?" No. "A Mediterranean house, why don't we do it Mediterranean?" No. Not, "No, and I don't want to hear any more about it." Her husband was a cool guy for his age, never raised his voice. But, really, it was all she thought about. She'd smoke a jay and scheme. Like hire a burglar; he takes it out a piece at a time. Or have it done all at once while they're in Cabo, or Maui.'

'Once her husband's gone,' Canavan said, 'why didn't she get an auction house in and sell it?'

'She felt it would be disloyal to his memory and it would be on her conscience.'

Canavan thought that was interesting. 'But it's okay if something happens to it.'

'Yeah, like an act of God.'

'Or a fire, in an area known for its fires. You know who you remind me of?'

'Linda Fiorentino?'

'You look just like her.'

'I know.'

'That movie where she goes in the bar . . . ?'

'*The Last Seduction*. She wants a Manhattan and the bartender won't look at her. So she goes, "Who does a girl have to suck around here to get a drink?" '

That was it. Not who do you have to blow.

'But as I was saying, when you come right down to it, Joe, who's out? Who's hurt? Who gives a shit outside of this person who owns the house?'

'I'll tell you who,' Canavan said, 'if you really want to

know. The law. Arson's a second-degree felony. A conviction can get you two to twenty years. There's a death as a result, it goes up to five to ninety-nine.'

Her reaction: 'For Christ sake, Joe, come on. You want to put me in *jail*?'

'I'm not the law. All I'm supposed to do is let 'em know when I see a crime's been committed.'

She said, 'Joe, come on, you're not a snitch. I can tell you're a very practical guy. How much you want?'

Like that, ready to pay him off.

He said, 'What's your best offer? So we don't waste time.'

'How about fifty grand?'

'You can do better'n that.'

'A hundred?'

He said, 'Mrs. Harris,' and paused. 'You mind if I call you Robin?'

Sounding formal now and he could see she didn't know what to expect, hesitating before she said, 'Sure, why not,' in a kind of vague tone of voice, her mind looking ahead.

He said, 'Robin, you've talked to a lot of people. Fire, law enforcement, insurance company stooges ... One of 'em even brought a dog out to sniff around. But no one's accused you of burning your house down, have they?'

She shook her head and brushed that soft, dark hair away from her face.

'You drive up to the house, the sky's full of smoke. You've already seen houses burning on the TV news, and they're right over in the next canyon, not half a mile away. You're thinking, Damn it, why can't my house catch on fire?'

She was nodding, staring at him with a thoughtful expression, following every word.

'You go inside and stand there surrounded by all this oriental stuff you hate.'

'You don't say oriental, you say Asian.'

'Either way, you hate it. You stand there looking at all that lacquered stuff, Buddhas and dragons, and you light a joint.'

He watched her raise her eyebrows.

'The joint is to take the edge off, calm you down. But now you look at the match in your hand. It goes out and you light another match and look at the flame.'

She was nodding again, staying with him.

'All that smoke, and remembering what you saw on the news, you're convinced sooner or later your house will catch fire.'

'I was, I was sure of it.'

'You're about to lose part of your life, and there's nothing you can do but stand back and watch. Five years up in smoke.'

Robin waited.

'What you do then is part acceptance and part a farewell gesture to the years you spent here with Sid.'

'Yeah . . . ?'

'You light the *Wall Street Journal*.'

He watched her nodding her head, thoughtful now. She looked up at him and said, 'You're not putting that in your report, are you?'

Canavan shook his head. 'I have no evidence to prove it, or disprove what you said. The house was burning when you got there.'

'What about the lady fire warden?'

'Mrs. Montaigne? She must've been mistaken.'

Robin paused and said, 'How do I pay you the hundred thousand?'

'You don't,' Canavan said, getting up from the sofa. 'I was playing with you, that's all. Seeing what I could score if I did that sort of thing. You should hear some of the offers I get. I come across a fraud situation and I can prove it. Some bozo in a neck brace looking for a million bucks, says he'll split it with me.'

'You turn them in?'

'If they're pros, like the ones that stage car accidents and people are injured. Or if they get ugly about it. Otherwise I tell 'em, forget the claim and don't try it again.'

'You're not turning me in?'

'I told you, I believe your story.'

'So what should I do?'

'If I were you?' Canavan said. 'I'd keep after the insurance company. Make 'em pay.' He turned to leave, saying, 'It was nice talking to you, Robin.'

And saw her raccoon eyes staring at him.

'You can't stay awhile, Joe?'

ERIC VAN LUSTBADER

....

Versatility in authors is even less common than it is among actors. One would be surprised at (and wary of the results of) Chuck Norris playing in a light romantic comedy, or Tom Hanks playing a bloodthirsty macho villain, or Madonna playing any role for which Donna Reed might have been appropriate. Equally unsettling would be to see the new Harlequin romance come from the pen of Norman Mailer, or to have Mary Higgins Clark walk the mean streets of drug dealers in the ghetto.

While it would be preposterous to suggest that Eric Van Lustbader's range equals Laurence Olivier's, it is, nonetheless, remarkable. The early books were martial arts thrillers, then he moved on to tales of oriental intrigue that have become highly successful best-sellers. His short stories, including the one that follows, have nothing to do with those huge canvases, but they are no less compelling. Had you read the entire collection of Van Lustbader's twenty novels, you would be unprepared for this very human story set in a small town.

SLOW BURN

By Eric Van Lustbader

Evil is in the details, my uncle Ben used to say to me. And he ought to know. He was a priest – a fine one, a man people looked up to in this community, a kind of principled hero they came to with their problems with the certain knowledge that he would help them – until he crossed the thin white line, did the unthinkable, and the Church turned its back on him. Even though that was seven years ago, a biblical interval, his advice has never left me. That was because he more or less raised me after my parents died. In fact, in many ways I thought of him as my father.

'Pris, looka how small Kent is with his jammies all crumpled up,' Mickey Brunt said, pointing his powerful flashlight down at the small blue-white body. At 2:00 A.M. of a dripping August night alive with tumbling, ominous clouds and the patio screened by huge Australian pines, it was inky dark out here, even with all the house lights on.

'Deceased,' Don Murtry said, giving up on the CPR. He was the town doctor, also its coroner and funeral director, as well as our forensics expert. In response to the emergency call, he'd arrived just before us, in the company of the paramedics from St. Francis. 'God rest his soul.'

From the other side of the teak pool fence, where two sweating patrolmen under Mickey's direction were keeping them away from the scene, Kent's parents reacted. Kitty Seams shrieked and tore at her hair; her husband, Morgan, pulled her to him with one hand and, with the other, clamped a cell phone to his ear.

'How pale the little tyke seems, jes like he's been drained of blood.' Mickey was my partner in the Placide sheriff's office. We'd been together five years. He'd hated being partnered with a woman and had made no bones about it. To be honest, I don't think a whole helluva lot had changed since then. Still, we managed to function okay as a team – see, down deep where it mattered we trusted each other, which is a damn sight more than you could say for most married couples of our acquaintance.

I saw Morgan Seams, the six-year-old's father, break away from the officers and stride toward us. 'I'm sorry for your loss, Morgan,' I murmured, but he didn't even give me so much as a look. He was a moose of a man, with craggy features below close-cut iron-and-steel hair. For the four years Don Murtry and I had been there he'd played linebacker at FSU – Florida State University – in a bruising style that some admired and others criticized as brutal intimidation. He'd ripped up his knee pretty good his first year in the pros in some kind of Old Testament retribution, I had thought. But, unfazed, he'd cleverly used his signing bonus to buy an auto dealership. Now he had a dozen throughout the state, as well as a couple of other even more lucrative businesses. He still walked with a slight limp, and it seemed to me he'd never lost his flair for brutal intimidation, save perhaps during the eight months he'd been wooing the former Kitty Winn, a striking deb from St. Augustine with all the right assets who over the years had blossomed into a real fine lady.

'Mr. Seams,' Mickey began, 'could you tell us what happened?'

Morgan stared at him. 'You already spoke to the boy's nanny—'

'Maria Escondido,' Mickey said, consulting his notepad. 'That's right. She found your son.'

'Then you know what happened.'

'We'd like to hear it in your own words,' I said.

'Maybe the nanny forgot something.' Mickey shrugged. 'Miz Escondido was very upset.'

'And I'm not?' Morgan shook his head. 'Gordon Lett is on his way over.'

I knew Gordon Lett only professionally. He was an eely attorney with a practice in Jacksonville who wouldn't let me or Mickey get away with a thing.

'I'm just asking for the facts as you know them, Mr. Seams.' I could see Mickey's patience was already wearing thin.

'Shit,' Morgan said under his breath. He still hadn't looked at me directly, even when I'd spoken to him. He told us how the nanny's scream had awoken him and his wife. It was approximately 2:40, he told us. They raced downstairs. Maria was crying, incoherent, but she was pointing outside toward the pool. Together, Morgan and Kitty ran outside. Once they broke through the stand of pines, he saw Kent floating face down in the pool. He had Kitty call 911 while he dove in and pulled his son out. He spent the remaining time until we got there trying to pump the water out of Kent's lungs. 'I got him to vomit some of it up,' he concluded, 'but then . . .' He shook his head.

'So he was alive when you got him out of the pool?' I asked.

Now his eyes met mine. They held in their depths a glittering coldness I knew was just for me. 'I don't know,' he said. 'Maybe the water came up by reflex. I tried to get a pulse . . .'

'Any idea how your son got through the gate and into the pool?'

'Ask the nanny,' he snapped. 'Kent was her job.' He stalked back to his wife before we had a chance to question him further.

'Charming as ever,' I said.

'Cold fucking bastard, ain't he?'

By the time we got back to Kent, Don had finished his prelim.

'You got anything for us?' Mickey said when we huddled down with him.

'Look here.' Don pushed Kent's left ear forward, revealing the tender flesh just behind. Training his pencil flash on the spot, he said, 'See it?'

Mickey nodded. 'Seems like an imprint of some kind.'

'That was my take.' Don turned to me. 'What do you think, Pris?'

All of a sudden, with Kent lying there and us talking about him as if we'd never known him, I began to cry a little bit, and Mickey turned away because this was one of the things he didn't like me doing. 'Officers of the law don't have no room for cryin',' he'd told me more than once.

'Anyone who's got a heart's got room for tears,' I'd tell him.

'Ain't it jes my luck I got you,' he'd shoot back.

'Take your time, Pris,' I heard Don saying now. 'I know it must be kind of weird you coming back here under these circumstances.' He meant about my uncle Ben, because it was here on this huge, moneyed estate Uncle Ben did the dirty deed that sent a knee-jerk spasm through the archdiocese and got him shit-canned. Weird wasn't all it was, not by half. But then there were a lot of weird things here in Placide. We were an honest-to-God backwater, a righteous rock sitting square in the stream of time, still heavily steeped in the nineteenth century, full of good old-fashioned values, friendly and neighborly but bigoted as all get-out and mighty suspicious of change. It was damn ironic us being right down the road from that postmodern experiment called Celebration, the Disney-made community that gets so much press.

I looked at Don gratefully. 'I'm okay.' He was handsome as sin: coffee-colored eyes that crinkled ever so nicely when he smiled, a shock of dirty-blond hair, the wide, muscular shoulders and long, narrow waist of a competition swimmer, which he had been when we'd been at FSU. I'd hoped the fact that I'd been on the varsity track team would have impressed him, but no dice. Cheerleaders were more his thing, the prettier and more pliant the better.

I forced myself to look at the oval welt behind Kent's left ear. 'It looks to me like the imprint a ring might make.'

Mickey snapped his fingers. 'A college ring, maybe.'

'Just the thing,' I said.

'That would mean pressure.'

'A lot of pressure,' Don agreed. He showed us the small bruise behind Kent's right ear.

'Someone held him under the water,' I said, 'while he fought.'

'With his left hand,' Mickey added, 'the mark of the ring being behind the left ear.'

'We're talking murder here,' Don said, 'aren't we?'

*

'You ain't never gonna get over him, are you?' Mickey growled as we walked back to our cruiser. Neither of us was yet prepared to talk about the horror we had just witnessed.

'What can I say?' I shrugged. 'I've been jonesing for Don ever since college.'

He made a rude sound. 'Why doncha go get him then?'

'Nah. I'm not that kind of girl.'

He paused. 'What kind of girl are you, Pris?'

The kind of girl who despite appearances drew lines in the sand. Take, for instance, last Friday night when we'd broke up that little fracas at the pool hall across the river. I call it that, but no doubt Mickey would have another name for it. He charged in and busted some heads, all black of course, and more blood would have been spilled if I hadn't taken a stand. Sometimes it just doesn't pay to deliberately take a backseat.

'You've got nothing more to prove here,' I'd said as I forcibly dragged him out of the pool hall.

Outside, he'd heaved a sigh as with his usual flourish he'd holstered his nightstick. You could still hear the juke merrily playing 'Blueberry Hill' just as if nobody had been hurt. As he climbed ponderously back into the cruiser, he'd said, 'Who you like on Sunday, Tampa Bay or the Jets?'

'Take the Bucs and the ten points,' I'd told him so he could win again and keep his life afloat. He had a witch of an ex who was just bleeding him dry.

'Excuse me a sec,' I said now. 'I'll be right back.'

The front door to the house was unlocked. In the living room, I found Kitty weeping on an oversize sofa that curved around her like an earth mother.

'Kitty, I'm so sorry about Kent.' I could hear her

shuddered breaths, and I poured her a glass of water from the black marble wet bar and made her drink half of it.

'Where's Morgan?' I asked, mainly to get her talking.

'Upstairs,' she said. 'On the phone.'

Not much had changed inside this house in seven years. It was as thoroughly oppressive as ever. I saw the same sweeping vista of immaculate cream-colored satin uphol- stered furniture, polished walnut wainscoting, Old World antiques, lush, gleaming Italian tile. And the enormous matriarchal portrait of Morgan's mother, Livia, peering hatefully at us from her position of dominance above the outsize stone fireplace. The place had the magnificent, musty air of a museum, with not one trace of the inevitable chaos with which, like a tyrant's edict, a six-year-old indelibly stamps a household. Instead, around every corner there was the same evil memory, ready to pop up and drag me back into the shadows that glimmered even when all the lights were blazing. That memory, God help me, had a life of its own.

'Kitty, when was the last time you saw Kent alive?' I asked softly.

She shook her head and, without facing me, said rather mechanically, 'Morgan told me not to say anything until Gordon gets here.'

'Can you think of why he would do that?' I kept my voice low and even and nonjudgmental. People in shock often revert to their younger, helpless selves. The thing is to guide them back, kindly but firmly, until they can again stand on their own emotional feet.

She looked at me just like I'd wanted her to, but she remained mute. That was okay; I just wanted her to begin thinking about it. Of course, it served no useful purpose to linger on how I might be manipulating her. I had a job to do, and it only took a tenth of a second for me to think of Kent Seams, made mute and bound by death, and I knew I had to forge on, no matter the cost. Mickey and I were his only advocates now.

'Did he suffer, do you think?' She said this in a tiny voice, clotted with shock and rampant emotion.

What could I tell her, knowing the truth.

'Of course you don't know. No one knows.' Her tear-filled eyes searched mine. 'How did he get out there? I mean, the gate should have been . . . Oh, Jesus God . . .' She buried her face in her hands, sobbing all over again.

'It's God's will,' I said, holding her. 'He will provide for you, no matter how shattered and despairing you feel at this moment.' But I knew that was my uncle talking, not me. How could a six-year-old's death be God's will? It couldn't; someone was to blame. This is why I had become a cop and not a priest.

'You're very kind, Priscilla.' Her head came up and for an instant her cornflower-blue eyes held mine. 'I never believed all the stories about your uncle. I know Morgan—' She choked on her words, and I couldn't say I blamed her. Morgan Seams despised me simply because Ben was my uncle. After all, it was largely his doing that Uncle Ben got hounded out of Placide. With a self-righteous fervor, he had taken up the archdiocese's official complaint and made sure that even in a secular way there was no longer room in Placide for my uncle. From him, I learned an important lesson in how easily public opinion could be aroused, how quickly it could be turned, and how irrational a thing it could become. Sentiment finally got so bad that one night my uncle just up and disappeared. Too late, I caught up with him inside a dingy motel room off I-75. It looked like he'd blown his brains out with a cheap pistol bought in a pawnshop. After that, Morgan and those who followed his lead were never wanting for verification of their accusations.

'Morgan and I will never be friends,' I said with ironic understatement.

'No,' she said in genuine sadness. 'Morgan never forgets anything. And his own particular view of the world—' She touched me then, just her fingertips against mine. 'I need to know—' Her soft eyes looked up at me. She was, indeed, very beautiful in the full flower of her womanhood. 'I need to make some kind of sense of this. Otherwise, Priscilla, I'll just go out of my mind.'

'I know, I—'

'No,' she said quickly, emphatically, 'you don't.' Her words seemed to catch in her throat, as if they were a swarm of bees. 'You see, it was—'

'Kitty, that's enough now.' Gordon Lett swept into the room as if let loose by the gods of Olympus. He was a small man with a barrel chest, a halo of silver hair on his otherwise bald pate, and one mother of a Napoleonic complex. His voice was nothing short of stentorian, so much so that I wondered how he ever handled sidebars in court, let alone pillow talk with his wife.

He inserted himself between us as if we were two boxers in the ring. 'I'll kindly ask you not to continue taking advantage of my client, detective. Even you should understand she's in a fragile emotional state.'

'Don't make a federal case out of it, counselor,' I said as I got up.

Lett's round, rosy-complexioned face was darkened by a

scowl as he planted his feet. 'I assure you there's nothing minor about invading my client's privacy. I am truly appalled at your callous lack of common decency.'

'Oh, for God's sake, get down off the stump,' I said.

Always ready for a good fight, he was about to respond when Kitty interrupted: 'Gordy, it's all right. Priscilla did me a great kindness, that's all.' She gave me a wan smile, which was as much as she was capable of at the moment. 'She was just being a friend.'

'Rule Number One: Cops don't have any friends.' Lett shot me a look heavy with menace. 'I'm putting you on notice, detective. I will not tolerate this kind of unprofessional behavior.'

'Lighten up, counselor,' I said to him. 'For the record, I wasn't asking for an official statement. That can wait until tomorrow.'

Mexican standoff.

Lett put his arm around Kitty and said in a deceptively offhand manner, 'It must have been a bitch coming back here.'

Not trusting myself to speak, I cursed him silently as I left.

'That sonuvabitch Lett.' Mickey blew smoke from his cigar out the cruiser's open window. That meant the air-conditioning was off and we were sitting in a pool of sweat. 'He loused up a couple of cases for me before you came along. He and I, we don't exactly see eye to eye.'

I laughed. 'That's because you both know how to massage the system.'

'That and the fact he's got a powerful hate on for cops.'

After my little go-round with Lett, I was in no position to

argue. The blue smoke seemed to release through the cracks in this town all the old hatreds, racial and otherwise, drifting aimlessly like the rotten smell of the mangroves. That rolled leaf burning was to me the smell of rich men conniving, of those in power wanting more, and getting it. Mickey had made no move to start the engine, which meant for sure he had something on his mind. I longed for a swim, then thinking of Kent, was immediately ashamed. How long would it be, I wondered, before I could sink into cool water without seeing his little blue-white body?

'You know when we was in church the other day, watchin' my daughter get confirmed,' Mickey said through a halo of smoke. 'Well, I didn't say nothin' to you at the time, but I'm thinkin' to myself, What the hell am I doin' here? The priest is spoutin' this mumbo-jumbo – means sumthin' to my wife, I guess, but it don't mean dick to me.' He hitched himself around on the well-worn seat. 'Anyways, I turn around an' look at you. An' I see that special light in your eyes an' I know you got your faith, an' all, from your uncle, who was about as devout a priest as I ever hope to meet. An' then I haul ass out here tonight to see this, an' I think, I wish I had your faith. I wish I could say a prayer an' know for a fact God was listenin', because I gotta tell ya, Pris, right now, seein' this here, I feel like dogshit.'

He seemed to listen to the high-pitched din of the tree frogs, then he picked a piece of tobacco off his lip and sighed deeply. 'Morgan's left-handed.'

'I know.'

'And he's got a college ring on the third finger of his left hand.'

'Plus, he lawyers up when he should be mourning the loss of his son,' I said. 'So far we're on the same page.'

'The very same paragraph, I'm thinkin'.'

'Morgan did for his own son.'

'Makes me sick to my stomach.' He flicked his butt, making it pinwheel into the darkness. 'Let's get some sleep. Seven A.M sharp we get all our ducks in a row. With Lett itchin' to earn his three hundred an hour, I don't wanna make no mistake when we charge the murderin' sonuvabitch.'

When I got home, I jumped into a cold shower, and while I was washing the night's filth off I had myself a good, long cry.

The phone woke me from a dream in which I had switched on my flashlight, only to discover that it was an upside-down cross, and felt dread clutch at me as it emitted a widening cone of purest pitch black. My eyes snapped open and, still half immersed in the dream, I snatched up the phone.

'Mickey?' I answered in reflex.

'No, it's Don. Don Murtry.' He waited a beat. 'Jesus, Pris, I didn't wake you, did I?'

'Uh-uh.' My heart pounded as I peered at the bedside clock. 6:03 A.M.

'Listen, Pris, I just finished my autopsy on Kent Seams.'

Wide awake now, I gripped the receiver more tightly. 'I'm listening.'

'Not over the phone,' he said in an odd, tight voice. 'How soon can you get over to my office?'

'Half an hour?'

'See you then.'

As I climbed into the shower I considered calling Mickey, then decided what the hell. To be honest, I suppose I should have, but I didn't often get a shot alone with Don Murtry, and even though the morgue had never been my idea of a romantic setting I was determined to make the most of it.

I don't know how it is in other towns, but in Placide the morgue is adjacent to Don's funeral parlor. The public building was a one-story brick-faced structure with a sober dark blue canopy out front to protect the mourners in inclement weather and a thoroughly depressing blacktop parking lot to one side. MURTRY'S FUNERAL HOME in simple stainless-steel letters was affixed to the concrete just to the left of one of the tasteful stained-glass sidelights that flanked the entrance.

The morgue was nothing more than a cinder-block bunker painted an incongruously frothy turquoise. Inside, the thermostat was set all the way down to tundra level, and all the lights were kept dim except where they burned purple-white bright in the single autopsy room.

Don jerked like a startled deer when I walked in. His skin seemed drained of all color. I thought it was an unfortunate effect of the lights, until I got near enough to see the haunted look in his eyes. He was clearly shaken.

'What is it?' I asked. Despite the cold, the place stank of chemicals and intimate human gases you just never got used to. 'Are you all right?'

'No.' He shook his head in that peculiar, distracted manner people have after they've been in a serious accident, as if the deepest part of them had fled to some safe inner place. 'Not nearly.' He glanced quickly, almost furtively over to the slab where Kent was lying. Then his eyes met mine. 'I've made a disturbing discovery. It's horrendous ... unthinkable.'

My eyes were drawn to the corpse as if it had become magnetic. The big raw T-incision seemed an abomination, an affront to God's handiwork, as Uncle Ben would have said. 'Don, what the hell is it?' It was so cold I could see my breath as I spoke.

He stared at me mutely for so long, I finally took him outside for a moment. We stood in the recessed doorway, watching the rain, hearing it hiss down like a thousand tiny swarming insects. The air was so heavy the clouds looked like they were going to crash down onto the rooftops. I shivered at the unnaturalness of his expression and, leaving him there a moment, ran across the slick street to Rosie's, where I bought us a couple of coffees.

He took his gratefully, sipping the rich, hot liquid from the Styrofoam container.

'Don, whatever it is you can tell me. I can deal with it, I promise.'

This little smile of his, so slight and shy, made him seem boyish, far younger than he had been in college when I'd first fallen for him. The dense, sopping air or the shot of caffeine seemed to give him courage. 'I'd better do this before I lose my nerve again.' Returning to the cold room, he snapped on a pair of disposable latex gloves. 'Cause of death looks to be drowning. No surprise there.' Gently, as if Kent were still alive, he turned the body over onto its stomach and pointed. 'But, Pris, this poor child was sodomized.'

I felt a profound shudder go through me. 'Before or after?'

'Before he died, I'm certain of that.' Don looked up at me and I saw again that awful haunted look in his eyes. 'But the fresh trauma hides an even more dreadful truth. This . . .

behavior was chronic.' He took a breath. 'Over a period of a year, I'd say.'

'God in heaven.'

'So you see, Pris, it appears there's some kind of demon at work here.'

'Demon.' I stared at him for a moment, despite my best efforts my mind rushing back in time. 'Why would you use that word?'

He shrugged. 'Can you think of a better way to describe this monster?'

The fact was I couldn't. 'But demon or no, we have him,' I said. 'The semen. We can do DNA testing on it.'

Don shook his head. 'This is one clever demon. I found no traces of semen.'

'What?'

Don appeared at once helpless and angry. 'I imagine you've read the same pathology texts I have. The offender doesn't always simply use his phallus. He could have inserted a lead pipe, a broom handle, almost anything of the right circumference.' He looked at me darkly. 'This form of rape is often as much about punishment as it is about sex. And, more often than not, it's a repeated behavior handed down from parent to child.'

It was taking some effort for the entire situation to sink in. 'Unbelievable that this is happening here in Placide. My God, this isn't New York City.'

'Maybe it just proves it can happen anywhere.'

'Not on my watch.' I considered a moment. 'Don, would you be okay holding the autopsy report for a while?'

'Sure. I'm not finished with the toxicology tests, anyway. I had to send out for those; no facilities here. It'll take a week, sure. But when they come back . . .'

'Gotcha.'

'There is one stipulation to my cooperation,' he added.

'What's that?' I said, instantly on my guard.

He paused, cocking his head to one side. 'You've changed your hair. It's shorter, isn't it?' He nodded. 'I like it, Pris.'

'Thanks.' I hardly knew what else to say, my heart was beating so fast. I was astonished he'd noticed.

'Anyway, I want to thank you for helping me over that bad patch.'

I waved away his words. 'Forget it. Anyone would have gotten unnerved by what you found.'

'I feel differently about it. And I'd take it kindly if you'd have dinner with me tonight.'

A hammer the size of the Everglades seemed to have landed on my throat. I made a pathetic little croak, which caused him to lean toward me. A clean, fresh scent – cologne mixed with fresh-washed clothes – wafted at me, and I felt a sudden thrilling wetness between my legs.

'Can I take that as a yes?'

I nodded, unable to utter a single word.

Because I was forty minutes late Mickey had already worked himself up into a lather.

'Well, shit,' he said. I thought he was going to spit right there on the scarred linoleum when I told him where I'd been. 'You know, skirt, you disappoint me sorely. Plenty people in the office say you're taking a job should be filled by a man with a family to support. They say you ain't got the expertise or the discipline to be a peace officer. Jeez, you sure know how t' make 'em look good.'

'Don't talk to me that way.'

'Brought it on yourself.' When he shrugged he looked

like a woolly mammoth I'd seen once in a museum diorama. 'Dammit, Pris, this is the thanks I get. Just 'cause I don't ask you t' get me my coffee every morning doesn't mean you have leeway to go do whatever the hell it is you want.'

'Don called and asked me to get on down there.'

'What, you forgot my home number?' Mickey pursed his lips, which meant he was digging in his heels.

'He made it sound personal.'

'I'll just bet he did.'

I shook a waxed-paper bag in front of his face and he snatched it away from me. Peering inside, he said, 'Shit, what's this, the baby portion? Jeez, you think you can buy me off for one of Rosie's goddamn sticky buns?'

'Nah.' I handed him the box I'd been hiding behind my back and watched his face as he opened it.

'A dozen!' He looked up. 'Now, *that's* a he-man-size bribe.' He shoved half a sticky bun into his mouth. 'Okay, I forgive your cute little ass. Now, why did Mr. Donald Juan have his jock in a knot?'

He whistled when I told him, and of course he got right away why I wanted Don to keep the report secret for the time being. With the Seamses already lawyered up, the sensation caused by the autopsy findings would just make all the suspects clam up. Right now, I told him, it would be best to keep the Seamses unsuspecting and as compliant as Gordon Lett would allow.

He licked the caramelized sugar off his fingertips. 'Speak of the devil, Lett called two minutes 'fore you showed up. We have an audience with the king and queen at ten this morning. I want you to interview Kitty.'

'Maybe it would be better if I take Morgan.'

Mickey's eyes narrowed. 'No fuckin' way. Morgan's the perp. His ass is mine.'

'Listen, Kitty was about to tell me something last night when Lett walked in and stopped her cold. If I depose Morgan, there's no way either Morgan or Lett will have a clue she wants to talk with me. Otherwise, they'll make sure she never sees me.'

'What is this all of a sudden, a goddamn democracy?' But I could see he was chewing the idea over. 'Okay, let's give it a shot.' He looked at me gimlet-eyed. 'Hey, you ain't angling for my job, are ya?'

Knowing him, he was only half kidding. 'Mick, you have nothing to fear from me.' I clapped him on his meaty back. 'I could never hope to fill your shoes.'

'Don't think you could,' he said smugly as he reached for the other half of that sticky bun. 'By the way—' I'd almost escaped. 'Mr. Juan didn't put any moves on you – I mean, you bein' alone with him an' all in the cold room.'

Vainly, I tried to keep the color out of my cheeks. 'As a matter of fact, he asked me out to dinner.'

I heard his derisive whoop all the way down the hall.

Sure as sugar Gordon Lett found a way to fuck us. He insisted that his clients make their statements together, and because as far as he knew this wasn't a criminal investigation, there was nothing we could do about it but grin and bear it. So in the end we did the best we could: I let Mickey do the talking while I sat back and observed everyone's reactions.

We convened back in the Seamses vast living room with Livia's forbidding countenance observing us like a presiding judge. It went something like this: Morgan went first. His story was in all respects identical to the one he'd given us last night, just here and there more detailed.

'Who normally got Kent ready for bed?' Mickey interrupted. The question, I knew, was meaningless for us, but it was Mickey's intention to break Morgan's rhythm. You always want to do that when you get the feeling statements have been carefully prepared. The more you do that, the better the chance the person will get rattled and say or do something that will be significant.

'Is this really necessary, detective?' Lett broke in rather testily.

'Just tryin' to get as complete a picture as we can, counselor,' Mickey replied in a voice like honey. He fixed Lett with a neutral stare. 'No harm in that, is there?'

'I don't want to prolong what is obviously a very painful procedure,' Lett said as if by rote. 'Mr. Seams needs to see to the final arrangements.'

This caused Kitty to expel a kind of moaning sob.

'Let's get on with it, then,' Mickey said directly to Morgan.

He nodded. 'The nanny had that particular chore,' he said with a curious edge. 'In fact, she has a lot to answer for, if I have anything to say about it.'

'That'll be enough,' Lett said warningly.

'Excuse me, Mr. Seams,' Mickey said, 'but I'm going to have to ask you to explain that statement.' I noticed that he had adopted the tactic of speaking directly, urgently, almost intimately to Morgan in order to try to cut Lett out of the loop.

'It's my opinion that the nanny is directly responsible for my son's drowning.'

'Morgan! How could you . . . !' Kitty gasped. They were

the first words she had uttered since we had entered their house. Her eyes were watery, sunken, and bruised-looking in that unmistakable way people get when they've been crying for hours on end.

'Someone's going to have to pay, Kitty, that's all there is to it. She left the pool gate open. That's negligence in my book.'

I felt immediately sorry for Maria Escondido, who had cared for Kent and had loved him when they were too busy.

'Morgan, this isn't the time or the place,' Lett admonished.

Morgan's face grew dark with rage. 'That's what you've been saying since you arrived. But I terminated her employment; what else could I do? So you tell me, when is the time or the place?'

'Excuse me, Mr. Seams,' I said, 'but was it among Maria's duties to make sure the pool gate was closed?'

'For Christ sake, it was her duty to make sure Kent was safe!'

'Even in the middle of the night?' I asked.

'*Especially* then!'

'My son—' Kitty began, but it ended in a deep-felt sob. She pulled herself together and began again. 'You see, Kent had a habit of sleepwalking.'

Morgan seemed even more incensed. 'Kitty, for God's sake—'

'He's dead, Morgan. My baby's dead.' Bowed, she put her head in her hands. 'What more harm can come to him now?'

In his extreme agitation, Morgan jumped up off the sofa. 'Goddammit, I will not have my son's disabilities paraded in public like a common—' He looked around him bewilderedly, as if he had woken up to a madman's ranting only to discover that the madman was him. He sank back onto the sofa as quickly as he had risen.

'You'll have to excuse my client,' Lett said. 'Grief and stress take a terrible toll.'

'Understandable,' Mickey said kindly. 'No problem.'

'Under the circumstances,' Lett continued in his oily manner, 'I think we should call a brief recess.'

'As long as we're taking a break,' I jumped in before Mickey could object, 'I'm wondering if I could get a cup of coffee.'

Kitty's head came up as Lett interjected himself once again: 'I think that would be a capital idea.' By his triumphant expression I could tell he thought I was an idiot. 'Kitty, would you be so kind?'

Mickey gave me a look like he was going to murder me on the spot, but I cheerfully ignored him. Now that he had Morgan wound up the last thing he wanted was a recess, but I had something else on my mind. When Kitty was in the kitchen, I excused myself. I could see Morgan's eyes on me as I headed down the hallway to the bathroom. It was the one, I recalled, that had two doors, the other one leading into the library. From there, I made my way around the other side of the house to the kitchen without the men seeing me.

I stood watching Kitty carefully measuring out the coffee. She wore black silk slacks and a man-tailored shirt of the same material. Her long, light-brown hair, alive with artful highlights, was pulled back in a bun. Unlike poor Maria Escondido, she had the knack of making the aura of intense sadness work for her, her grief revealing other facets of her beauty.

'How you doing, Kitty?' I said as I came in.

She turned, one hand clutched between her breasts. Some ground coffee spilled onto the granite countertop and I smelled its pungent aroma. 'Oh, you startled me.'

'Did you get any sleep?'

'A little.' Her eyes slid away. 'No, not much. I dreamed of Kent. He was laughing, running toward me, but when I woke up his death hit me all over again. So this is the nightmare – I'd like to sleep for a year and just dream him back to life.'

'It would be wonderful, wouldn't it.' I went over and stood behind her as she cleaned up the coffee. 'I know you want to talk to me.'

'It's not—' She put the pot of water on the stove. 'I've been told it's not a good idea.'

'Did Lett forbid you to talk to me?'

She stared straight ahead. 'Gordy has been occupied with other matters.'

She meant Morgan had told her to keep her mouth shut. 'Listen, Kitty,' I said in a low tone, 'I'm going to tell you something confidential. No one else knows, except my partner. Someone violated Kent.'

She turned to face me. 'What do you mean?'

'The coroner discovered that Kent had been sodomized just before he drowned. Wounds in that area indicate there had been a pattern of abuse for quite some time.'

I wanted to go on, but she had pressed her fists against her ears. Her mouth was open in a soundless scream and all the color had drained from her face. Her mouth worked for a moment before she whispered, 'How could you . . . How can you say that?'

I saw her begin to shake and I held her for a moment.

'Kitty,' I said. 'I've taken a big risk telling you – and only you. But I feel you have a right to know – to try to make sense of—'

'Stop!' Her paper-thin voice went through me like a knife. 'Please stop! I can't take any more.'

'But there is more. Someone raped your son, then held him forcibly underwater until he drowned.'

She gave a tiny inarticulate cry and I held her silently, rocking her a little, until she stopped shaking. Her heart was still beating fast, and I thought of how I used to hold my little sister, Jenna, when she got scared at night of sounds outside or shadows moving. I felt now as protective of Kitty as I had then of Jenna. At the hospital where Jenna was dying of cancer five years ago, I had held her as the dark came down and reassured her that I had banished all the ghosts and goblins to a land far away.

'Kitty, I know you have something you need to tell me.' She bit her lip and turned away. The coffee began to perk, filling the kitchen with its rich, homey steam.

I was astonished how calmly and dispassionately she dispatched her statement. If it had been me, given what she'd just been told, I couldn't have managed it. For his part, Lett just couldn't hide his smug pleasure at the way her statement coincided with Morgan's.

'Are you quite finished, detectives,' Lett said after her voice trailed off. It was not a question. 'My clients need time to themselves now.'

'Sure.' Mickey slapped shut his notepad and stood up. 'Long as it's understood that we may need a couple more questions answered at a later date.'

This got Lett's attention. His head came around like a dog at point. 'What questions?'

Mickey had an evil little grin lying in wait for him. 'Questions that may arise in the course of our investigation.'

'What investigation?' Lett said as we were leaving. 'This is an accidental death, pure and simple.'

'Pure and simple,' Mickey said to me outside. 'Far as I can see, that's exactly what this here is. Morgan did it. I can feel it in my bones.' He lighted a cigar. 'Why the fuck did you peel him off the ropes?' He was trying to be calm, but his fingers were trembling. 'He was getting woozy, carried away by his emotions. I was getting to him.'

'Wishful thinking. Lett wasn't going to allow you to go much further. Besides, it was a perfect excuse to corner Kitty without anyone seeing.'

His eyes had that red shift, and I knew he was nearing his boiling point. 'You are so fuckin' lucky I'm your partner, because sure as shit no one else would let you get away with this kinda crap.'

'Guess I'm just blessed.'

He gave me a wicked sidelong glance as he smoked in silence for a time. 'So was it worth it? What did she give up?'

'Nothing yet.' We headed for the cruiser. 'I told her about Don's findings.'

He pounded the top of the car with his fist. 'Christ on a crutch, Priscilla, you are some fuckin' piece of work.' He peered at me over the light bar. 'Why?'

'The faster she comes apart, the quicker she'll come to me,' I said. 'She's got a bone caught in her throat, and she needs to get it out. She only wants a helping hand.'

'I hope you're right,' he said, 'because it could be

dangerous to give Lett too much—' He broke off prematurely. 'Holy shit,' he said under his breath, 'Morgan Seams is heading our way.'

I looked back at the front door. Sure enough, Morgan, a light raincoat across his shoulders, was heading straight for me. 'Quick,' I hissed at Mickey, 'go off somewhere.'

'An' do what?'

'How should I know? Take a leak or something.'

Grumbling, he did as I asked so that I was alone by the cruiser by the time Morgan came up. 'I suppose you're surprised to see me here.' Not, 'Hello, how are you?' Not, 'Sorry I nailed your uncle's ass to the wall.' Not, 'Let's let bygones be bygones.' Jesus.

I gazed at him levelly. Just the sight of him made my stomach churn. His face, baby-pink, clean-shaven, expensively scented, was in such stark contrast to Kitty's sad, dark, sunken-eyed appearance I wanted to lash out at him or at the very least scream so loudly that everyone in Placide would at last know what a demon he was. 'Today, I don't believe anything would surprise me.'

'I suppose that's admirable in your profession,' he said rather vaguely. Was he kidding or what? 'The reason I wanted to speak to you ... confidentially' – his eyes now locked on mine in that intense manner I'd seen before when self-interest caused his awareness to be fully engaged – 'is to find out your thoughts on this matter. Your plans, as it were.'

'For what?' I said.

He appeared genuinely surprised. 'For bringing Maria Escondido to justice, of course.' When I said nothing, he was forced onward. 'She's gone, you see. Packed up after I fired her. All but an admission of guilt, don't you think? But

I found out where she is. I have my sources. I thought you should know. Unlawful flight and such.' He frowned. 'Shouldn't you be taking notes?'

'So far I can remember this conversation perfectly.'

'I see.' He paused for a moment, perhaps wondering if he detected sarcasm in my voice. 'In any event, she's at the bus terminal, preparing to flee like a common felon. You need to get over there as quickly as possible.'

'You can be sure we'll do our best.' I saw Mickey ambling back toward us. I went around the cruiser and got in. Mickey slid in behind the wheel and started it up.

'What was that all about?' he asked as he pulled out in a spray of gravel and a squeal of tires.

'Morgan dropped a dime on Maria. She's at the bus terminal with a ticket to wherever. Unlawful flight, in his eyes. As far as he's concerned, she's just confessed to the crime of negligent homicide.'

'Oh, boy,' Mickey said. He was about to go on about that sonuvabitch Morgan, no doubt at length, when Lydia, our operator, patched through a call from Don.

'Hi, how you doing?' he said in my ear.

I would dearly have liked to have told him, but all I said was a neutral 'Tolerably well.'

'I've got a bit more news. First, I got a good impression of that oval. Get me the ring and I'll be able to tell you if it's a match.'

'Great.'

He sighed. 'Also, I went back in and pulled out a microscopic particle of wood. So we can rule out a pipe or something metal. You're looking for a broom or a baseball bat.'

I said nothing; my stomach was too busy trying to rebel against gravity.

'Pris?' Don said.

'Here.'

'I thought maybe I lost the connection. How's the investigation going?'

'Slow but sure.'

'There's progress, then. Good.' He paused. 'You know, Pris, being here with Kent, going over him so intimately, hours go by and I can't help thinking of the boy's pain and suffering. It's not just professional. I guess I've become an interested party.'

'That makes all of us.' The glorious warm spot in my heart for him was growing. As I turned the corner, I saw the bus depot come into view.

'I also seem to be thinking about your new hairstyle.' He laughed a little as if he was embarrassed. I found my cheeks were hot. 'So I'll see you tonight then. Seven at the Glades.'

'Looking forward to it,' I said as I hung up. Was I ever.

I told Mickey Don's latest forensic discoveries as we got out of the cruiser.

'That why you're flushed all over?'

'Stop it,' I snapped.

He made disgusting smooching sounds with his lips, but then immediately sobered up. 'A baseball bat.' He shook his woolly head. 'Jesus H. Christ, what kinda sick people in this world.'

We found Maria Escondido inside the terminal sitting on a slatted wooden bench smoothed to glass by ten thousand patient passengers. She sat with her full striped skirt and her woven cloth bags around her like surf lapping at her feet.

She had a ticket to Miami clutched in one hand, which we took from her.

'Maria,' I said, 'do you remember me from last night?'

She nodded even while she gave Mickey a long fearful look; he held her ticket. Sorrow and fear and disillusion had done their insidious work. The face of the once-pretty señorita from Colombia now looked like so much crumpled up gum wrapper.

'That's my partner. Mickey Brunt.'

'I'm afraid you'll have to come with us, Miz Escondido,' Mickey said, half bending over her.

'I got fired,' she said. 'The señor, he let me go just like that, no money in my pocket, nothing.'

'We're sorry, Maria,' I said as we led her to the cruiser and put her inside. Already battered by a fate she could scarcely fathom, her face shut tight as a clam all the way over. We put her in a room with a wooden table and a couple of chairs. The one window had thick wire mesh over it. I gave her some iced tea while Mickey glowered at her.

'Why you want to talk to me again?' she finally blurted out. 'I told you what I told you last night.'

Mickey waved her ticket in her face. 'That was before you decided to run away.'

She turned her head away and fiercely bit her lip.

'Listen, lady,' Mickey told her, 'your ass is to the wall.'

Maria's eyes got big around. 'For why does he talk to me that way?' she asked me.

I pushed the tea toward her. 'Maria, for whatever reason, Mr. Seams has it in his head that you are the cause of Kent's death. He says he's going to sue you.'

She burst into tears. '*Ay de mí!* I loved that little one like I gave birth to him, but I no have eyes when I am asleep!' She looked at me. 'What am I to do? This is America, yes?'

'Yes, and we want to protect you,' I said.

'But unless you cooperate with us – tell us everything – our hands are tied,' Mickey continued. 'I'm afraid Mr. Seams will –' He drew a forefinger horizontally across his throat.

I sat down opposite her. 'Maria, listen to me, your only hope is to help us here. If you do, if we solve the case, Mr. Seams won't be able to sue you.'

Maria pulled out a handkerchief, blew her nose, then looked from Mickey to me. 'All right.' She nodded. 'What is it you want to know?'

'See, here's the thing,' Mickey said. 'We don't think Kent's death was accidental.'

'*Ay, ay, ay!*' Maria cried. 'Who would do such a thing?'

'We were hoping you could tell us.'

'Me?' Her eyes opened wide.

'Well, you live with the Seamses, you're with Kent almost all the time,' I said. 'It stands to reason that maybe you saw something.'

Maria sat very still and erect, her hands folded in her lap. She had not touched the tea. Mickey leaned over her. 'C'mon, Maria, give us something – anything. Did the Seamses fight?'

'Fight? No, they never fight.' She eyed him suspiciously. 'Okay, so then maybe they don't agree about the *pobrecito*.'

'What about him?' I said.

'He goes into fits. They argued about how to fix it. Señora Kitty wanted to take him up to Atlanta, to a clinic, but the señor refused.'

'Why?' I asked.

'It is a secret. Now I tell you and they will be more angry with me.' Tears welled up in her eyes. 'So then the *pobrecito* wasn't perfect, but all the better to love him, no?'

'Excuse us a minute, Maria.' I grabbed Mickey and we went out of the room. 'Good Christ, this is like what happened to my uncle all over again,' I said to him.

'You mean Kent and his grandmother—'

'It's hereditary.' I nodded. 'They wouldn't acknowledge that Livia had it; they wouldn't acknowledge Kent had it, either.'

'Looks like we got our motive for murder, anyway.' I could almost see Mickey licking his chops just like the Big Bad Wolf. 'Oh, man, Morgan, we are gonna take your ass down.'

We spent the next hour formally deposing Maria. When she had signed her statement and it had been duly witnessed, I took her over to the rooming house where we'd set her up for the time being. If everything went as planned, she was going to become a state's witness. She seemed grateful enough when I told her I'd keep her ticket personally and give it back to her after the trial.

We stood on either side of the bed, she unpacking her clothes and personal things, me thinking about what a frightening thing it must be to be a stranger held in a land for criminal proceedings.

'Is there anything I can get you?' I asked her.

She shook her head as she set out a small folding frame. Inside were a pair of photographs.

I held out my hand. 'May I?'

'My parents,' she said as she handed it over.

I saw a handsome woman with a lace shawl and a shy

smile, an imposing man with a huge, curling mustache and beetling brows.

'My mother, she is still alive, but my father is dead.'

'Mine, too.'

'Was an *abagado*, a lawyer.' She cocked her head. 'Do you speak Spanish?'

When I nodded, she switched to her native language. 'My father fought the drug cartels until they murdered him.'

'My uncle was murdered, too,' I said. 'By Morgan Seams.'

Nothing stirred in the room save the swampy air pressed down on us by the slowly circling ceiling fan. Something seemed to swim at last behind Maria's eyes. I could almost see it work its way to her mouth.

'When I was a child,' she said, 'I found in the forest near our house a horned beetle. It was bound by thin threads to the center of a large leaf the shape of a knife blade. Sometimes, I think that life is like that leaf, that secrets are like the horned beetle, bound to its fabric. My father died because of the secrets he had found out about the cartel. I am leaving here because of the secrets I know.'

'Like what?'

'Señora Kitty gave me money; she bought me the bus ticket. She wished me Godspeed.' She turned away from me and sat on the bed. I came around so that I could face her. I could see the renewed agony on her face.

'Maria, listen to me, no matter what, your loyalty right now must be to yourself. You understand that, don't you?'

'I understand that the choices in life are always hard. Always.' She squared her shoulders. 'So then I promised myself I would remain silent. But now, because of the child, because of how he died, I think I must tell you what I have seen. Secrets. I hate secrets.' She shuddered. 'It may mean nothing, but then ...' Her voice trailed off. Then she looked up at me. 'You see, the way it was ... There was a change in the air. It seems to me that Mrs. Kitty became fed up with the little one. For the past several months she was short with him, saw him less.' Her gaze dropped to her restless hands. 'Her tongue was sharp even with Mr. Seams. And then she would not meet my eyes, as if there was much to hide, as if she was planning something difficult, dark, permanent.'

I went home at six and spent forty harrowing minutes after emerging from the shower trying on one outfit after another. Not that I had that many. When I realized I had my dark blue pleated skirt on for the third time, I groaned at my nervousness, decided to wear the skirt, and then discovered I was in such a sweat I needed another application of antiperspirant. Nothing has ruined a date more effectively than having those dark half-moons appear under my armpits.

I did not want to think about what Maria had told me, not yet. I needed to let it percolate through so I could get a sense of how it changed things – or even if it did at all. In any event, tomorrow morning would be soon enough to decide on a course of action.

In the restaurant parking lot, the normally friendly pink and pale-green neon sign of The Glades winked at me; even the alligator logo seemed to be leering, making fun of my expectations. I felt like fifteen again, going out on my first real date.

The restaurant was as dead as a used matchstick, just a couple of old barflies sucking down gin and one lonely-looking businessman no doubt on his way north to

Jacksonville or Tallahassee. The Glades might be empty, but it was the only restaurant in town that wasn't a complete dump. Don was waiting for me at a corner table near the back. He stood as soon as he saw me.

'Hi,' he said, 'you look great.'

'Thanks,' I mumbled, my cheeks flaming again.

Marge, the waitress, saved me from further embarrassment. I ordered a vodka and tonic. 'Bloody Mary?' I asked him as I sat down.

'Virgin,' he said. 'Ever since I turned forty, my body doesn't react well to alcohol. Just like my father.'

When my drink had been set in front of me, Don offered a toast. 'Here's to getting reacquainted,' he said. I laughed a little as we drank.

'I guess we both had a hard day today,' he said with his dark eyes on me. I felt their weight as clearly as if his body was pressed against mine.

'It was nice what you said on the phone, about how involved you'd gotten.'

'How could I help it?'

It was wonderful how unself-conscious he was about his compassion. 'But you see death every day.'

'Not like this I don't.' He shook his head. 'Poor kid. I really feel for him.'

I found myself staring into his eyes and wanting with all my soul to get lost in there. But the more I thought about that the more tongue-tied I got, and the silence between us just got longer and more embarrassing. Finally, Don grabbed my hand and said, 'I'm not really hungry, are you?' When I shook my head, he grinned. 'I've got a better idea.'

He took me across the river to Neddy's Place, an old roadhouse, more or less off-limits to whites, filled with blacks, jazz, and abandoned dancing. The place was jumping. Don glided through this throng with the ease of a regular. People shook his hand or gave him the hi-sign or slapped him on the back. He led me to the crowded dance floor, took me in his arms, and said, 'Ready?'

Was I ever. For me, dancing is the great liberator. In its grip, I forget everything. The music flows around me, through me, energizing and elating.

'How did you know I love to dance?' I asked him an hour later. We were sitting at a small table. I was on my second vodka and tonic and he was nursing another Virgin Mary. My head was spinning and I felt more alive than I had in years.

'Took a chance.'

Which was just what I was going to do. With my heart in my throat, I said, 'You know, I used to dream about this moment.'

'How d'you mean?'

It seemed to me an odd smile was frozen on my lips and I thought, Oh God, Priscilla, you are a fool. But I'd crossed some kind of Rubicon and, despite the wild detonations of my pulse, I couldn't turn back. 'At FSU, I used to watch you practice when I was finished with my sprints. I remember watching your big shoulders glistening as they came out of the water and wishing with all my heart you'd ask me out.'

He appeared startled. 'I never knew.'

'Would it have mattered if you had?' I screwed up my mouth. 'I wasn't your type.'

His gaze dropped to his drink.

Stupidly, I felt ashamed. 'That was a cheap shot. Sorry.'

'A cheap shot?' His eyes found mine. 'No. I don't believe you're capable of a cheap shot, Pris. Sure, I saw lots of girls.

But it wasn't what you imagine. Back then I could never keep a relationship going for more than a couple of months.'

'Really? That's the truth?'

'As far as it goes.' He held his hand out to me. When I took it, he said, 'The real truth is I watched all your races, too.'

My heart went *kuh-thump*! 'You did?' I could hardly believe it.

'Yeah, but I never – God, I'm embarrassed to admit this. You know, I could never get up the nerve to approach you.'

I was stunned. 'For heaven's sake, why not?'

'You were intimidating, that's why not. Dean's list student, champion track star, first contralto in chapel choir, campus fundraiser – Jesus, you were so damn accomplished in *everything*.'

I was astonished at how my own opinion of myself could differ so radically from that of other people. Good lord, I thought, melting, I wish we'd had this conversation in college.

'And if that wasn't enough,' he went on, 'there was your uncle. He was famous – *infamous*. Everyone at FSU knew about him, even before he gave his legendary 'Hellfire and Brimstone' sermon the night before Easter recess of our junior year.'

'He wasn't as intimidating as all that,' I said, going into my all-too-familiar defensive mode. Even in death I was fiercely protective of him. But privately, at the center of my soul, what I could tell no one because it was so painful to admit even to myself was what a struggle it had been for me to hold everything right side up for him. 'He was a

wonderful man – warm and sweet and forgiving ...
especially forgiving.'

'Maybe so,' Don said. 'But when he was in the pulpit he
sure could put the fear of God – or the Devil – into you.'

'That was his job,' I said. 'Or part of it, anyway. He was
into saving souls, especially those he saw in torment.'

A waiter arrived with the gator popcorn Don had
ordered – deep-fried chunks of alligator tail – and we both
dug in. I don't know about you, but dancing makes me
hungry as well as happy. We laughed a little over our
mutual appetites.

When the band took a short break, Don said, 'Speaking
of souls in torment, Pris, what happened that night out at
the Seams estate?'

Something inside of me irised closed. 'You know what
happened. Everyone does.'

'They *think* they know. But I've often wondered what
really happened with your uncle and Morgan's mother. Did
he perform an unsanctioned exorcism like the archdiocese
claimed?'

'Yes,' I said. 'That much is true.'

'But the rest is all conjecture – and, I've always imagined,
lies.'

'All right.' I took a breath. It had been a long time since I
had spoken to anyone about it. Like battery acid, the facts
of Uncle Ben's demise had been eating away at me. And
now to be confessing them to Don Murtry of all people!
This was truly, as my uncle would say, a night of
revelations.

I asked him to order me coffee before I began. 'As you
know, Morgan's mother, Livia, was a devout Catholic. My
uncle had been her confessor for years. She was a strange,

domineering woman who ruled the Seams household with absolute authority. Even Morgan's father deferred to her. It was her family's insurance business, after all, that supported him once they were married – and it was he who finally ran it into the ground.' I paused as the coffee came. I drank some to steady my nerves; caffeine has that effect on me. Like my mother, I often brewed myself a cup before I went to sleep. 'Anyway, Livia adored my uncle, attended all his sermons. One day, she came to him after services. She was very concerned, almost panic-stricken. She told my uncle that she had started having visions.'

Don frowned. 'You mean like Joan of Arc or Thomas Aquinas?'

'In a sense. It was clear by her descriptions that she was in an altered state.' I stopped suddenly. 'She'd had them once or twice when she was young, but now she firmly believed that she was being periodically invaded by a demon.'

Honestly, I thought Don was going to laugh at me, but instead he looked away for a moment, and I saw him staring through the smoke-filled room. Then he turned back to me and said, 'Go on. Please.'

'Before I do, you have to understand something. My uncle was a profoundly religious man, but he was in no way superstitious. He had never before performed an exorcism and he did not take the possibility lightly. In fact, he tried to explore every alternative avenue. He suggested bringing in a psychotherapist friend of his from Atlanta, other specialists to test her for a brain tumor or epilepsy. She refused, and Morgan became increasingly hostile to his interventions. By that time, my uncle had begun a habit of looking in on

Livia three or four nights a week because she was having more and more visions.'

Feeling anew the weight of my agitation, I sucked down more coffee. 'Anyway, one night while my uncle was visiting, she was gripped by a vision so horrible, so relentless, he grew frightened for her. She begged him to help her in the way only he could. She wanted to be exorcised.'

'And he hadn't gotten his bishop's approval.'

'The archdiocese was firm on the issue. They'd never had an exorcism performed, and they weren't about to start now.' I shook my head. 'But even worse for my uncle, Morgan was against it. He'd been raised as Catholic, as Livia decreed, but in college—'

'He was as irreligious as could be. I remember.'

'Besides that, he had grown jealous of all the attention my uncle was paying Livia. He had become suspicious that some kind of hanky-panky was going on between them.' There was a sour taste in my mouth just saying it.

'But your uncle ignored all that—'

'It simply wasn't true.'

'—just as he ignored the ruling of his archdiocese.'

'The archdiocese had made a political decision. It was far removed from the front line. All that aside, however, he would not abandon a parishioner in spiritual agony. He performed the exorcism.'

Don, who had been gripped by the events once again come so vividly to life, leaned forward. 'What happened?'

'Basically, he failed,' I said.

'The story was he raped Livia and she went mad.'

'Yes, that was Morgan's story,' I said. 'But it was a lie. As my uncle had come to suspect, Livia was suffering from an insidious form of dementia. He could see it happening as her "visions" accelerated. She was a proud woman, from a proud and prominent family. The shame of premature dementia was intolerable for them.'

'Then why did your uncle put himself on the line to perform a meaningless exorcism?'

'But it wasn't meaningless, you see. He hoped that the ritual might arrest the progress of her affliction, or if that weren't possible at least ease her suffering.'

'But it did neither.'

'No. He had waited too long. Livia was too far gone.' I still had nightmares about it. 'Within six weeks she was dead.'

'So Morgan blamed your uncle.'

'With a vengeance.' I drained my cup.

'He killed himself, if I remember right. Put a gun in his mouth.'

A twist inside me, as if an old wound was alive, tearing open its sutures. 'That's what the county coroner ruled.'

'Who was that? Duke Peterson, right?'

I nodded. The band returned and broke into a heartfelt rendition of Thelma Houston's 'Don't Leave Me This Way.'

'Retired now,' Don said reflectively. 'I see him from time to time. Still plays golf with Morgan, doesn't he?'

'Uh-huh.' The coffee seemed to be turning to battery acid in my stomach. 'They were pals from way—'

We both looked up as a beautiful young woman with skin the color of coffee-and-cream and a skirt cut way too high brushed by the table. She was pulling behind her a tall man with very dark skin and wavy hair that looked like it had been polished. The way his eyes devoured her, you could see he was thrilled to be anywhere she wanted to take him. As she passed, her hip bumped provocatively against Don, and she turned to him, giving him a dazzling five-hundred-watt smile. Her eyes slid from his face to mine, where they emitted the chill, penetrating pall of an X-ray. Then the two of them were twirling out on the dance floor. Don tried not to look, but the urge was apparently too powerful.

'Someone you know,' I said, appalled at the vicious surge of jealousy washing over me.

'Colette. We used to go out.' He turned back to me. 'It wasn't good for either of us, but you know how it is with forbidden things.'

'No,' I said snappishly. 'How is it?'

'Oh, c'mon, Pris,' he said immediately. 'Don't be like that. You already have enough anger on your plate.' He took my hand and pulled me out onto the dance floor. 'Let's have some fun tonight.'

The band was playing the Dreamlovers' 'If I Should Lose You,' a sad, nostalgic song for me. At FSU, I used to play it late at night, swaying dreamily to its beat while silent tears rolled down my cheeks. Thinking, as always in those small hours, of Don.

Now I was in his arms, he was holding me close, and I was nearly fainting with the sensation. I nestled my head against his shoulder, his hand went to the small of my back, drawing me a little closer, his right leg slipped between my thighs, and my mouth opened in a silent moan. Occasionally, I could see Colette staring at us as she and her partner whirled by on the dance floor, but I no longer cared. When, at three-thirty, Neddy's Place closed down, I let him take me back to my house. There was no point in either of us being coy; we both knew what we wanted and it was the same thing.

When I was a kid, I'd sometimes drift off during the day and dream of waking up in a bed of rose petals. That's what making love with Don felt like: soft and fragrant and heady and sensuous and oh, so delicious. I had one bad moment. It had been so long since I'd been with a man I was stupidly afraid I wouldn't remember what to do or how to do it, but as soon as I stopped thinking and used my body everything flowed from there. The weight of him on me was like a soothing balm. He seemed to melt into me, filling that dark and aching space I had reserved for him from the nights of my fantasies, fueled by the sight of his gorgeous body knifing at speed through the water. We fell asleep to the ticking of the alarm clock and the somnolent purring of Lama, my watchful Tibetan cat.

Sunlight stroking across the bed like a swimmer woke me, and the insistent ring of the phone. I stretched across the bed, realized that Don wasn't there, and fumbled the receiver to my ear. I felt a small clutch at my stomach. It was Kitty Seams. I looked at the clock: It was just after eight. She sounded breathless, as if something very nasty was nipping at her heels. Morgan was out and she was able to escape the house – those were her words. We agreed to meet down by the river in forty minutes. Glancing around the bedroom, I came upon the note Don had left me telling me he had an early appointment, that he'd made grits and left enough for me, and that we'd catch up with one another later today. Which blissfully buried my fear that this had been a one-night stand.

She was waiting for me, a large-brimmed expensive sun hat

and Chanel sunglasses all but obliterating her from view. I thought of Audrey Hepburn in *Charade*. Growing up, I'd skinny-dipped many times in this cool, tree-shaded place with just the bees and crickets droning obsessively. I'd often imagined being swept away on a sudden swift current, swirled like a leaf far from here, as if the river could take me all the way to Oz.

Kitty held on to the bole of a weeping willow as if for dear life. It was scarred with my initials, as well as those of so many other kids who were now grown up, with their own children and curious thoughts of the past.

She handed me a small package, hastily wrapped, as if it were burning her flesh. 'Here. I brought his ring, just as you asked.'

'Thank you,' I said.

Kitty looked out over the water. 'When we were courting, Morgan used to take me here.' She shook her head ruefully. 'It seems like a million years ago.'

I opened the package, making sure I didn't touch the ring. 'Maybe it *was* a million years ago, emotionally.' Rewrapping it, I put it carefully away.

'It's like this,' she whispered. 'Morgan never wanted this child. I forced the issue, more or less.'

I couldn't see her eyes. Those damn sunglasses. 'I didn't know anything could be forced on Morgan.'

'You're right, of course. Except in certain matters where females have the edge.' She gave me a knowing smile that had no humor in it at all. 'When we made love I lied to him about using the pill.'

'Why didn't he want a child?'

'You know,' Kitty said. 'You of all people.' She took a breath. 'Because of Livia. Morgan was terrified his child would inherit her premature dementia.' The tip of her tongue circled her lips. 'Morgan doesn't have the disease, but Kent did. Apparently, this hereditary condition has a tendency to skip a generation.' She paused, as if lost within herself. 'Morgan was furious. Naturally, I was prepared for him to take it out on me. But no, he did something far, far worse. He punished his own child for being imperfect.'

'Kitty—' My heart was in my throat. 'What do you mean, Morgan punished Kent?'

'You know.' She was not looking directly at me, and sunlight flared off the dark, convex lenses. All at once, she fell to her knees, clawing off her sunglasses. 'You know exactly what I mean!' she cried, and, burying her face in her hands, bowed down until her forehead touched the saw grass.

'My God, Kitty.' I knelt down beside her, but she violently brushed aside my attempt to throw my arms around her.

'No, no, leave me alone,' she moaned. 'I want to die.' And she collapsed, slipping quickly into the water.

'Kitty!' I reached down after her, and her sunglasses snapped beneath my weight. Hauling her back up the bank, I drew her, dripping and shaking and weeping, into my lap. The wide-brimmed hat, upended and filled with water, was whirling away to that lost place of my childhood imagination. So much for the Audrey Hepburn fantasy. Kitty looked now like what she was: a mother faced with the unthinkable – the mutilation and murder of her child.

'If you save me this will be on your head,' she whispered thinly. 'I deserve to die. For letting him ... For saying nothing while he defiled my child.' Her eyes rolled upward. 'How could I be so weak. I'm vile, filth ...'

'Hush, Kitty.' I stroked tendrils of hair off her face. 'Hush now. We're all locked inside ourselves. We all do what we have to do in order to survive.'

'How often I dreamed of leaving,' she cried. 'But with what? To go where? To live what kind of life? He'd drag me down in a settlement, and you know him, he'd hold a grudge for the rest of his life. He would find all the ways to make my life without him miserable.'

It all seemed so sad, so needlessly wretched. I felt her heart beating close to mine, felt the communal bond of our shared gender. It was clear that what Maria had told me had no bearing whatsoever on the case. It was cut and dried. Morgan was a monster and had to be put away for the rest of his life. 'As a child, when I swam here I had nothing but dreams,' I said. 'Now I find only complications, duties, responsibilities, and I wonder where all those sweet simple dreams went.' I was near to tears, thinking of her heartbreak, which chimed with intimacy in the sudden and unexpected flowering of my own life. This morning, waking up smeared with his scent, I could for the first time imagine myself a mother.

'Now you have a way out,' I told her. 'You have the ammunition to fight him, if you have the will.'

'Mrs. Seams wants to make a statement,' I told Mickey when I brought her back to the office. 'She's implicated Morgan.'

'I'm gonna kill that stinking rat bastard myself.' Mickey's eyes bulged in their sockets and it was all I could do to restrain him. 'A child, a helpless *child.*'

'Everyone was helpless in that household,' I said, sneaking a glance at Kitty. 'He made damn sure of that.'

We took her into a back room, gave her a yellow legal pad and a pen. Mickey made her a fresh pot of coffee; it was good therapy for him. He stared out the window, glowering at the live oaks hung with Spanish moss, while her pen scratched like a huge beetle over the paper. A vein in his temple throbbed with terrible menace. Once, I approached him, but his rage seemed to repel me like the wrong end of a magnet, and I stepped back, returning my attention to Kitty, who was weeping as she wrote. I placed a box of tissues at her left hand and gripped one shoulder in an effort to keep her from coming apart.

When she was finished, Mickey and I read the statement. It was all there, everything she had told me.

Mickey's hands trembled as he stalked in a frightening stiff-legged manner around the room. 'Take her out of here,' he whispered hoarsely to me. 'Now.' I did as he asked and, as soon as I shut the door behind him, I heard the sharp crack of a chair being hurled against a wall. Kitty, startled, tried to turn around, but I led her to my desk, where I put my hand on the phone. 'If I remember right you had a sister in St. Augustine. She still there?'

Kitty nodded almost numbly as I gave her the phone.

'Why don't you stay with her for a while.'

Mickey emerged from his den of pain while Kitty was speaking with her sister. I left her in the care of one of the other officers while he and I went to round up Morgan.

'What? Are the two of you insane?' he said when we snapped the cuffs on him at his dealership. 'I want to speak with my attorney.'

Mickey read him his rights as we herded him into our cruiser. 'You've got the wrong person,' he said. 'Christ, the two of you are completely incompetent.'

'Shut up, you.' Mickey boxed him on the side of the head. 'You ain't even shed one tear for your son.'

Morgan gathered himself in the backseat like a fulminating volcano. 'My private life isn't on display for the likes of you.' To my surprise, he turned and spoke directly to me: 'What shocks me gravely is the accusatory statement my wife has written. It's all a pack of disgusting lies.'

Lett wasted no time getting Morgan out on bail. You can guess how he did it: son of Livia Seams, family roots in Placide, pillar of the community, yadda yadda. 'Don't worry,' I heard him tell Morgan, 'their case is so ludicrous it won't even make probable cause.'

Three days later, at the hearing before Judge Kronos, we trotted out for the assistant district attorney the county had assigned to the case the baseball bat Morgan had bought for Kent for his last birthday.

'My partner and I found this in Kent Seams's room,' I testified, 'and it's covered with Morgan Seams's fingerprints.'

'Is this some kind of joke?' Morgan looked incredulous as he jumped up. 'I live in that house; I gave the bat to Kent; I spent time showing him how to hit a ball. Of course my prints are all over it.'

The judge instructed him to keep quiet, and the assistant D.A. called Don to the stand, who identified the bat as being the instrument used to sodomize Kent.

This news took the wind out of Morgan's sails. He slumped in his chair beside Gordon Lett, his face drained of blood. 'There must be some mistake,' I heard him say to no one in particular.

That was the moment the assistant D.A. chose to introduce the ring into evidence. The judge asked Morgan to identify it. 'It's my college ring,' Morgan said. He appeared confused. He turned to Lett. 'Where did they get it?' But Lett was too busy hyperventilating to answer.

'See the face of it?' Don turned it around. 'It matches the imprint found behind Kent Seams's left ear.'

'And in your expert opinion, Mr. Murtry, that would be indicative of what?' the assistant D.A. asked as Judge Kronos compared the ring with the close-up photo of the side of Kent's head.

'That imprint, along with the bruise mark behind the deceased's right ear, would be consistent with someone pressing down with some force.'

'As in pushing Kent Seams's head underwater.'

Don nodded. 'Yes.'

'Against the child's will.'

'Of course. Yes.'

Lett jumped to his feet. 'Objection!'

But the damage was done. The case was bound over for trial.

That night, I made love to Don with a passion I scarcely knew I had inside me. Its intensity brought about an elation as well as a fright I had not felt since I was six years old. That was the moment I discovered that I wasn't an extension of my parents, that there was inside me a force wholly independent of either of them. I learned, in other words, that I possessed the power of deception. Up until then, it had been my perception that the scope of my life – private, unalterable, complete – had been written in my uncle's hand. I was to be the vessel from which he would sip the heady liquor of immortality. Into me he would pour all that he had learned, all that he had been, so that when the time came for the Last Rites to be murmured over him in an officious cloud of incense, he could take with him into the endless night the certain knowledge that he would live on through me.

Climbing atop Don, taking control of his organ as well as my own, I was feverish, avid to do all the lascivious things I had dreamed of but had never done before. Hours afterward, when he had left, I sat drinking iced coffee, staring with blind eyes out onto the street. I had turned off all the lights, had even in the face of the unrelenting humidity thrown open all the windows. Listening to the tree frogs, the crickets, the gentle patter of the rain that had rolled through sometime when Don and I had been insensate, I considered the matter of Morgan Seams. After all this time, all the rage and bitterness, it was a distinct letdown to see him in jail. What did his incarceration mean, after all, but a temporary blow to his sense of propriety? He had Gordon Lett and pretty much anyone else he cared to hire. Looking ahead, I imagined how he would assemble a crack team of lawyers: forensics, technical, and psychological experts who would use their high-priced razzle-dazzle to convince a jury that he was innocent because there was more than a shadow of a doubt as to his guilt or – failing that – that the abuse he himself had, no doubt, suffered at the hands of his father when a child would absolve him of any willful volition or culpability in atrocities visited upon his son. This future was an abomination, utterly contemptible.

I padded into the kitchen, refilled my mug, and returned to where I had been sitting. This time, I looked out into the night. A dog ran down the center of the street, its tongue lolling, its nails making rhythmic skittering sounds like sand draining through an hourglass. Far away, I could hear the soft susurrus of the interstate. Nothing else moved, save the dripping from the eaves in the aftermath of the rain, like someone from long ago inconsolably weeping. There was an old Ford Mustang parked outside my house that had seen better days – it had been repainted by hand in an ugly matte finish. Here and there, it had been eaten away by rust as if with the pointed teeth of tiny gremlins, and its antenna was bent into the shape of a pretzel. The odd thing was that it had been there when I'd let Don in hours ago.

As I watched, someone opened the driver's side door and got out – a woman, slim and sinuous as she walked up the path to my front door. I heard the soft rapping of her knuckles reverberate through the darkened house like an evil omen, and I almost did nothing. For a moment longer I sat still, the sweat popping out on me in the sluggish darkness. I could hear the rushing of my pulse in my ears. Then the rapping came again, more insistent this time, and I put aside my mug. I imagined I heard again the skittering sound, not of time passing, but of it draining away.

'Do you remembah me?' she said when I opened the door.

Even in the mean yellow porch light I recognized her from the night Don and I had spent dancing at Neddy's.

'Colette, isn't it?'

She nodded and, despite the heat, drew her long shiny raincoat more tightly about her. 'May Ah come in? Ah'm not comfortable here'bouts at night.' She meant the white section.

How beautiful she was. I stepped back, too late remembering the malignant look with which she had meant to paralyze me.

'Coffee?' I asked automatically, heading for the kitchen.

'No.'

That one word brought me up short, the resonance in the syllable making the hair stir at the nape of my neck. We stood facing each other in the darkness of my living room. Don's scent was still in my nostrils and no doubt on my skin like some exotic moisturizer, and I was at once triumphant and chagrined.

'Ah have sumthin' t' say t'yo.'

I was close enough to her to see the small pulse at the corner of one eye.

'Don told me all about the relationship you and he had,' I said as much in defense as to cut her off at the knees, because I was dead certain this was what she had come to tell me. She'd had poison in her eyes that night at Neddy's, and it was surely on her tongue now.

'That's as may be,' she said simply, 'but did he tell yo 'bout his relationship wid Kitty Seams?'

'Excuse me?' It was all I could say with my heart suspended like a cold stone in my chest.

A slow smile spread across her face, making her, incongruously, even more beautiful. 'Of course he hasn't.' When I turned away, she went on. 'Ah guess yo think Ah came here crazy wid jealousy, but yo'd be wrong. Ah got over Don fast when Ah found out he was ballin' Kitty Seams same as he was me. Ah ain't that kinda girl.' She said this in such a straightforward, unself-conscious manner it had the unmistakable ring of truth.

'How long?' I knew it was my voice, but I wondered where it was coming from. Some tiny part of me concerned solely with my survival had taken over and was directing me with a general's icy control.

'Kitty Seams, Ah s'pose yo mean, 'cause you sure as shoot wouldn't concern yo'self wid how long him 'n' me were hittin' the sheets. Lessee now, it mus' be goin' on a year now, an' Ah like t' say that's the least o' it.'

'Did you ask him to break it off with her?'

'Did Ah? Shee-it, course Ah did, sugah. We got some mighty fine mojo kickin'. But he refused. Said he wanted us both.'

'Does she—' I swallowed. 'Does she have some kind of hold over him?'

'Seem like it's the other way round. Took all I had t' walk away, tha's the truth. T' this day, I can feel his hands on me. But no, it be a evil thang. They had plans.'

That was really the first inkling I got that Kitty had been lying to me all along. My scalp began to crawl. 'What kind of plans?'

'Wouldn't know nuthin' 'bout that. Don never said specifics, why would he? But Ah knows it.' She bared her fine teeth. 'Ah knows when a married woman won't leave a man they's got be a pow'ful reason.'

I sat down on the arm of an oversize upholstered chair. My head was spinning. Don was Kitty's lover? I was too numb to yet feel the depth of his betrayal. As I said, this hyperefficient little part of me was too busy keeping my head above water. No time for recriminations, my little general ordered. No time for self-pity. I stood up. 'I'm very much obliged to you for coming here tonight.'

She nodded gravely and gazed deep into my eyes. As with everything she did or said, these small, passing gestures were imbued with the weight of inner conviction. Perhaps we'd never be friends, exactly, but we wouldn't be enemies, either. 'Ah do believe Ah'll take that cup o'coffee now.'

*

Don opened the door to my knock. 'Pris.' He grinned. 'Here for more?'

'More.' I nodded as I came in, backing him up. 'I want everything.'

'Well, now.' His grin widened. 'I think that can be arranged.'

I stared at him. 'Do you always answer the door naked?'

'I saw you coming up the walk.'

Vigilant little fuck, I thought. I kicked the door closed behind me. As he took me in his arms, I could feel my skin break out into goose bumps. Then I unwound myself from him and started to walk around the place. I'd never been here before. It was paneled in cypress, furnished in pieces from the fifties that must have come from the odd lawn sale. A couple of oval rag rugs hugged the floor between stacks of books on anatomy, forensics procedure, and criminal psychology. The pictures on the wall, of flowers and hillsides, looked as if they had been left behind by the previous owner.

'What is it?' he asked in a bantering tone. 'Looking for ghosts?'

'No,' I said. 'I'm looking for Kitty.'

Revealed in the swell of lamplight, his face had become ridged, like the stone facade of a well-defended fortress. In this same illumination, his long, lean swimmer's muscles had taken on a bristling menace. 'Kitty Seams?' His laugh was brittle, false. 'What in the world would she be doing here?'

'That would be what I was wondering.'

'I mean, I barely know the woman.'

I stood in front of him and smiled. My hand reached out and took hold of his penis. 'You barely know me, and just look at us.' I began a rough pulling, just as he liked, and he got hard.

He began to unbutton my blouse. 'Pris – ' His hands cupped my breasts.

'No, really, I mean it.' I squeezed him so hard his eyes fairly popped. 'How long have you and Kitty been getting it on?'

'Who told you that?' he gasped.

'Colette.'

'Ah, that explains it.' Sweat had broken out across his upper lip. 'Colette hates my guts. She'd say anything to –'

He gave a little yelp as I applied more pressure. 'Don't treat me like a moron, Don.'

'I don't –' He gasped again in pain. 'I don't think that of you. I know you're different from all the others.'

'Even Kitty Seams?'

His nostrils were flared, and now his eyes closed. 'Even her.'

'No, it's Kitty you love, Don. That's clear enough.' I leaned forward and whispered in his ear: 'Still, you're right about one thing. I *am* different. Because I'm the one who can keep you and Kitty apart.'

His eyes opened like windows into a dark and mysterious world I had never suspected. 'Why on earth would you do that?' he said. 'You hate Morgan as much as she does. Maybe more.'

Who was being more devious, Don or Kitty? 'So we all want to see Morgan fry, is that it?'

'Yes.' He said this as if the wish were the most natural thing in the world. 'We're all in this together, Pris.' His smile was gentle, sensuous. 'And as far as I'm concerned, whatever I have going with Kitty has absolutely nothing to do with you and me.' He kissed me once. 'Different animal.' He kissed me twice. 'Different ride.' I felt his tongue. 'Colette couldn't handle it, but I know you can. You're better, you're stronger. I know you and Kitty can become good friends. I don't want to lose either of you.'

'So – what? – we'll all become Mormons and live happily ever after?'

He laughed, certain now we'd turned a corner. 'Those Mormons certainly have the right idea, don't they?'

I could hear Colette's soft drawl in my head: *They had plans.*

'With your cock dangling between us?'

He was so hard he was throbbing. He put his hands on my thighs. 'You know, Pris, your skin is as smooth as candy.'

'And where do I fit in?'

'What d'you mean?' His fingers had slipped higher and, despite myself, I felt a small thrill like a flame flickering in the night. The danger was palpable, his lure intoxicating.

I pressed my thumb against the moist tip of him. 'You know what I mean. You need me, don't you?'

'That's right.' His eyes fluttered closed and he swayed a little in rising ecstasy. 'I was right when I told Kitty we'd never be able to fool you. You're too smart, Pris. Too smart by half.'

He hit me then, the heel of his hand smashing into my nose. My head flew backward, and he kicked me so that I lost my balance. He took my gun while I slid down the wall. Tears of pain inflated his image, so that he seemed to tower over me like an ancient god in a thunderous rage.

'Too smart to live, maybe.'

He hauled me to my feet and dragged me into his

bedroom. That's when I saw them: the photos of Kent Seams covering the walls like an obscene wound. Impossible to hold the horrific images in the mind's eye for long, let alone to describe. The boy was naked in all of them, and the positions . . .

'It was you, not Morgan!'

He shrugged. 'We all have our hobby.'

'Is that what you call it?'

'Among other things.' He considered a minute. 'The irony is, I could empathize with Kent, really I could. He'd inherited his disability from his grandmother; I inherited mine from my father.' He reared back, a dangerous look transfiguring his face. 'Oh, how he exulted in punishing me. I never did anything right, and the consequences of my fucking up was . . . a good fuck!'

I felt chilled to the marrow of my bones. 'But how could Kitty –'

'She doesn't know. As far as she's concerned, Morgan's the villain of this piece, just like he was in the death of your uncle. In her case, it bound her to me ever so tightly.' He slapped me down. 'Why do you fight me, Pris? I'm doing you a favor – the biggest goddamn favor of your life, if I can be so immodest. Morgan Seams will never be tried for murdering your uncle, but he sure as hell will go upriver for this.' His face twisted. 'Isn't that revenge?'

'No,' I said. 'It's obsession.'

'In the book of my life a sweet, sweet word.' He put his face between my breasts and licked me while he flipped off the gun's safety and pressed the muzzle between my thighs. He arched away without warning, his face a mask of rage. 'I don't want to pull the trigger, Pris. I like you, honest to God I do. You make love like a fucking priestess, like you're tuned in to some holy channel. You take possession of me in a way even my hot little Kitty can't.' He jammed the muzzle inward. 'But so help me if you don't stop fighting me you'll be nothing but a goddamn mess all over my bed.'

I lay back and listened to the jangling of my nerves. My heart beat painfully in my chest, and the adrenaline was rushing in my ears like a summer torrent.

'There's still a way to save this,' he said. 'You were right, we needed you to back up my autopsy report, which I must say is here and there fudged in favor of implicating Morgan. See, people around here trust you – even the blacks on the other side of the river. You think I could have brought Mickey into Neddy's like I did you? Mickey's got a temper like a wasp, he's as bigoted as shit, and nobody thinks he's straight.'

'He is straight.'

'Doesn't mean squat. Didn't you learn anything by your uncle's death, Pris? The truth doesn't matter. All that matters is what people think.' He grinned. 'Everybody trusts me, everybody likes me.'

'Colette doesn't.' Now, there was a dumb thing to say.

His expression darkened. 'I'll take care of Colette in time.' He wiggled the gun barrel. 'But right now I've got to concern myself with you. What the hell am I going to do with you?'

'Shoot me,' I said. 'Go ahead. It's what you want to do.'

'But I don't want to do it, Pris. I told you—'

I slapped him so hard I could feel it all the way up my arm.

'Bitch!' he cried, and, putting the gun under my chin, pulled the trigger.

As soon as I heard the dry snap of the hammer hitting

home I moved fast. I had deliberately left the first chamber empty, but if I gave him the chance to pull the trigger a second time ...

I didn't. I jammed my knee into his groin and, at the same time, slapped the gun to one side. He cursed again, but I was already inside his defense and, locking his elbow against mine and, with a quick, fierce release of energy, I broke his left arm. But even maimed, he came after me. He almost dislocated my jaw, swinging the gun barrel into my face, and then he dropped it and his hands were around my throat and I had no air to breathe.

My world was turning red. I could hear the tiny gasps sawing out of my mouth, and there was a frantic beating in my temples as of a caged beast fighting to be set free. In short bursts, I glimpsed the gun, already half off the edge of the bed. My hand scrabbled over the covers for it, I felt its cool, reassuring surface against my fingers. I reached for it and it dropped to the floor. I moaned in despair. Don bore down on me. A moment more and my life would wink out. Just like that.

Never.

I reared up, pushing him, if not off me, then over so that we both tumbled off the bed. We landed hard on the cypress floorboards. I felt the gun against my right hip and I closed my hand around it, brought it up, tilted the barrel toward him.

I pulled the trigger.

I sat next to Kitty all during the trial. I had a lot of time to savor the story of Don's death because there were no loopholes. The first thing I had done was to call Colette. I did this from a phone booth so there would be no record of a call coming from Don's house. She was only too happy to back up my story of rape, by coming forward to say he'd tried the same thing with her. Then I went back to Don's and stripped the place of all the photos of Kent and the other children I found stuffed in his drawers. I set fire to them out back, stamping on the ashes until they melted like mud into the ground. Then I called Mickey. My voice was shaky and frightened enough to bring him at the run. That excellent actress Kitty Seams would have been proud of my performance. The rest laid itself out like the Yellow Brick Road. There was a very brief inquest, but all the forensics evidence – my bruises and scratches, the state of Don's apartment as well as his own wounds – was entirely consistent with the forcible rape story.

During the trial I looked for Colette, but she never appeared. Mickey took me out to dinner on the nights when Kitty and I didn't get together, and I asked to spend more time with his kids. Their shouts of laughter acted as an annealing balm to my fractured psyche. When I was with Kitty, she preferred to listen to me talk about my uncle and the days before she had been married to Morgan. As a consequence of this, I think, she started attending Sunday services. I could see her always as I sang in the choir, and knew she was watching me as her sweet alto lifted and fell, the hymnal open before her. I thought often of Maria Escondido and her theory of secrets. I recalled her brave, handsome father and his bitter, premature death.

Don was the enigma. Why had he revealed himself to me – first through the autopsy, which he could so easily have suppressed, then showing me his bedroom? He could have gone to Mickey, who, wearing his hatred of Morgan on his chest like a medal of honor, wouldn't have questioned a thing Don had told him. In the end, I suppose there had been a part of Don that had wanted to be stopped – finally, irrevocably.

When, at the end of the second week, the foreman of the jury pronounced the verdict, I was watching Morgan Seams's face just as Kitty was. Guilty, on all counts. Of course, at that moment, we must have been consumed by completely different thoughts.

Then again, maybe not. We had both been possessed by a demon, and now he was gone. For me – as well as for her, I think, despite her deep and lasting pain – it was a blessing that the Seams house had been exorcised.

After it was all over and Morgan had been moved to the state penitentiary, I took myself to Neddy's. Colette and I sat together, drinking ice-cold beers, listening to the band play 'Time Is Tight' and 'I'm Walkin',' songs I'd adored in college, when I'd had nothing more on my mind than Uncle Ben's impending guest sermon. I wondered what he thought of me, of what I'd done deliberately and calculatedly. *I make it a point never to judge anyone,* he often told me. *I leave that particular bit of nasty business to the Heavenly Father.* The band was so hot that Colette and I danced together until two lithe, dark-skinned guys joined us. It was molten in there, abandoned and sweaty, with the smoke rising in arabesques just like in the movies, and the music was like liquor in my veins. I was conscious of the river of life, filled with a boundless energy, flowing through me, and my heart was as light as the notes streaming out of the tenor sax.

Angel or devil, how would Uncle Ben see me? Maybe,

tonight as on that night out at the Seams estate when he'd performed the exorcism, there was very little difference between the two.

MICHAEL MALONE

....

A few years ago, Michael Malone wrote his first short story in more than a decade. 'Red Clay' went on to win an Edgar Allan Poe Award from the Mystery Writers of America, a nomination for an Agatha, and was selected for Best American Mystery Stories, 1997.

The following is his first mystery story since then, and it is a worthy successor. The northern milieu of 'Invitation to the Ball' is very different from the southern locale of 'Red Clay,' and the sophisticated young socialites of this story are very different from the simple small-town folks of the previous one, but the style is as pure and rich in one as in the other. It is recognizably a Michael Malone story, than which there can be no greater compliment.

The author has recently completed his long-awaited third novel in the Justin Savile and Cuddy Mangun detective series, following the impeccable Uncivil Seasons *and* Time's Witness.

INVITATION TO THE BALL

By Michael Malone

'A dinner invitation once accepted is a sacred obligation. If you die before the dinner takes place, your executor must attend.'

> – Ward McAllister,
> the man who made up
> 'the Four Hundred'

Mark told Tugger Whitelaw, who was Chanler's best friend, that something had to be done, and that he'd found a girl, the perfect girl. Mark had been telling their whole group for months that Chanler was in a bad way, that he was getting weird about this woman in the picture. Now Mark brought Tugger along to witness what he meant. Later, when Tugger testified for the prosecution in what the tabloids called the 'Honeymoon Murder,' he would refer to this meeting as 'the day it all started.' But that was from his perspective. According to the prosecutor, the original plan had been set up for over a year when it was replaced by a daring improvisation. He said that's the thing about the most successful con artists. They have qualities not often combined in the same personality – both a ruthless patience and an imperturbable spontaneity.

At the Parnassus Club, in the high-ceilinged, oak-paneled

dining room, they found Chanler seated in front of the painting again. The Parnassus was a private arts club in the Forties just off Fifth Avenue, though very few members were in the arts anymore. It was an easy walk from everyone's office, and the young group to which these friends belonged had all joined, but only Chanler appeared to feel at home there.

Mark gave Tugger a nudge, pointed at the painting, and asked Chanler if they could talk. Ruffling his sandy hair, straightening his expensive thin glasses, Chanler was happy to see them. Had something happened to Mark? As he ordered Parnassus cups for them all, Tugger affably noted that it was true, they were usually talking about Mark – whether Mark was in trouble again at the brokerage firm where he and Chanler worked, or whether he was broke again (Mark had an impulsive way of playing around with stocks that no one had ever heard of – usually for good reason). They'd been talking about Mark's problems since the three had been in prep school together.

Mark interrupted; this time *he* was fine.

'Channie,' Mark began, squinting over the disk of his silver cup. 'It's you. We're all getting worried about you. Aren't we, Tug?'

'Sure are.' Tugger smiled to show that his concern for his best friend was benign.

Turning his face back to the painting he'd been looking at, Chanler asked, 'Worried about what?'

Mark pointed at the picture of the woman over the mantelpiece. 'This. You're like Dana Andrews in *Laura*. Isn't he, Tug?'

Chanler was surprised. 'I'm like *Laura*? The old movie?' (This was an easy guess for Chanler, as so many of Mark's analogies came from the classic Hollywood films he'd spent most of his Yale years watching.)

'Yeah. Dana Andrews fell in love with Laura's portrait, remember? Laura.' Mark sang a line of the song.

Popping cashews in his mouth, Tugger tried to help. 'Kim Novak played her.'

Impatiently Mark grabbed the silver bowl of nuts away from Tugger. 'Not *Vertigo*, jerk.' He glowered at such ignorance. 'Gene Tierney, Laura. They thought she was murdered but she wasn't. This cop had a fixation on her portrait. That's the point, Channie, okay. You're spending way too much time with old Mrs. DeWitt Rawlings here.'

Chanler considered the life-size portrait of Mrs. Rawlings in front of him. 'I thought *not* having a fixation on a woman was my problem.'

It was true that friends of Chanler Swaine's, and he was famous for having the most friends of anyone in his young group, were always telling him he didn't want things enough. Of course, they'd also agreed that the same equanimity was what made him so pleasant to be around. Born into a fashionable family and an enviable trust fund, blessed with reasonable looks and brains, he appeared to be entirely satisfied with his life – a state of mind that was, if not unnatural, certainly unusual. Didn't even the rich always want more money, the successful more success, didn't the beautiful labor to make themselves more beautiful? Mark, with his black hair and startling blue eyes, so handsome that women stared at him in public places, certainly wanted a great many things he didn't have.

Chanler, on the other hand, had seemed able, in a lackadaisical way that charmed and frustrated his friends, to win or lose without much caring which happened. It was the way he played his little old-fashioned tunes on the piano, his long fingers wandering softly over the keys. But if he tended to drift, he did so in a fairly steady direction, steered by virtues that his friends had come to rely on. He'd been a good boy; he was a good man. He just wasn't a passionate one, although he'd always admired the passions in others.

Yet, as Mark was trying to get everyone to see, Chanler had changed. He had begun to develop a bizarre infatuation with Mrs. DeWitt Rawlings. He gave every indication of having fallen in love with the woman, or rather with her portrait, which hung in the dining room of the Parnassus Club, above a green marble mantelpiece ripped a century earlier from some hapless Veronese palazzo. In this painting, the 'ravishing' Mrs. Rawlings (as the nineteenth-century social arbiter Ward McAllister had christened her) stood in a gold gown on a curved stairway, half turned, but looking back as if she had just whispered the viewer's name in an intimate way.

The portrait had made the reputation of a struggling young artist and it was one of the prizes of the Parnassus Club's famous collection. The Rawlings family had sold it years ago to the club, where the artist himself, Jacob Zanski, had once applied for membership and been blackballed. Chanler had discovered in the records of the membership committee this instance of a time when prejudices were so sure of themselves that they kept records. Though some of the old ways were still sequestered behind the varnished doors, it was a far more diverse group of young Parnassus members who met there monthly to plan the BGC – Ball for a Good Cause – that Chanler hosted every Christmas at his mother's town house on East Fifty-fifth. (Chanler was chair of the Invitations Committee, and invitations were avidly sought by New Yorkers of twenty- and thirty-something.)

Lately at these meetings, as Mark pointed out to their friends, Chanler had made certain to sit facing the portrait of Mrs. Rawlings, even if he had to ask someone to change places with him, so that her strange low-lidded seductive green eyes stared straight into his. Even Tugger, who'd resisted Mark's alarm, was growing concerned about the way Chanler had started dropping in at the club every night, pulling up a chair, ordering a champagne Diana, and staring at Mrs. Rawlings for an hour or more. He couldn't seem to keep his eyes off a woman a hundred years older than he was.

'This wasn't,' said Mark, 'what we meant when we told you to really go after somebody.'

Tugger nodded. 'We meant find somebody you love and get married.'

Chanler said he hoped Mark wasn't about to matchmake again. Apart from Tugger (who'd been recovering for years from the heartache of a broken engagement), Chanler was the only bachelor left in their group. Thanks to Mark, he'd once been briefly on the verge of proposing to a bond trader named Belinda, but the moment had passed. Asked why, he admitted that when he wasn't with Belinda, he couldn't remember what she looked like. But Chanler now spent so much time gathering information on Mrs. Rawlings's life in the Gilded Age (for example, that the drink 'the Diana,' brut champagne with a dash of Cointreau, had been named for her) and so much time staring at her portrait here at the club that he could have picked Diana Rawlings out of a large crowd in a fog, from the lobe of her ear alone, from the nail on her little finger. 'Which is why we're just all getting a little worried about you, aren't we, Tug?'

'A little. I mean, Mark here likes old movies and stuff, but there's such a thing as too much of the past, Channie. I don't even know why we joined this place. The old farts here just snooze around and complain about their prostates.'

Now, Chanler's friends, many of them raised on the Upper East Side, had nothing against the past; in fact they thought of themselves as stylistic reconstructionists, social neo-classicists. After all, they put on fancy dress balls for charity, just as their great-grandparents had. Like their grandparents, they knew how to dress and how to fox-trot. Tugger enjoyed his Broadway shows and porterhouse steaks; Mark, his film noir, braces and Borsolino hats, martinis and cigars. But Channie's falling in love with a woman in a fin de siècle painting was taking the traditional too far.

'Here's the point,' Tugger admitted. 'She's dead.'

'That's the whole point,' Mark agreed. 'He finally picks somebody and she's been dead a hundred years. You see the problem, Channie?'

'She's only been dead since 1951.' Chanler smiled.

'In 1999, that's still a problem.' Mark stroked his new mustache with a tan, well-manicured hand. 'Not that you should have married Belinda.' (Mark's former wife had been Belinda's best friend, and Chanler's breakup with her had caused some awkwardness in the group until Mark had left his wife.) 'I mean, Belinda and my wife both turned out to be real class-A bitches.'

That night Mark called Tugger for his views on Chanler's

fixation. Everyone in their group relied on Tugger's dogged literalism as a 'reality check,' trusting him despite (or because of) his inability to play the social games at which Mark was far more skilled. 'So, okay, Tug? Am I right, Channie's got a problem, and we need to fix it?'

Tugger admitted that Chanler appeared to be determined to fall in love, and therefore it might be better if a real woman could be substituted for the one on canvas.

The next week, Mark had Tugger bring Chanler to the club. He found them sitting in front of the portrait. He told Chanler, 'I want you to meet somebody tonight. You're gonna thank me.'

Chanler gestured that Mark should step backward. 'Don't try to fix me up again, Mark, please. Fix Tugger up.'

'Not me,' said Tugger. 'Let me finish my diet.' But Mark was hurrying away down the wide stairs, presumably to bring back the perfect female for Chanler, who asked, 'Has he got some girl hidden down in the coatroom? Do you know who she is?'

'He thinks you'll like her.' Tugger was looking at the painting of Mrs. Rawlings. 'So what is it about this picture?'

Chanler confessed that he'd never seen a contemporary woman in the same class as Mrs. Rawlings.

Tugger gave a closer look. 'Are those real, painted on her dress?'

Chanler drew Tugger even closer to examine the jewels sewn all over the gold gown. 'They're real.' (Mrs. DeWitt Rawlings's husband had inherited a rather large copper mine at a time when there was no income tax.) 'But,' he added, 'you should have seen Alice Vanderbilt that night. Alva's sister-in-law. She came to the party as "The Electric Light." Her whole head was covered with diamonds.'

'What night, what party?' Tugger asked. Chanler pointed at the portrait's title. *Mrs. Rawlings as Dido. Mrs. Vanderbilt's Ball, 1883.* It had been a fancy dress affair, which was why Mrs. Rawlings was costumed in this jeweled outfit: She'd come as the Queen of Carthage – or at least the fashionable tailor Lanouette's bizarre notion of what that ancient queen might have looked like. Chanler explained to Tugger how this picture, painted a year afterward, commemorated Diana Rawlings's great triumph at the most famous ball ever given in New York City, when Alva Vanderbilt had spent $250,000 on a dance and dinner in order to break into Society. Chanler told Tugger $250,000 then would be about four and half million today.

'For a party?! Four and a half million?'

Chanler agreed, it was no small change, even for a Vanderbilt. But it was worth every cent to the social-climbing Alva because it had done what it was meant to do. It had forced Mrs. Astor to pay a visit to her home, and where Mrs. Astor went (and she went wherever a man named Ward McAllister advised her to go), the Four Hundred followed.

'But what exactly is it about Mrs. Rawlings here that you like so much?' Tugger persisted.

Chanler's answer surprised him. 'I like her because she's a pirate,' he said.

'You mean like a thief?'

Chanler shook his head. 'No. And not just reckless, like Mark. I mean like a pirate captain, flying her own flag, taking no prisoners. The opposite of me.'

'Or me,' agreed Tugger. 'Or anybody else in here.' He gestured around the private club, where the members chatted at one another in a room designed by Stanford White; they looked and dressed and talked alike.

Chanler nodded. Yes, the first and most powerful rule of Society, he said, is that Society rules, that it is impossible to break those rules without dreadful penalties. 'But, of course,' he added, placing his long thin legs on the leather chair across from him, 'the rules only have power over those who agree to believe in them.' A portly man frowned fiercely at him, and Chanler quickly removed his feet from the chair. But, he added, there have always been pirates who did as they pleased and got away with it. One such pirate was Alva Vanderbilt. Diana Rawlings was another.

'And what did she do?' Tugger asked.

'She murdered her husband.' Chanler smiled. 'Nobody knows it, and I can't prove it, but I'm sure she did. And got away with it.'

Tugger frowned, his concern growing that Mark was right: Their friend was in the grip of a strange fixation.

Chanler squeezed his arm, his mild gray eyes brightened. 'That's what makes her so beautiful.'

'That's she a murderer?'

'That she's letting you know she's going to act on her desires. It's in her eyes. See how she looks right at you.'

Chanler took something from his pocket. It was a small framed photogravure that just that afternoon he'd come across at the antiques fair at the Armory. It was a picture of Diana Rawlings taken for the society pages some ten years after the death of her husband; she sat in a fashionable group at the races at Saratoga. Behind her in the group stood the artist Jacob Zanski, by then a successful man. 'And Jacob Zanski knew she was a pirate. He saw it from the beginning and put it in the portrait.'

Tugger, alarmed, looked from the photo to the painting. He saw a woman in a long golden gown, beaded with hundreds of small rubies, emeralds and pearls, low-cut and strapless, except for two thin strands of rubies curling over her shoulders. Her head was a flame of auburn hair, piled high and sprinkled with rubies. She wore no necklace, and the white nakedness of her neck and bare arms was, even today, a shock to viewers. On her right hand, the one resting on the newel of the marble banister, she wore a bracelet of intricate design, of rubies twined in gold. The dress had cost more money than a thousand mill workers could earn in a year of long, backbreaking days at a thousand looms.

Chanler said the dress had caused a sensation at Mrs. Vanderbilt's ball. So had the fact that Diana Rawlings (who was not one of the Four Hundred) arrived unescorted by her husband (who was). In fact, no one had ever heard of Diana before she'd married DeWitt Rawlings six months earlier. His family had been surprised, and not at all pleased, and had tried to keep the marriage to a shop girl as quiet as possible. They'd thought DeWitt, an amateur archaeologist, would never marry anybody, much less a beauty half his age with no connections. But while Diana had arrived at the Vanderbilts' essentially uninvited, she'd been accompanied by the Reverend DeLancey, rector of a large Fifth Avenue church, who came dressed as El Cid, and by his wife, a lumber heiress, who came as Bo Peep. Between them, Mrs. Rawlings had walked past the police squads into the white limestone château, up the marble stairway lined by the rows of footmen in maroon knee britches, buckled shoes and powdered wigs, who guarded every step. Beneath the circular frescoed ceiling, she'd offered her hand to Alva Vanderbilt as if she'd done so daily for the past dozen years, while she explained that her husband, DeWitt, sent his regrets; he'd been unexpectedly delayed returning from an archaeological trip to Greece.

Despite the shock of her décolletage, her beauty, and the fact that no one really knew who she was, Diana Rawlings then joined the thousand socialite guests dancing to an orchestra under a canopy of all the roses for sale that day in New York City. The moral standing of her escorts protected her as she climbed into a world where she was to live unchallenged until her death some sixty years later. If this Dido was all right with the Reverend and Mrs. DeLancey, well, then ... And she managed to remain all right, from that night on, even when, the very next day, her husband was found lying dead on the terrace of the family's country house, having presumably fallen, or jumped, from a bedroom balcony. 'Or,' said Chanler, 'been pushed.'

Mark still hadn't returned with the girl. Tugger tried to stop himself from eating the mixed nuts the waiter kept replenishing. 'Channie, you do sound a little weird, you know that?'

'Oh, I'm not making this up. There were rumors even back then, but nobody ever—'

At that moment, Mark interrupted. 'Channie. Got a minute?'

Chanler turned and saw the young woman. She stood at the top of the stairs beside Mark and looked right at him. Even from a distance, he could see the shocking resemblance, even in the tailored black suit and pageboy haircut. She had the same slender figure and cream-white glow to her skin. The same auburn hair and the green, oddly tilted eyes that one couldn't look away from.

Mark was grinning as Chanler hurried to his feet, pulling Tugger with him. 'Right,' Mark said. 'Mattie, this is Tugger Whitelaw.'

'Tim,' insisted Tugger.

'And this is Chanler Swaine, the guy I've been telling you about.'

As she held out her hand, Chanler noticed the bracelet. He couldn't believe it. 'Hi, Chanler.' She smiled. 'Mark tells me you know all about my great-grandmother. Well, I don't know a thing. I don't think my dad ever mentioned her.' She laughed, a low conspiratorial chuckle.

'Your great-grandmother?'

'Diana Rawlings. There.' She pointed at the portrait. 'Look at that. Just like you said, Mark. It is my bracelet.' She spun the bracelet with its gold-tangled rubies, showing it to them. Tugger asked her where she'd gotten it. Mark told her she'd have to get used to Tugger; he was notorious for asking personal questions.

She answered. 'My dad gave it to me. He told me it had belonged to his family, but he didn't say it was in a famous painting. He wasn't much for old memories.' She spun the bracelet. 'So, Chanler, Mark says you can tell me everything?'

Chanler told her that Mrs. Rawlings's husband had been found dead the morning after the Vanderbilt ball. There were rumors of suicide, rumors that Diana had been having an affair, even rumors of murder.

Mattie laughed. 'Why do men think that just because a woman may be capable of adultery, she must be capable of murder too?'

'You gotta admit, Tug' – Mark grinned as later they followed Mattie and Chanler to the club dining room –

'she's got it. Like Bogie says, the stuff dreams are made of. Look at Channie!' Chanler was talking to the young woman with an animation unusual for him. She nodded, smiling as they went.

'I guess,' said Tugger. 'I don't know. I thought the idea was to get him away from this stupid painting, not bring it to life.'

A week after this first dinner together, Chanler invited Mattie Rawlings to be his date at the BGC. That made her one of their group. Only two months later, he proposed. They got along beautifully; it turned out that everything Chanler liked, Mattie liked as well. She shared his taste in restaurants, in politics, in movies, furniture, and friends. She liked to ballroom dance and jog in the park, she liked the History channel, and she collected things – old autographs, art deco lacquer. In fact, had Mattie been trained like Gigi since childhood to take her place as Chanler's mate, she couldn't have been more perfectly suited. She didn't even mind having dinner once a week with his mother, whose sarcasm had reduced earlier dates of Chanler's to tears; Mattie appeared to enjoy the undeclared war of thrusts and parries.

She had her own life too, in fact would occasionally be unavailable for an evening out or would go away for a weekend, and Chanler found this independence reassuring. Their only incompatibility was Mattie's pleasure in gambling; like Mark, she loved betting on long shots at Belmont, and Mark and she would occasionally go to the track together, where they seemed always to lose. It was a kind of recklessness that Chanler lacked but – he admitted to Tugger – secretly admired.

'Is she a pirate too?' Tugger asked.

Chanler responded, puzzled, 'A pirate?' He seemed to have forgotten his theories about Mrs. DeWitt Rawlings; her great-granddaughter had effaced her completely. She looked so much like her ancestor's portrait that Mark made a quip that went the rounds – that Chanler and Mattie were a match made in the fin de siècle. And in fact, Chanler grew so obsessed with her that he neglected his work at the brokerage firm where he had once been the odds-on favorite to be the first of their group to make partner. Instead, that honor went to Mark, who confessed he could use the raise; things were a little tight financially. 'Besides, what do you care, Channie? You're richer than God.'

'Not really,' Chanler modestly protested. He was, however, indisputably better off than Mark, and he congratulated his friend on his promotion. When Tugger claimed that Chanler was too decent to see how much less Mark had done to deserve the promotion, Chanler said he owed Mark a lot, for it was Mark who had given him Mattie.

Tugger sat looking at the portrait. 'Where did Mark say he met Mattie?'

'The Yale Club.'

'She went to Yale? When?'

'No, she was just there.'

'She and Mark were both in L.A. the year before.'

'It's a big town.'

'You know more about her family than she does—'

'What are you getting at, Tugger?'

Tugger blurted out: 'Channie, are you going to marry her?'

'Yes ... Is that a problem?'

'... I hope not.'

But there were problems. Chanler's mother, alarmed by

the speed of the engagement, let Mattie know in a general way of her fears that some lower-class girl would try to marry Chanler for his money. Mattie sweetly replied that she hoped Mrs. Swaine would do everything in her considerable power to thwart that tragedy. Even Mrs. Swaine, something of an East Side fixture and by her own proud admission a snob, could have no social objection to her son's choice. Mrs. Swaine still believed it took four generations to make a gentleman, which gave Mattie's father, DeWitt Rawlings IV, the rights to that title, even if he had drunk himself to death in a succession of cheap motel rooms, having long since squandered what little of the copper fortune his father hadn't managed to mislay in the Crash of '29. Society had lost track of the Rawlings since they'd moved west, and downhill. The Rawlings's house on Fifty-third Street had fallen to the wreckers' ball, their country estate was a girls' school, and who knew where the gold gown of Dido, so heavy with real jewels, had gotten to. Nevertheless, they had had a name, and that still meant something, at least to New Yorkers like Mrs. Swaine.

Mattie, the only child born to her father in his late middle age, was, she said, the last of the Rawlings. She worked at Sotheby's and roomed with two other pretty young women in a Chelsea walk-up the size of one of the bathrooms at the Parnassus Club. She had no great stake in either job or apartment but, nevertheless, the first three times Chanler proposed, she declined. Nearly a year went by before she said yes. It was this firm reluctance that finally won over his mother, who confessed to her minister that she'd originally thought Mattie a gold-digger, but the gold had been lying around for the picking a long time, untouched, and what fortune hunter of Mattie's generation would have the patience not to pounce at once.

Everyone seemed to like Mattie except, more and more obviously, Tugger. Finally Chanler had to warn his best friend to stop challenging Mattie with questions about her past. Tugger defended his reservations. Why should she object to such straightforward questions? He offered to resign as Chanler's best man, but Chanler told him not to be silly.

That Christmas, the engagement was announced at the BGC, to which Chanler and Mattie came dressed as Nick and Nora Charles, although everyone thought they were Fred Astaire and Ginger Rogers. Mrs. Swaine's friends were struck by Mattie's beauty and congratulated Chanler. In the end it was Mrs. Swaine herself who insisted on (and financed – Mattie didn't have a cent) the formal wedding at the Fifth Avenue church. She also paid for the big reception at the Parnassus Club. Her wedding present to Chanler was to frame the life-size painting of Mattie he'd commissioned and to hang it in the town house – the bottom floors of which Mrs. Swaine planned to turn over to the newlyweds when they returned from their month-long honeymoon cruise in the Mediterranean.

The wedding itself was perfect. The trouble began at the reception. People commented on Tugger Whitelaw's toast to Chanler and Mattie, filled with curiously ominous fears for his friend's happiness. They couldn't help but notice his intense quarrel with the bride off in a corner (where no one could hear what they were arguing about), which was broken up by Mark, with whom Tugger also quarreled. Afterward, the best man abruptly left the party, despite his duties, presumably too upset over the loss of his sole fellow bachelor to stay. The older Mrs. Swaine then took the younger Mrs. Swaine aside for a few words about finances that the bride said she found insulting; Chanler's mother said they weren't accusations, merely clarification. All of Chanler's money was in Mrs. Swaine's control, not her son's. In the event of a divorce, or even an indiscretion, Mattie should expect to leave the marriage as unencumbered by wealth as she had entered it.

Later on, a drunken Mark offended Chanler's mother by his boorish conduct on the dance floor; he kept cutting in on the bride until Mrs. Swaine finally asked two friends to take him home. He kicked over a chair as they dragged him out. Chanler's mother announced to her minister that Mark Toral was no gentleman, he just looked like one – usually a successful substitute on social occasions, but only as long as one stayed sober. It was soon after this that Mattie realized that she'd lost her heirloom bracelet. She was as close to frantic as anyone had ever seen her. Chanler was distressed by her loss. The ballroom was searched to no avail. Sadly, despite its value, it wasn't insured.

By morning, as the newlyweds left to fly to Athens, Mattie had recovered her typical cheerfulness. She was even conciliatory toward Tugger when he showed up at the airport to apologize for his behavior at the reception. Mattie had even kissed Tugger on the cheek, then gone off to buy magazines so the friends could be alone. It was then that Tugger gave Chanler a special present; it was a daguerreotype of Mrs. DeWitt Rawlings that Tugger had located through an autograph dealer. Dated the night of the Vanderbilt ball, taken during that event, it showed her in her Dido gown, looking exactly like the portrait painted a year later, down to the rubies in the hair and the ruby bracelet. Tugger and Chanler embraced, reminding one another that they'd always be friends.

On the flight, Chanler didn't mention Tugger's gift. Nor did he ask what Mattie and Tugger had fought about at the reception. Chanler was never one to invade privacy, to gossip, to confide suspicions that he considered unjustified.

Two weeks after their honeymoon ship sailed out of Athens, Mattie gave Chanler a present as well. They'd had a good morning climbing among the ruins of Delos, then Chanler had returned to the ship for a swim while she went alone into Mykonos to do some shopping. She was gone so long she almost missed the last tender back to the ship. Now, as they pulled away from the island's postcard hills of white houses, the newlyweds stretched out on their private balcony on deck chairs whose cushions were as blue as the sky and the sea. 'Are you happy, Mr. Swaine?' Mattie asked him, raising her champagne flute to his. He nodded; he'd never been this happy. She toasted him. 'I was almost this happy one day in my life,' she confided. 'It was a doll, a stupid doll I wanted like crazy, a very expensive Madame Alexander doll, and my dad kept telling me we couldn't afford it.'

'But you got it?'

She smiled at him. 'I stole it ... Does that shock you? I bet you've never stolen anything.'

He shook his head. 'I guess I never wanted anything that much, till I met you.'

Mattie leaned over, kissed Chanler, then handed him a cheerfully wrapped package. 'Here, I want to give you something for a change.'

He took her hand and kissed the wrist, near where she had once worn the ruby bracelet. She was still upset about its loss; no doubt, thought Chanler, because she had held on to so little of her past. It apparently had been a painful one; she'd once described 'memory lane' as 'a real nightmare alley.' He'd seen a few things in her apartment: family photos, her father's watch and cuff links, old books, a couple of letters her father had written her, and a few that his father had written him. Her present for Chanler was a part of that past. Among the jumble of odds and ends of furniture stored by her father in a friend's garage, she'd found an old suitcase. There was something in it she thought Chanler would enjoy seeing.

Chanler carefully opened the package, taking out a battered travel journal, its leather covers cracked and dry. In faded ink, in thin, regular script, it was dated 1883 and inscribed *DeWitt Rawlings, Vol. 3.* Chanler read the first entry aloud.

> After the remarkable ruins at Mycenae, Eleusis is at first sight something of a disappointment. Still, it is fresh territory for us, and Trimmer is confident we shall have a successful dig. I miss Diana dreadfully. It is hard, as she says, that we should be separated these two months after so brief a time together. But I couldn't back out of this chance, having waited so long for a respite in my responsibilities to family business. Trimmer's team is the absolute best in the field, and working under them I am learning at such a great rate that Trimmer pleasantly jokes that all the new copper my father dug up has robbed the academy of a good digger of old bronze.

Chanler looked up, thrilled. Diana Rawlings's husband, DeWitt, the grandfather of Mattie's dad, had kept a diary on that Mediterranean voyage to ancient archaeological sites – the trip that had brought him back to the States, unknown to his wife, too late to attend Mrs. Vanderbilt's ball. 'The perfect present,' said Chanler.

She smiled. 'But what else from the perfect wife? ... Don't stay out here long. With that sunburn you'll get a chill. And a storm's coming.'

'Thank you.' He smiled.

Mattie turned, the white caftan caught by the Mediterranean breeze, blew a kiss. Then she was gone, headed to the ship's spa, to make herself beautiful for the captain's table tonight. He teased that it was a waste to spend so much time off at that spa; what could they do to improve her?

Chanler settled in his deck chair and re-opened the journal. On the surface DeWitt Rawlings was a contained, ironical man, whose meticulous notes about broken shards of the Peloponnesian past filled the bulk of his diary. But flaring up now and then from the yellowed pages were the man's two passions – his love of Greek art and his love of his young wife:

> Diana says she has received not a single visit from anyone in my family. Their snobbery and cruelty disgust me. How can they not see her worth? I know they still think me mad for marrying her, and no doubt had Father not passed away before I met her, it might well have cost me his estate. But I would happily trade all the copper in this earth, and a thousand times more, to have her in my life. Before her there was nothing and, without her, nothing again.

As he read, Chanler could see that DeWitt Rawlings was not blind to his wife's shortcomings, her vanity, ambitions, propulsive desires; he simply loved her so much everything in her nature gave him pleasure: *Diana has met a painter who has flattered her into a commission. How she likes to have her beauty appreciated. And why shouldn't she?* And then this:

> Letter from Diana waiting here at the hotel, sent on from Athens. She talks of nothing but an idiotic ball Alva Vanderbilt is planning, at God knows what cost to poor Willie. My darling obviously would give her soul to be included and keeps hurling hints, heavy as cannonballs, that I might, even from this distance, somehow manage to get her invited, and adorned, no doubt, like Cinderella in some astonishing gown for which Lanouette will triple-charge her. I've decided to write Ted DeLancey to ask a favor. He and his wife go everywhere; indeed, one wonders when he has time to compose his sermons.
>
> This morning, we unearthed a bronze mirror, nearly intact, with a figure of Eros at its base. A great excitement.

Chanler was mesmerized, reading the journal on the balcony, with the Mediterranean sun like a great blood orange set on the blue plate of the ocean. Here was the actual life only hinted at in the public records, the microfiche of old newspapers where he had first searched for the facts behind the painting. He read on, page after page of the dead man's diary, finding, among the lists of Attic amphora fragments, DeWitt's poignant hopes for children with Diana. Then, near the end of the entries, Chanler came to a page that stopped him cold. He shivered, looked up; the sun had gone down, and his burn was chilling him in the cooler air.

After hurriedly dressing, Chanler got out the little daguerreotype of Mrs. Rawlings that Tugger had given him at the airport and took it to the ship's library, where he'd noticed a magnifying glass beside a globe. He found it and carefully examined the figure of Diana Rawlings in the old photo. Chanler had guessed right. She had lied. At the brief inquest that followed her husband's death, she'd testified that she had not known that his ship had already docked before she left for the Vanderbilt ball, nor, she'd said, was there any indication that he'd come to their town house while she was away attending the ball. She said DeWitt must have gone for some reason straight to their country home, where he'd somehow fallen to his death. She said it was not until the police officers came with news of his accident that she'd had any idea her husband was not still off in the Mediterranean. None of that was true. Chanler had once checked the arrival time in New York of DeWitt Rawlings's ship and knew that Rawlings *could* have come to his town house that night in time for the ball. Now he knew he had to have been there!

Chanler went to the bridge and asked the captain a question: Would it be possible to verify a specific piece of historical maritime information? Chanler wondered if the time he'd once seen listed for a certain ship to dock in New York harbor on a certain day in 1883 was the scheduled time or the actual time? Yes, the captain thought it would be possible to assist Chanler, who was staying in the most expensive suite on the cruise. In fact, it took only fifteen minutes to learn that the ship had actually arrived ahead of schedule.

With the computer printout, Chanler hurried back up the stairs and along the hallway to their suite. The predicted rain was blowing in, the seas growing rough, and he had to catch his balance against the bulkhead as he went. As he came round a corner, he saw a dark-haired man heading into the elevator. Two women getting off it turned back to look at him; for an instant Chanler had the oddest sensation that the man was Mark Toral.

Back in the stateroom, he placed a ship-to-shore call to New York, to Tugger Whitelaw. He woke Tugger out of a deep sleep and there was a lot of static, so he wasn't sure how much Tugger understood about what he needed him to check out about Diana Rawlings's family. Tugger was happy to do it. In fact, Tugger had already done some research into the Rawlings family on his own. Furthermore, there was a lot he needed to talk to Channie about, though perhaps this wasn't the right time or the right way. Could they meet as soon as the Swaines returned from their cruise next week? Chanler set a lunch date at the Parnassus Club but warned Tugger that he wasn't going to listen to any more negative talk about Mattie. He'd hoped that Tugger's apology for that scene at the wedding reception was the end of it. Parenthetically, Chanler mentioned just seeing a guy aboard ship who'd reminded him of Mark, and he asked Tugger how Mark was doing. Tugger hadn't seen him lately; someone at the club had mentioned that Mark was on vacation somewhere. Tugger admitted that he and Mark hadn't really spoken since Chanler's wedding. 'We had sort of a falling out.'

'Oh?' Chanler said.

'About Mattie, to tell you the truth,' Tugger blurted out. 'Channie, I'm sorry, but I'm going to tell you this one thing and I don't care if you want to hear it or not.' Then he told him.

There was a long pause. Then Chanler asked, 'Are you sure?'

'I'm sure. I took it to a guy at Tiffany's. If they don't know, who does?'

Chanler asked Tugger to fax him the information aboard the ship. The storm suddenly cut the connection and the operator wasn't able to get through again. Chanler sat on the bed, trying to decide what to say to Mattie. In the end, he decided to say nothing.

An hour later, when Mattie returned from the spa, Chanler was still seated on the bed in his khakis and T-shirt, looking at the journal.

'I guess you like your present,' she said.

'. . . Yes. Thank you. Did you read it?'

'Glanced at it,' she said, coming close. 'Why aren't you in your tux?'

Chanler held up the diary. 'Diana lied at DeWitt's inquest. I can prove it now.'

'What are you talking about?' She leaned over, took off his glasses, kissed him. 'You know, Mark was right. You're kind of nuts on the subject of my family.'

He put the glasses back. 'I know why she lied.'

'Why?'

'She killed her husband.'

Mattie's head pulled quickly back. '. . . Channie, come on.'

'No, I'm serious. Diana Rawlings killed your great-grandfather. If that's who he was.'

Mattie stared at him with that strange, straight-on look that was so like the look of Mrs. Rawlings in the painting. 'What's that supposed to mean?' He didn't answer. 'First you're madly in love with her. Now you think she's a murderer. And she's just a painting.' Slowly she smiled and shrugged. 'Okay. So why do you think she killed him? Tell me while we get dressed.'

Chanler followed Mattie back to their bedroom. 'She was having an affair. And he found out.'

Mattie picked out a red dress. 'Oh? ... Who with?'

'Jacob Zanski.'

'Who?' Mattie sat at the vanity, began applying make-up.

'I told you about him. Remember?'

'... Oh, right. The painter.'

'Yes. Zanski, who painted her portrait. They were lovers.'
And sitting on the bed, Chanler read to her from DeWitt's journal.

> I cannot shake off Corinne's – ['His older sister, that would
> be your great-great-aunt,' Chanler explained] – disturbing
> letter. Her distasteful insinuations about Diana and this
> Zanski fellow ... Why shouldn't she walk with him in the
> park, or picnic with him by the lake for that matter? But
> Corinne can't bear the thought that the bulk of Father's
> estate should go to Diana, or to our children if we have
> them. I've written my sister to keep her base suspicions to
> herself.

Mattie looked into her vanity mirror, at Chanler standing behind her. 'That's it?' She frowned. Both spoke to their reflections in the glass. 'All that means is her husband's sister tried to make him *think* she was having an affair. It doesn't mean she was. Why shouldn't they picnic in the damn park? And even if she was, so what?'

Chanler looked at her in the mirror. 'They'd been married less than a year.'

'Well, you know what I mean.' Mattie handed Chanler the pearls his mother had given her the night before the wedding. He fastened the clasp. 'What I mean is, how do you get from that to she murdered him?'

Chanler held up the journal. 'Listen. "This evening in a shop in the Plaka, I found the most extraordinary bracelet, rubies set in twists of gold. Very Byzantine."' Chanler paused, looked up. 'The one you lost at our reception.' He read again. ' "The shopkeeper, a fat, keen-eyed woman absurdly claiming direct descent from Agamemnon, soon had me at her mercy, and I bought the damn thing for Diana. So I've said my good-byes at the dig – Trimmer was so kind as to be disappointed – and we sail in the morning. My return should put a stop to Corinne's innuendoes. Perhaps I'll take Diana to Alva and Willie's party myself." ' Chanler straightened his glasses, looked at Mattie.

Mattie shrugged at the mirror. 'I guess I don't get your point.'

His mild gray eyes moved down the line of her perfect neck to the white cream of her shoulder. 'You don't? Remember, Diana told everyone she didn't even know DeWitt had returned to the States before she went to the Vanderbilts'. But he brought the bracelet with him. He was bringing it to her. You see? She wore it the night of the ball. That means she had to have seen him that night.'

Mattie reminded Chanler that he'd told her himself that the portrait of Mrs. Rawlings as Dido at the Vanderbilt ball had been painted a whole year after the event. No doubt someone had found the bracelet in DeWitt's effects, had given it to his widow, and she'd added it to her costume when she'd sat for the painting.

Chanler shook his head. 'No. She wore it to Alva Vanderbilt's ball.'

'How do you know?'

'Tugger.'

'Oh, great. Tugger.'

Chanler then showed Mattie the daguerreotype of Mrs. Rawlings taken at the Vanderbilt mansion, the gift from Tugger that she had not yet seen. He pointed out the bracelet clearly visible on Diana's wrist.

'Tugger gave this picture to you at the airport? Why didn't he show it to me?'

Chanler made a gesture; it assumed that she was aware of Tugger's dislike of her and that Chanler wouldn't wish to remind her of that unpleasantness by mentioning Tugger at all. He said, 'She wore the bracelet to the ball. So what happened to DeWitt after he gave it to her? I have a theory about how she killed him.' He watched as Mattie slipped on the red dress. 'You gave me the proof, and I've worked it out.'

She turned for Chanler to do her zipper. 'You'll have to tell me later,' she said. 'We're going to be late.'

While Chanler was starting toward the shower, the phone rang; in the other room, Mattie told him to go ahead, she'd answer it. When he returned, she said it had just been their steward, reminding them they were to go to the captain's table.

At dinner, Mattie was at her most charming, and Chanler was generously congratulated on his marriage to so engaging a young woman.

'Yes,' Chanler said to the banker's wife to his right. 'I was in love with her before I even met her.' Months later, this woman told her husband back in Cleveland (when the 'Honeymoon Murder' made the papers even there) that she'd thought it such a romantic thing for a newly-wed to say.

Mattie left the table to return to their rooms to get casino chips she'd left in their safe; she wouldn't let Chanler go for her. She was talking with a stranger at their door when the steward appeared with a fax that had been sent to Mr. Swaine from the States. Mrs. Swaine said she'd take it to her husband. But when she returned to the dining room, she didn't mention the fax, nor the casino. She suggested they go to the Perseus Lounge at the stern of the ship instead. There were never many people there, and she loved listening to Chanler play his romantic old songs on the white baby grand.

Soon, with the bar closed, they were alone in the place with their bottle of champagne, the storm having driven the other passengers back to their cabins. Waves sprayed the decks and wind rattled the glass windows and doors. Although Mattie was cold, she didn't want to leave; she draped Chanler's tuxedo jacket over her shoulders. She kept filling his champagne glass as he answered her questions about what he'd learned of DeWitt and Diana Rawlings.

Chanler told her that the more he assembled the facts that he'd been unearthing for so long, the more they took the shape of a murder. The old rumors were true. Diana Rawlings was having an affair with the man who'd painted her portrait; in fact, now Chanler suspected she'd been involved with Zanski *before* she married DeWitt; DeWitt's sister Corinne had discovered (and written to inform her brother) that the painter's Battery studio was on the same block as the milliner's shop in which Diana McBride had worked. Zanski had talent but no money. Diana had ambition enough for two. She'd married DeWitt Rawlings so that, with his money and his name, she could make her way in Society, and make her lover's way as well. Perhaps that's as far as she planned the future.

But things went wrong. First, DeWitt's sister saw the lovers together. Worse, Diana found out she was pregnant and knew that if anyone calculated carefully enough (as apparently no one ever did, not until Chanler worked out the arithmetic a hundred years later), it would be clear when she delivered that she'd conceived while her husband was inconveniently on the other side of the Atlantic. So the child had to be Zanski's. Still, Chanler admitted, Diana might have somehow managed to squirm out of everything; DeWitt was deeply enamored of her and refused to listen to her detractors. But something catastrophic had happened the night of the Vanderbilt ball. Somehow, the betrayed husband had been confronted with evidence even he could no longer evade.

Chanler showed Mattie the computer printout that listed exactly when DeWitt's ship had docked in the New York harbor on March 26, 1883. It was a good six hours before Diana would have left with the DeLanceys to walk around the corner to the Vanderbilts' on Fifty-second Street.

'And that means?' asked Mattie, pouring him more champagne.

'That means DeWitt came home, completely unexpected, and caught Zanski and Diana in bed together or doing something he couldn't pretend was something else. Something that meant his sister was right. It was all over.'

Mattie jumped. With a sharp bang, the wind slapped open the glass door, sucking the flapping curtains out into the rain. Chanler had to throw himself against the door to get it closed. He was, he noticed, a little drunk, and he suddenly felt very sleepy. He suggested they go back to their cabin.

'No. Finish your story,' Mattie told him. 'It's fascinating. DeWitt came home that night and saw the lovers together . . .'

Removing his glasses to rub his eyes, Chanler nodded. 'Zanski left the room. DeWitt made it clear the marriage was over. Maybe he lost his temper and flung that bracelet at her. Diana saw herself losing everything. Social position. Wealth. A future for herself, for her unborn child, Zanski's child. I think she made her decision quickly. Her only hope was if no one ever knew he'd been there. Either the servants weren't at home or she avoided them. She pushed DeWitt down the stairs, or hit him with something. She killed him.'

Mattie nodded. 'To stop the divorce?'

'And everything that went with it.'

Mattie stared out at the black night. The wind smashed a deck chair against the glass, startling them. 'And then what?' she asked. 'She picks up the body, hails a hansom cab, hauls him out to their country house, and tosses him off the balcony? Come on!'

Chanler smiled at his wife sadly. 'No, I think Jacob Zanski did all that for her. He took care of it while she put on that gold gown, sprinkled rubies in her hair, and set out with Reverend and Mrs. DeLancey to the Vanderbilts' ball. Funny, if she hadn't been so vain that she couldn't resist wearing the bracelet, her secret would have been safe forever.'

Mattie laughed. 'Sweetheart, sometimes I think Diana Rawlings's life is more interesting to you than your own.' She yawned, turned the empty champagne bottle upside down in its bucket. 'So she steps over her husband's body and heads off to the Vanderbilts'. Pretty gutsy lady.'

'Very gutsy lady,' Chanler agreed.

'That invitation to the ball meant a lot to her ... But then, maybe that sounds unbelievable to you; like you say, you never wanted anything that much.'

'... Except you.'

'Well, darling, you've got me.' She showed him the channel-set, multiple-carat diamond wedding ring they'd bought at Tiffany's. 'And Diana, did she get what she wanted?'

'I think she always did.' After her great triumph at the ball, Mrs. Rawlings had returned home at dawn and waited in bed to be brought the shocking news of her husband's demise. Of course, Chanler wasn't the first to suspect something wasn't right; even back then questions were raised. There were inconsistencies in the evidence, rumors of adultery. But in the end, DeWitt's death was ruled an unfortunate accident. And in the end, despite Corinne Rawlings's long legal battle to contest her brother's will, Diana and her new-born baby, DeWitt Rawlings the Third, inherited everything. Diana never married Jacob Zanski, and their son never knew his father was not a Rawlings but an immigrant portrait painter. Maybe the lovers didn't dare risk marriage. Or maybe their passion was killed by the murder they concealed. Maybe it just wore itself out.

'And that,' concluded Chanler, unsteadily rising to his feet, 'is the end of the story. Mrs. Rawlings died in her bed, a grande dame of ninety. Her son, DeWitt the Third, lost most of the family fortune in the twenties' Crash. His son DeWitt took care of the rest.'

'My dad.'

'So you tell us.' Chanler loosened his tie.

She turned to him. 'Are we talking about something we're not talking about, Chanler? I mean, that is your style.'

'We're talking about pirates,' Chanler said. He made his way to the curved glass of the stern, looked out at the storm waves spuming over the rail. He thought he saw the shape of a man on the observation deck behind some cable housing, but it made no sense that anyone would be out in that kind of weather, and when he looked again whatever he'd seen was gone.

Mattie asked, 'Does it change how you feel about your beloved Mrs. Rawlings, now that you've proven she's a killer?'

Chanler turned back, shook his head, his eyes on hers. 'No, it doesn't change a thing. Funny.'

'Funny,' Mattie said. 'So, what do you do about it, even if it's true? Everybody's dead. And the money's all gone. I didn't inherit a cent.'

'Just the bracelet. And you lost that.' He waited for her to say something, but she just looked at him curiously. Finally, he added, 'Here's something else that's funny. Zanski died in his early forties. In his will, he left a dozen paintings "to his son." But since he didn't have a son, as far as anybody knew, and since Diana certainly wasn't about to admit that her little boy was Zanski's son, all the paintings went to some distant cousin. You know how much the last Zanski portrait sold for at Sotheby's?'

She shook her head.

'No? ... Three and a half million dollars,' Chanler replied. 'Actually, I thought you'd know, working there. I got that figure from a Sotheby's catalogue in your apartment.'

'Oh, maybe I knew it, I guess it didn't really register. Three and a half million? And he was so poor, she wouldn't marry him. Ironic.'

'Ironic. Also ironic that you seem to be a Zanski heir.'

She smiled at him. 'Maybe I ought to get in touch with the Zanskis, then. That is, if you think I'll be needing an income.'

Chanler staggered slightly when he took back the tuxedo jacket she held out; he'd drunk more champagne than he was used to. 'That's really ironic. You'd have to be a Rawlings to be a Zanski.'

'Chanler, I don't know what you're talking about.'

He smiled at her. 'I'm not an idiot, Mattie; I just love you.'

'I love you too.' She moved against him, pulled him against the glass door, kissed him, then kissed him again. 'I'm going to the casino; see you back at the suite.' He took her arm, feeling suddenly queasy, and fell back into his seat.

Mattie asked if he was all right and, being told that he felt nauseated, suggested that he stand outside just for a minute to clear his head, then they'd go back to their cabin. He said no, he'd be okay, go on to the casino. Handing him the tuxedo jacket he'd dropped, she helped him tug the glass door open. But she didn't follow him onto the deck.

The croupier congratulated Mattie; she was unusually lucky, and a crowd gathered to watch her win.

Early the next morning, the storm behind them, just before they docked in Santorini, a horrified Mattie frantically called the steward. She couldn't find her husband anywhere!

She said she'd left him the night before in the Perseus

Lounge. She'd assumed he was still there when she'd returned from the casino and, as she'd felt a little seasick, she'd taken a sedative and quickly fallen asleep. When she awoke early that morning, she thought he'd already gone down for breakfast, perhaps even gone ashore. But he wasn't in the dining room, and no tenders had yet left the disembarking station. Besides, his boarding pass was on the bureau, and why would he leave without it? Back in their suite, she realized that there were no traces of his having come back at all last night. She was growing alarmed.

They paged Chanler throughout the ship. There were twelve decks and fifteen hundred passengers, but they searched everywhere. Nothing. They interviewed the morning bartender in the Perseus Lounge, who said when he'd come on shift he'd found an empty bottle of champagne overturned in an ice bucket, and wet curtains caught in the starboard door to the observation deck. They sent out radio messages to all other ships in the vicinity. No one had rescued a passenger fallen overboard.

A solemn captain and ship's doctor spoke privately with young Mrs. Swaine. It distressed the captain deeply to have to ask her whether there was any cause that might lead her husband to take his own life. Stricken, indignant, Mattie dismissed the possibility. Her husband had to be somewhere on the ship. They continued looking. Other passengers assured the honeymooning bride that their prayers were with her, that surely her husband would show up safe and sound. But at three that afternoon, one of the crew found Chanler's tuxedo jacket, still soaked, in a heap under an overturned chair, right beside the rail on the observation deck. And by dusk, when the ship had to set sail for its next port, a man's patent-leather dress shoe had washed ashore.

Mattie identified it as Chanler's. Then they found bloodstains on the cable housing. The Santorini police arrived.

The captain felt he should prepare Mrs. Swaine for the probability that her husband – after drinking more than he was accustomed to – had walked out on deck for a breath of fresh air, tripped, and hit his head, disorienting him even further, recklessly climbed up on a railing (despite the posted warnings) and, losing his balance in the rough weather, fallen overboard. His cries unheard, he had been swept away to his death. Mrs. Swaine began to shake violently; the ship's doctor offered her tranquilizers, but she declined. She said she wouldn't give up hope for Chanler's return, but she would call his mother.

Chanler's mother took the next plane to Athens. She and Mattie were a comfort to each other; after a week, they were forced to accept the verdict of the Santorini police. Chanler was dead. His mother's only consolation was that her son's wife was pregnant with his child. She was very solicitous of Mattie, terrified that she would miscarry in her grief. Mattie phoned Chanler's best friend, Tugger Whitelaw, to tell him the news. She asked him to speak at Chanler's memorial service. As soon as she hung up, Tugger took six pages of notes to a friend at his firm who specialized in criminal law and who gave him the name of a homicide detective.

Two weeks after Chanler's memorial service, the detective, a good-looking young man from Queens, paid a call on the younger Mrs. Swaine at her mother-in-law's town house in the East Fifties. Mattie found him waiting for her in the living room, looking at her portrait in the gold BGC gown. It was, he said, a good likeness. The picture hung over the marble mantel, where it had been waiting to surprise Chanler on his return. The widow looked ill despite her lingering tan. Detective Eisenberg wondered if she'd mind a few questions. She wouldn't mind; she'd answered so many back in Greece. But questions about what?

The detective felt it only fair to tell her that certain accusations had been made by Mr. Timothy Whitelaw. Mattie confessed she was not surprised. Tugger had always been jealous of her, resented her taking Chanler away from him, and was spreading rumors about her even before the marriage. But as Mr. Whitelaw had been three thousand miles away from the site of her husband's accident, she hardly thought he could have anything useful to say about it.

Probably not, the detective agreed. But he guessed Mrs. Swaine knew how it was, how the system made them check things out, even things that probably weren't useful. Mrs. Swaine understood the detective's problem. How could she help? What was Tugger's accusation?

First the detective nonchalantly wondered if she would mind telling him a little about her background: for example, where she and her father, DeWitt Rawlings IV, had lived in California, where she'd gone to school, when she'd first come to New York. He appeared to be almost uninterested in her answers to his bland questions. Mattie noted that she could hardly see the point in them, but she answered pleasantly enough; after about twenty minutes, however, she admitted she was still under an emotional strain, and she hoped Mr. Eisenberg would excuse her.

'No problem. I just got a couple more things here.'

Mattie politely sat back down.

'How 'bout this guy, Mark Toral? What's your relationship with him?'

'I don't care for the insinuation.' She stood back up. 'I assume it originated with Mr. Whitelaw.'

'What insinuation?'

'Don't be coy, Mr. Eisenberg. Mark and I dated a few times years ago. Nothing serious. I haven't seen him since my wedding day.'

Eisenberg looked from her to the painting. 'You sure? See, Mr. Toral is kinda telling us something a little bit different.'

Mrs. Swaine blinked just once, then said that she didn't care what Mr. Toral might or might not be telling them. And now she would ask the detective to leave. He stood, rummaging through his jacket pockets until he found a balled-up handkerchief. Mattie's face stayed perfectly still as Eisenberg pulled out the bracelet of rubies twisted in gold. 'Mr. Whitelaw says he found this thing of yours at your wedding reception.' Eisenberg pointed at the portrait, where the same bracelet circled Mattie's perfect white wrist.

Mattie reached for the bracelet. 'Found it? I suspect he stole it.'

'Could be. He admits he wanted it real bad. Had an idea about it. Maybe,' Detective Eisenberg said, 'you could help me out with that. According to Mr. Whitelaw—'

She surprised him by interrupting. 'It's fake.'

Detective Eisenberg lost his bearings for a moment, not expecting the admission. 'You admit you told folks that this was a bracelet your dad inherited from some turn-of-the-century lady named Diana Rawlings, and that wasn't true?' She nodded. 'Well, then you know what the problem is. Mr. Whitelaw's appraiser at Tiffany's claims it's a couple of years old. And it's paste.'

'That's right.' Mattie looked at the young man coolly. Finally she said, '. . . So?'

'So.' He smiled.

'So, what's this got to do with Mark Toral?'

'That's what I need you to come to the station and tell me, Mrs. Swaine. Mr. Whitelaw's got his ideas. And I've had a lot of talks with your friend Mark and he's says he was on that honeymoon ship, whereas you'd think three would be a crowd. Which I guess is what he was thinking too. But the version I really want to hear is yours, ma'am. For instance, how 'bout telling me what's your real name?'

'Mrs. Chanler Swaine,' she replied.

'Yeah.' He nodded at her slowly. 'I guess that's true.'

Mattie walked to the door. 'I think I'll call my attorney, Mr. Eisenberg. Would you excuse me?'

'No problem.' He sat down, facing the portrait.

In the end, Mattie confessed to a number of things. But not the murder. And only the murder was a crime. Besides, Mark Toral had already confessed to that, before his lawyer could stop him. Tugger told him that he should have known from his love of film noir that he didn't have anywhere near the nerves of Mattie Rawlings Swaine – born Madeline Gart – and that she'd throw him over in the end. Mark insisted Mattie knew nothing about his killing Chanler and she agreed with him, but they put her on trial anyhow. Many were sympathetic to Mattie, especially the elderly Mrs. Swaine, who'd lost her only child and lived for the birth of her grandchild. Mattie asked their friends to forgive Tugger's animosity to her; he'd lost his best friend and was irrational from grief. She could understand.

'The Honeymoon Murder,' the papers called it. Tugger sat in the courtroom day after day, taking notes as Mattie admitted the things Tugger had helped the prosecution already prove. Of course, she and her defense team put a very different construction on them. In their version Mattie had been a poor, hardworking young woman seduced by a good-looking sophisticate (Mark) into playing a prank on his friend Chanler (by pretending to be descended from Diana Rawlings). In their version, during the playing of this prank, she'd fallen in love with Chanler and broken off with Mark. But she'd been too ashamed to confess her original lie and so allowed Chanler to go on believing she was a Rawlings when she was no more real than the bracelet. She'd tried over and over to say no to his marriage proposals, feeling unworthy, but she'd loved him so much. She cried when she said that. Her defense attorney told her she was fantastic on the stand.

The prosecution told a very different story. According to the prosecution, Madeline Gart had met Mark at a cigar and martini club in Los Angeles and had promptly started an affair with him, one of many she'd had, despite her youth. Mark had just been let go from his job in his uncle's brokerage firm for buying a stock he was sure was going to double, with funds he was sure no one would find out didn't belong to him; his uncle covered the loss. Madeline was at a shop in Beverly Hills, selling to naive millionaires in search of a heritage overpriced antiquarian prints and autographs, many of them forged, some of them by her – by no means her first con, despite her youth. She had a knack for such things.

Mark fell in love; he wanted to marry Mattie. She declined, and he didn't take it well. The second time he came to her apartment and caused a scene, she had her neighbor throw him in the pool. She refused to answer his calls when he tried to apologize.

Around this time, the alcoholic DeWitt Rawlings IV came into Mattie's store to try to sell off little bits of his past, just enough to allow him to finish drinking himself to death. From Rawlings, Mattie learned how amazingly she resembled the portrait of his grandmother Diana that was hanging in a place called the Parnassus Club back in New York. He invited her out for a drink and, sensing something big yet undefined in this connection, Mattie said yes. The lonely, childless, dying old man developed a kind of crush on her; she would listen for hours to all the stories about his once-grand family, including the old rumors about the famous painter Jacob Zanski. One day he brought Mattie his grandfather's 'Mediterranean journal' and she read it, much more closely than she'd admitted to Chanler. If she'd noticed the implication that Mrs. Rawlings was a murderer, it didn't interest her. What interested her was that Mrs. Rawlings had slept with Zanski. She got an idea. If she could 'prove' that Diana's son, DeWitt Rawlings III, was really the son of Jacob Zanski, and 'prove' that she, Mattie, was the daughter of DeWitt Rawlings IV, then Mattie was in line to inherit, not Rawlings money (there wasn't any), but Zanski money (there were dozens of Zanski portraits still in the private collection of the family of a distant cousin who'd wrongly inherited them, and they were worth millions of dollars each). Rawlings grew quite dependent on Mattie in his last months; she was very sweet to him, his only visitor. She had pictures taken of them together. She pored over his letters, photos, little mementos, and the day he died, she took them all. She was in a way his only heir. For with Rawlings now in no position to argue, Mattie was set to become a Zanski by claiming to be Rawlings's daughter; she worked on the plan patiently for over a year, including the forging of the legal documents and personal letters needed to make her case.

And here – as the prosecutor said – here's the thing about successful con artists like Madeline Gart. After all that preparation to file her claim to be the true Zanski heir, she threw the whole plan away. Why? Because something better came along, something simpler and quicker and much, much less risky. That something was Chanler Swaine.

By this point Mark had returned to New York, but he wasn't over Mattie. He called her, sent her roses, told her he was back on his feet: A college friend (Chanler) had helped him secure a job in the best brokerage firm in Manhattan. Mark wanted Mattie to move to New York and marry him. She said no, but she didn't hang up. Then one night during their phone talk, Mark happened to mention his friend Chanler's fascination with the painting of Diana Rawlings in the Parnassus Club, where Mark, too, was now a member; he mentioned it to Mattie because she'd told him she was supposed to resemble the portrait, and he wanted her to know that she certainly did.

According to the prosecution, it was this news about Mark's very wealthy friend's peculiar obsession with Diana Rawlings that gave Mattie her next idea.

To Mark's delight, she decided to come East. She found a job at Sotheby's. (Her recommendations – most of them forged – were impressive.) She and Mark resumed their affair. Although she refused to live with him, they went out nearly every night; they both had expensive tastes in restaurants and a reckless habit of betting extravagantly on horses with large odds. Soon Mark was playing the market to try to cover his credit cards; it didn't work. It was then that Mattie told him the new plan. It was simple. Since Mark was always trying to find a girl for the reluctant Chanler, it would be easy for him to introduce Chanler to Mattie Rawlings. His bizarre infatuation with the portrait would make things even easier. She would marry Chanler, divorce him, keep half his assets and, after a decent interval, return to Mark. Mark didn't like the part that involved her marrying Chanler, but by now he would do anything Mattie wanted. She had Mark bring her to the Parnassus Club, where they took a photograph of the portrait of Diana Rawlings in order to have a cheap copy made of the bracelet in the picture.

Chanler was smitten the moment he saw her in the Parnassus Club. The rest, said the prosecutor, was as easy as Mattie predicted: She seduced Chanler Swaine through her resemblance to Mrs. Rawlings, whose descendant she pretended to be. She married Chanler Swaine for his money. But when she learned that Chanler's mother would stop her from getting the money if she divorced Chanler or was caught out in an affair, she had to change her plan. Now, claimed the prosecutor, she needed to maneuver her lover, Mark Toral, into killing her husband. She began by telling Mark at the wedding reception that she was going to try to make the marriage to Chanler work.

The day after Mattie and Chanler left on their honeymoon, a disconsolate Mark flew to Athens and, according to his confession, tracked down their ship. He admitted to a fatal passion for Mattie that made the reality of her marriage to another man unbearable. He began calling the ship and, finally, at Mykonos, she agreed to meet him, which she did on her island 'shopping trip.' It was then that she told Mark that divorcing Chanler would not solve their problems; his mother had taken care of that. She was going to stay with her husband, and Mark had to leave them alone. Forever. Then she kissed him. And kissed him again. How, she whispered, could she ever give him up? She agreed to meet him onboard and gave him Chanler's pass so he could board the ship. According to the prosecutor, she knew exactly what she was doing. That night, his passion and jealousy heated to a boil, Mark called Mattie, and they arranged to meet. But when Mattie met Mark at the suite (where the steward saw him and later identified him from a photograph), she told him Chanler had grown suspicious; they couldn't risk ever being together again. Not ever. It was over. This was not something Mark was willing to accept and, according to the prosecutor, Mattie knew that. The question was, did she know that Mark was following them, was hiding out on the stern deck, when she took Chanler back to the deserted Perseus Lounge; did she get him drunk and lure him outside? There was no doubt that that was when Mark saw his chance, knocked Chanler out, and shoved him over the railing, then sneaked off the ship with the early-morning crowd headed for the Santorini shops. DNA analysis showed traces of Chanler's blood on Mark's jacket sleeve. And Mark admitted the crime to Detective Eisenberg.

The prosecutor told the jury that there was no doubt that Mattie had put Mark up to the murder. Her defense team told the jury that Mattie was a victim; she had followed Mark to New York because she loved him. Once there, she'd agreed, at his request, to play a foolish but innocent trick on his friend Chanler by pretending to be a Rawlings. But in the process, she'd fallen in love with Chanler, broken off with Mark, and accepted Chanler's marriage proposal. It wasn't her fault that Mark wouldn't give her up. He'd caused such a scene at her wedding that she'd had to ask him to leave (many witnesses confirmed this). She had no idea Mark had somehow sneaked aboard the ship with them in Santorini, and certainly no idea that his violent obsession would lead him to murder her husband. Mattie broke down when she said this, blaming herself for Chanler's death.

The jury believed the defense team. They felt sorry for Mattie, just as the defense advised them to do. There the poor young widow sat, after all, pregnant with her dead husband's baby. After some hours of deliberation, they found Mattie not guilty. Mark would not testify against her. Tugger couldn't get him to see that Mattie had used him. Mark still thought they were in love. Mattie walked out of the courtroom, pausing to nod at Tugger Whitelaw, who turned his back on her. A few days later, Mark was sentenced to ten years in prison for second-degree murder. It was a good deal; there were, after all, no witnesses, no corpse, and possibly no premeditation. The judge agreed with the press, who didn't believe Mark had murdered Chanler for money but on the spur of the moment, driven to the act by his jealousy over Mattie. Mark had the looks of a man who'd murder for love.

Naturally Mattie stayed in the Swaine town house with her mother-in-law. Sadly, the elder Mrs. Swaine, broken by grief, died of a sudden stroke before ever seeing the grandchild she'd been living for. The baby was a boy, with (Tugger heard) very blue eyes. Tugger told Mark about the child when he visited him at the prison. Mark hadn't heard about the birth and was upset when Tugger told him how much the boy looked like him. Mattie, Mark admitted, hadn't kept in touch.

About a year later, Tugger started dating a young woman who worked at the courthouse, someone he'd known back in his home town in Maryland. She called him Tim. She didn't run with his old group, and slowly Tugger drifted away as well, although a few friends from Yale did give him a bachelor party when he (the last of the bachelors) married the young woman.

He took her once to eat at the Parnassus Club and, on their way out, he ran into Mattie Swaine, hosting a dinner to plan the upcoming BGC. She was chair of the invitation committee, and the chair always hosted the dinner that decided what the year's good cause should be. Mattie was seated beside her fiancé, one of the old group, one of the wealthiest – and although Mattie had plenty of money of her own by now, Tugger suspected she didn't feel it was enough. From the time of the trial, this young man (another friend of Chanler's) had been a staunch supporter of Mattie's innocence, absolutely sure that she had had nothing to do with Mark's 'craziness.' A few months ago, the young man had warned Tugger that if he didn't quit talking against Mattie, they'd have to stop seeing each other. So Tugger walked past the table without speaking to him. To his surprise, Mattie called out, 'Tugger,' and asked if they could talk for a second. She smiled. 'You're looking good, Tug.'

'Yes, I've lost some weight,' Tugger said. 'You oughta go see Mark, Mattie. I mean, after all, he killed Channie for you; it's the least you could do.'

She smiled at him. 'Never one to beat around the bush, were you?'

'No.'

It was a diamond bracelet that Mattie now wore. It looked real, and no doubt this one was. She pointed at her wrist. 'Tug, you remember that fax you sent Chanler on the ship, about how I'd faked Diana Rawlings's bracelet? I'm just wondering, had you told him about it before you sent the fax?'

'Yes. He called me that night.'

'I thought so. He was acting funny.'

Tugger shook his head. 'Is that why you had him murdered? He knew the truth about you?'

She smiled again. 'You think it would have made any difference to Channie? That's *why* he loved me.' She pointed over at the painting above the green marble mantelpiece, *Mrs. Rawlings as Dido. Mrs. Vanderbilt's Ball, 1883*. 'That's why he loved *her*. That was the whole point, Tugger; you didn't get it.'

'I don't think Mark got it either.'

She nodded. 'Mark always had a serious problem with impulse control. He had no patience. He wanted what he wanted and he could never wait.'

Tugger smiled. 'I think he's going to feel that way about getting his son back, too.'

He left her standing there and was convinced that he'd shaken her; not much maybe, and not for long, but he felt good about it.

Tugger's wife was waiting. She looked back at Mattie Swaine, standing alone near the painting of Diana Rawlings. 'I see what you meant. If you hadn't told me,' she said to Tugger, 'I would have thought they were the same woman.'

He put his arm through his wife's as he led her out of the room. He said, 'They were.'

ED MCBAIN

....

The question asked most frequently of writers is, 'Where do you get your ideas?' Stephen King says, 'Utica. There's a little shop that sells them.' It's the question we all want answered, and it's the one many authors would like answered, too. They mostly don't know.

This little story by Evan Hunter, using his famous pseudonym, does have a recognizable genesis. He was recently married to a lovely woman who brought many things to their marriage – including a small dog. While the dog and the husband get along wonderfully now, it was not mutual love at first sight. What most of us might fantasize about in the quiet of the night becomes a story idea for an author.

Although this bizarre tale is quite different from his best-selling 87th Precinct sagas, it should come as no surprise at all. He is one of the most versatile writers alive, having written children's stories, science fiction, serious popular fiction, films, and, currently, a Broadway-bound musical, The Night They Raided Minsky's.

BARKING AT BUTTERFLIES

By Ed McBain

Damn dog barked at everything.

Sounds nobody else could hear, in the middle of the night the damn dog barked at them.

'He's protecting us,' Carrie would say.

Protecting us. Damn dog weighs eight pounds soaking wet, he's what's called a Maltese poodle, he's protecting us. His name is Valletta, which is the capital of Malta. That's where the breed originated, I suppose. Some sissy Maltese nobleman must've decided he needed a yappy little lapdog that looked like a white feather duster. Little black nose. Black lips. Black button eyes. Shaggy little pipsqueak named Valletta. Who barked at everything from a fart to a butterfly. Is that someone ringing the bell? The damn dog would hurl himself at the door like a grizzly bear, yelping and growling and raising a fuss that could wake the dead in the entire county.

'He's just protecting us,' Carrie would say.

Protecting us.

I hated that damn dog.

I still do.

He was Carrie's dog, you see. She rescued him from a husband-and-wife team who used to beat him when he was just a puppy – gee, I wonder why. This was two years before we got married. I used to think he was cute while she was training him. She'd say, 'Sit, Valletta,' and he'd walk away. She'd say, 'Stay, Valletta,' and he'd bark. She'd say, 'Come, Valletta,' and he'd take a nap. This went on for six months. He still isn't trained.

Carrie loved him to death.

As for El Mutto, the only thing on earth *he* loved was Carrie. Well, you save a person's life, he naturally feels indebted. But this went beyond mere gratitude. Whenever Carrie left the house, Valletta would lie down just inside the door, waiting for her to come home. Serve him a hot pastrami on rye, tell him, 'Come, Valletta, time to eat,' he'd look at me as if he'd been abandoned by the love of his life and never cared to breathe again. When he heard her car in the driveway, he'd start squealing and peeing on the rug. The minute she put her key in the lock, he jumped up in the air like a Chinese acrobat, danced and pranced on his hind legs when she opened the door, began squealing and leaping all around her until she knelt beside him and scooped him into her embrace and made comforting little sounds to him: 'Yes, Valletta, yes, Mommy, what a good boy, oh, yes, what a beautiful little puppyboy.'

I used to joke about cooking him.

'Maltese meatloaf is delicious,' I used to tell Carrie. 'We'll pluck him first, and then wash him real good, and stuff him and put him in the oven for what, an hour? Maybe forty-five minutes, the size of him. Serve him with roast potatoes and—'

'He understands every word you say,' she'd tell me.

Damn dog would just cock his head and look up at me. Pretended to be bewildered, the canny little son of a bitch.

'Would you like to be a meatloaf?' I'd ask him.

He'd yawn.

'You'd better be a good dog or I'll sell you to a Filipino man.'

'He understands you.'

'You want to go home with a Filipino man?'

'Why do you talk to him that way?'

'In the Philippines they *eat* dogs, did you know that, Valletta? Dogs are a delicacy in the Philippines. You want to go home with a Filipino man?'

'You're hurting him.'

'He'll turn you into a rack of Maltese chops, would you like that, Valletta?'

'You're hurting *me*, too.'

'Or some breaded Maltese cutlets, what do you say, Valletta? You want to go to Manila?'

'Please don't, John. You know I love him.'

Damn dog would rush into the bathroom after her, sit by the tub while she took her shower, lick the water from her toes while she dried herself. Damn dog would sit at her feet while she was peeing on the toilet. Damn dog would even sit beside the bed whenever we made love. I asked her once to please put him out in the hall.

'I feel as if there's a *pervert* here in the bedroom watching us,' I said.

'He's not watching us.'

'He's sitting there *staring* at us.'

'No, he's not.'

'Yes, he is. It embarrasses me, him staring at my privates that way.'

'Your privates? When did you start using *that* expression?'

'Ever since he started staring at it.'

'He's not staring at it.'

'He is. In fact, he's *glaring* at it. He doesn't like me making love to you.'

'Don't be silly, John. He's just a cute little puppydog.'

One day, cute little puppydog began barking at *me*.

I came in the front door, and the stupid little animal was sitting smack in the middle of the entry, snarling and barking at me as if I were a person come to read the gas meter.

'What?' I said.

He kept barking.

'You're barking at *me*?' I said. 'This is *my* house, I *live* here, you little shit, how *dare* you bark at me?'

'What is it, what is it?' Carrie yelled, rushing into the hallway.

'He's barking at me,' I said.

'Shhh, Valletta,' she said. 'Don't bark at John.'

He kept barking, the little well-trained bastard.

'How would you like to become a Maltese hamburger?' I asked him.

He kept barking.

I don't know when I decided to kill him.

Perhaps it was the night Carrie seated him at the dinner table with us. Until then, she'd been content to have him sitting at our feet like the despicable little beggar he was, studying every bite we took, waiting for scraps from the table.

'Go ahead,' I'd say, 'watch every morsel we put in our mouths. You're *not* getting fed from the table.'

'Oh, John,' Carrie would say.

'I can't enjoy my meal with him staring at me that way.'

'He's not staring at you.'

'What do you call what he's doing right this minute? Look at him! If that isn't staring, what is it?'

'I think you're obsessed with this idea of the dog staring at you.'

'Maybe because he *is* staring at me.'

'If he is, it's because he loves you.'

'He doesn't love me, Carrie.'

'Yes, he does.'

'He loves *you*.'

'He loves you, too, John.'

'No, just you. In fact, if you want to talk about obsession, *that's* obsession. What that damn mutt feels for you is *obsession*.'

'He's not a mutt, and he's not obsessed. He just wants to be part of the family. He sees us eating, he wants to join us. Come, Valletta, come sweet puppyboy, come to little Mommy, come sit with your family,' she said, and hoisted him off the floor and plunked him down on a chair between us.

'I'll get your dish, sweet babypup,' she said.

'Carrie,' I said, 'I will not have that mutt sitting at the table with us.'

'He's not a mutt,' she said. 'He's purebred.'

'Valletta,' I said, 'get the hell off that chair or I'll—'

He began barking.

'You mustn't raise your hand to him,' Carrie said. 'He was abused. He thinks you're about to hit him.'

'*Hit* him?' I said. 'I'm about to *kill* him!'

The dog kept barking.

And barking.

And barking.

I guess that's when I decided to do it.

October is a good time for dying.

'Come, Valletta,' I said, 'let's go for a walk.'

He heard me say 'Come,' so naturally he decided to go watch television.

'Is Daddy taking you for a walk?' Carrie asked.

Daddy.

Daddy had Mr. Smith and Mr. Wesson in the pocket of his bush jacket. Daddy was going to walk little pisspot here into the woods far from the house and put a few bullets in his head and then sell his carcass to a passing Filipino man or toss it to a wayward coyote or drop it in the river. Daddy was going to tell Carrie that her prized purebred mutt had run away, naturally, when I commanded him to come. I called and called, I would tell her, but he ran and ran, and God knows where he is now.

'Don't forget his leash,' Carrie called from the kitchen.

'I won't, darling.'

'Be careful,' she said. 'Don't step on any snakes.'

'Valletta will protect me,' I said, and off we went.

The leaves were in full voice, brassy overhead, rasping underfoot. Valletta kept backing off on the red leather leash, stubbornly planting himself every ten feet or so into the woods, trying to turn back to the house where his beloved mistress awaited his return. I kept assuring him that we were safe here under the trees, leaves dropping gently everywhere around us. 'Come, little babypup,' I cooed, 'come little woofikins, there's nothing can hurt you here in the woods.'

The air was as crisp as a cleric's collar.

When we had come a far-enough distance from the house, I reached into my pocket and took out the gun. 'See this, Valletta?' I said. 'I am going to shoot you with this. You are never going to bark again, Valletta. You are going to be the most silent dog on earth. Do you understand, Valletta?'

He began barking.

'Quiet,' I said.

He would not stop barking.

'Damn you!' I shouted. 'Shut up!'

And suddenly he yanked the leash from my hands and darted away like the sneaky little sissydog he was, all white and furry against the orange and yellow and brown of the forest floor, racing like a ragged whisper through the carpet of leaves, trailing the red leash behind him like a narrow trickle of blood. I came thrashing after him. I was no more than six feet behind him when he ran into a clearing saturated with golden light. I followed him with the gun hand, aiming at him. Just as my finger tightened on the trigger, Carrie burst into the clearing from the opposite end.

'No!' she shouted, and dropped to her knees to scoop him protectively into her arms, the explosion shattering the incessant whisper of the leaves, the dog leaping into her embrace, blood flowering on her chest, oh dear God, no, I thought, oh dear sweet Jesus, no, and dropped the gun and ran to her and pressed her bleeding and still against me while the damn dumb dog barked and barked.

He has not barked since.

For him, it must seem as if she's gone someplace very far away, somewhere never even remotely perceived in his tiny Maltese mentality. In a sense this is true. In fact, I have repeated the story so often to so many people that I've come to believe it myself. I told her family and mine, I told all our friends, I even told the police, whom her brother was suspicious and vile enough to call, that I came home from work one day and she was simply gone. Not a hint that she was leaving. Not even a note. All she'd left behind was the dog. And she hadn't even bothered to feed him before her departure.

Valletta often wanders into the woods looking for her.

He circles the spot where two autumns ago her blood seeped into the earth. The area is bursting with fresh spring growth now, but he circles and sniffs the bright green shoots, searching, searching. He will never find her, of course. She is wrapped in a tarpaulin and buried deep in the woods some fifty miles north of where the three of us once lived together, Carrie and I and the dog.

There are only the two of us now.

He is all I have left to remind me of her.

He never barks and I never speak to him.

He eats when I feed him, but then he walks away from his bowl without once looking at me and falls to the floor just inside the entrance door, waiting for her return.

I can't honestly say I like him any better now that he's stopped barking. But sometimes . . .

Sometimes when he cocks his head in bewilderment to observe a floating butterfly, he looks so cute I could eat him alive.

JOYCE CAROL OATES

....

As a writer of serious literary fiction, in both the novel and short-story form, Joyce Carol Oates has achieved extraordinary success by any standard of measurement.

In recent years, it seems that an avid interest in reading mystery fiction has influenced her enough so that she has begun to write in the mystery genre – broadly defined, true, but still genuine mystery fiction – with greater and greater frequency.

Having already written psychological suspense novels under the Rosamond Smith pseudonym, as well as a Gothick and a fictional account of the murder of Mary Jo Kopechne at the hands of Ted Kennedy, she has recently written My Heart Laid Bare, *an epic novel about a family of nineteenth-century con artists, and numerous short stories about crime and punishment. She has had a story selected for each of the first two annual editions of* Best American Mystery Stories. *There is no reason to think she won't have one in* every *issue. As one of the shining literary lights of our age, and one of the hardest-working, most dedicated authors in America, she will have earned the honor.*

THE VAMPIRE

By Joyce Carol Oates

1.

Through the rifle scope the woman's head silhouetted by light drifts like a wayward balloon.

Staring into darkness. Into him.

No. She can't see. The part-shuttered windowpanes, the bright-lit room behind her, would reflect light.

Seeing her own face, her fleshy torso.

Seeing her eclipsed eyes. Seeing nothing.

Now she's sighted through the rifle scope from the rear of the tall narrow house where there's a shallow ridge of grassy earth.

Through the rifle scope hair-fine lines crossing to indicate that lethal spot at the very base of the skull.

His forefinger on the trigger. Squeezing.

Except now seen at an angle, in fact barely seen, through the rifle scope as she moves through the kitchen into that alcove off the kitchen, what is it – the pantry. She's in the pantry. Where there's a second, waist-high refrigerator and a freezer.

That freezer stocked with venison. One of Carlin's fans

brought them. Just a token of my esteem. My admiration for your good work. Bless you.

Through the rifle scope the woman's eyes glisten.

Through the rifle scope she's seen now from beneath. Not twelve feet away. Yet (there's music playing inside the house, loud) she hasn't heard a sound, no footstep. His quickened breath, a faint steaming breath in the just-freezing air she hasn't seen and will not see.

No moon tonight. Yes, a moon, a crescent moon (he's checked the newspaper, the weather box), but massed cumulus clouds, gusty autumn, and no moonlight to expose him. In his night clothes. Night-camouflage. Hooded canvas jacket purchased for this night. The color of night.

Beneath the side window, spongy leafy earth. He knows he's leaving footprints, which is why he'd purchased, at a Sears in Morgantown, not the same store in which he'd purchased the jacket, a pair of rubber boots two sizes larger than his own.

Which he'll dispose of hundreds of miles away from the house in which the dead woman will be discovered, encircled by footprints in spongy leafy earth.

Through the rifle scope – is the woman smiling? Smiling!

She's speaking on a cellular phone tucked into the crook of her neck. That slow sensuous smile. Greedy gloating smile. Incisors damply glistening.

Through the rifle scope the crossed hairs, that fleshy face, smiling.

Through the rifle scope moving about idly as she speaks on the phone. Unconsciously caressing her breasts. Smiling, and laughing. Speaking to a lover. One of the widow's lovers. *Since your death. Since she's begun to feed.*

Through the rifle scope the woman's head large as a

dinner plate. He wonders will it shatter like a dinner plate. He wonders whether anyone will hear the shattering.

In Buckhannon, West Virginia. On a moon-shrouded autumn night.

How many months, now it's been more than a year, since Carlin Ritchie's death he isn't sure. He'd count on his fingers except his forefinger is in use.

But his arms ache! This heavy rifle he isn't used to, the long barrel. Purchased especially for tonight. His arms, his shoulders, his backbone and his wrists ache. His jaws ache from that fixed grimace he isn't conscious of, next time he sees his face, examines his stubbled face in a mirror (in a motel near Easton, Pennsylvania) he'll see the creases etched in the skin as with a knife blade. How he's aged.

Through the rifle scope, a woman's torso. Shapely breasts, shoulders. He'd caressed, once: he knows. In layers of clothing, gypsy-clothing Carlin called it, admiring, lovesick, velvets and silks and Indian muslin, long gauzy skirts swishing against the floor. Even at home, by herself, she's in costume. Through the rifle scope laughing like a girl, eager, shrewd, wetting her lips, unconsciously stroking her breasts. Through the rifle scope on display as if she knows (but of course she can't know) she's observed.

On TV it looked as if she'd dyed her hair a darker, richer red. Tincture of purple. Yet streaks of silvery-white, theatrical as bars of paint. *How does it feel? Widow? His name, his memory. Dedicating her life.*

Through the rifle scope, that life. Will it shatter, like crockery? Will any neighbors hear?

But the nearest neighbors are at least a quarter mile away. And this wind tonight. A low rumbling, a sound of thunder in the mountains. No one will hear.

Through the rifle scope she's moving toward the stairs. Still talking on the phone. Slow hip-swaying walk. She's gained how many pounds since becoming a widow, twenty pounds, twenty-five, not a fat woman but fleshy, ample. Solid. Those solid breasts. Skin that exudes heat. Burning to the touch. He knows!

His finger on the trigger. For in another minute she'll have climbed the stairs. In another minute she'll be out of the rifle sight. He's anxious, on the veranda. Peering through a side window. Risking being seen. Boots trailing mud. Nudging the barrel of the rifle against the very glass. This wide, old-fashioned veranda on which Carlin lay. *Don't want to die. Yes, but I'm ready. I want to be brave. I'm a coward, I want to be brave. Help me.* On this moonward side of the house, if there were a moon this October night, which there isn't. *Like God watching over me* Carlin said *if there's a God but I guess there is not.*

Which is why, through the rifle scope, or not, we die.

2.

It might be that I know of a murder soon to be committed, and it might be that I don't. I mean – I don't know if the murder will be committed, if the murderer is serious. (Though he surely seems serious.) Does this make me an accessory? Am I involved, whether I wish to be or not? I don't mean just legally, I mean morally. What's the right thing to do here? Say I make a call to the potential victim, what do I say? 'Ma'am, you don't know me, but your life is in danger. You're hated, and you're wanted dead.' The woman would say, 'Is this some kind of joke? Who are you?' I'd say, 'It doesn't matter who I am. Your life is in danger.' She'd be getting upset, maybe hysterical, and what could I tell her, really? How could I save her, if the man who wants to kill her is determined to kill her? I surely couldn't give her his name. Even if that makes me an accessory. And I surely couldn't inform the police, any police. And anyway – does such a woman deserve to be saved?

My cousin Rafe has said, *There are folks who deserve to die because they don't deserve to live, it's that simple. They must be stopped in their paths of destruction.*

I've known about this murder, this potential murder, for less than a week. Never did I ask for such knowledge. I'm not a man who thinks obsessively. I mean, I'm not a man who broods. I'm a tool-and-die designer, I'm skilled at my job, working with my brains and my hands, and when I'm working I'm focused like a laser beam – I put in an eight-hour day (we're on computers now doing three-dimensional design) and when I'm through for the day, I'm through. Like, wiped out. And now knowing of this murder-to-be, I'm having trouble concentrating at work. I'm having trouble driving my car. Even eating. Trying to listen to my wife, to tune in to something besides my thoughts. *She is one of these, an emissary of Satan. A vampire. Must be stopped.* My life at home is a quiet life. We've been married a long time and neither of us will surprise the other except if my wife knew my thoughts she'd be surprised, shocked. Last night was the worst yet. Trying to sleep. Kicking at the bedclothes like they're something trying to smother me and grinding my molars (a habit I'd gotten into when our two boys were young teenagers making our lives hell, but I hadn't done for years) so my wife wakes me, frightened – 'Honey, what is it? What's wrong?' She switches on the light to look at me and I try to hide my face. I know what she's thinking: I might be having a heart attack – her father died of a heart attack at around my age, forty-four. That's young, but not too young. My own father had a saying – *You're never too young to die.* And it's true; my heart is pounding so hard you can feel the bed shake and I'm covered in cold sweat and shivering and for a minute I don't even know where I am. I'd had a few drinks before going to bed and my mind's like cobwebs. I tell her, 'Nothing! Nothing is wrong. Leave me alone.'

What the hell can I tell my wife, who loves me and who I love that when she woke me up I was crouched in the dark outside some house I'd never seen before, in some place I'd never been, peeking at a woman inside the house through a long-range rifle scope? A woman who's a total stranger to me? And my finger on the trigger of the rifle? Me, Harrison Healy, who's never even touched a gun in my life, let alone aimed it at another human being?

3.

I never asked for such knowledge, God knows. It was my cousin Rafe spilled it into me like you'd tip something poisonous into a stream.

There I was at the county courthouse. Kind of anxious and self-conscious, first time I'd been summoned for jury duty in my life. And practically the first person I see in this big drafty windowless room in the basement where we're told to wait is my cousin Rafe. Rafe Healy. Who's two years younger than me, at least three inches taller, and thirty pounds heavier – a tall, husky, sort of shuffling man in overalls, a gingery beard and thinning hair sticking up around his head so he looks like (my wife used to say when we saw Rafe, which hasn't been lately) an accident getting ready to happen. Rafe commands attention in any situation because of his height and girth and his mode of dress and that look in his face like a beacon turned on high – his pebbly eyes sort of shining out. He's always looked younger than his age, even with that scruffy beard and hair and the hard-drinking life he's led. And the drugs. Rafe's an artist, you'd have to call him; he does clay pots, ceramics, latch hook rugs, and quilts. He's been written up in magazines and has had exhibits in museums, even in New York. You don't think of a man making quilts, but Rafe Healy is said to be one of the leading quilters in the United States. Nobody in the family knows what to make of him. Mostly, they're sort of embarrassed. You could be switching TV channels seeing what's on and there on PBS there's Rafe Healy's broad earnest sunburned face, he's being inter-viewed standing in front of a quilt that looks like a constellation in the night sky, saying something weird like *I need to talk to myself when I'm working. Otherwise I'd disappear into my hands, I'd cease to exist.* My wife disapproves of Rafe for a number of reasons and I can't argue she's wrong. Mainly it has to do with Rafe and drugs. Maybe ten, twelve years ago we were on friendly terms and we'd have Rafe over for dinner and he'd think nothing of taking out a pipe, smoking some sweetish-stale-smelling weed right in our living room, and looking surprised when Rosalind got upset and told him to put it out. Another time he showed up for dinner bringing a woman with him, an

Amazon-type 'sculptress' in soiled overalls just like Rafe's, loud and sassy. You just don't behave that way if you have any manners, Rosalind says. She's possibly a little jealous of Rafe and me, for we'd grown up like brothers when Rafe's father, who was my dad's younger brother, was killed (in a car crash) and Rafe's mother wasn't well enough (mentally) to keep him so he came to live, age four, with my family. I was older than Rafe and so felt protective of him until he passed me by physically and in other ways, already in junior high school. And in high school he ran with a wild crowd, had a reputation for being hot-tempered and already a drinker, quick to get into fights. Nobody would've figured him for an artist in those years, except Rafe always had a strange imagination, a sort of impassioned exaggerated attitude, as likely to burst into tears if something made him sad as he was to lash out with his fists, face boiling up like a tomato ready to burst, if something made him angry. By sixteen he'd been arrested more than once for brawling, usually with older guys in some tavern or another, and my parents couldn't handle him though they loved him, we all loved him – it was just Rafe was too much for any ordinary family to deal with. So he moved out. Left town. Bummed around for years, up into Canada, Alaska, Oregon, and California and back to the East, and somehow he wins a scholarship to the Shenandoah School of the Arts, in Virginia – when he hadn't even graduated from high school! – so that was a real surprise, and nobody in the family knew how to take it except possibly me. I told Rafe when he visited I was proud of him and Rafe said, I remember his words clear as if he'd uttered them just yesterday and not twenty years ago, 'Hell, pride's a risky thing. It "goeth before a fall."' And he glowered at me like

I'd said the wrong thing, making him think worried thoughts.

The past fifteen years or so, Rafe's been living just outside town. On a forty-acre rundown farm, beautiful hilly countryside we've been told (we've never visited), with people coming and going, fellow artists, so it's said that Rafe Healy is living in some sort of hippie-style commune, which I frankly doubt – Rafe was never one to tolerate anybody's bullshit. He's a hard worker, maybe a little obsessed. For an artist, as I see it, is one who works nonstop – nobody's paying him for an eight-hour day. You'd have to be a little crazy to work so hard, or maybe it's the hard work that makes you a little crazy. What's sad is that I'm living in town, a half hour's drive from Rafe's place, and we never see each other, who'd once been so close. About five years ago there was a TV documentary about the famous West Virginia artist Carlin Ritchie, who had some sort of wasting disease, and it was a surprise to see my cousin Rafe included in a segment on Ritchie's generation of 'crafts' artists, and to see that Rafe was apparently a friend of Ritchie's; they'd all been at the Shenandoah School together. It made me a little dazed to think of something you could call 'history' (if only 'art history') and Rafe Healy included in it (if only in a brief segment). I called for Rosalind to come and see this on TV, but by the time she got there the part about Rafe was over. I said, 'I don't care what you think of Rafe, I'm proud of him. He's my cousin.' And Rosalind, who's got this sweet, prim little face and placid eyes but never misses a beat, says, 'Makes no difference whose cousin he is. Even if he was mine. He's a loose, careless, dangerous man of no true morals and he isn't welcome in this house, if that's what you're edging toward.' And back in April, just this year, there was Rafe Healy honored at the White House! And this is on network TV, and a big spread on the front page of our local paper so Rosalind, like everybody else in the vicinity, can't ignore it. But she says, 'There were fifty other "artists" honored at the ceremony, it couldn't have been too selective. Don't tell me there are fifty great artists like Rembrandt or Picasso living in the United States at one time. And there's absolutely no morals at the White House. So Rafe Healy would fit in just fine.' I can't argue my wife is wrong but a few weeks ago for her birthday I brought home a sea-green ceramic bowl purchased at a crafts store in town, she's blinking back tears lifting it from the wrapping paper saying, 'Oh, Harrison – I never saw anything so beautiful.' And she looks at me surprised like I could select something so beautiful for her, and kisses me. How many times she's admired this bowl, and showed it off to visitors, and examined it, running her fingers over the potter's initials on the bottom, *RH* she's never caught on whose work it is. And I'm surely never going to tell her.

All this was passing swiftly through my head when I saw Rafe in the jury selection room, a big, tall, fattish man with gingery hair and beard, bib overalls splattered with what looked like paint or manure, and the other potential jurors, and the brisk efficient ladies who run the jury selection, looking at him like he's either a freak or somebody of local renown, or both. He'd sighted me and came excitedly over to me, shaking my hand so hard I couldn't help but wince, and if I hadn't blocked him he would've hugged me, cracking a rib or two, with everybody in the room gaping at us. Rafe was so happy to see me he was practically crying. His big, bulgy, pebble-colored eyes shining with tears. We went out into the corridor and before we'd even exchanged greetings, caught up on news, Rafe was leading me out of earshot of others, puffing hard, saying, 'Oh, Jesus. Harrison. This place is like a prison. A morgue. I'm scared here. It's a bad sign I'm here. I don't want to be here.' I said, 'Well, I don't want to be here, either. Nobody does. It's called "jury duty." ' Rafe just kept on, in a voice more hoarse and cracked than I remembered, but in that same intense manner – like he's in his head so much, and you're inside his head, too, so he doesn't need to listen to anything you might actually say – 'Harrison, listen. I was up all night. My brain is about to explode. I need to work, I need to use my hands. I work in the morning from six-thirty till noon and I couldn't work this morning worrying about coming here, I didn't even know if I could find the courthouse, it's not even nine A.M. and we have to be here until five P.M. and I'm scared I'm going to explode. All week it's going to be like this, and if I'm seated on a jury it could be longer. I'm not a man who belongs on a jury, not at this time in my life. Oh Jesus.' He whimpered like he felt actual pain. Here I hadn't seen Rafe in years and already I was feeling that mixture of impatience and affection he used to stir in me, that feeling that, in whatever intense mental state he's in, if you can get him to listen to you, which he will sometimes do, you can have a calming effect on him, so it makes you want to try. I said, 'Rafe, it isn't the end of the world, for God's sake. Chances are you won't be seated on a jury, there's two hundred ninety of us and they won't be needing any more than seventy, somebody said.' Rafe was gripping my upper arm; he'd walked me to the far end of the corridor, which was just a deadend, an EMERGENCY EXIT ONLY door with warning red light, DO NOT OPEN ALARM WILL SOUND. He was saying, puffing, his eyes swerving in their sockets, 'I tried to get another postponement but I failed. I tried to get an exemption, I pleaded "I can't be a juror, I believe in *Judge not lest ye be judged* – I believe in *Let he who is without sin cast the first stone.*" But all I could get when I called the number was a recorded message! I never spoke to a living human being! And that lady who's in charge, she warns me I'll be in contempt of court if I address any judge like that and if I walk out of here like I'm thinking of doing. I don't mind paying the five-hundred-dollar fine but there's a chance I'd be "incarcerated," too. Harrison, I feel like I'm going to burst.' Rafe's face was heavy with blood, a nerve or artery was twitching on his forehead, his eyes blinking in virtual panic. I didn't know whether to laugh at him or take him seriously. That was the way of Rafe Healy – of artists, I suppose – they draw you into their moods no matter how extreme, you can see something's truly possessing them, they're in pain and you want to help. I said, leading Rafe back toward the jury selection room the way you'd lead a dazed, upright bear back to his cage (we'd been summoned inside, though I doubt Rafe noticed), 'Come on, Rafe. If I can do it, you can do it. Just calm down. Can't you make some sketches while you're waiting? Work on your art?' As if I'd insulted him Rafe said, 'Work on my *art*? In a place like this? Where I'm being detained against my will? Fuck you, Harrison. I thought you were my friend.'

But he allowed me to lead him back inside the jury selection room where we picked up plastic JUROR badges to pin to our shirts. I was JUROR 121 and Rafe was JUROR 93. We sat in uncomfortable folding chairs and watched, or anyway looked at, a fifteen-minute TV documentary on the justice system in the county, which must've been prepared for junior-high kids, and then we were made to listen to a forty-minute monotone recitation on jury selection by a middle-aged female court officer who looked as if she'd been living in this windowless musty-smelling underground space most of her life, and then we were told to wait 'until such time as your jury panel is called.' A TV set was turned on loudly, to what appeared to be a morning talk show. All this while Rafe was breathing quickly, wiping at his damp face with a wadded tissue, sighing and squirming in his seat. He reminded me of one of those hyperactive children no one knows how to treat except to dose with drugs. As Rafe said, he seemed about to burst. What if he had a stroke? A heart attack? He was making me anxious. I'd brought along the morning paper, and tried to read it, and an old back issue of *Time* someone had discarded, but couldn't help but glance sidelong at my poor cousin, with concern. The twitchy nerve or artery in his forehead was throbbing. I wondered if he was on a drug, but, no – if he'd taken any drug it would've been one to calm him down. And he hadn't been drinking, he was stone cold sober. That was the problem, I thought. Whatever was troubling Rafe (which had to be more than just jury duty) was pure and unalloyed, as real to him as a fever burning in his veins.

Every ten minutes or so Rafe would jump up, excuse himself to the court officer to use the men's room, or get a drink from a fountain in the corridor, or just pace out there like a trapped beast. I'd see him glance through the doorway at me, and I knew he wanted me to join him, but I stayed where I was. I'd been nerved-up well into my twenties but I was grown up now, or God knows I tried to be.

If you've ever been drafted for jury duty, you know that

what you do, like the lady told us, is wait. You sit, or you stand, and you wait. You're relaxed, or you're restless, but you wait. You wait until you're officially discharged for the day. Somewhere in the courthouse there are judges preparing for trials, at least in theory, and an army of potential jurors has to be in readiness for their use; a juror is a disposable unit, just a badge and a number. In fact, the judges are hearing motions, talking and arguing with their fellow lawyers; prosecuting and defense attorneys are trying to work out pleas and settlements in order to avoid trials. Guilt or innocence doesn't much matter, except to the defendant. Everyone else is a lawyer, and the lawyers are drawing salaries. The court system is a factory that works most efficiently when what happens today is exactly what happened yesterday. I suppose I sound cynical and I'm not a cynical man but this is the wisdom I came away with after my week of jury duty and it's been confirmed by others who've had the identical experience, though nobody who hasn't had it can comprehend – 'But it must be exciting, to be on a jury. At a trial.' That's what everybody says who doesn't know better. The truth is, most potential jurors are never seated on a jury and don't get within fifty feet of any trial. A trial means that a deal between the lawyers couldn't be worked out. If things moved smoothly in the justice system, there would be no trials. Potential jurors would be summoned, hundreds of us, made to sit like zombies in rows and wait hour after hour, day after day, until the week of jury duty is concluded, and we're sent back home with phony thanks and the promise that our payment will be mailed to us within six weeks – a salary of five dollars per day.

Maybe if Rafe had understood this, and hadn't exaggerated the likelihood of being a juror at an actual trial, he wouldn't have confessed to me what he did, and I'd have been spared these miserable hours, a roaring in my ears and my stomach in knots. For in my soul I'm like a newborn baby *not knowing what to do*. It's like my conscience is a sheet of transparent glass and I can't figure out if it's there or not, if it exists. How do I know what's the right thing to do? But even if I do nothing I will have done something. *I'm trapped.*

4.

At 1:10 p.m. our panel of jurors was released for a forty-minute lunch, with severe warnings from the court officer to return on time, and Rafe and I were about the first out of the courthouse; Rafe might've looked like a shambling bear in those overalls, and his facial expression sort of dazed and glassy-eyed, but like a bear the man could move fast when motivated. In the open air he laughed wildly. 'Freedom! We can breathe! Let's celebrate, man.' I didn't think it was a wise idea to drink right then, but like when we were kids I found myself going along with Rafe, Rafe's enthusiasm, so we ended up in a tavern a block from the courthouse. Rafe downed his first beer straight from the can, rubbed his knuckles over his bloodshot eyes, and said, lowering his voice so no one else could hear, 'Harrison. It's meant for me to tell you. I got to tell somebody. I'm going to explode if I don't.' I asked Rafe what was it, feeling a tinge of alarm, and Rafe leaned over the table toward me and said with a grimace, as of pain, 'I'm being forced to – kill someone. I think. I don't have a choice.'

I wasn't sure I'd heard right. I laughed. I wiped my mouth. Moisture glistened in my cousin's beard that was threaded with gray. I heard myself asking, 'Rafe, what?' and he didn't reply for so long I thought he'd decided not to tell me; then he said, his eyes fixed on mine with that look of his of profound sadness, yet with excitement glimmering beneath, that I remembered from when we were kids, and struck a spark of excitement in me, despite my good judgment, 'There are folks who deserve to die because they don't deserve to live. It's that simple. They must be stopped in their paths of destruction.'

'Folks? . . . What folks?'

'From the beginning of time they must've lived. Victimizing the innocent. Do you believe in Satan?'

'Satan?'

'I'm not sure if I believe in Satan myself. Probably I don't. You know how we were brought up – your mom would take us to that Lutheran church, and the minister talked of "Satan" but you had the idea he didn't really mean it. Like a man speaks of "death" – "dying" – but has no idea what he's saying. But I do believe in evil. I believe that there are individuals among us who are evil, who've chosen evil, who might believe in Satan themselves and are emissaries of Satan in their hearts.' Rafe was speaking quickly in his low, hoarse voice, and gripping my wrist in a way I didn't like as if to keep me where I was, in the booth listening to him. A waitress brought us more beers, set down plates before us, and Rafe scarcely noticed. He said, breathing quickly, 'I believe in vampires.'

'Rafe, what? *Vampires*? . . .'

'What the hell's wrong with you? Everything I say you repeat like a parrot! Not actual vampires, of course – mortal men – and women – who are vampires. Who destroy others. Suck away their lives. And even after their deaths – their victims' deaths – a vampire can continue. A man's work, a man's reputation – he can't protect it if he's dead. I'm thinking of a man, a good man, a man who was a great artist, a man who was my friend, who trusted me, a man now dead, who can't protect himself, whom I must protect.' These were like prepared words, uttered with passion. I didn't know how to reply. I felt like an empty vessel waiting to be filled.

So Rafe began telling me about Carlin Ritchie, who'd died the previous summer (I guess I knew that Ritchie had died, there'd been tributes to him in the media) at his mountain place in West Virginia that his second wife had made into a shrine for him; he'd died in 'suspicious circumstances' and since his death his widow was stealing his art, his reputation, claiming the two of them had been 'collaborators' on the important work Ritchie had been doing the last five or six years of his life; she'd hidden away a dozen silk screens – 'Carlin's Appalachia series, some of the best work he'd ever done' – that Carlin had designated in his will should go to Rafe Healy. 'She's taken from me! Stolen from me! Who was a friend of Carlin's, who loved him like a brother! Not just me but other old friends of his, she'd prevented from seeing him the last months of his life, this vicious woman, this vampire, sucking a helpless man's blood, and it goes on and on after his death – "Janessa Ritchie" she calls herself. I've tried to reason with her, Harrison. I'm not the only one, there's Carlin's first wife, and his grown children, relatives of his – she's cut us all out.

She wants him for herself. Herself alone. A great American artist, an artist people loved, now he's dead and can't protect himself – it's killing me, tearing me apart. I have to stop her.'

'Stop her – how?'

'A gun, I think. Rifle. I'm not a man of violence, no more than Carlin was, but – it's like there's a cancer inside me, eating me up. The vampire has got to be *stopped.*'

I was astonished. I was shocked. My cousin Rafe telling me such things! I saw he was serious, dead serious, and I didn't know what to say. There was this queer tawny light coming up in his eyes I'd never seen before. I didn't have much appetite for lunch but sat there staring as Rafe devoured his, a sandwich and french fries doused with ketchup, ducking his head toward his plate, turning it slightly to one side, his incisors tearing at the thick crust of a roll, slices of rare-done roast beef.

5.

This is what Rafe told me, over the broken-up course of the next three days.

'The last time I saw Carlin Ritchie, at his place in Buckhannon, West Virginia, that she'd made into a tourist shrine before he even died, it was eight weeks before she killed him, I swear he pleaded with his eyes – *I'm not ready to die. Rafe, don't abandon me!* Putting out his hand to me. His good hand, the left. Squeezing my fingers. Jesus, I loved that man! Even when I don't remember too clearly, I know I've been dreaming about him. Like last night. And the night before. *Rafe? Rafe? Don't abandon me, okay?*

'How I knew he'd died, a friend called. Mutual friend. "Carlin's dead, she's killed him," my friend was screaming. I made calls, I turned on the TV but there was nothing, got a copy of *The New York Times* and there was the obituary across the full top of the page— CARLIN RITCHIE, 49, "PRIMITIVE" ARTIST, DIES IN WEST VIRGINIA. Now I saw it was real, I started sobbing like a baby.

'That's bullshit that Carlin was a "primitive" artist. He was a born talent, no one could capture the human face, eyes, soul like Carlin, but he'd trained himself too; there was a phase, when he was in his twenties, he turned out these ugly, wrenching silk screens modeled after Goya. At the Shenandoah School, we were just kids then, Carlin was the "classicist" – *You can't overcome the past unless you know it.* And he'd quote Blake – *Drive your cart over the bones of the dead.*

'Yeah. The last lines of an obituary tell you who the survivors are. Carlin's first wife was named, and his three grown kids. Then – "Janessa Ritchie, his widow." *His murderer.*

'"Janessa"? – that isn't even her name, her name's something like Agnes, Adelaide – and she'd been married at least once before, and wasn't so young as everybody thought. I found this out later. I never did tell Carlin. He was crazy in love with her, enthralled by her – wouldn't listen to a word against her even from his old friends. Even from his kids. They're the ones who're hurting – she'd gotten him to change his will, leaving her mostly everything and naming her the executor of his estate. Carlin never spent much, money didn't seem to mean anything to him except as a means of buying art supplies, but we're talking millions of dollars here. And the way she's marketing him –

we're talking double-digit millions. She's gonna suck that name for all it's worth.

'Sure I knew Carlin's first wife, his family, not intimately but I knew them and counted myself a friend. Carlin had married his high-school sweetheart, both of them just kids when they started having babies. They were together for twenty-six years. Nobody could believe they'd broken up, Carlin was living with another woman – "That just can't be. Carlin isn't that type" was what everybody said. And it was true, Carlin wasn't. But *she* was – the vampire, I mean. Just took him over. Like she'd put her hand, her nail-polished talons, on the man's living heart.

'No, I don't cast any blame on Carlin. I believe he was enthralled – enchanted. Like under an evil spell. He'd been sick with MS – that's multiple sclerosis, in case you don't know – "mucho shit" Carlin called it – struck him down when he was twenty-nine, just starting to sell his work, make a name for himself, win prizes – and he's in a wheelchair, like that. Except he gets better, he's in remission for a while, then struck down again, can't use his legs, then he's into some holistic health regimen and actually improves – back in remission is what they call it, though in fact, as Carlin said, nobody knows what MS actually is, it's like a syndrome, what works for one person doesn't work for another, one person shrivels away and dies in five years and another person can be on his feet, walking and healthy for twenty years – *it can't be calculated. Like life.* But Carlin was lucky, I think it had to do with his attitude, his heart – he just wasn't going to let that disease eat him away.

'First time any of us knew about "Janessa" – it was a summer arts festival in Virginia, and there was Carlin Ritchie, a guest of honor, without his wife – surrounded by admirers, one of them this strange-looking young woman, this slender sort of snaky-sexy girl, with a constant, nervous smile, showing her gums and white, slightly protruding teeth, enormous dark eyes, you'd have to call them beautiful eyes though they were sort of weird, with bluish, hooded lids, and a way of staring like she was memorizing you. Carlin was embarrassed being with her, that shamed, lovesick look in his face, but he introduced us, saying Janessa's a photographer from New York, very talented, and I thought oh yeah? and didn't say much. The girl looked about twenty. (In fact, she was over thirty.) She wasn't embarrassed in the slightest. Her eyes hooked on to mine, and her skin gave off a musky heat. She pushed her hand into mine like a squirmy little creature, and there's the pink tip of her tongue between her teeth – Jesus! Did I feel a charge. She said, "Rafe Healy! I'm sure honored to meet *you*." Like there was some immediate understanding between us and even Carlin was out of it. I was disgusted by her, but I have to admit sort of intrigued, at that time it wasn't altogether clear how serious Carlin was about her, whether they were a couple, or just together in Virginia. Nobody would've predicted Carlin would leave Laurette for her, after all they'd been through together, and Carlin making money now, famous. I watched Carlin and the girl for the rest of the week, keeping my distance, so Carlin would get the message I didn't approve, not that I'm a puritan or anything, not that I even take marriage all that seriously, most marriages at least – you make vows to be broken, is my experience. But the last night of the festival I got drunk and spoke to Janessa in private, I said, "You know, Carlin Ritchie is a married man, a devoted family man, he hasn't been well and his wife has taken care of him and before he began to make money she supported him for years, and they've got three kids – keep that in mind." And Janessa says, all eager and girlish, wide-eyed, laying her hand on my arm and giving me goose bumps, "Oh, Rafe, I know!" like she knew me, she'd been calling me "Rafe" for years, " – Carlin has told me all about that wonderful woman, 'My first love' he calls her." Janessa lowered her eyes, and made this simpering face like she knew she was being naughty, flirtatious and naughty, but couldn't help it, " – but I'm thinking, Rafe, y'know? – I'd rather be Carlin Ritchie's last love than his first."

'With his medication, Carlin wasn't supposed to be drinking. He'd had a whole life practically before he got sick when he drank – serious drinking. Without Laurette around he'd relapse, and in this situation he was drinking, and people were worried about him, but not Janessa – I watched the two of them walk off together, from a party, it was late, past three A.M., Carlin was leaning on the girl, and she had her arm around his waist, she was skinny but strong, practically holding him up, and Carlin was a tight-packed, heavy little guy, those muscular shoulders and torso, but Janessa supported him walking up this hill to the cabin Carlin was staying in, a white-birch log cabin, and I stood in the shadows watching, I don't believe I was drunk but stone cold sober, watching after those two, after they'd gone inside the cabin, and the cabin lights were off.

'Next thing we knew, Carlin was separated from Laurette. He was living with Janessa in New York, going to parties, gallery openings, being photographed by Avedon for *The New Yorker* – Carlin's haggard-homely face, like a kid's, yet he was beautiful in his way, his unique way, like his Appalachian Faces silk screens that made him famous –

there's something about faces like that, that touch you deep
in the heart. A few of Carlin's friends turned against him,
but not me – I'd forgive him anything, almost. Also, I'm
not so innocent myself, with women. I wasn't anyone to
judge. I never judged *him* – only *her*. It happened pretty fast
that Carlin divorced Laurette and married Janessa, let her
take over running his life, his exhibits, his correspondence,
his finances; let her talk him into buying the house in
Buckhannon and renovating it, the shrine to Carlin Ritchie,
having it painted lavender with purple trim, and putting up
a spike fence with a gate and a little bronze plaque CARLIN
RITCHIE RESIDENCE PRIVATE PLEASE so admirers could take
pictures of it from the road – "Jesus, Carlin, it's like you're
on display, marketing yourself, how can you tolerate it?" I
asked him, I was frankly pissed, and Carlin said, embarrassed, "It's got nothing to do with *me*. It's just the idea.
Janessa says – "People love your art, so they want to love
you. You can't deny them." "Hell you can't deny them," I
said, " – you denied them in the past." Carlin said, in a flat,
sad voice, "Well – the past is past." We were talking over
the phone, Carlin was in his studio, it was about the only
way we could talk and even then Janessa was monitoring his
incoming calls, lifting the receiver so you'd hear a hissing
breath. Most of the time when Carlin's friends called,
Janessa would answer the phone with this mock-girlish
greeting, "Oh *hel*-lo! Of course I know who you are. Of
course Carlin would love to speak with you. But—" and
she'd explain how it was a day Carlin had worn himself out
in the studio, or a day he hadn't been able to use his legs, or
focus his eyes; a day he was "fighting the demon" –
meaning the MS. More and more when we called we'd be
told that Carlin "isn't available, regretfully." His sons

complained they were told repeatedly, the last fifteen months of their father's life, that he "isn't available, regretfully." Yet there was a steady stream of photographers, interviewers, TV and videotape crews traveling to the Carlin Ritchie residence in Buckhannon, from as far away as Japan and Australia, and these people, you can be sure, who never failed to include "Janessa Ritchie" in their profiles, were always welcome.

'When Carlin left Buckhannon it wasn't ever to visit his old friends as he used to. After he married that woman, he never came to see me again. She'd take him to arts festivals, to fancy events where Carlin was the guest of honor, black-tie evenings in New York and Washington, but she'd never take him to the Shenandoah summer festival, or anywhere ordinary. Carlin went as a star, or he didn't go at all. She demanded high fees for him, and he seemed embarrassed but proud, too; he'd never forgotten his West Virginia background, he'd been born in a small town twenty miles from Buckhannon, just a crossroads, and his folks were poor; despite the Carlin Ritchie legend that's sprung up, Carlin hadn't been happy in his childhood, I happen to know; not as happy as I was – and I'd lost both parents. (But I had good, kind, generous stepparents, you could say. And even a brother close to my heart.) Janessa wouldn't ever let Carlin talk about his real home, his real folks, everything had to be pretense, sentiment. In Carlin's best work there was always a melancholy tone, like Hopper's paintings, but with more texture and subtlety than Hopper, sort of dreamy, meditative, after-the-fact – posthumous, almost. Like these Appalachian people and places were really gone, vanished. And Carlin Ritchie was remembering them. (And Janessa started taking these phony, posed pictures in West Virginia, "companion pieces" she called them to Carlin's art, and when he was too sick to prevent her, and after his death, she published them side by side with his work claiming she'd been his "collaborator" for all of their marriage. Carlin Ritchie's "collaborator"! But that wouldn't be the worst.)

'The last time I saw Carlin in public, it was a black-tie awards ceremony at the American Academy in New York. Carlin was a member of the Academy, and I was getting an award. And some other friends of ours, from the old days at Shenandoah, the days of our youth, were there. And celebrating. But, hell, we couldn't get within twenty feet of Carlin. He'd cast sort of wistful, embarrassed looks at us – but he was in his wheelchair, and Janessa had him surrounded by rich, important people – "Carlin's privileged patrons" she called them. It would be revealed afterward that she'd been selling Carlin's work, drawing up actual contracts, before he'd created it; she was getting the poor bastard to sign contracts, naming her as agent, without knowing what he was signing – he'd always been a careless kind of guy with contracts and money, worse even than I am. We got drunk on champagne and watched our friend Carlin in his tux that made him look embalmed, in his wheelchair that was an expensive motorized chair but guided by this white-skinned female in a black velvet gown cut so low her breasts were almost falling out, strands of pearls around her neck, looking like the real thing, not cultured, surely not West Virginia-type costume-jewelry pearls, her glossy red hair upswept on her head and her face beautiful, radiant – this was the second Mrs. Ritchie? No wonder photographers loved snapping her and poor Carlin, sunken-chested in his chair, wearing thick glasses now, and his right hand palsied, lifting his ghastly-hopeful smile and managing to shake hands with his left hand as "privileged patrons" hovered over him. Janessa wasn't a skinny strung-out anorexic-type any longer, she'd packed on serious, solid female flesh and looked good enough to eat. Her face was pale as a geisha's and made up like a cosmetic mask, flawless – crimson mouth, inky-black mascara accentuating her big eyes, flaring eyebrows that looked as if they'd been drawn on with Crayola. She didn't look any age at all now – like Elizabeth Taylor in those glamour photos you used to see on the covers of supermarket tabloids, generic female vamp-beauty. Totally phony, but glamorous as hell. I have to admit that Carlin looked happy enough that night, under the sharp eye of Janessa, and her shapely bust nudging the back of his head so if he was nodding off (on medication, probably) he'd wake up with a startled smile. I managed to get near enough to him to shake his hand – hell, I leaned over to hug the guy, and Carlin hugged me, hard, like a drowning man – though the second Mrs. Ritchie didn't like this at all. Carlin was saying, almost begging, "Rafe? Where've you been? Why don't you visit me anymore? Come see me! Come soon! Next week! Show me what you're doing these days, man! I'm into some new, terrific work – I'm gonna surprise you, man!" while that bitch Janessa is smiling a tight, angry smile, pushing Carlin's wheelchair away saying, "Mr. Healy, you're over-exciting my husband. He's on medication, he doesn't know what he's saying. *Excuse us.*" And she'd gotten him to an elevator, blocking me from entering with them, though there was plenty of room, and there was the artist Robert Rauschenberg in the elevator; Janessa recognized a famous name and it was like she'd been shot with pure adrenaline, her big hungry eyes glistened, her sexy mouth lost its stiffness, her breasts sort of burgeoned out, there she was cooing and cawing over Rauschenberg, saying how she'd loved his "big wild collage paintings" since she was a young girl, all the while blocking me, and pretending not to be aware of me, while Carlin looked on, confused and anxious – it would've been a comic scene on TV, but in real life, if you had to live through it, it wasn't so pleasant. Anyway, you know me, I kept pushing onto the elevator, nudging up against Janessa, her perfume in my nostrils like rotted gardenias, and I was trying to talk to Carlin, and Janessa loses control and slaps at me, actually slaps at me, and says, "Damn you! You're harassing my husband, and you're harassing me! We don't know you! I'm going to call a security guard if you don't let us alone!" I say, "What the fuck do you mean, you don't know me? I'm Carlin's friend – who the fuck are *you*?" So maybe I was a little drunk, and belligerent, and my black tie was coming untied, but Janessa provoked me, and I'd like to haul off and hit her, except she starts screaming, "Help! Police!" so I back off the elevator quick; everybody's glaring at me, even Rauschenberg.

'It's then I realize that that woman, "Janessa," is my sworn enemy. And she's Carlin's enemy, too. Though the poor guy wasn't in any condition to know it.

'The last time I saw Carlin Ritchie in private, it was at his place in Buckhannon, West Virginia, that I'd visited only once before. This was about eight weeks before Carlin died. I'd gotten a call from him, inviting me down; he was trying to sound in good spirits on the phone, but his voice was weak, and I had the distinct idea that our conversation was being monitored by Janessa, but I was damned happy to hear from my friend, and if I figured anything I figured that

Janessa was embarrassed at her treatment of me and worried I might make trouble somehow. So she was allowing Carlin to invite me to Buckhannon. And this was more or less what it was, I think. Also she was preparing to murder him and may have believed she needed some credible witness beforehand, to testify that the poor guy was in bad shape. "Lost the use of his legs!" as she'd say, in this wailing breathy voice like it was a total surprise to her, or to Carlin, that he wasn't walking just then.

'So I drove to Buckhannon, grateful to be invited if it was only for overnight, and I loaded the van with some of my new quilts to show Carlin, who'd always been a strong supporter of my work, even if it was totally different from his own, and there was Janessa opening the door for me in this weird Disney-type theme house, "West Virginia ginger-bread classic-Victorian" was how she described it in interviews, "an exact duplicate of Carlin's family home lost in the Depression" – bullshit you'd think Carlin would be ashamed of, but he had to endure it; and instead of my enemy, Janessa was now my friend, or so it seemed – hugging me with her strong, fleshy arms, dazzling me with her perfume and a wet high-school-girl kiss right on the mouth – "Rafe Healy! We've been missing you! Come *in*! How long can you *stay*?" (Like she hadn't worked it out with me that a single night was the limit.) You'd have thought the scene was being televised; here's Mrs. Carlin Ritchie, the gracious hostess, in some long, floor-length, swishing Indian skirt, layers of gauze and silk, red hair tumbling down her back, welcoming an artist-friend of her husband's, a woman who'd sacrificed her professional photography career to tend to a crippled husband she adored. And Rafe's a sap, a sucker; she kisses me on the mouth and pokes me with her tongue and Jesus! – I feel such a charge I'm thinking I'll forgive this female anything. It's a total surprise to me that the mood between us is completely different from what it had been in New York, in that elevator, which I understand now is typical of a certain kind of psychopath, the most devious kind, who isn't predictable from one occasion to another but is coolly improvising, trying out different methods for deception, manipulation, and control. (This would explain what Carlin's children said of her: that sometimes, when they'd spoken with their father on the phone, in the days she'd allowed it, they could hear Janessa screaming at him, or at someone, in the background, while at other times she was cooing and welcoming, saying how nice it was of them to call, how happy their father would be hearing from them – "And that makes me happy, too!")

'This visit with Carlin, this final visit, was painful to me, but very powerful, memorable – it was like I was in the presence of a saint, yet a saint who was also a good-hearted guy, a friend, with no pretensions, no sense of who he was, what stature he'd attained. Just Carlin Ritchie I'd known since we'd been kids together at Shenandoah, groping our way into our "careers." It shocked me to see how he'd lost more weight and seemed to have resigned himself to the wheelchair. His legs looked shriveled, even his socks were baggy. But his mind was clear, sharp. He told me he was supposed to be taking a certain medication, Janessa would be upset if she learned he'd skipped it that day, "But it makes my head fuzzy, and my tongue so thick I can't talk – so the hell with it, right? For now." We spent most of the visit out on the veranda where Carlin could lie back on a wicker divan, it was a mild May evening, and it pissed

Janessa off that Carlin wanted just to eat off plates, no formal dinner like she'd planned in the dining room, and no Polaroids – "Janessa is the most posterity-minded individual I've ever known," Carlin told me, winking, "she'd snap me on the toilet if I didn't lock the door." Janessa laughed, hurt, and said, "Well, somebody's got to be posterity-minded around here. This is a living archive, and you're "Carlin Ritchie" lest you forget. You're not *nobody*." Looking sort of bold-provocative at me, like she's saying Rafe Healy is *nobody*. After a while Janessa got bored with us and went inside; I'd catch glimpses of her through a curtained window, drifting around, talking on a cellular phone, simpering, laughing so it seemed to me she must have a boyfriend, sure she's got a boyfriend, a female like that, and poor Carlin a cripple. But I was grateful she'd let us alone, and I could see Carlin was, too. He'd never say a word against that woman but there was a sad-ironic tone of his, a way he'd shrug his shoulders when she said some preposterous thing, his eyes locking with mine like we were boys and some adult female was bullshitting us. But then he'd say, a few minutes later, talking about his new work, "Rafe, I don't know how I would continue, without Janessa. She hires my assistants, she screens my calls, my business – the world." I wanted to retort, "Well, Laurette would know, if you don't." But I didn't. I knew better. The vampire had her fangs in him deep, there must've been an anesthetic effect, a comforting delusion. I get drunk for more or less the same reason, maybe I shouldn't judge. We just sat out there on Carlin's veranda and talked. Must've been three hours – and Janessa fuming and stewing inside. Carlin wasn't supposed to drink, but he had a couple of beers, and I put away a six-pack at least. It was like we both knew this might be the final time we saw each other. I said, "Carlin. I wish the fuck there was something I could do, y'know? Like donate a kidney. A spleen transplant. Hell – half my cerebral cortex." And Carlin laughed, and said, "I know you do, Rafe. I know." "It's a goddam thing. It's fate, it's unfair. Like, why *you*?" I said. My eyes were stinging with tears, I was about to bawl. Carlin groped out for me with his left, good hand and said, like he was feeling a little impatient with me, he'd worked through this logic himself and was impatient I hadn't yet, 'But my fate was to be "Carlin Ritchie" one hundred percent. It's one big package deal.' Then he started telling me how 'we' – meaning himself and Janessa – were making 'plans of expediency.' For when, finally, he got too sick. Which might be coming a little more quickly than he'd hoped. Stockpiling pills, barbiturates. It would have to be, Carlin said, without his doctors knowing. Without anyone 'legal' knowing. No one in his family – 'They're old-style Baptists, they don't hold with taking your life, let alone your death, in your own hands.' I was shocked to hear this, I said, 'Carlin, what? You're planning – what?' Carlin said, lowering his voice, 'I don't want to be a burden on Janessa. Not any more than I am. When – if – I become "incontinent," as it's called, I know what to do.' 'Carlin, I don't like to hear such talk. You're young, for Christ's sake – not even fifty.' 'That's the problem, man, I'm young enough to be around, in a vegetable state, for a long time.' 'You've got more work to do – lots of work to do. What the fuck are you telling me, you're thinking of pulling out?' 'Rafe, I didn't tell you what I did, I didn't share it, for you to condemn me,' Carlin says, with dignity, '– I didn't invite you even to have an opinion. I'm telling you. That's that.' So I sat there, shaking. I'm an aggressive guy I've been told,

I talk before I think, so I tried to absorb this, tried to see Carlin's logic. I could see it, I suppose. Back inside the house, that was lit up like a movie set, Janessa was watching TV and it sounded like she was still talking on the phone. Carlin said apologetically that he'd been thinking, a few years ago, of asking me to be his estate executor if something premature happened to him – 'Laurette was real enthusiastic' – but now of course things were different; Janessa was to be his executor. I swallowed hard and said okay, I could see that, I understood. Carlin said, embarrassed, 'You know how Janessa is – she loves me so. She's a little jealous of me and some of my old friends. I can't blame her, she's a hot-blooded woman, y'know? She's an artist too. She gave up her art for me.' 'Did she.' 'She gave up the possibility of having children, she said, for me.' 'Did she.' 'She doesn't want me to suffer, she says. She's worried sick about me, it's almost more upsetting to her than to me, that I might suffer. "Interminably" as she says.' 'So you're stockpiling barbiturates for her,' I said, sort of meanly, '– you don't want her to suffer.' Carlin blinked like he didn't exactly get this, and I said, louder, 'She's rehearsing your death, is that it? She's urging you to die? Has she picked the date yet?' Carlin said quickly, 'No, no – my wife isn't urging me to do anything. It's my own best interests she has in mind. If – when – it comes time I can't walk, can't move, can't eat, can't control my bowels – I don't want to live, man.' 'But that won't be for a long time. That might be never.' 'It might be next month.' 'I might beat you to it, Carlin. It's like shooting dice.' Carlin finished his beer, or tried to – a trickle of beer ran down his chin. He said, shrugging, 'Okay, I don't want to die. Yes, but I'm ready. I want to be brave. Fuck it, I'm a coward, I want to be brave.

Help me.' 'Help you? How?' But Carlin laughed, and repeated what he'd said, adding something about God watching over him – 'If there's a God but I guess there is not. We've got to grow up sometime, right?' And I said, uneasy, not knowing what the subject was any longer, 'Hell, no. Not me.' And we both laughed.

'That visit in May of last year was the last time I saw Carlin Ritchie alive, though I tried to speak with him on the phone once or twice. But Janessa always answered the phone, saying in this breathy little-girl voice, "Who? Oh – you. Well, I'm truly sorry, Rafe Healy, but my husband isn't taking calls today." "When do you think he will be taking calls, Mrs. Ritchie?" I asked, trying to keep my voice steady, and she said, as rehearsed as if she was being taped for posterity, "That's in the hands of the Lord." '

At this point, my cousin Rafe paused. He'd come close to breaking down. And I was feeling kind of strange myself – exhausted by Rafe's story, but excited, too. And a little suspicious just suddenly.

We weren't at the tavern near the courthouse, nor in the basement corridor of the old building. As it happened, we were having a few beers in a bar called Domino's; it was early evening of the second day of jury duty, and our panel of jurors had been dismissed that afternoon still without being summoned to any courtroom. Since Rafe had begun telling me his story, though, the hours flew past, and neither of us seemed to mind our enforced idleness. I was so caught up in Rafe's words I could feel pity for Carlin Ritchie, whom I'd never known, as intense as any I'd ever felt for anyone, and I could feel hatred fermenting in my heart for that woman Janessa. I could sympathize why Rafe hated her so but I wouldn't have gone so far as to wish her dead – that's a pretty extreme state after all.

The evening before I'd come home late, past 7 P.M., having stopped at Domino's with Rafe, and Rosalind was waiting for me, worried – 'Since when does jury duty last so long? Were you called for a trial?' I'd decided not to tell her about meeting up with Rafe at the courthouse, and I knew it was futile to pretend to this sharp-nosed woman that I hadn't stopped at a bar and had a few beers, so I told her, yes, I'd been selected for a trial, and it was a damned ugly trial, and we were forbidden to talk about it until it was over – 'So don't ask me, Rosalind. Please.' 'A trial! You actually got chosen!' Rosalind cried. 'Is it a ... murder case?' 'I told you, Rosalind, I can't discuss it. I'd be in contempt of court.' 'But, honey, who would know? I wouldn't tell.' 'I would know. I've given my word, I've sworn on the Bible to execute my duties as the law demands. So don't tease me, I'm not going to say another word about it.' And I was feeling so nerved-up, anyway, about the ugly story my cousin was telling me, it didn't really seem that I was lying to Rosalind; there was a deeper truth, lodged in my heart, my cousin's secret he was sharing with me, which I would never tell to another living soul.

But Rafe was shifting his shoulders in that way he'd had when he was a kid, and you knew he wasn't telling all of the truth. So I said, on a hunch, 'Rafe, back up just a bit. To the last time you saw Carlin Ritchie. That visit in Buckhannon.' 'Why? I already told you about Buckhannon.' 'But was there anything more? Between you and Mrs. Ritchie, maybe?' 'That's a crude accusation,' Rafe said. 'Fuck you, man.' 'Well – was there? You'd better tell me.' 'Tell you what, man?' Rafe was defying me, but his pebble-colored eyes were clouded and evasive, and I kept pushing, until finally he admitted yes, there was more. And he wasn't proud of it.

'Already, by eleven P.M., Carlin was exhausted. Where in the old days he'd stay up much of the night talking art and ideas and drinking, now I could see he was ready for bed when Janessa came to fetch him. She wheeled him away to a specially equipped room at the rear of the house, and when she returned she said with a sigh and a sad-seeming smile, "That poor, brave man. Thank you for making this pilgrimage, Rafe Healy." Pilgrimage! Like I was some kind of fawning pilgrim. I thought *Fuck you, lady* and should've gone off to bed myself (I was staying in a guest room upstairs) except I let her talk me into having a nightcap with her – "Just one. For old time's sake. So there's no hard feelings between us." There was this coquettish way about the woman, yet an edge of reproach, too, as if she knew full well how certain people valued her, and was defying them, yet wanted them to like her, at least be attracted to her, just the same. So she pours us both bourbon. She's wearing a gauzy cream-colored dress like a nightgown, and her hair in ringlets like a little girl's, and her eyes like an owl's ringed in mascara, and there was this hungry, ugly lipstick mouth of hers I couldn't stop staring at. *Yes, I knew I should've gotten the hell out of that house. All I can say is, I was drunk, I was a fool.* Janessa slipped her arm through mine and led me around showing off the house, which had been her idea, she boasted, a "shrine of memories" for Carlin while he was still in good-enough condition to appreciate it. I said, "Hell, he'll be in good-enough condition to appreciate lots of things, for a long time," but she wasn't even listening. This cold, sickish sensation came over me that, to her, Carlin Ritchie was already dead and she was the surviving widow, the proprietor of the shrine, keeper of the legend. Executor of the estate. Heiress. She'd been drinking earlier in the evening, too. She showed me this display-case room, a parlor, which was papered in deep purple silk wallpaper with recessed lighting in the ceiling, photos of Carlin from the time he was a baby till the present time (except there was no evidence of Carlin with his first wife or his children), an entire wall covered with framed photos of Carlin and Janessa, posed in front of his artworks or at public ceremonies shaking hands with important people. I flattered the woman by saying, "Is this the President of the United States?" and she said, pleased, yet a little rueful, "Yes, it sure is. But it was Carlin he made a big fuss over, not me." I laughed, and said, "Janessa, the President would've made a bigger fuss over you, if it hadn't been such a public occasion," and she laughed hard at that, she liked that kind of humor.

'After that, things got a little confused.

'I mean – I know how it ended. I sure do. But how it got to where it ended – that's confused.

'We were in the living room, which was mostly darkened. And having another bourbon. And this hot-skinned, good-looking woman is sort of pressing up against me like she doesn't know what she's doing. And I'm not supposed to catch on till it's too late. She's complaining how Carlin's family is spreading slander about her, then she's boasting how Carlin's art was fetching higher and higher prices now it was being marketed more professionally – "Thanks to my intervention. *He'd* be happy giving it away." She's complaining, or boasting, how so many folks make the pilgrimage to Buckhannon, a lot of them bringing gifts like needlepoint-Bible pillows, glow-in-the-dark crucifixes, a hundred pounds of venison steak Carlin's too kindly or too weak to decline – "So it's jamming our freezer. Can you believe it?" "Well, if people love him," I mumbled, or words like that. Janessa starts saying how lonely she is amid all this commotion, and how frightened, "like a little girl," of the future. How painful it is, married to a man who's not really a man any longer – "My husband, but not my lover. And I'm still *young*." There's the pink tip of her tongue between her teeth, and suddenly she's in my arms, and we're kissing, panting like dogs like we'd been waiting for this for hours, for all of our lifetimes and now there's nothing to hold us back. Except – I'm pushing her away, disgusted. The taste of her mouth was like something rotten. Like you'd imagine old, stale blood – ugh! If I'd been drunk I was stone cold sober now, on my feet and out of there, upstairs to get my duffel bag and back down again and there's this furious, shamed woman saying, "You! God damn you! Who do you think you are, you!" – she slapped at me, shut her fist, and punched like a man; I pushed her away and she lunged back like a wildcat, clawing me in the face, and I was a little scared of her, knowing she'd have loved to murder me, she'd been so insulted, but she wasn't strong enough to do any real injury, didn't have time to rush into the kitchen for a knife, shouting after me from the veranda as I pulled away in my van, "You fucker! You sorry excuse for a man! Don't you ever darken this house again! You're no better than he is – cripple! *Cripple*!" And a few weeks later, Carlin Ritchie was dead.

6.

On the third day of jury duty, which was a Wednesday, our panel of jurors was taken at last upstairs to the fifth floor, to a judge's courtroom, where there was an aggravated-assault case to be tried. After a ninety-minute voir dire session, during which time neither JUROR 93 (Rafe Healy) nor JUROR 121 (Harrison Healy) was called, meaning that Rafe and I just sat, sat, sat in enforced silence, Rafe so tense I could feel him quivering, a panel of twelve jurors and two alternates was seated, and the rest of us were dismissed for lunch with a severe warning to be back in the courthouse in forty minutes. Rafe groaned in my ear thank God he hadn't been chosen, he wasn't in any mental state to be questioned by any judge.

I wanted to say: *If you're so torn up about this, maybe you shouldn't be planning to commit a murder. Maybe you're not a murderer.* But I never said a word. It was like I didn't want to interfere with this strange, scary thing that was happening in my cousin's soul, of such magnitude and danger it could never have happened (I was certain) in mine, as if I didn't have the right, but could only be a witness.

Again we went to the tavern up the street. Again we had several quick beers, to soothe our nerves. Rafe held out his big, burly hand – 'Jesus, Harrison: I got the shakes.' But he only laughed. He said, 'I hope you don't think too lowly of me, Harrison, for behaving like I did. With that vicious woman.' I said, truthfully, 'I believe you did the right thing. Getting out like you did.' 'I drove all night to get back home. I was so disgusted with myself! And with her, for making a fool of me like she did. Jesus, the taste of her! – it's still with me, I swear.' Rafe wiped at his mouth and ordered another beer to assuage that taste; it was almost so I could taste something rotten and bloody-stale on my own lips.

Rafe continued with his story, and now I already knew parts of it, and could feel I'd lived through some of it myself, and was feeling tense and agitated at what was to come. It was like I'd been with him when he opened *The New York Times* to see CARLIN RITCHIE, 49, 'PRIMITIVE' ARTIST, DIES IN WEST VIRGINIA. And Carlin's photo, taken how many years before. The county coroner ruled 'complications caused by multiple sclerosis' but the actual cause of death, as Rafe hadn't been surprised to learn from the Ritchie family, was that, during a siege of bad health, and depression, Carlin had 'accidentally' ingested a lethal quantity of alcohol and barbiturates. 'And guess what? Janessa hadn't been there. Carlin had been alone. For the first time in years, the second Mrs. Ritchie had left her husband out of her sight long enough to travel to New York.

'So she'd killed him and would get away with it. For who was to blame *her*?

'Now, the wake. Harrison, you are not going to believe the wake.

'The wake was held in the shrine-house in Buckhannon, and – Jesus! – what a mob scene. I'd been prepared for Janessa to forbid me to come, and every other old friend of Carlin's, but that wasn't the case – Janessa hired an assistant to call us, wanting to make sure that as many people came to the wake and funeral as possible. Even Carlin's first wife and children were invited. We were advised to fly into Charleston, secure a motel room, rent a car, and drive to Buckhannon, which is what most of us did. I was in a state

of shock, though I'd known what was coming. I'd about
written off Carlin as a doomed man, after that visit. Though
the Ritchie family was claiming he hadn't been that sick,
only just depressed because he hadn't been able to work for
some time. "He was too young to die. There were doctors
who'd given him hope. How could Carlin do such a
desperate thing?" I knew, but I wasn't going to say. I was
feeling sick and guilty myself, as if I'd betrayed Carlin, left
him with the vampire to die. And Janessa was the bereaved
widow, with her dead-white powdered skin and black velvet
gown, even a black velvet band around her throat, and her
hair streaked at her temples with silver. She stood at the
door greeting everyone like a hostess. Her eyes were manic-
bright and her mouth crimson like a wound. Seeing me, she
pressed herself into my arms with a wail, as if we were old,
intimate friends. We were on camera: There was a German
documentary film-maker on the site, who'd apparently
been interviewing Carlin up to a few days before his death.
There were "selected" journalists from *Vanity Fair, People,
The New York Times;* from England, France, Japan, and
Israel. The interior of the house was packed with people,
most of them strangers to me. There were flowers
everywhere. What appeared to be a lavish cocktail buffet
had been set up in the dining room, and white-costumed
caterer's assistants were serving. The shock, and I mean it
was a shock, was Carlin himself – I mean, Carlin's body. It
was lying, in an expensive tuxedo, on the white lace spread
of a brass four-poster bed (the marital bed, carried down
from upstairs) in the parlor. Dozens of candles reeking
incense had been lighted. Exclusively white lilies were
banked around the bed. I stood there trembling, staring at
my friend who'd been made to appear younger and

healthier, you could say more garish with health, than he'd looked in years. Pan-Cake makeup skillfully disguised the hollows beneath his eyes, his sallow cheeks were rouged. "It's like Carlin is only just sleeping, and he'll be waking any minute to say *What's going on here?*" – this remark was repeated numerous times. I said it myself. I said it seriously, and I said it as a joke. I was in that metaphysical-drunk stage where the saddest truth in the world can be the funniest. Photos were being taken of Carlin Ritchie's beautiful, grieving widow, standing at the bier-bedside, her fingers linked with those of her dead husband. A tape of mournful country-and-western rock music played. Janessa was taking photos herself, avidly. From time to time she disappeared to freshen her makeup, which was elaborate and effective; at some point she changed into another black dress, low-cut, taffeta, with a startling slit up the side to mid-thigh. Later that night she called for testimonials from "those who'd known and loved Carlin" and I was one who stood by the four-poster bed speaking of Carlin Ritchie's great talent, his great spirit, and his great courage, and tears ran down my cheeks and others wept with me, as at a gospel ceremony. Janessa pushed into my arms, embraced me hard, her talon fingernails in my neck – "Rafe Healy! I thank you in Carlin's name." The wake continued through the night. The problem with grief is it reaches a peak, and another peak, and quickly you begin to repeat yourself. What is spontaneous becomes a performance. Repeated. More people arrived, distraught and needing to expend their shock, grief, loss. They wept in the widow's arms. Some wept in my arms. Food had fallen underfoot in the dining room, but fresh platters were being hauled in from the kitchen, and bottles of whiskey, bourbon, wine. Carlin had always appreciated a good party, hadn't stinted when it came to quality, and he'd have been proud of this one. Except there was an encounter, caught on videotape, between some Ritchie relatives and Janessa, and there was an encounter between Laurette (who proudly called herself "Laurette Ritchie") and Janessa, and harsh words were said. Carlin's twenty-seven-year-old daughter, Mandy, screamed and slapped Janessa – "You stole Daddy! Like a thief! He'd be alive this minute but for you!" – and had to be carried, hysterically weeping, out of the house. The German film-maker hurried after her. More mourners pushed into the parlor, there was a roaring of motorcycles in the drive. Near dawn, Janessa requested several old friends of Carlin's to lift him from the bed and place him in a casket beside the bed, and we were a little unsteady on our feet, shy about touching our dead, embalmed, sleeping-looking friend with the rouged cheeks and shoe-polish hair; also Carlin was heavier than he appeared. I said under my breath, "Man, what'd they inject you with? Lead?" My buddies laughed. We were sweating like hogs but Carlin was cold. You could feel the cold lifting from him. I believe he was sucking the heat from our hands as cold water will do. Janessa had her camera, taking flash shots of us. I muttered, "Fuck you, you bitch, a man has died for fuck's sake, we must respect him." My buddies muttered, "Amen!" But Janessa chose not to hear. She gave her camera to someone so that her picture might be taken beside us, fitting Carlin into his casket, which was silver-onyx-mahogany, purchased in Charleston and shipped to Buckhannon. We were having a hard time keeping from laughing, fitting poor Carlin into the silk-cushioned casket, and everybody looking on, gaping and drinking. Carlin's toupee was askew, and Janessa hurriedly adjusted it, and I was trying to remember if I'd realized that my friend had been wearing a toupee in life but I couldn't. The funeral was scheduled for nine A.M. but didn't take place until 10:20 A.M. Some folks, driving from the Ritchie house to the cemetery a mile away, became lost, or disappeared. Yet others appeared. A raw-boned preacher from the Gospel Church of Jesus of Buckhannon, whom Carlin hadn't known, spoke at the grave site, quoting Scripture. This was "Americana" for the foreign journalists, I suppose – Carlin hadn't belonged to any church, though he'd been baptized Baptist. I tried to interrupt the preacher to say what Carlin had said – "I believe in God but not in man believing in God" – but everybody hushed me. I was pissed, and would've left before the casket was lowered into the grave, but Janessa gripped my arm in her talon-claws and held me there. She'd been glancing at me at the grave site, using her eyes on me; I wondered if she was worried that Carlin might've told me of the plan to stockpile barbiturates and I might tell the authorities. Sure, the woman was guilty of aiding and abetting a suicide, probably under West Virginia law she'd be vulnerable to arrest, but no one could prove her involvement, any good lawyer would've gotten her off. Anyway that wasn't her truest crime, an act of murder. And soul-murder. But what she wanted from me was that I'd stay for the funeral luncheon at the Buckhannon Inn and come back to the house that afternoon – "There's just a select few of Carlin's artist-friends I'm inviting; Heinz Muller wants to interview you and wrap up his film."

'When I left Buckhannon that day, which was immediately following the funeral, I could not have believed that I would ever plan to return. For any purpose possible.

'Yet now I'm being called. It's Carlin calling me. He'd been the one to own firearms, as a kid. He'd been a hunter, with rifle and shotgun.

'Only a few weeks after Carlin's death, it began to happen. Her calculated acts. Not honoring Carlin's will, getting a lawyer to help her break it, contesting the provisions Carlin had made for his first wife and his children, refusing even to surrender the artworks he'd left to museums in West Virginia and to certain of his friends, like me. Those silk screens Carlin wanted me to have – from his Appalachia series – she's claiming she doesn't have. People try to excuse her – "Poor Janessa, she's devastated with grief. Cries all the time, she says." Bullshit. But this isn't the worst.

'This behavior, it's mean, cruel, vicious, conniving – criminal. But you wouldn't wish to kill because of it. At least, I wouldn't.

'What's unforgivable in her, what's purely evil, is that she's a vampire. She's sucking from the living, and from the dead. On TV, for instance, interviewed by Barbara Walters. Network TV. And she's reminiscing about Carlin Ritchie's last years, how they collaborated together on mostly everything, Carlin had even worked from sketches she'd provided him, and suggestions; saying theirs was "one of the great loves of the century, like Georgia O'Keeffe and Alfred Stieglitz." Work of Carlin's he'd done years before he met her, work he'd had in his studio but hadn't shown, turns out it's "collaborative." Janessa Ritchie is "co-artist." Right there on TV, her hair dyed almost purple, with grief-streaks of silver, and the big owl-eyes brimming with tears as Barbara Walters pretends to take this bullshit seriously. There's even a journal of Carlin's Janessa reads from, conveniently not handwritten but typed, a so-called log of the final year of his life – "My heart is full! My love for Janessa and for my work is God's grace! I will die not out of sorrow or despair but out of love, in the ecstasy of pure love, knowing my soul is complete." And her and Barbara Walters practically bawling together. I came close to kicking in my TV, I was so furious.

'Furious, and sick in my soul. For *my* soul is sure not complete!

'Now she's being invited everywhere. "Janessa Ritchie" is as famous as Carlin, almost. Exhibits in Berlin, Paris, London. This exhibit at the Whitney – it's up right now. Go and see for your own eyes. Big features in glossy magazines – *The New Yorker, Mirabella,* even *Art in America,* where you'd expect the editors to be more discerning. Some people in the art world have called her to protest, Carlin's ex-dealer drew up a letter, which dozens of us signed, and which was sent certified mail to her, but none of it does any good, and it won't. To stop a creature like her you must destroy her. Trying to reason with her, pleading, even threats of lawsuits – none of that will work. This exhibit at the Whitney – that did it, for me. Tipped me over. It's more of this "collaborative" bullshit except this time Janessa has dared to put her name to art that was Carlin's, that he hadn't finished and signed. The title of the exhibit is "The Ritchies" – like she, the woman who killed him, the vampire, is an equal of her victim! It's a nightmare. It's like the media know what's happening but go along with it, Janessa's a glamorous woman, they can champion "an exemplary female artist," as she's been called.

'I wasn't invited to the champagne opening at the Whitney, of course. But I got in anyway. I saw what was on the walls and walked right up to her, the bitch, the thief, the "grieving widow"; she's lovey-dovey with this guy who's Carlin's new dealer at a wealthy uptown gallery, and she's dressed in sexy black silk, spike-heeled shoes, and textured black stockings, she's put on more weight, in her bust and hips, fleshy but not fat, and sexy, though her skin is powdered dead-white and looks bloated like a corpse that's been in water. And that crimson mouth that's wider than ever, thick with greasy lipstick. *Ugh! – I remember the taste of her.* She sights me coming at her and I see the guilty panic in her eyes, though right away she puts on this pose of innocence so I'm the one who comes off badly. I say, "Goddamn you, woman, what do you mean claiming this work is yours? It's Carlin's and you know it," and she says to her companion in this scared little-girl voice, "He's a deranged man! I don't know who he is! He's been threatening me for months!" and I say, "Don't know who I am! I'm Carlin's friend. I'm here to speak for him. To tell the world that you are thieving from him, and betraying him. Jesus, woman, didn't you love that man at all?" But by this time two security guards are on me and I'm being hustled out onto the street – Madison Avenue. And I know better than to stick around and get arrested by some real cops.

'So what'd I do – drove home here. Sick in my heart. Wanting to commit a murder right then if only I had the power. I saw Carlin on that veranda, as dusk came on, wrapped in a flimsy blanket, shivering, trying to smile at me, pleading. *I don't want to die. Yes, but I'm ready. Help me.*'

We were still in the tavern, but it was almost time to return to the courthouse. Rafe had showed me a newspaper photo of 'Janessa Ritchie' and she looked just like he'd said:

glamorous, fleshy, with hungry eyes and mouth. I felt my heart beating hard and heavy, Rafe's hot, angry blood streaming through my veins. He said, 'Every day it gets worse. It's hanging over me always. Can't sleep, can't work. And this week of jury duty – at the courthouse – in that atmosphere – it's like somebody is fucking with me, y'know? – mocking me. Every defendant who's on trial had the courage to do what he needed to do – there's that way of thinking. But Rafe Healy doesn't have the courage, so far, to do what I need to do.'

I could see how agitated he was, so I paid the bill for both of us and got him out of there, walking in the sunshine and trying to talk to him, reason with him. It was like we'd been imprisoned together in a small cell that, even though we were in the open air now and in the eyes of observers free, unconfined men, continued to press in upon us. I said, 'Maybe it's a sign, Rafe? If you don't have the "courage"? That you shouldn't do it? That you should just forget about it? Since your friend is dead anyway—'

Rafe stopped on the sidewalk, glared at me like I was his mortal enemy. 'Fuck you, man, what're you saying? Carlin's *dead*, that means – what? I should abandon him?'

'No, Rafe. Only just that—'

'She's a vicious, evil woman. I swear, an emissary of Satan. That's more and more clear to me, Harrison. Last night I was in my studio, trying to work, drinking and trying to work, and my hands shook so badly I couldn't do a thing – I heard her laughing at me, and saw those eyes, I tasted that mouth sort of nuzzling at me, teasing. She's moving onto me, now. The vampire's moving onto me.'

'Rafe, that isn't right. You know that isn't right. Listen to you.'

At the courthouse steps, Rafe wiped his face on his sleeve, tried to compose himself. Just since Monday, I believed he'd lost some weight. There were knifelike vertical creases in his cheeks. He said, 'I believe you're right. I can hear my own voice, and it's become a deranged voice. I'm not me – I'm a deranged man. And it's that woman who's to blame. So long as she lives, I am her victim.'

7.

You could rent a car. Two cars. In sequence. The first you'd rent at an airport, perhaps in New Jersey. You'd leave your van in a parking lot. The second car you'd rent in Pennsylvania. And drive to Buckhannon, West Virginia, to arrive there by first dark. Because you would need to seek your target in a lighted house, yourself hidden in darkness. But wait: Before this, at a Sears or Kmart in any large mall (some distance from your home), you could purchase a dark jacket with a hood. Rubber boots a size or two larger than your own. Gloves. But wait: Before this, you will need to buy the rifle. The rifle with the scope. Ammunition. You're going deer hunting, you'll tell the sales clerk. You'll purchase the rifle upstate, where hunting is common, and you'll need to practice shooting at a target. Somewhere private. Maybe we could practice together. I don't mean that I'd be coming with you to West Virginia. I could not do that. But I could help you. I could buy the rifle, possibly. I could give you moral support. I can see you are in need of moral support. I'm your cousin but we're closer than most cousins. You could say I'm your lost brother. And I'm lonely.

Rosalind woke me, gently. Telling me I'd been grinding my teeth.

A bad dream? she asked, and I said. No. Not a bad dream. Not at all.

8.

Thursday afternoon at 2:25 P.M., Rafe's luck runs out. JUROR 93 is called to take his seat in a jury box – our panel of jurors was sent up to a sixth-floor courtroom where there's a murder case scheduled, a nasty case it looks to be, burly black man with a downlooking, gnarled face accused of having killed his wife. Rafe shudders and gives my arm a quick scared squeeze as he stumbles out of his seat to step forward. Poor Rafe: Everybody's staring at him, he's unsteady on his feet as a sleepwalker (or a drunk: He'd had at least six beers at lunch, in spite of my telling him to go easy), the tallest of all the jurors and, judging by the look in his mottled face, the shyest. He's wearing his bib overalls, which look as if he's been sleeping in them (I wouldn't doubt he has), and his beard and hair are scruffy. I'm worried that my cousin will get into trouble if it's discovered he's been drinking while on jury duty: Does that mean contempt of court? I'd been drinking, too, but not as much as Rafe, and I believe I'm fully sober.

This trial will be for first-degree murder. Which is to say, it's a capital case. New York State reinstated the death penalty a few years ago, by lethal injection.

As Rafe Healy passes by the defense counsel's table, the defendant turns to stare at him. It's the first time in the approximate ninety minutes we've been in this courtroom that the defendant, a muscular, near-bald man of about fifty, has roused himself to take such an interest. But Rafe, a vague, dazed smile on his face or a grimace of the lips that might be mistaken for a smile, makes it a point not to look at him.

Not many jurors, Caucasians or persons of color (as we're told they wish now to be called), are anxious to be assigned to this case. Downstairs the rumor circulated that it could last for weeks. And there's a death-penalty trial that follows, if the verdict is guilty. I swear Rafe was actually praying, moving his lips during the voir dire as potential jurors were questioned one by one, a few retained in the jury box but most dismissed. Now JUROR 93 is seated in the box being asked, 'Occupation?' ('self-employed craftsman' – which makes a few people smile) and whether he's associated in any way with the case, heard anything about it, or believes he might be in any way disqualified to remain on the jury, and Rafe is staring pained at the judge, moving his lips but not speaking. I'm feeling – Jesus! – just so excruciatingly embarrassed for my cousin, and anxious for him; I'm worried as hell what he's going to say. *I can't sit in judgment of any murderer. I am not the man.* The way Rafe and I've worked it through these past few days, less than a week but it feels like we've been together for a long, long time, there are times when murdering another human being isn't just not wrong but morally and ethically right. The law just can't cover that. The judge rephrases his question, and again Rafe tries to answer, but can't seem to speak; his face is mottled now like he's got a sudden case of measles, and his eyes are glassy. 'Mr. Healy, is something wrong? Mr. Healy?' the judge inquires, concerned; he's a middle-aged man, friendly-seeming most of the time though he's been a little impatient with some of the jurors who'd clearly wanted to be dismissed, and now with Rafe he doesn't know how to proceed. Is this juror just being difficult, to be excused, or is there something really wrong with him? I raise my hand like a kid in school and say, 'Excuse me? Your Honor? That man is my cousin and he's kind of a – nervous type? He's on medication, I think – probably he shouldn't be here.' Now everybody's staring at *me*.

But it's okay. It's the right, inspired thing. The judge contemplates me for a minute, frowning, then thanks me for the information and calls Rafe over to speak with him in private. After a few minutes' consultation (I'm watching Rafe's earnest face and hoping to hell he isn't uttering any sort of blunt truth, only just improvising a reasonable excuse to get him out of here) JUROR 93 is formally dismissed for the day.

In fact, it will be for the rest of the week. Rafe Healy is finished with jury duty, probably forever.

For me, the remainder of the voir dire passes in a blur. I keep waiting for my number to be called, but it isn't. By 5:20 P.M. the jury box is finally filled, twelve jurors and two alternates and the rest of us dismissed for the day.

I'd been wondering if Rafe would be downstairs waiting for me, but he isn't. He's in the parking lot, leaning against the fender of my car. 'Jesus, Harrison! You saved me up there. Man, I'm grateful.' Rafe actually hugs me, it's that weird. But I know I did the right, shrewd thing. It just seems like my brain's been revved up lately, like a machine working faster and more efficiently. Things falling into place.

9.

It's past 8 P.M. by the time I get home, Thursday night. Should've called Rosalind from the bar but forgot. And the woman's in my face as soon as I get in the door, asking, 'how's the trial?' and I say, 'Trial? What trial?' (Goddamn, I'd kind of forgotten what I'd told her the other day) then – 'Oh, that. It's pretty ugly stuff, like I said. I'll be glad when it's over.' Rosalind says, with that blinking little frown of hers that isn't an accusation, but means to make you think along those lines, 'I looked everywhere in the paper but I didn't find anything. About any trial that sounded like yours.' I say, beginning to get pissed at her, 'Look, Rosalind, I explained to you I can't discuss it. Didn't I explain to you I can't discuss it?' and she says, 'It's got to be something terrible for you to get drunk every night on the way home, like you haven't done for twelve years,' and I say, 'What? You've been counting?' like it's a joke, or I'm willing to grant her the possibility that it's a joke. I'm an hour late for supper, but what the fuck, I get a beer from the refrigerator and Rosalind's pulling at my arm in that way I don't like, and she knows I don't like, saying, 'Don't be ridiculous, Harrison, you can hint about it, can't you? Is it a murder case? Some kind of murder case?' I'm drinking from the can, saying nothing, trying to walk away and the woman keeps pushing, 'Is it a woman killed, and a man on trial? Is it some pervert? It isn't a child killed, is it? And some disgusting pervert on trial? Just wink your left eye, honey, and give me a clue,' and I'm beginning to lose it, I say, 'Look, we could both be in trouble if I breathe a word of this trial to anyone, including even my fellow jurors, before the judge gives permission, didn't I explain that to you?

Can't you comprehend? Violating the judge's order is called contempt of court and you can be jailed,' and she's in my face persisting, in that way she used to do with the boys, and that pisses me for sure, saying, 'Harrison? Come *on*. Just wink your left eye if—' And I shove her back against the edge of the kitchen table, and she gives a little scream of pain and surprise and I'm out of the kitchen, I'm slamming out of the goddamned room, I'm shaking, muttering to myself words I've never heard myself speak aloud in this house, in such a voice, I'm thinking I've never touched my wife, or any woman, in anger in my life, never in anger like this, like flame, never until now and it feels right, it feels good, it feels goddamned good.

Like Rafe knows.

ANNE PERRY

....

When this story found its way to my desk, the author acknowledged that she thought it was the best short story she had ever written. She is right. This wonderfully evocative tale of the trenches in World War I and the terrible crime it reports will haunt your memory for a long time to come.

It doesn't seem, at first blush, to be a crime story at all, but as you continue along you will learn that it surely is.

This is a different era for Anne Perry, who has achieved great success with her Victorian era mystery novels, but it must have been important to her as she has produced such a vivid account of the place and time.

Perhaps the reason for the power of this unusual tale is that it was inspired by a real-life person. The kindly but strong chaplain who understands the obsession of an officer who wants to be a hero was based very closely on the author's grandfather.

Heroes won the Edgar Allan Poe Award from the Mystery Writers of America as the best short story in 2000.

HEROES

By Anne Perry

Nights were always the worst, and in winter they lasted from dusk at about four o'clock until dawn again toward eight the following morning. Sometimes star shells lit the sky, showing the black zigzags of the trenches stretching as far as the eye could see to left and right. Apparently now they went right across France and Belgium all the way from the Alps to the Channel. But Joseph was only concerned with this short stretch of the Ypres Salient.

In the gloom near him someone coughed, a deep, hacking sound coming from down in the chest. They were in the support line, farthest from the front, the most complex of the three rows of trenches. Here were the kitchens, the latrines and the stores and mortar positions. Fifteen-foot shafts led to caves about five paces wide and high enough for most men to stand upright. Joseph made his way in the half dark now, the slippery wood under his boots and his hands feeling the mud walls, held up by timber and wire. There was an awful lot of water. One of the sumps must be blocked.

There was a glow of light ahead and a moment later he was in the comparative warmth of the dugout. There were two candles burning and the brazier gave off heat and a sharp smell of soot. The air was blue with tobacco smoke, and a pile of boots and greatcoats steamed a little. Two officers sat on canvas chairs talking together. One of them recited a joke – gallows humor, and they both laughed. A gramophone sat silent on a camp table, and a small pile of records of the latest music-hall songs was carefully protected in a tin box.

'Hello, Chaplain,' one of them said cheerfully. 'How's God these days?'

'Gone home on sick leave,' the other answered quickly, before Joseph could reply. There was disgust in his voice, but no intended irreverence. Death was too close here for men to mock faith.

'Have a seat,' the first offered, waving toward a third chair. 'Morris got it today. Killed outright. That bloody sniper again.'

'He's somewhere out there, just about opposite us,' the second said grimly. 'One of those blighters the other day claimed he'd got forty-three for sure.'

'I can believe it,' Joseph answered, accepting the seat. He knew better than most what the casualties were. It was his job to comfort the terrified, the dying, to carry stretchers, often to write letters to the bereaved. Sometimes he thought it was harder than actually fighting, but he refused to stay back in the comparative safety of the field hospitals and depots. This was where he was most needed.

'Thought about setting up a trench raid,' the major said slowly, weighing his words and looking at Joseph. 'Good for morale. Make it seem as if we were actually doing something. But our chances of getting the blighter are pretty small. Only lose a lot of men for nothing. Feel even worse afterward.'

The captain did not add anything. They all knew morale was sinking. Losses were high, the news bad. Word of terrible slaughter seeped through from the Somme and Verdun and all along the line right to the sea. Physical hardship took its toll, the dirt, the cold, and the alternation between boredom and terror. The winter of 1916 lay ahead.

'Cigarette?' The major held out his pack to Joseph.

'No thanks,' Joseph declined with a smile. 'Got any tea going?'

They poured him a mugful, strong and bitter, but hot. He drank it, and half an hour later made his way forward to the open air again and the travel trench. A star shell exploded high and bright. Automatically he ducked, keeping his head below the rim. They were about four feet deep, and in order not to provide a target, a man had to move in a half crouch. There was a rattle of machine-gun fire out ahead and, closer to, a thud as a rat was dislodged and fell into the mud beside the duckboards.

Other men were moving about close to him. The normal order of things was reversed here. Nothing much happened during the day. Trench repair work was done, munitions shifted, weapons cleaned, a little rest taken. Most of the activity was at night, most of the death.

''Lo, Chaplain,' a voice whispered in the dark. 'Say a prayer we get that bloody sniper, will you?'

'Maybe God's a Jerry?' someone suggested in the dark.

'Don't be stupid!' a third retorted derisively. 'Everyone knows God's an Englishman! Didn't they teach you nothing at school?'

There was a burst of laughter. Joseph joined in. He promised to offer up the appropriate prayers and moved on forward. He had known many of the men all his life. They came from the same Northumbrian town as he did, or the surrounding villages. They had gone to school together, nicked apples from the same trees, fished in the same rivers, and walked the same lanes.

It was a little after six when he reached the firing trench beyond whose sandbag parapet lay no-man's-land with its four or five hundred yards of mud, barbed wire, and shell holes. Half a dozen burnt tree stumps looked in the sudden flares like men. Those gray wraiths could be fog, or gas.

Funny that in summer this blood- and horror-soaked soil could still bloom with honeysuckle, forget-me-nots, and wild larkspur, and most of all with poppies. You would think nothing would ever grow there again.

More star shells went up, lighting the ground, the jagged scars of the trenches black, the men on the fire steps with rifles on their shoulders illuminated for a few, blinding moments. Sniper shots rang out.

Joseph stood still. He knew the terror of the night watch out beyond the parapet, crawling around in the mud. Some of them would be at the head of saps out from the trench, most would be in shell holes, surrounded by heavy barricades of wire. Their purpose was to check enemy patrols for unusual movement, any signs of increased activity, as if there might be an attack planned.

More star shells lit the sky. It was beginning to rain. A crackle of machine-gun fire, and heavier artillery some-where over to the left. Then the sharp whine of sniper fire, again and again.

Joseph shuddered. He thought of the men out there, beyond his vision, and prayed for strength to endure with them in their pain, not to try to deaden himself to it.

There were shouts somewhere ahead, heavy shells now,

shrapnel bursting. There was a flurry of movement, flares, and a man came sliding over the parapet, shouting for help.

Joseph plunged forward, slithering in the mud, grabbing for the wooden props to hold himself up. Another flare of light. He saw quite clearly Captain Holt lurching toward him, another man over his shoulder, deadweight.

'He's hurt!' Holt gasped. 'Pretty badly. One of the night patrol. Panicked. Just about got us all killed.' He eased the man down into Joseph's arms and let his rifle slide forward, bayonet covered in an old sock to hide its gleam. His face was grotesque in the lantern light, smeared with mud and a wide streak of blood over the burnt cork that blackened it, as all night patrol had.

Others were coming to help. There was still a terrible noise of fire going on and the occasional flare.

The man in Joseph's arms did not stir. His body was limp and it was difficult to support him. Joseph felt the wetness and the smell of blood. Wordlessly others materialized out of the gloom and took the weight.

'Is he alive?' Holt said urgently. 'There was a hell of a lot of shot up there.' His voice was shaking, almost on the edge of control.

'Don't know,' Joseph answered. 'We'll get him back to the bunker and see. You've done all you can.' He knew how desperate men felt when they risked their lives to save another man and did not succeed. A kind of despair set in, a sense of very personal failure, almost a guilt for having survived themselves. 'Are you hurt?'

'Not much,' Holt answered. 'Couple of grazes.'

'Better have them dressed, before they get poisoned,' Joseph advised, his feet slipping on the wet boards and banging his shoulder against a jutting post. The whole

Anne Perry

trench wall was crooked, giving way under the weight of mud. The founds had eroded.

The man helping him swore.

Awkwardly carrying the wounded man, they staggered back through the travel line to the support trench and into the light and shelter of a bunker.

Holt looked dreadful. Beneath the cork and blood his face was ashen. He was soaked with rain and mud and there were dark patches of blood across his back and shoulders.

Someone gave him a cigarette. Back here it was safe to strike a match. He drew in smoke deeply. 'Thanks,' he murmured, still staring at the wounded man.

Joseph looked down at him now, and it was only too plain where the blood had come from. It was young Ashton. He knew him quite well. He had been at school with his older brother.

The soldier who had helped carry him in let out a cry of dismay, strangled in his throat. It was Mordaff, Ashton's closest friend, and he could see what Joseph now could also. Ashton was dead, his chest torn open, the blood no longer pumping, and a bullet hole through his head.

'I'm sorry,' Holt said quietly. 'I did what I could. I can't have got to him in time. He panicked.'

Mordaff jerked his head up. 'He never would!' The cry was desperate, a shout of denial against a shame too great to be borne.

'Not Will!'

Holt stiffened. 'I'm sorry,' he said hoarsely. 'It happens.'

'Not with Will Ashton, it don't!' Mordaff retorted, his eyes blazing, pupils circled with white in the candlelight, his face gray. He had been in the front line two weeks now, a long stretch without a break from the ceaseless tension,

476

filth, cold, and intermittent silence and noise. He was nineteen.

'You'd better go and get that arm dressed, and your side,' Joseph said to Holt. He made his voice firm, as to a child.

Holt glanced again at the body of Ashton, then up at Joseph.

'Don't stand there bleeding,' Joseph ordered. 'You did all you could. There's nothing else. I'll look after Mordaff.'

'I tried!' Holt repeated. 'There's nothing but mud and darkness and wire, and bullets coming in all directions.' There was a sharp thread of terror under his shell-thin veneer of control. He had seen too many men die. 'It's enough to make anyone lose his nerve. You want to be a hero – you mean to be – and then it overwhelms you—'

'Not Will!' Mordaff said again, his voice choking off in a sob.

Holt looked at Joseph again, then staggered out.

Joseph turned to Mordaff. He had done this before, too many times, tried to comfort men who had just seen childhood friends blown to pieces, or killed by a sniper's bullet, looking as if they should still be alive, perfect except for the small, blue hole through the brain. There was little to say. Most men found talk of God meaningless at that moment. They were shocked, fighting against belief and yet seeing all the terrible waste and loss in front of them. Usually it was best just to stay with them, let them speak about the past, what the friend had been like, times they had shared, just as if he were only wounded and would be back, at the end of the war, in some world one could only imagine, in England, perhaps on a summer day with sunlight on the grass, birds singing, a quiet riverbank somewhere, the sound of laughter, and women's voices.

Mordaff refused to be comforted. He accepted Ashton's death; the physical reality of that was too clear to deny, and he had seen too many other men he knew killed in the year and a half he had been in Belgium. But he could not, would not accept that Ashton had panicked. He knew what panic out there cost, how many other lives it jeopardized. It was the ultimate failure.

'How am I going to tell his mam?' he begged Joseph. 'It'll be all I can do to tell her he's dead! His pa'll never get over it. That proud of him, they were. He's the only boy. Three sisters he had, Mary, Lizzie, and Alice. Thought he was the greatest lad in the world. I can't tell 'em he panicked! He couldn't have, Chaplain! He just wouldn't!'

Joseph did not know what to say. How could people at home in England even begin to imagine what it was like in the mud and noise out here? But he knew how deep shame burned. A lifetime could be consumed by it.

'Maybe he just lost sense of direction,' he said gently. 'He wouldn't be the first.' War changed men. People did panic. Mordaff knew that, and half his horror was because it could be true. But Joseph did not say so. 'I'll write to his family,' he went on. 'There's a lot of good to say about him. I could send pages. I'll not need to tell them much about tonight.'

'Will you?' Mordaff was eager. 'Thanks ... thanks, Chaplain. Can I stay with him ... until they come for him?'

'Yes, of course,' Joseph agreed. 'I'm going forward anyway. Get yourself a hot cup of tea. See you in an hour or so.'

He left Mordaff squatting on the earth floor beside Ashton's body and fumbled his way back over the slimy duckboards toward the travel line, then forward again to the front and the crack of gunfire and the occasional high flare of a star shell.

He did not see Mordaff again, but he thought nothing of it. He could have passed twenty men he knew and not recognized them, muffled in greatcoats, heads bent as they moved, rattling along the duckboards, or standing on the fire steps, rifles to shoulder, trying to see in the gloom for something to aim at.

Now and again he heard a cough, or the scamper of rats' feet and the splash of rain and mud. He spent a little time with two men swapping jokes, joining in their laughter. It was black humor, self-mocking, but he did not miss the courage in it, or the fellowship, the need to release emotion in some sane and human way.

About midnight the rain stopped.

A little after five the night patrol came scrambling through the wire, whispered passwords to the sentries, then came tumbling over the parapet of sandbags down into the trench, shivering with cold and relief. One of them had caught a shot in the arm.

Joseph went back with them to the support line. In one of the dugouts a gramophone was playing a music-hall song. A couple of men sang along with it; one of them had a beautiful voice, a soft, lyric tenor. It was a silly song, trivial, but it sounded almost like a hymn out here, a praise of life.

A couple of hours and the day would begin: endless, methodical duties of housekeeping, mindless routine, but it was better than doing nothing.

There was still a sporadic crackle of machine-gun fire and the whine of sniper bullets.

An hour till dawn.

Joseph was sitting on an upturned ration case when

Sergeant Renshaw came into the bunker, pulling the gas curtain aside to peer in.

'Chaplain?'

Joseph looked up. He could see bad news in the man's face.

'I'm afraid Mordaff got it tonight,' he said, coming in and letting the curtain fall again. 'Sorry. Don't really know what happened. Ashton's death seems to have ... well, he lost his nerve. More or less went over the top all by himself. Suppose he was determined to go and give Fritz a bloody nose, on Ashton's account. Stupid bastard! Sorry, Chaplain.'

He did not need to explain himself, or to apologize. Joseph knew exactly the fury and the grief he felt at such a futile waste. To this was added a sense of guilt that he had not stopped it. He should have realized Mordaff was so close to breaking. He should have seen it. That was his job.

He stood up slowly. 'Thanks for telling me, Sergeant. Where is he?'

'He's gone, Chaplain.' Renshaw remained near the doorway. 'You can't help 'im now.'

'I know that. I just want to ... I don't know ... apologize to him. I let him down. I didn't understand he was ... so ...'

'You can't be everybody's keeper,' Renshaw said gently. 'Too many of us. It's not been a bad night otherwise. Got a trench raid coming off soon. Just wish we could get that damn sniper across the way there.' He scraped a match and lit his cigarette. 'But morale's good. That was a brave thing Captain Holt did out there. He wanted the chance to do something to hearten the men. He saw it and took it. Pity about Ashton, but that doesn't alter Holt's courage. Could see him, you know, by the star shells. Right out there beyond the last wire, bent double, carrying Ashton on his back. Poor devil went crazy. Running around like a fool. Have got the whole patrol killed if Holt hadn't gone after him. Hell of a job getting him back. Fell a couple of times. Reckon that's worth a mention in dispatches, at least. Heartens the men, knowing our officers have got that kind of spirit.'

'Yes . . . I'm sure,' Joseph agreed. He could only think of Ashton's white face, and Mordaff's desperate denial, and how Ashton's mother would feel, and the rest of his family. 'I think I'll go and see Mordaff just the same.'

'Right you are,' Renshaw conceded reluctantly, standing aside for Joseph to pass.

Mordaff lay in the support trench just outside the bunker two hundred yards to the west. He looked even younger than he had in life, as if he were asleep. His face was oddly calm, even though it was smeared with mud. Someone had tried to clean most of it off in a kind of dignity, so that at least he was recognizable. There was a large wound in the left side of his forehead. It was bigger than most sniper wounds. He must have been a lot closer.

Joseph stood in the first paling of the darkness and looked at him by candlelight from the open bunker curtain. He had been so alive only a few hours ago, so full of anger and loyalty and dismay. What had made him throw his life away in a useless gesture? Joseph racked his mind for some sign that should have warned him Mordaff was so close to breaking, but he could not see it even now.

There was a cough a few feet away, and the tramp of boots on duckboards. The men were stood down, just one sentry per platoon left. They had returned for breakfast. If he thought about it he could smell cooking.

Now would be the time to ask around and find out what had happened to Mordaff.

He made his way to the field kitchen. It was packed with men, some standing to be close to the stoves and catch a bit of their warmth, others choosing to sit, albeit farther away. They had survived the night. They were laughing and telling stories, most of them unfit for delicate ears, but Joseph was too used to it to take any offense. Now and then someone new would apologize for such language in front of a chaplain, but most knew he understood too well.

'Yeah,' one answered his question through a mouthful of bread and jam. 'He came and asked me if I saw what happened to Ashton. Very cut up, he was.'

'And what did you tell him?' Joseph asked.

The man swallowed. 'Told him Ashton seemed fine to me when he went over. Just like anyone else, nervous ... but, then, only a fool isn't scared to go over the top!'

Joseph thanked him and moved on. He needed to know who else was on the patrol.

'Captain Holt,' the next man told him, a ring of pride in his voice. Word had got around about Holt's courage. Everyone stood a little taller because of it, felt a little braver, more confident. 'We'll pay Fritz back for that,' he added. 'Next raid – you'll see.'

There was a chorus of agreement.

'Who else?' Joseph pressed.

'Seagrove, Noakes, Willis,' a thin man replied, standing up. 'Want some breakfast, Chaplain? Anything you like, on the house – as long as it's bread and jam and half a cup of tea. But you're not particular, are you? Not one of those fussy eaters who'll only take kippers and toast?'

'What I wouldn't give for a fresh Craster kipper,' another sighed, a faraway look in his eyes. 'I can smell them in my dreams.'

Someone told him good-naturedly to shut up.

'Went over the top beside me,' Willis said when Joseph found him quarter of an hour later. 'All blacked up like the rest of us. Seemed okay to me then. Lost him in no-man's-land. Had a hell of a job with the wire. As bloody usual, it wasn't where we'd been told. Got through all right, then Fritz opened up on us. Star shells all over the sky.' He sniffed and then coughed violently. When he had control of himself again, he continued. 'Then I saw someone outlined against the flares, arms high, like a wild man, running around. He was going toward the German lines, shouting something. Couldn't hear what in the noise.'

Joseph did not interrupt. It was now broad daylight and beginning to drizzle again. Around them men were starting the duties of the day: digging, filling sandbags, carrying ammunition, strengthening the wire, resetting duckboards. Men took an hour's work, an hour's sentry duty, and an hour's rest.

Near them somebody was expending his entire vocabulary of curses against lice. Two more were planning elaborate schemes to hold the water at bay.

'Of course that lit us up like a target, didn't it!' Willis went on. 'Sniper fire and machine guns all over the place. Even a couple of shells. How none of us got hit I'll never know. Perhaps the row woke God up, and He came back on duty!' He laughed hollowly. 'Sorry, Chaplain. Didn't mean it. I'm just so damn sorry poor Ashton got it. Holt just came out of nowhere and ran after him. Obsessed with being a hero, or he'd not even have tried. I can see him in my mind's eye floundering through the mud. If Ashton hadn't got caught in the wire he'd never have got him.'

'Caught in the wire?' Joseph asked, memory pricking at him.

'Yeah. Ashton must have run right into the wire, because he stopped sudden – teetering, like – and fell over. A hell of a barrage came over just after that. We all threw ourselves down.'

'What happened then?' Joseph said urgently, a slow, sick thought taking shape in his mind.

'When it died down I looked up again, and there was Holt staggering back with poor Ashton across his shoulders. Hell of a job he had carrying him, even though he's bigger than Ashton – well, taller, anyway. Up to his knees in mud, he was, shot and shell all over, sky lit up like a Christmas tree. Of course we gave him what covering fire we could. Maybe it helped.' He coughed again. 'Reckon he'll be mentioned in dispatches, Chaplain? He deserves it.' There was admiration in his voice, a lift of hope.

Joseph forced himself to answer. 'I should think so.' The words were stiff.

'Well, if he isn't, the men'll want to know why!' Willis said fiercely. 'Bloody hero, he is.'

Joseph thanked him and went to find Seagrove and Noakes. They told him pretty much the same story.

'You going to have him recommended?' Noakes asked. 'He earned it this time. Mordaff came and we said just the same to him. Reckon he wanted the Captain given a medal. He made us say it over and over again, exactly what happened.'

'That's right.' Seagrove nodded, leaning on a sandbag.

'You told him the same?' Joseph asked. 'About the wire, and Ashton getting caught in it?'

'Yes, of course. If he hadn't got caught by the legs he'd have gone straight on and landed up in Fritz's lap, poor devil.'

'Thank you.'

'Welcome, Chaplain. You going to write up Captain Holt?'

Joseph did not answer, but turned away, sick at heart.

He did not need to look again, but he trudged all the way back to the field hospital anyway. It would be his job to say the services for both Ashton and Mordaff. The graves would be already dug.

He looked at Ashton's body again, looked carefully at his trousers. They were stained with mud, but there were no tears in them, no marks of wire. The fabric was perfect.

He straightened up.

'I'm sorry,' he said quietly to the dead man. 'Rest in peace.' And he turned and walked away.

He went back to where he had left Mordaff's body, but it had been removed. Half an hour more took him to where it also was laid out. He touched the cold hand and looked at the brow. He would ask. He would be sure. But in his mind he already was. He needed time to know what he must do about it. The men would be going over the top on another trench raid soon. Today morale was high. They had a hero in their number, a man who would risk his own life to bring back a soldier who had lost his nerve and panicked. Led by someone like that, they were equal to Fritz any day. Was one pistol bullet, one family's shame, worth all that?

What were they fighting for anyway? The issues were so very big, and at the same time so very small and immediate.

He found Captain Holt alone just after dusk, standing on the duckboards below the parapet, near one of the firing steps.

'Oh, it's you, Chaplain. Ready for another night?'

'It'll come, whether I am or not,' Joseph replied.

Holt gave a short bark of laughter. 'That doesn't sound like you. Tired of the firing line, are you? You've been up here a couple of weeks; you should be in turn for a step back any day. Me too, thank God.'

Joseph faced forward, peering through the gloom toward no-man's-land and the German lines beyond. He was shaking. He must control himself. This must be done in the silence, before the shooting started up again. Then he might not get away with it.

'Pity about that sniper over there,' he remarked. 'He's taken out a lot of our men.'

'Damnable,' Holt agreed. 'Can't get a line on him, though. Keeps his own head well down.'

'Oh, yes.' Joseph nodded. 'We'd never get him from here. It needs a man to go over in the dark and find him.'

'Not a good idea, Chaplain. He'd not come back. Not advocating suicide, are you?'

Joseph chose his words very carefully and kept his voice as unemotional as he could.

'I wouldn't have put it like that,' he answered. 'But he has cost us a lot of men. Mordaff today, you know?'

'Yes ... I heard. Pity.'

'Except that wasn't the sniper, of course. But the men

think it was, so it comes to the same thing, as far as morale is concerned.'

'Don't know what you mean, Chaplain.' There was a slight hesitation in Holt's voice in the darkness.

'Wasn't a rifle wound, it was a pistol,' Joseph replied. 'You can tell the difference, if you're actually looking for it.'

'Then he was a fool to be that close to German lines,' Holt said, facing forward over the parapet and the mud. 'Lost his nerve, I'm afraid.'

'Like Ashton,' Joseph said. 'Can understand that, up there in no-man's-land, mud everywhere, wire catching hold of you, tearing at you, stopping you from moving. Terrible thing to be caught in the wire with the star shells lighting up the night. Makes you a sitting target. Takes an exceptional man not to panic, in those circumstances ... a hero.'

Holt did not answer.

There was silence ahead of them, only the dull thump of feet and a squelch of duckboards in mud behind, and the trickle of water along the bottom of the trench.

'I expect you know what it feels like,' Joseph went on. 'I notice you have some pretty bad tears in your trousers, even one in your blouse. Haven't had time to mend them yet.'

'I daresay I got caught in a bit of wire out there last night,' Holt said stiffly. He shifted his weight from one foot to the other.

'I'm sure you did,' Joseph agreed with him. 'Ashton didn't. His clothes were muddy, but no wire tears.'

There were several minutes of silence. A group of men passed by behind them, muttering words of greeting. When they were gone the darkness closed in again. Someone threw up a star shell and there was a crackle of machine-gun fire.

'I wouldn't repeat that, if I were you, Chaplain,' Holt said at last. 'You might make people think unpleasant things, doubts. And right at the moment morale is high. We need that. We've had a hard time recently. We're going over the top in a trench raid soon. Morale is important . . . trust. I'm sure you know that, maybe even better than I do. That's your job, isn't it? Morale, spiritual welfare of the men?'

'Yes . . . spiritual welfare is a good way of putting it. Remember what it is we are fighting for, and that it is worth all that it costs . . . even this.' Joseph gestured in the dark to all that surrounded them.

More star shells went up, illuminating the night for a few garish moments, then a greater darkness closed in.

'We need our heroes,' Holt said very clearly. 'You should know that. Any man who would tear them down would be very unpopular, even if he said he was doing it in the name of truth, or justice, or whatever it was he believed in. He would do a lot of harm, Chaplain. I expect you can see that . . .'

'Oh, yes,' Joseph agreed. 'To have their hero shown to be a coward who laid the blame for his panic on another man, and let him be buried in shame, and then committed murder to hide that, would devastate men who are already wretched and exhausted by war.'

'You are perfectly right.' Holt sounded as if he were smiling. 'A very wise man, Chaplain. Good of the regiment first. The right sort of loyalty.'

'I could prove it,' Joseph said very carefully.

'But you won't. Think what it would do to the men.'

Joseph turned a little to face the parapet. He stood up

onto the fire step and looked forward over the dark expanse of mud and wire.

'We should take that sniper out. That would be a very heroic thing to do. Good thing to try, even if you didn't succeed. You'd deserve a mention in dispatches for that, possibly a medal.'

'It would be posthumous!' Holt said bitterly.

'Possibly. But you might succeed and come back. It would be so daring, Fritz would never expect it,' Joseph pointed out.

'Then you do it, Chaplain!' Holt said sarcastically.

'It wouldn't help you, Captain. Even if I die, I have written a full account of what I have learned today, to be opened should anything happen to me. On the other hand, if you were to mount such a raid, whether you returned or not, I should destroy it.'

There was silence again, except for the distant crack of sniper fire a thousand yards away and the drip of mud.

'Do you understand me, Captain Holt?'

Holt turned slowly. A star shell lit his face for an instant. His voice was hoarse.

'You're sending me to my death!'

'I'm letting you be the hero you're pretending to be and Ashton really was,' Joseph answered. 'The hero the men need. Thousands of us have died out here, no one knows how many more there will be. Others will be maimed or blinded. It isn't whether you die or not, it's how well.'

A shell exploded a dozen yards from them. Both men ducked, crouching automatically.

Silence again.

Slowly Joseph unbent.

Holt lifted his head. 'You're a hard man, Chaplain. I misjudged you.'

'Spiritual care, Captain,' Joseph said quietly. 'You wanted the men to think you a hero, to admire you. Now you're going to justify that and become one.'

Holt stood still, looking toward him in the gloom, then slowly he turned and began to walk away, his feet sliding on the wet duckboards. Then he climbed up the next fire step and up over the parapet.

Joseph stood still and prayed.

SHEL SILVERSTEIN

A prolific author and illustrator, who wrote regularly for Playboy *and other magazines, Shel Silverstein died last year. His impossible-to-categorize books, such as* The Giving Tree, The Light in the Attic *and* Where the Pavement Ends, *made the best-seller lists with regularity and often remained on them for a year or two more.*

THE GUILTY PARTY

Shel Silverstein

Judge Vernon Hobbs had been known for some unusual and unorthodox rulings.

There was the occasion when Leon Poole and Maurice Stehner came before him for a judgment on a 1938 De Soto.

It seems they had bought the vehicle together from Orville Clayton's lot with Leon's three hundred dollars, eighty-seven of which was owed by Orville to Maurice to settle a wager on the World Series. Maurice then did what was disputed to be six hundred and forty-two dollars worth of repair and restoration, for which he demanded full payment or the De Soto.

Judge Hobbs suggested joint ownership or selling the damn thing and splitting the profits – but by then there was too much bad blood between the boys, as to who said what, and who promised which, and who indeed was the De Soto's rightful owner.

'Well then,' said Judge Hobbs, 'I am gonna render a decision based upon the wisdom of Solomon. Is either one of you boys versed in or acquainted with the Biblical tale of Solomon and the two mothers?'

The boys had to admit that Scripture was not their long suit.

'Good,' said Judge Hobbs, 'I wouldn't want either of you anticipating my ruling, which is – that the aforementioned De Soto be cut in half, and one half awarded to each of the claimants. Leon, is that all right with you?'

'Fine with me,' said Leon.

'And Maurice, do you find this acceptable?'

'I'll go for that,' said Maurice, 'but who gets the front half and who gets the back half?'

'I'll take the front half,' said Leon.

'The hell you will,' shouted Maurice, 'the front half's got the engine, the radio, the hood ornament, and the—'

'Order,' called Judge Hobbs, banging down the claw hammer he used as a gavel. 'I'm amending my decision – the De Soto will be split lengthwise – thereby giving each of you an equal—'

'Well, who gets the driver's side?' demanded Leon. 'That's got the mahogany wheel, the transmission, gearshift, the—'

'And who's supposed to saw that damn engine in half?' Leon whined. 'You try cuttin' through a windshield and an engine, with a chainsaw, and you're sure as hell gonna mess up a—'

Judge Hobbs banged his hammer.

'Well,' sighed Judge Hobbs, 'I can see from the incredible willingness of both claimants to gladly destroy this unique and classic example of automotive art that neither one of them is the rightful owner. And the court hereby impounds said vehicle as property of the court to be used at the court's discretion on various court business on weekends and holidays, and if there is any question as to the right of the court to impound said De Soto, I'm sure that something can and will be found in the trunk or glove compartment to justify my decision. These proceedings are concluded – everybody go home.

'And that,' said Judge Hobbs later, as he and Clarence Sawyer, his bailiff, sat sipping some good apricot brandy, 'is the last time I try to render a verdict based upon anybody's wisdom but my own.'

It was too damn hot.

Judge Hobbs leaned back in his swivel chair and turned up the fan as high as it would go. He didn't want to lean too far back. They might see that he was wearing short pants underneath his robe. That might be interpreted as being unjudicial or, at best, undignified.

Carefully, Judge Hobbs rolled up the brief that lay upon his desk. The fly was on the rim of the coffee cup. One swat – *justice* – swift and sure. But *was* it just? What was the fly doing but exercising its nature? What was young Billy Ray doing but exercising his? But if that were the case, who deserved to be punished for anything?

Judge Hobbs closed his eyes and tapped the rolled papers against his palm. He hoped that this would look contemplative. The fly was moving down the inside of the cup now. As long as it stayed there it was safe. Did the sonofabitch know that?

'All right,' said Judge Hobbs, unrolling the brief and flattening it out, 'all right, let's proceed with these – *Clarence*, will you turn that damn thing off.'

'I got the sound down, Judge,' said the bailiff.

'Well, I can still hear it,' said Judge Hobbs. 'What's the score, anyway?'

'Eight to two, Bluebirds, top of the fifth – they just brought in that Binky Lewis. He's as wild as a—'

'Well, I think that Lewis boy might be able to hold a

six-run lead,' said Judge Hobbs, wiping his neck with his handkerchief.

'Judge, they got two men on and—'

'Damn it, Clarence, at least turn the *sound* off – and announce these proceedings – in a proper and official manner.'

Clarence snapped off the sound and stood up, pouting.

'Hear ye, hear ye, first district court, Menasha County, now in session. *Honorable* Vernon Hobbs presiding – all rise.'

He had hit the *Honorable* a little too hard.

'Too hot to rise,' said Judge Hobbs, throwing Clarence his stern look. 'Stay sittin'.'

'The state versus William Raymond Brockley,' continued Clarence. 'The charge, sexual battery, assault with a deadly weapon, kidnapping, resisting arrest—'

'All right,' said Judge Hobbs, 'I'm tired of list'nin'.'

The fly had taken off.

Judge Hobbs turned toward Billy Ray. Damn, the boy was too good-looking to have to force anyone into anything.

'Billy Ray, you've decided to forgo and dispense with a trial by a jury of your peers.'

'Yes, sir,' said Billy Ray.

'Well,' said Judge Hobbs, 'that may be a wise decision, since most of your peers around here would like to see you strung up slow and sliced down a piece at a time. A few of 'em might even be blood-related to Eunice Tillman.'

'The young lady is in critical condition at Baptist Hospital,' said Lew Porter, district attorney and proprietor of Porter Brothers General Contracting, Roofing and Aluminum Siding, 'and is at this time physically and emotionally unfit to attend this hearing. Therefore, Your Honor, the state requests a one-week postponement until the young lady—'

'The young *lady*'s condition has been upgraded to stable,' interjected Buddy Linz, defense attorney and co-owner of Buddy's Four Alarm Chili And Pit Bar-B-Cue.

'Well, I think we can proceed ahead,' said Judge Hobbs. 'I want to get this over and done with as soon as possible.'

Lew Porter stood up. How did he manage to look so dry and unwrinkled in a three-piece suit on a day like this?

'Your Honor,' said Lew Porter, 'the state will prove that on the night of—'

'*Attempt* to prove,' snapped Judge Hobbs. Lew Porter sighed.

'*Attempt* to prove that on the night of April seventeenth, the accused, Billy Ray Brockley, did willfully and forcibly—'

'Come to think of it, Lew, you don't even have to attempt to prove anything,' said Judge Hobbs. 'Sit back down – I have all the pertinent facts right here.' He tapped the rumpled brief. 'This don't look like that big of a deal.'

'We know you'll render a fair and impartial judgment, Your Honor,' said Buddy Linz.

Lew Porter groaned and sat back down.

Judge Hobbs had the reputation of being one of the goodest and oldest of the county's good old boys, two of his favorite expressions being 'Boys will be boys' and 'Let he who has never been young cast the first stone.' Also Judge Hobbs had been heard to remark on more than one occasion that it didn't serve much purpose slappin' young people in jail.

'In the spring the sap will rise,' he would sigh, his eyes looking back a long time ago. 'The fruit turns ripe and the pickers come. That's nature – you can't stop it or slow it down.'

'All right,' says Judge Hobbs, tossing the brief aside and turning to Billy Ray Brockley, 'Billy Ray, you've been advised by counsel that my decision will be binding?'

'Yes, sir,' said Billy Ray.

' 'Cause I sure as hell don't want to hear no bitchin' or moanin' later that I been too severe – or too lenient – and I sure as hell don't want to hear the word *appeal* interjected anywhere into these proceedings. I mean I don't want to even sniff the word *appeal*, and anybody – defense attorney or prosecutor – who even breathes or whispers that word is gonna find me somewhat prejudicial in my rulings on his future cases – is that understood? All right, you wanted my decision on this case and you'll get it – and abide by it. Billy Ray – how do you plead to these charges?'

'I didn't do it.'

'You didn't meet Eunice Tillman at the VFW Blue Moon Dance on the night of ... April seventeenth?'

'I met her.'

'You didn't dance with her?'

'We danced ... awhile.'

'You didn't get her drunk?'

'You don't have to get Eunice drunk,' said Billy Ray. 'She's always—'

'You didn't drive her to the Larkspur Underpass?'

'Yes, sir – But I didn't do it.'

'Didn't do ... what?'

'The rest of it. I'm not guilty.'

'You sayin' she led you on? 'Cause if she led you on—'

'I'm sayin' I didn't do it.'

'You didn't do it.'

'Not ... really.'

'Not really?'

'I ... witnessed it.'

'You witnessed it.'

'Bein' done – yes, sir.'

'Bein' done – by who?'

'I don't like to name names, Judge. I just—'

'Bein' done by *who*, damn it?'

Billy Ray closed his eyes.

'By ... Sam.'

'Sam?'

'Sam Johnson, Your Honor.'

'Sam Johnson?' Judge Hobbs picked up the brief. 'I don't see any Sam Johnson listed in this—'

'Sam Johnson,' said Billy Ray. 'My ... thing.'

'Your ... thing?'

Buddy Linz stood up.

'My client is referring to his ... member, Your Honor, his ... sexual member, his—'

'I can see what he's referring to,' said Judge Hobbs. 'He's clutchin' the damn thing.'

Judge Hobbs leaned forward.

'Billy Ray – you're sayin' that *that* is Sam Johnson?'

'Yes, sir.'

'You've givin' him a ... name?'

'That's his name, Judge. *Sam.*'

'A first name too.'

'Well, sir, there's a lot of Johnsons out there.'

'Hopefully not related to this case,' said Judge Hobbs, picking up his pen and beginning to write. 'Mister Johnson? *J-O-H-N-S-O-N?* He's the guilty party?'

'I call him Sam,' said Billy Ray. 'It's not so formal.'

'Well, I want to keep things formal as possible,' said Judge Hobbs. 'Samuel Johnson. No middle initial?'

'No, sir.'

'Just first and last name – you didn't make a little checkered coat for the sonofabitch, did you? With a little straw hat and a cane?'

'No, sir.'

'And you say that this "Samuel Johnson" on the night of April seventeenth, and against the person of Eunice Tillman, did willfully and forcibly, without your aid, cooperation, or collaboration—'

'He's got a mind of his own, Judge,' said Billy Ray. 'There's no reasoning with him – he just gets a notion and does . . . anything that comes into his head.'

'I know, son,' sighed Judge Hobbs, 'but as an innocent observer and witness to the alleged attack, did you do anything to restrain the aforementioned Samuel Johnson from—'

'There's no holding him, Your Honor,' said Billy Ray. 'He's . . . unrestrainable – I tried – he just . . . shook me off.'

Lew Porter was on his feet.

'And what the hell were *you* doing, while Sam Johnson was forcing Eunice Tillman into the backseat? What were you doing when your buddy Sam was forcing Eunice Tillman to perform a—'

'I couldn't have gone against him,' Billy Ray pleaded. 'I was afraid.'

'Afraid?' asked Judge Hobbs. 'Afraid of what?'

'Of what he might . . . do . . . to me.'

'To *you*?' Judge Hobbs was wide awake now. 'What could he have done to you?'

'You don't know him, Your Honor. The bastard's got no

conscience – he might do ... anything. He's got a ... power, Judge. He just ... takes over. You don't know Sam Johnson.'

Lew Porter was up and screaming now – the veins in his neck about to bust. His face was right in Billy Ray's.

'And I imagine it was the same Sam Johnson who drove your Thunderbird to the Larkspur Underpass. I wanna see it, Your Honor, I want a demonstration of Sam Johnson drivin' a stick shift, I wanna see Sam Johnson holdin' a knife to somebody's throat – this knife. Your Honor – I'm introducin' this barlow as Exhibit A. And I wanna see—'

'You don't have to introduce that knife to me,' said Judge Hobbs, picking up the barlow and turning it over slowly. 'This was your daddy's fishin' knife, wasn't it, Billy? I believe if he knew you were leavin' it layin' around within easy reach of such unsavory characters as this Sam Johnson, he'd be spinnin' in his grave.' He turned to Buddy Linz.

'Buddy, this defense that you've cooked up is highly unique and creative, I must say. You realize if I allow it and it becomes a precedent, any forger can claim that it was his hands that did it, and not him. Anybody can kick somebody to death and claim it was his feet.'

'Next thing you know,' chimed in Lew Porter, picking up the line of reasoning, 'next thing you know the arsonist is blaming the match, the sniper is blamin' the bullet, the ax murderer—'

'That's our defense,' said Buddy Linz, 'and I've got a trunkload of psychiatric books and psychological studies and psychiatrists' opinions that'll back me up.'

'Sam Johnson did it,' said Billy Ray. 'I'll swear to it.'

Lew Porter was swearing now. That three-piece suit was beginning to look like wet cardboard.

'Your Honor,' he said, 'this ... this incredible "my-pee-pee-did-it-not-me plea" is so outrageous – so desperate – so without any legal foundation, that no one can possibly—'

'I'm going to allow it,' said Judge Hobbs, 'and if it brings down upon my head a torrent of legal criticism and controversy, well, then, they'll just have to put me on the same bench with boys like John Marshall, Louis Brandeis, and Oliver Wendell Holmes – in presenting a ruling that will forever influence future jurisprudence.

'Because, gentlemen, I find this theory of a ... member ... having a will of its own to be reasonable and within the scope of human experience.

'Have we all not at some time or other been led down pathways dark and devious? By something stronger than our hearts or heads? And is justice not to be tempered with mercy? And who indeed can stop the sap from rising in the young sapling?'

Lew Porter groaned and held his head in his hands.

'Billy Ray, I find you innocent of all charges specified here. I do find you guilty of witnessing a felony and not immediately reporting it, but in light of your coming forth now and identifying the guilty party, I'm suspending sentence. I don't suppose Sam Johnson has any money.'

'Not a cent, Your Honor,' said a cheerful Billy Ray.

'Well, then, seein' as how he's a friend of yours—'

'Former friend,' said Billy Ray.

'Whatever – I'm ordering you to pay whatever medical costs Eunice Tillman may run up due to the actions of your former friend Sam Johnson. And I hope this serves as a lesson to you to refrain from any associations with violent, abusive members.'

'Thank you, Judge,' said Billy Ray, getting up with a grin.

'And I'm sure gonna be more selective in the future about hangin' out with bad company.'

Judge Hobbs sat there. Billy Ray was hugging Buddy Linz. Lew Porter was putting his papers together. Clarence was fiddling with the horizontal. Billy Ray started toward the door. Judge Hobbs picked up his gavel.

'Where you goin', son?' asked Judge Hobbs.

'Home ... to dinner ... like you said. I think my momma is makin' a meat loaf.'

'Well, good,' said Judge Hobbs, 'but who you takin' with you?'

'Buddy ... if he wants to come – hell, all of you, if you like meat loaf. There'll be plenty.'

'Well, you ain't takin' no convicted felon home to your momma's table, are you?' asked Judge Hobbs.

Billy Ray looked confused.

'I mean, son, you're innocent and free to go – free as a bird.'

Billy Ray sighed.

'But that heartless, cold-blooded sex fiend, Sam Johnson, I'm findin' him *guilty*' – Judge Hobbs banged his gavel – 'of aggravated sexual assault and kidnapping, I'm sentencing the ruthless sonofabitch to twelve years' confinement in the state correctional facility at Joliet.'

'Judge—' said Billy Ray.

'Son,' said Judge Hobbs, raising a restraining finger, 'I know how hard it is to take leave of a loved one for an extended period of time, so as a special consideration, I'm gonna give you the opportunity to accompany your friend, your former friend, to Joliet, or you can stay behind and let him go on alone ... You look pale, son ... Mr. Linz, why don't you escort your client to the men's room. I think he needs a glass of water . . . Oh, and Clarence – give Billy Ray his daddy's barlow – he's innocent and it's his property. Take all the time you need, son,' he said softly to Billy Ray, 'but when you come out of there, Sam Johnson *is* goin' to prison. . . . Next case—'

'There ain't no next case, Judge,' said Clarence.

'Well, then, turn up the sound,' said Judge Hobbs, 'and let's find out whether or not that Lewis kid can hold a six-run lead for five damn innings.'